A WELL-FOUNDED FEAR OF DEATH

Stepping Out, Book 2

By Sherri Stewart

DEDICATION

For Dorothy Rossman Nixon Weber,
You are my greatest encourager. You delight in your children and
grandchildren. You always seek what is good. Even at 87, you search for
ways to serve. You are cherished.

Chapter One

Delicate fingers grasped Julie's arm. She'd been so intent on
getting the fruit merchant's attention, their touch caught her off
guard. "You scared me. What's wrong? I've been waiting twenty-
two and a half minutes to pay for these mangos."

"I saw Amber." Sun's dark, worried eyes demanded Julie's
attention.

The humid Colombian summer air draped the marketplace,
making her and fellow shoppers edgy and impatient. Sweat soaked
Julie's neck and the underside of her chestnut hair. She wiped her
cheek against her shoulder, surprised and annoyed by her teenage
assistant's pleading face. "Amber who?"

"Just Amber … Dae didn't let us know each other's last names.
She was with me in the van last summer, but she went missing. But
she's here in the market." She twisted side to side and cast swift
glances at the crowd, then leaned close to Julie. "Please, we must
find her." She pulled Julie's arm again, almond eyes melting her
resistance.

Exaggerating a groan, she released the mangos and gave the
frazzled seller a mournful glance, then stepped away from the
cacophony of requests from a dozen locals.

Sun charged into the main aisle, gripping Julie's hand as she
struggled to keep up. Julie shouted at the back of Sun's head.
"What does she look like?"

She yelled over her shoulder, "My age—fifteen or sixteen.

Blond hair. Long. Thin."

Sun wove deftly through the congestion with the ease of youth, past booths sporting multi-colored fabrics, skin cleansers, and picture frames made of shells. The noisy swell of the crowd made it impossible to talk. Every step assaulted Julie with smells from coconut to incense to seasoned beef.

She did her best to avoid collisions with tourist families and barely managed to sidestep a stroller. Meanwhile, Sun's long black hair rippled as she bobbed up and down trying to peer over the shoulders of the people surrounding them.

When they reached a crossroad, Sun spun toward Julie, her lower lip quivering. "She's gone…again." She brushed away tears with the back of her hand.

After a last panoramic view around them, Julie steered her toward a spot between empty booths. "If she's here, we'll do our best to find her. I promise." She bent down to get eye-to-eye with her four-foot-ten assistant. "Angela's waiting for us by the produce. We have to go back." She straightened. "Tell me more about Amber on the way, but you'll have to talk loud."

Worry creased Sun's youthful forehead. "Don't know much. She's one of the nine girls in the van—the only one nice to me. She cried a lot. When I told her my name, she said in my ear, 'I just want to go home.' When we stopped at the—how you say in English—ware-building—the place where the men bid for us, she didn't get back in the van. And Dae, our master, said we had to leave before the cops came. That was the last time I saw her. Until today—here in Bogotá. Amber's in trouble—we must help her."

A crowd still surrounded the fruit and vegetable tables, waiting for the solitary merchant to take their orders. Pungent fruit smells filled the air. Heat radiated from customers bumping into each other. Julie was standing on her tiptoes peering over people when her cousin Angela approached from behind and linked arms with her and Sun.

"Where did y'all go? I thought you had abandoned me."

"Sorry. Sun thought she saw a friend of hers and didn't want to lose her. Amber—the girl who vanished last summer." After glancing at her wristwatch, Julie scanned the crowd for the elusive blonde she'd never met. "We have about an hour before the bus picks us up. Do you want to go search for her? You love an adventure."

Angela's eyes sparkled. "You know it." She focused on Sun. "What was she wearing?"

"It was so fast. Maybe a pink or red dress. I didn't know it was her 'til I saw her face." She touched her own. "She wore lots of makeup. Blue stuff on her eyes. Like last summer."

"Did she see you?"

"Yes, Miss. When I called her name, her eyes got real big. She shook her head at me and said 'no.' Then she ran into the crowd." Sun dropped her head. "I wish I followed her."

Julie squeezed Sun's shoulder. "We'll go now. But let's not lose sight of each other, so there'll be three of us to help her." What she didn't say out loud was she was too much of a coward to deal with a troubled teenager on her own.

Crowds hampered their progress. If Amber was in the market, she was well hidden. Sun's gaze darted from booth to booth. When they reached the far end, she blotted her eyes against her sleeve. "I can't give up. She's in trouble."

"It's time to get on the bus." Julie said. They retraced their steps and met their transport and fellow volunteers at the market's entrance. Sun asked to take the window seat so she could keep scanning the crowd.

Once the twelve-member mission group settled in, the team leader, Don, tapped the microphone. "Welcome back. Hope y'all had a great time sampling the local color. It's going to be lights out at 10:00 because we have to be at the orphanage at 7:30 sharp. We'll talk more over dinner." He motioned for the bus driver to go.

The heat made Julie's head hurt. Pulling her long, damp curls into a pony tail with a scrunchy, she took a sip of tepid water, leaned back against the high headrest, and closed her eyes. They eased into traffic. Heat billowing through the open window combined with the engine's drone, lulling her to sleep.

Sun shook Julie's arm. "She's over there." A thin wisp of a girl stood on the curb, hand on hip, facing the passing cars. Julie leaned across Sun and pressed her face against the window to focus on the slight figure with scraggly hair who was falling further behind. Then the bus jerked to a stop, the driver blasting the horn. He called back to the passengers that a stalled car was blocking their way.

"Are you sure it's her?" Julie asked.

"Oh yes." Her voice was louder than usual. "Please tell the driver to let me out. I have to go to her."

Julie's green eyes darted from the back of the driver's head to the fragile girl on the street corner. A man with crossed arms stood a few feet away staring at her … or guarding her. Julie's fingers tightened on Sun's arm. "See that guy leaning against the pole. He's watching your friend. Could he be … what did you call Dae … a *master*?"

Sun's face grew grim. "Yes, that's her master. They're always close by their girls watching." Her brows knit together. "What should we do?" At Julie's silence, she focused her attention out the window.

Angela twisted in her seat toward them. "I see her. Should we ask the driver to let us off?"

Then it hit. The familiar sound akin to a train engine was deafening. Julie knew it heralded an oncoming panic attack. Her hands went to her ears. No way could she handle rescuing a troubled teenager from her trafficker. It was too dangerous—too risky. She jerked her head toward the aisle. Why now? She didn't want Sun to see her like this—weak and afraid.

The only reason she'd agreed to come on this trip was to prove she was over her agoraphobia, but the fact was—she wasn't. If all she had to do was work in the orphanage kitchen, she could keep her fears hidden under the surface. But this was way out of her safety zone. She calculated the hours until she'd be back in Florida—back in her house in Celebration with the security system activated.

Angela's eyes narrowed. "You don't look so good."

"I'm fine. It's just …" The bus lurched forward and people clapped. The stalled car apparently was moving.

Angela cupped Sun's chin in her hands. "Don't worry, sweetie. It's not the right time. We've got to plan this carefully if we want to succeed. We'll only get one chance. How about coming back tomorrow? What do you think?"

Sun paused. "You are right. And we can pray tonight."

Julie let out a silent sigh of relief.

***

The sleepy trio met in the dorm lobby the next morning.

Angela yawned audibly, stretching her arms above her head. "If anyone sings lullabies to the babies today, don't be surprised if you find me in a crib snoring next to them. I need coffee." She headed for the dining room, then spun around. "By the way, Don said he'd get one of the interns to drive us to the market about five."

Sun's worry lines vanished. "Thank you." A small smile erupted on her face. Angela bowed in return.

Julie wrapped her arm around Sun's thin shoulders. "See? We'll find her, don't you worry." She tilted her head toward Angela. "Just bring me a half a cup. You know how I spill everything. I don't have any clean shirts left."

The room filled with fellow teammates, all eagerly seeking the coffee pot. Julie secured three seats in the dining room while Angela waited in line for the drinks. Sun returned with yogurt and fruit for the three of them.

Angela joined them with cups of steaming coffee and a bottle of orange juice. "Here you go, Julie. Be careful. I'm out of clothes for you to borrow."

"Yes ma'am. How come you never spill anything on your clothes?"

"I'm a flight attendant. I carry drinks for a living."

Julie sipped from her half-full cup and set it on the table. "You know the bus will be late. We might as well come up with a plan for this afternoon." She bit into her banana. "Sun, you know more about these things than we do. What should we do to help Amber escape?"

"Not sure, Miss. She could be harmed, maybe tortured. We must be careful."

Angela's eyes narrowed, then lit up. "What if I created a diversion near the dude watching her? You two whisk Amber away. Then we'll meet up later."

This trip was getting out of hand, Julie thought. "I don't want you to get hurt. These are dangerous people." Pain welled up like an anvil pressing against her sternum.

Angela's eyes danced with excitement. "I can handle it. You know me—I live for danger. But what about you. A year ago, you were afraid of everything—I couldn't get you to leave your house. You haven't had a single panic attack on this trip, and now you're ready to rescue a human trafficking victim? Wow, girl, I am proud of you."

Tucking stray curls away from her face, she managed a weak smile, "This was a giant baby step agreeing to come on this trip with you two. But—rescuing Amber is a bit daunting for me."

Sun said, "*You* rescued me last summer, Miss Julie. Now *Amber* needs us." She twisted her hands. "But, what if she refuses to come with us?"

"Hadn't thought about that. Hm." Julie twirled a strand of hair around her finger, catching it in the tangles. "I don't think she weighs much, and you're a friend of hers. We should be able to handle her." Then she thought of something else. "We should take a change of clothes, so if that guy follows us, she won't be so easy to identify."

Their bus arrived, but Julie hardly noticed the sights on the way to the orphanage. When they arrived, they checked the duty roster. Sun was assigned to the nursery. She'd spend the day with the eight babies in the crib room. Angela cheered when she found out she had outdoor duty playing soccer with a dozen rambunctious boys. Children made Julie break out in hives; she did a mental happy dance because she was assigned kitchen duty once again.

***

Julie was cutting up sandwiches when Sun entered the kitchen to warm some bottles of formula. She spoke so softly Julie had to sidle up to her.

"My heart breaks for the babies," pointing at her heart. "All day, all night, they lie in those cribs, and no one picks them up or changes their diapers after we go home. Smell this bottle."

Julie jerked away from the sour smell and waved her hand in front of her face.

Sun's eyes were plaintive. "Can we take the babies back with us?"

"It's not that easy." She marveled at Sun's child-like idealism.

"The ladies probably wouldn't even notice they were gone." Holding a bottle under the spout, Sun washed the old formula out with dish soap.

Julie put her arm around Sun's shoulder. "You have such a tender heart. Enjoy them while you can."

"Each day, I rock them and sing Korean songs my mother sang to my little sisters. If I could save just one baby. You rescued me.

Now I want to help them."

Julie wiped the bottles and handed them to Sun. "I feel sorry for them too, although I'm not much of a baby person." Indeed, an understatement. She wouldn't know what to do with one of them.

Angela rushed into the room breathing hard yet hardly breaking a sweat. Julie could never understand how Angela remained so fresh after playing soccer while she was dripping wet.

Angela opened the refrigerator. "When is lunch? They're wearing me out. I have to keep some reserve of energy for tomorrow night. Friday night trips to Miami are always a challenge for us flight attendants; I'll have my work cut out for me."

Julie poured her a glass of ginger limeade from the pitcher on the table. "There's a plate of burritos for the boys on the counter. I'll bring out some pineapple and a keg of limeade. After lunch, why don't you read them a story to calm them? Settle them down and give yourself a break at the same time. Then you won't be too worn out for your passengers."

"Good idea. By the way, the bus will pick us up early at three."

***

Throngs of people overflowed the market onto the streets. Instead of talking, the three girls rode in silence, staring out the window. Amber's grave situation weighed heavily on Julie's mind. As they neared their destination, Scott, the driver, circled the area and parked a few blocks from the spot where they had seen Amber the day before. He had agreed to help Angela with the diversion.

As they rounded the corner, Angela pointed. "Hey, she's there again. Green shorts, white top, and miserable high heels. And the same guy is leaning against the telephone pole."

Julie shielded her eyes from the sun with her hand and watched the girl coyly waving at passing cars, but the girl didn't smile. "Are you sure it's Amber?"

"Yes, but I'm worried. I don't want to put her in danger. Masters don't like—how you say—interfering. She will be punished." Despite the heat, she shivered.

Julie squinted at the man. No more than twenty, he sported heavily gelled hair, sunglasses, a jean jacket, and a white t-shirt. Despite his illusion of disinterest and shielded eyes, she felt sure he monitored Amber's every move.

Angela said, "She's not going anywhere. We'll pray and then

split up. Scott and I'll position ourselves between them and pretend to be focused on a map. Meanwhile, Julie and Sun, get as close as possible. When you're in place, I'll trip and fall, pretending to be injured. I'll make a lot of racket. Scott, you can ask "sunglasses" to help me get up and to a seat. Lucky we both speak Spanish."

"Will do," said Scott.

Angela continued, "So when I fall, you two catch hold of Amber and take off. The second little store you pass sells baskets—go in there. Leave through the back door to the apartment entrance across the alley. Scott checked it earlier today. It's unlocked." She swallowed. "Hide there and watch for us. We'll pick you up out front, but stay out of sight until you see the bus. Then run."

Scott said. "We might need a plan B if something goes wrong. If he sees you leaving with Amber and comes after you, hide and call me." He handed Sun a phone. "Just hit one."

Sun said, "Amber can't run in those shoes. I know because I wore heels like that when I was rescued last year." Pulling a pair of sneakers out of her bag, she said, "So I found these. I hope they fit."

Sun's voice grew fainter. Although Julie tried hard to concentrate on what she was saying, it was if she were talking from an underground tunnel. Focusing grew difficult. The already hot temperature was burning a hole in her head. She concentrated on taking measured breaths, but nothing worked this time. This trip was too much for her to handle.

Scott's body seemed distorted, moving sideways and blending with the colors behind him like a kaleidoscope. Frustration rose. She thought she was winning the battle over her fears. Wasn't that why she agreed to come on this trip? Darkness swallowed the moving colors. She felt herself swoon and fall to the sidewalk. She was powerless to help herself. Then nothing.

***

Why was Angela shaking her and calling her name? Couldn't she let her sleep? Her eyelids were heavy, but she forced them open. Three faces hovered so close their breath warmed her cheeks. Garlic combined with spearmint. Why were they talking about her as if she wasn't there?

"She's coming to."

"What's Miss Julie mumbling? Something about kitchens."

"Jules, wake up."

She squinted until the dizziness subsided, then pushed up on her elbows. She shook her head to dispel the fugue. Her face felt warm and moist. "What happened?"

"You fainted." Angela handed her a bottle of water. "Drink some."

"I think it's the heat. I'm okay. Let's do this."

"No, I think it was a panic attack. Like the ones you had last year whenever you left your house." Angela brushed damp strands of hair off of Julie's face. "Let's just wait a few minutes. Nothing's happening. Why don't you sit over there in the shade?"

It wasn't easy for Julie to push herself to her feet. The trees spun around her like a merry-go-round. Her wobbly legs almost gave out. She smoothed her crumpled clothes and managed a shallow breath. "I'm fine." She wasn't, but they didn't need to know.

Angela's eyes narrowed, and Julie knew she wasn't fooling her. Then she glanced at the others in the group and apparently changed her mind. "Let's go." Splitting into two groups, they crossed the street.

Something was happening near Amber. A small crowd formed to her right. Whatever was going on inside, the circle of onlookers blocked Julie's view of Angela and Scott. Amber remained on the curb, but her attention was focused on the source of the commotion beside her.

As Julie and Sun joined the crowd, she bent toward Sun. "Find the guy. I'll keep my eyes open for Angela."

The crowd's attention was riveted on a barefoot girl of six or seven. Clad in dirty clothes, her snarled hair needed a wash. The tiny acrobat effortlessly bent backward, forming an arch with her feet planted on either side of her head.

Three musicians dressed in white, sporting sombreros and sunglasses, banged their drums to a calypso beat, a hat at their feet for tips. The audience clapped and squealed at the little girl's every maneuver. She knew how to work the crowd. As the beat got faster, the small contortionist sprang up and did a series of flips onto a barrel. Another flip put her on the low-hanging roof. A double flip brought her back to the ground ending in splits. A final spin brought her to Angela's feet. Glancing up, the tiny performer grinned shyly at Angela, then twirled away. The audience roared its approval.

Angela tilted her head in Amber's direction and mouthed the word "Go."

At that moment, Sun slipped next to her, out of breath. "He's there, but he can't see around the crowd."

Julie touched Sun's arm. "It's time." They approached Amber—so close they could touch her. Sun whispered in her ear. Julie touched her elbow and tried to draw her away from the spot, but Amber flinched and resisted.

She hissed through her teeth. "Don't do this. He'll kill me."

Julie and Sun locked their arms in hers. "C'mon. Let's get you home to your family. Now."

She stopped resisting, but she wobbled and swayed, nearly falling. Her clenched fists and rigid shoulders fought the heaving of Julie's chest.

Amber peered back over her shoulder—the pull of her master straining to hold her back. Yet she let them prop her up by the elbows and pull her away in the opposite direction.

They entered a store filled with baskets of all sorts and sizes, scurried around the displays, and hid behind a pole.

The fetid air and rank wood made Julie nauseous. She knew a panic attack was forthcoming, but she didn't have time for it. She was the adult here; she needed to be in control. Taking a shallow breath, she moved toward Amber and managed a weak smile. "Hi, I'm Julie. You know Sun. Change into these." She held out the sneakers.

Amber's lips were pursed, but she unfastened her straps without a word.

Sun kept watch at the door. Once Amber stood, Sun rushed over and threw her arms around her neck. "I thought they killed you."

Amber averted her eyes. Her voice was barely audible. "It's been ... okay." Her eyes darted to the door and widened when a man walked past. "This won't work. He won't let me go. He always finds me."

The nausea finally vanished. Julie handed her a bag of clothes, locking eyes with her to relay assurance. "We're not going to let that happen. Here, put these on."

The shopkeeper stopped dusting when Amber pulled on a shirt over the one she was wearing. Worried they'd get kicked out if she didn't say something, Julie approached the woman whose narrowed eyes were trained on the three girls. She searched her memory of high-school Spanish, then said. "Esculpe. Mi amiga…my friend…in danger." She pointed at the back door. "La puerta?"

The woman's lips tightened. "Ladrones!"

The three girls shook their heads. Julie said, "No, Senora. We are not thieves."

The woman's gaze went from face to face. Then she flicked her hand toward the curtain at the back.

"Muchos gracias." Julie's voice trailed as they scrambled through a darkened room toward the exit. Not a wisp of light allowed them to see where they were going. Julie barreled into Sun, who had stopped short. "Sorry."

"I almost tripped over something. What is that smell?"

"I know. Like raw sewage. Can you find the door?"

They gripped one another's hands as Sun grappled for the knob. The door opened, bathing the room in light. Julie said, "Don't think about it. We don't need to know."

Julie squinted in the bright light. Across the alley was a door. She asked Amber, "What does it say?"

"It says 'Private Entrance'."

"That must be the apartment Angela was talking about." The door swung open revealing a beautifully landscaped swimming pool. Julie tried to appear nonchalant as she slowed her pace, and skirted the edge of the pool, with the apartment lobby ahead.

A mother splashing water on her children stopped and stared at the strange trio, suspicion written on her face.

They slinked past with heads down. Sun held the door open for the other two. Once out of sight, they leaned against the bank of mailboxes.

Julie opened her bag and said, "Let's put on these baseball caps and hide our hair underneath." Then she handed each a pair of sunglasses.

Sun blew out an audible breath. "That was close." Tiptoeing to the front entrance, she peeked past the tall shrubs and stared across the expanse of grass bordering the road. "I don't see Angela and Scott."

Julie tugged the two of them into the concealment of a large bush. "Stay here. I don't want the guy to find us. What's his name?"

"Miguel," Amber said wistfully, eyeing the door, "his name is Miguel."

Julie ushered them behind a stand of four palms and an immense shrub, a sprawling fortress that could conceal a dozen people. An insect crawled up her leg. She slapped at it; then at the mosquito buzzing near her ear. Sweat ran down her back. She glanced at her watch for the third time. Had she misunderstood Angela? Had they gone to the wrong apartment? "Wait, we have the phone. I'll call and find out where they are."

Sun fished it out of her pocket and passed it to her. Julie had to release Amber's arm to take the phone. She did so reluctantly, not trusting Amber yet. Would she run back to Miguel the moment she had the chance?

Scott's number rang. No answer. Her breath echoed in the silence as she peeked through the branches. This was not how she'd imagined her first trip after overcoming her agoraphobia. She'd only agreed to go because of Angela's persistence, with the understanding she wouldn't be overly stressed. And Angela had promised her she could have kitchen duty away from the children in the orphanage. She didn't know how much more she could take.

A rumbling vehicle slowed, drawing her attention away from the phone. A closer look revealed a gray bus idling at the curb. Scott leaped from it and flung the side door open, frantically motioning them in.

Julie ran like a deer being chased, gripping a girl with each hand. "Run."

As Sun and Amber scrambled in, Julie's eyes made a sweep of the street. An ancient sedan eased from a side road and inched up behind them. In spite of its heavily tinted windows, she could tell the driver was a male. She leaped in the bus, throwing all her weight into slamming the door, then collapsed against Sun, knocking her over. "Go. Go. Go." Scott gunned the engine, tires squealing as the bus pulled away from the curb.

Angela thrust her hand toward Amber. "What a rush. I'm Angela. Happy to meet you." She twisted toward Scott. "Can you cut this trip short and take me to the dorm to get my suitcase and then to the airport? I have to work a flight to Miami and Atlanta in three hours."

Julie hit her forehead with the palm of her hand. She'd forgotten Angela had to work. "It'll be close. I know you can't be late."

Angela patted her hand. "Not to worry. I wouldn't have missed this for the world. Whew, this was too exciting for my heart."

Sun was quiet; she rubbed Amber's arm as if the simple act would offer her comfort. Amber stared out the side window.

Julie twisted in her seat to check out the back window, then swiveled back toward Scott. "Do you see the car following us? Could you—how do they say in the movies—lose it, to be on the safe side? It's been following us ever since we got on the bus."

"Leave it to me. Buckle up." The bus swung onto a congested thoroughfare. Julie clenched the edge of her seat and wished she had a seatbelt. "Breathe, breathe, breathe."

Scott forced his way into the next lane, then veered into the parking lot of a sushi restaurant. Careening behind the building, they detoured into an alley and exited into a quiet residential road. They drove a mile before reentering a busy street. Julie kept watch out the back window for the car. They had lost it.

Angela's fingers tapped on her handbag. Julie knew that gesture well—she was worried about getting to the airport on time.

Scott glanced at Angela. "Not to worry. I know a shortcut. We'll get you there quick."

Twenty long minutes later at the dorm, Angela opened the door before the bus came to a complete stop and ran to get her suitcase. Julie knew she had her uniform laid out and could dress faster than anyone. She tried to think of something casual to talk about with Amber, yet she detested trivial conversation. This wasn't the time for serious inquiry or her plethora of questions. She settled for talking about the heat as she checked her watch again and again.

Seven minutes later, Angela walked toward the bus, her long honey curls glistening in the sun, and climbed in holding her pumps in one hand and her suitcase in the other. The bus headed for the airport.

With her cousin gone, she wouldn't have anyone to hide behind. "I wish you weren't leaving. They might move me from the kitchen to outdoor pursuits. What am I going to do with all those little boys? I don't know how to play soccer. And my Spanish is *nada*."

Angela laughed. "Ha, the thought of you playing any sport with boys. I can't get the picture out of my head now. Make it stop." She patted Julie's hand. "You'll be back in Orlando in three days. You only have one more at the orphanage. One day. You can do it."

"I hope so." She wilted in her seat. "But I'd feel better if you were here."

"C'mon, did you see yourself today? You were a rock star. Not one excuse. Only one panic attack. The old Julie is back."

At the airport curb, Angela hopped out of the bus, blew kisses at them, and disappeared into the terminal. Julie's arms wrapped around her chest; a glacial fear filled her to the extent that she shivered. She glanced out the back window. Was that the same sedan with tinted windows from earlier? Her gaze flickered toward Amber whose fingers clung to the window ledge as if she was being held against her will.

And she stared longingly at the same sedan.

Chapter Two

Julie glanced at her watch—again. Only fifteen minutes had crawled past since the last time she checked. Did nine-year-old boys take naps? She hoped so. They hadn't been too impressed with her suggestion to help clean the kitchen. Instead, she allowed herself to be led into the yard for a soccer game, but she drew the line at joining. So she sat, dodging errant balls and thinking of all the productive things she could be doing. Like working on a brief she had left in the dorm or making a list of errands to do when she got back to Orlando.

Sun kneeled by her chair. "How you doing?"

"I'm fine, but I'd be better if I could finish making lunch for these ... boys."

"I'll give you a break. Amber can watch the babies." They sat in silence watching the boys pummel one another. Then Sun said, "I want to go home. I miss my mom. But it's hard to leave the babies without someone to love them. What will happen to them?"

"Hopefully, another mission group will come and take our place. I think I'm ready to go home, too. Ouch." She flung her arm up to deflect a ball and put it on her lap.

"I want them to be safe and have their own families. Just like me." Sun's voice trailed off as she disappeared into the house.

"Sorry, Miss." A boy with chubby cheeks and a brush cut needing a trim stuck out his hands for the ball.

Using her limited Spanish, Julie said, "I'll be fine. Tell the boys to finish in five minutes and wash their hands for lunch."

"Yes, ma'am." But the boy remained next to her, kicking a pebble with his toe.

Why didn't he leave? Was there some cultural protocol she didn't know about to dismiss someone? "Is there something else?"

"You abogado, Miss, a lawyer?"

"Si. How did you know?"

"The ladies en la casa—they … talked about you. They say you are too young to be an abogado."

"Well, I am. Porque?"

The boy wiped his nose with the back of his hand. "Mi tio … uncle … needs a lawyer."

"There are many *abogados* here in Bogotá." She stood and signaled the boys to form a line in front of her and hold out their hands. She shook her head at three of them. "Back to the baño and use soap this time." She felt a tug on her shorts.

"Will you talk to my uncle, please? Today? Just for a minute. He needs an abogado americano."

She wished he would leave; she didn't have time to work on a case down here. Besides, it would be too out of her comfort zone. His worried eyes overcame her reluctance just as Sun's had at the market. Using her whiniest voice, she responded, "Okay, but I don't know what I can do. What's your name?"

"Alejandro, Alex." He thrust his hand out to shake hers, whipped around, and ran to the back of the line forming at the outhouse.

Putting the little boy out of her mind, she quickly threw together some empanadas—following a recipe Angela had left her; piled chips on paper plates; cut up pieces of an unfamiliar type of banana, and poured lemonade.

The boys devoured the lunch and pounded their fists on the table for more food. She found some wilted-looking ice cream bars in the freezer and tossed them on the table. When Sun showed up, Julie murmured a heartfelt thank you, and ran into the kitchen to clean up.

As she scoured the sink with an emaciated steel-wool pad, her mind went to the orphans. What happened to them when volunteers weren't there to do all the work? Not once had the women who ran the place left the living room to check on the children. An empty refrigerator, garbage pails teeming with flies, the smell of decay in the air had welcomed the volunteers a week ago. She couldn't think about it anymore, so she did what she always did when plagued with uncomfortable thoughts—she compartmentalized. Push the delete button when they popped up.

Children weren't her thing anyway. But that little Alex was rather charming.

A knock on the kitchen door jarred her musings. She opened it to a man about thirty, hair thinning, dressed in khakis and a polo shirt—clean-cut came to mind. He entered the kitchen hand in hand with Alex. She had a swift desire to hide.

"You are Senora Julie?"

She stuck out her hand, then pulled it back, not quite sure what the proper etiquette in Colombia was with regard to shaking hands. Hoping he didn't notice, she clasped them in front of her. "Yes, I am Julie Richards. What can I do for you?"

His eyes were dark and warm. "I am Kevin Perez. My nephew said you are an attorney. I'm searching for one—an American attorney."

Julie was surprised at his fluent English. "Why an American one?"

He coughed, pulled out a handkerchief, and mopped his forehead. "I want asylum in your country."

"Asylum? Seriously? Are you in danger?"

"Yes, as is my family."

She pointed at a chair and sat next to him. "I'm not an attorney in this country, but I can tell you what you'll need to prove you're eligible for asylum. It's an extremely high standard. By the way, your English is excellent."

"My father worked in the states when I was in elementary school. We lived in Virginia for eight years." He paused, then said something to Alex, who waved good-bye and departed. "I never thought I'd be in this position." His mouth worked as if he was choosing his words carefully. "I work for the Colombian government. I'm in charge of setting up communication networks and am privy to government information many groups would like to access." He leaned toward her, tugged at his collar, and surveyed the room as if the walls had ears.

"Please continue."

"One night my team and I were returning from setting up a system at a remote location outside of Bogotá. The equipment in the back of our truck was worth a lot of money, and all I could think about was getting back to the safety of the base. Then it happened—we were ambushed. FARC, a paramilitary organization, stopped our truck, put guns to our heads, and demanded we unload the equipment. Six of them; only three of us. They were armed; we weren't." He coughed. "Do you have something to drink?"

Julie went to the refrigerator. "Water or juice?"

"Water's fine." He took a swig from the bottle she handed him. "I knew it was up to me to guard the equipment with my life. The computers held information catastrophic in the wrong hands. I told them the equipment was worthless; couldn't be fixed. I think I said we were going to scrap it. Fortunately, they believed me. One of them said they didn't have any way to cart off the equipment anyway."

He drank again and wiped the sweat off his brow with the back of his hand. "They weren't done with us. They seized our identification badges, phones, and wallets, and drove us in their van to an ATM machine. With guns to our heads, they forced us to withdraw our money. I remember thinking they weren't going to be happy since I only had eighty dollars in my account. They weren't. One guy pulled out my kid's and my wife's pictures and said, 'Take a good look. We know where you live. We know who you work for. Not a word to anyone, or you can kiss your family goodbye. You'll be dead meat.' One of them hit me in the back of the head—probably with the gun he was holding. I woke up in an alley a few hours later." He set the bottle down, stood, and walked to the other side of the room facing away.

Once she had finished scribbling notes on a napkin, she asked, "What happened after that? Did they follow up on their threat? Show up at your house? Harass your children? Did you go to the police or to the hospital?"

"No, I took what they said seriously. I didn't want my family to be killed. I did go to a clinic to have my head checked out because I needed stitches. My head bled a lot. I also told my boss because the equipment might have been compromised when they abducted us." He took another sip of his drink. "Then the calls started. Hang ups at first. Then breathing and laughter. In the middle of the night, there'd be pounding on the door. One morning, I found a dead dog on the driveway—threats in blood on my car window. I'm so glad my children didn't witness that. The next night, my little girl woke up to a man's face in the window. She won't sleep in her room anymore. That's when I knew we had to leave the country."

Julie swallowed hard. Her dry mouth yearned for water. "I've never heard of FARC, but they sound like a violent gang of thugs. In order to qualify for asylum in the United States, you need to fulfill two requirements. You must belong to an identifiable group—a religion, a race, a political or ethnic group, and because of your association with the group, you have a well-founded fear of persecution in your country. I would assume your association with the government of Colombia is the reason you and your family are being harassed by FARC. I need to tell you the standard of persecution is extremely high to meet these days. So far your family has been harassed but not attacked. Also, it's not clear whether you are being harassed because you belong to a political group or because they want to scare you into not going to the police."

He rubbed his temples. "You don't understand. FARC is more than a bunch of thugs; it's a terrorist organization—extremely powerful and dangerous. They're involved in drug trafficking and kidnapping. They kill for sport. We can move, but they'll find us. And their actions are escalating. Soon it'll be my daughter who is kidnapped or my wife who is raped. I can't let that happen." His voice rose with every word, and he pounded the table with his fist. "I'm sorry. I don't know what to do. Don't know where to go." He covered his face with his hands.

They sat in silence for a moment. Julie gnawed on her pencil as she considered what to do; then she stood. "I'll take your case, Mr. Perez. I'll do my best for you, but I can't promise results. I suggest you meet me at the American embassy tomorrow. I have to go there anyway. We'll be leaving Colombia the day after tomorrow. You need to go into hiding with your family. We'll be in touch."

He grasped her hand in his. "Thank you, Miss Julie." Tears appeared in his eyes, and he blinked them away. She fished in her pocket for a business card, wrote a time for them to meet, and handed it to him.

Sun and Amber bounced into the kitchen arm in arm. Years had vanished from Amber's face with the makeup. She appeared like any other teenage girl. Sun said, "The bus is here. Time to say goodbye."

Julie extended her hand to her new client. "I guess we're leaving. We'll see you tomorrow at the embassy."

"I can't thank you enough. I'll be there—you can be sure. Now I have to go find my nephew and say goodbye to him."

What had she gotten herself into? What if she let Mr. Perez down because of her lack of experience? Sure, she had filled out forms for applicants before, but this was a real family in danger. What if, because of her ineptitude, the family was denied entry into the United States and was attacked or worse? Ice-cold fear seared her spine. She should never have said yes. It would be best if she told him she couldn't take the case. She ran out to the curb to catch him, but it was too late—he was gone.

Trudging back into the kitchen, she gave it a final inspection, satisfied that it was far cleaner than ten days earlier when she'd arrived. She ran her finger along the counter. Others would have preferred working with the local people, but not her. She was happy to be in the background. The place smelled like household cleaner—much better than eau de garbage. She poked her head into the living room to say a quick goodbye to the women in charge and joined Sun and Amber in the bus. "We have to take Amber to the embassy tomorrow. She'll need papers for the trip back to the States. How are you feeling?"

Amber peered at the ground, at the house, anywhere but at Julie. "I'm okay. But I miss him."

"Who?"

"Miguel."

"Seriously?"

"He wasn't all bad. He loved me."

Julie cringed. "I don't understand. Think about what he made you do. If he loved you, why would he hurt you?"

Amber's shoulders stiffened, and she crossed her arms across her chest. "He didn't hurt me much. Only when I deserved it. I don't want to talk about it." Her lips pressed together in a single line. Sun rubbed her arm and laid her head against her shoulder.

Stockholm Syndrome.

If they could get Amber out of the country and back to her family, there'd be time for healing. She changed the subject. "Tell me about your family? Where do they live? Do you have any sisters or brothers?"

Amber didn't answer at first. Then she chafed as if Julie was forcing the words from her. "I have a little brother. His name is Oliver, and a twin sister—Aubrey. My family lives in Wichita. My dad's a pastor there."

Sun squeezed Amber's arm. "You are a lucky girl. I wanted a twin when I was little. Someone to share secrets with. And clothes."

"Not so lucky. We're nothing alike. She's Miss Perfect. It's one of the reasons I left. I couldn't stand always being asked why I wasn't more like her."

Julie didn't want to appear too pushy. "When was the last time you were home?"

A line formed between Amber's eyebrows. "Almost two years ago."

"What happened?"

"I got in a fight with my mom over my friends and my grades. She was always on my case."

"And that particular day?"

"I got caught skipping, and the office called home. My parents overreacted and said horrible things. I vowed it was the last time I would ever be compared to Aubrey."

"What did you do?"

"I called my friend Vanessa to meet me at the mall. We did the usual. Hung out in the food court; then we checked out a few stores like Hot Topic. We met some guys in the store, and we walked around with them for a while. One of them, Nick, told me I was pretty. I knew he was lying, but it felt good to hear it. Aubrey got the pretty genes—I mean, we're identical, but she knows how to work it. The mall was closing, and Vanessa had to go home. I didn't have anywhere to go, so the guys told me I could crash at their apartment. I ended up staying with them for a long time." Her lips closed tight, and Julie knew not to dig deeper.

Don came on the microphone and thanked them for a hard day's work. He told them to enjoy their last day in Colombia and described a number of available excursions. Julie paid little attention. Their morning would be taken up visiting the embassy.

*****

Sleeping an hour later without an alarm clock to wake her was what Julie needed. She shuffled into the dining room at nine, magnetized by the heavenly aroma of the coffee. Colombian coffee smelled delicious—rich, full, and nutty. But her cloudy head needed the taste.

Once the caffeine had done its work, Julie went to wake the girls. She glanced at her watch. They needed to get a move on. Kevin Perez would be meeting her at the embassy in two hours. She knocked, expecting them to be asleep, but Sun swung open the door—fully dressed and smiling. The room was a disaster, but they were ready.

Amber's sullenness had disappeared. She and Sun acted like typical teenagers, giggling over memories only the two of them shared. Julie used the time to rehearse what she would say to the officials at the embassy. It would be tricky persuading them that Amber was a victim. She didn't have a passport, so she was in the country illegally. Julie would have to convince them she was brought to Colombia against her will. Problem was—Amber was resistant to disclose what had happened to her, and she still was loyal to Miguel.

Julie broke into their conversation. "Amber, the officials are going to ask you a lot of personal questions. We need them to see you as a victim. I know you don't like to talk about your situation, but tell them exactly what happened when you were brought here and what has occurred since."

Amber became quiet and stared straight ahead.

As they climbed out of the bus, Julie spotted the sedan parked a few spaces behind. Was it Miguel's car? The last thing she needed was for Amber to see him and run. Julie whipped out a long scarf she'd bought at the market and draped it over Amber's head. "You need to stay in disguise—for your own protection." She could only hope the scarf would do double duty in keeping the two star-crossed lovers apart.

When they'd almost reached the top of the stairs near the entrance to the embassy, a voice called out, "Amber, what are you doing?" Julie hazarded a glance back at the car. The guy who had guarded Amber leaned against the bumper, arms crossed, staring in their direction. Amber didn't seem to hear. Julie pushed her through the door before he called her name again.

Entering the American embassy felt like coming home. She released the breath she'd been holding in since she saw the car. The place was surprisingly empty except for a couple with a baby, sitting next to a man in a suit, presumably their lawyer.

When their number was called, Julie accompanied Amber into a small office with a massive desk that took up most the space. A man with wisps of gray hair parted and swept to one side stood as they entered and pointed to the folded chairs across from him. Pictures of grandchildren graced the bookshelves behind him. Julie hoped it meant he was compassionate. As he busied himself searching for something, she rehearsed what she would say. Not having long to make her case for Amber; she had to get it right. *Think opening statement—precise but compelling.*

His glanced up from a file. "Tell me, why are you here?"

Julie cleared her throat. "Sir, my name is Julie Richards. I'm an attorney, and this is Amber … Amber …" It occurred to her she didn't know her last name; she didn't even know if Amber was her real name.

"Siemens. Amber Marie Siemens," the girl spoke up.

The man switched his focus away from Julie toward Amber. "Why are you here?"

She glanced at Julie, then back to the man. "I was kidnapped and brought here about a year ago. I want to go home." Tears popped and rolled down her cheeks, and pink blotches appeared on her neck.

The man stared at Amber as if he was having difficulty processing what she said, yet his face betrayed no emotion. He stood, shuffled the papers in front of him, and said. "Excuse me for a minute."

Julie felt dismissed, as if he hadn't believed them. She covered the stain on her shirt. "Sir, please, her kidnapper is outside at this moment, standing by an old sedan parked at the curb. Please don't send her out there." Now Amber knew. She could kick herself.

"I'll be back." He cast a sideways glance at Amber before leaving the room.

Amber chewed on a nail, and her leg tapped at lightning speed.

"I think I made a mistake in coming here. I should go." She stood and hastened toward the door.

"No." Bolting from her chair, Julie lunged at her, wondering what she could say or do to keep her from leaving the room.

At the same moment, the man entered and seemed confused. "You're leaving? Please don't. I have your file here." He pointed toward her seat, and a smile crossed his face for the first time. "Amber, I don't know if you know it or not, but you are on the national list of missing and exploited children. The last time you were seen was …" He scanned the file, "Wichita, Kansas, about eighteen months ago." He glanced at Julie. "We'll take it from here. Thank you for bringing her in."

Julie crossed her arms. "But, but what are you going to do?"

"We'll take care of her, don't you worry." His hand flicked toward the door.

Leaning toward Amber, she said, "We'll be right out in the lobby." She surveyed the room before leaving it. Breathe, she told herself.

Sun was standing with Kevin Perez, arms laden with files. "Where's Amber?"

"With the officer." Julie had completely forgotten about Mr. Perez. "Sun, I'll be right back. Mr. Perez, come with me." She joined the short line waiting at a glass window with a microphone and a small opening for passing documents back and forth. When they advanced to the window, she bent toward the microphone. "This is my client, Mr. Kevin Perez. He is seeking asylum in the United States of America."

The woman glanced at her and Mr. Perez, then passed a document through the sliver of an opening. "Read the forms, fill them out, and bring all required documents. Next."

What? She'd expected a bigger reaction to a request for asylum. But this was Colombia, and it probably happened every day. As she returned to Sun, she searched through her purse for signature tabs to highlight where Kevin should sign. In the process, she bumped into the officer who had interviewed Amber. "Sorry."

"You don't need to stay," the man said. "We've already contacted her parents. They'll be waiting for her at the Wichita airport tonight."

Julie was speechless and amazed. The government never

worked that fast. She didn't trust it. Was this man in cahoots with Miguel? She eyed the man, rifled through her purse for a business card, and thrust it into his hand. "Please, give this to Amber. Tell her to call if she needs us."

Sun's face vacillated from sad to joyful to confused. "Will we be able to say goodbye to her?"

"I don't think so."

"She not going to be happy."

"About not saying goodbye to us?"

"No, the last thing Amber wants is to go home."

Chapter Three

Angela made a cursory check of each seat on the plane for teddy
bears and sweaters—the kind of things passengers leave when
they're in a hurry to reach their destination. She was more than
ready to sleep in her own bed. In the meantime, she sat on the jump
seat, removed her pumps, and massaged her feet.

Combining this working trip with her church's volunteer
opportunity was hard on the body. And that dorm bed had such a
hard mattress, it was like sleeping on a sheet of slate. A few more
things to check and she could go home. First, count the liquor
bottles and make sure the money balanced. Next, check the galley
drawers, so the incoming crew wouldn't have to stock them.

She made one more sweep of the cabin. As A-line for the
flight, she had to make sure she left it in perfect shape. Luckily,
this had been a normal night with no surprises. The overhead bin
where her bag was stored was the only one still closed. She tugged
on it, but it wouldn't budge.

Great. Why was it stuck? Her bag wasn't that big.

She steadied her feet against the armrests for better leverage to
grip the bin handle. One-two-three. Tugging with all the strength
her precarious stance allowed, she could only persuade the bin to
open a few inches. Something was catching, and it better not be her
bag, which had cost most of a paycheck. With one last grunt, she
put all her weight into lifting the handle.

The door inched open. Two eyes stared back at her. Two

scared dark saucers and trembling lips and tousled dark hair needing a comb, although the child couldn't be more than six or seven.

"Hey, how did you get in there"

The child said nothing.

"C'mon. We've got to get you out."

She leaned as far in as she could to grip the child's arm. "That's why the door wouldn't budge. How long have you been in there anyway? I don't remember seeing you on the flight."

The bin opened a few more inches revealing the child was a girl. Her eyes widened, and she shook her head. To Angela's consternation, she pulled away and scooted backward in the tight space and pulled away from Angela's grip.

"Hablas espanol?'

More silence.

Couldn't she talk? "Come on now, honey. You have to come out of there. Your parents are probably worried sick. Work with me." The more she tried to catch her arms, the more she slipped through her fingers. "Okay, enough. Come on. The cleaning crew will be here in a minute, so we have to go now."

Even though the child couldn't have been more than thirty pounds, the space was so small her knees touched her ears. The girl encircled her knees with her arms. Matted brown hair covered her frightened eyes. Her lips trembled.

Something about her was familiar.

Angela covered her nose with her hand. The smell of unwashed clothes was overwhelming. "I'll have to go for help. You stay here. Don't try to jump out on your own. I'll be right back."

What to do? She knew she hadn't seen her on the flight. It was her routine to hand out mini-wings and little toys to children. She would have remembered those eyes. Of course, one of the other flight attendants might have tended to this one. But what was familiar about her? She was dirty. Was she wearing shoes? Parents usually made sure their kids were properly dressed for flights.

Stowaway.

The word entered her mind in bold letters with an exclamation point. There had been quiz questions about stowaways during training, but she hadn't heard of an actual case. She couldn't remember the protocol. Well, logic told her to get the gate agent.

She rushed off the plane and into the waiting area—no one was in sight. She ran to the next gate where two busy agents checked boarding passes for a flight to Cincinnati. She glanced in all directions and decided her best bet was to call the airport police. Tell them to meet her at gate … she twirled back around. Gate 54B.

The busy agent handed her the phone without asking why. After quickly relaying the information, she returned to her gate. She paced in front of the jet-way door, willing the police officer to hurry. Orlando airport was always hectic; she hoped it wouldn't take too long. Where was the officer?

She dredged up old procedures, ordering them in her brain.

1. Do not leave the stowaway alone. Well, great. But what was she to do? She had to get help, didn't she?

2. Call the authorities. Check.

3. File report. She'd do it once the child was secured.

Angela shook her watch to make sure it was working. Where were the girl's parents? They must be frantic. Or maybe there weren't any. Had the girl sneaked on the plane by herself? Not possible, not since nine eleven. How could a six-year-old girl pass through security and board a plane without anyone noticing? No, there had to be parents. But where were they? Her throat constricted. She borrowed Julie's remedy and managed three cleansing breaths.

"Miss? Did you call for me?" Angela whirled around to see a young officer wearing police garb too big for his body.

"Thanks for coming so fast. We have a stowaway on this plane. I know it's hard to believe. I need your help to get the little girl out of the bin. Follow me."

He hiked his pants up by the waist a la Steve Urkel. "Did you talk to her?"

"She hasn't said anything, so I don't know if she speaks English. Our flight originated in Colombia. I don't know how she got on. This hasn't happened before. We're so careful to check our manifest against the passengers." They stopped in front of the bin and she pointed. "There."

The bin was empty.

The agent's face registered impatience.

"She. Was. Right. There." She could feel herself scowling as she strode to the back of the plane, surveying each row of seats she passed. "We need to check everywhere. She might be hiding. I'll start back here; you start in the galley, and we'll meet in the middle." She knew it was a lost cause. If the girl had boarded the flight with no one seeing, she could have easily escaped. Still, she couldn't give up.

Following the agent, she paused at the bin for a final glance. Something round and shiny reflected the light. Balancing on the armrest, she gripped the edge of the bin with her left hand and wriggled it forward with her finger tips, pulling out a grayish stuffed animal. It was surprisingly heavy. The single ragged ear indicated it had once been a bunny. One shiny brown eye watched her. The agent was already off the plane when she stuffed it in her purse.

Taking hold of her suitcase, she reviewed her training. Notify the police and file a report with the base. Her feet hurt; she longed for sleep, but she needed to do her job.

***

Alone on the elevator to the parking level, she reflected on the whole ordeal. Funny. Both the police officer and the flight attendant supervisor treated her as if it was her fault the little girl was on the flight and got away under her watch. Feeling in her purse for her car keys, her fingers touched something soft—ah, the bunny. She'd forgotten the bunny.

On any other day, crossing an empty parking deck in the dark didn't bother her. But tonight it did. The clip of her heels and the squeaky wheel on her suitcase heralded her presence to anyone watching as she headed to the far end where her car was parked. Shadows loomed from the familiar concrete buttresses. She imagined the man from the sedan jumping out. Her head bounced back and forth like a tennis ball alert to any stranger nearby—too many places for someone to lurk and leap out. She'd never live it down if Julie ever heard that she was afraid of the dark.

But something didn't feel right.

After she put her suitcase in the trunk, she fumbled with the purse strap when her keys clattered to the ground. As she bent, a shudder went down her spine.

Who was there?

Her eyes darted back and forth. She needed to get in the car.

29

Clicking it open, she bolted upright, and scanned the area. No one in sight. No sound except for the whish-whish of the elevator as it changed floors. Her hand went to the door handle.

Something touched the back of her pants. Someone was right behind her; she could sense it. Her eyes darted behind and choked back a scream.

Big eyes peered up at her. A small dirty finger pointed at her hand. Angela glanced at the bunny she held. "How did you … where … is this yours?"

The girl nodded and dislodged it from Angela's hand. Hugging it against her neck, she patted it like it was a baby, and her little face relaxed.

Angela's hands twisted the purse straps as she scanned the still-empty area. "You can't stay here. I don't know how you found me, but we have to take you back. I don't want to be charged with kidnapping." She went to seize the stowaway's hand but stopped short when the girl backed up. She repeated her words in Spanish. The little girl shook her head, and a petulant expression enveloped her face.

Angela put her hands on her knees. "Where are your parents?"

She stared at the ground. "No padres."

She put her hand on her chest. "Angela." She pointed at her. "What's your name? Cómo te llamas?"

Silence. The girl jerked away.

"We have to go back." She stood and grasped the child's hand tightly. No way would she lose her again. She glanced at her charge, and then it struck her. "I know where I saw you before. You're the street performer—the contortionist. That's how you got past everyone and climbed into the bin."

Although the child weighed thirty pounds at best, it took all of Angela's strength to pull the resistant child toward the elevator door. They'd only gone about eight parking spaces when a car squealed around the far corner and stopped. Two men got out and ran toward them.

With a feral scream, the girl yanked away and dashed into the shadows of the closest vehicle.

Angela didn't have time for this. The car moved toward her. The men slowed down to a brisk walk, searching the shadows on each side.

Something shiny in one of the man's hands reflected the overhead light. Angela's fight-or-flight instinct took over, and she dove between two minivans. They were definitely not the good guys. Squatting low, she crept toward the girl and huddled next to her.

Footsteps got louder, approached, and slowed down. Words were exchanged in muffled Spanish. The little girl's heart beat against her chest when she pulled her close and stroked her tangled hair. Had they seen her?

They had to get to her car and lock themselves in. Then she could call for help. She pointed in that direction. The girl held tightly onto to her wrist. Peeking around the front of the bumper, they crept past one car at a time. Footsteps slowed and then stopped. Peering under the car, Angela saw their shoes on the other side. Trapped. They were going to die in this dark, cavernous, mildew-smelling place. Not if God could help. She prayed.

A scene from an old movie popped into her mind. Taking a hairbrush from her purse, she lobbed it as hard as she could behind them. It bounced off the hood of a car and clattered to the ground. The shoes spun toward the sound and ran.

Angela nudged the girl's back, and they scurried to her car. So close. Surely, the men had found her hairbrush by now and were headed back. The remote thundered when it clicked. They clambered into the front seat, scrunched down, and she locked the doors. When she tried to put the key in, like in a bad dream, her hand shook so hard she couldn't fit it in the ignition.

C'mon.

Pounding footsteps.

Finally, the key connected as did the engine. She slammed the Audi into reverse without even checking, and peeled out. Voices cursed her in Spanish. Doors slammed. An engine gunned, and tires squealed behind them.

Who were those men? And why were they chasing them? The girl hugged her bunny—so short, her feet stuck straight out. "Put on your seat belt…" What was *seat belt* in Spanish? She knew what a seatbelt was on an airplane. "Cinturón de seguridad?" The girl complied.

Angela almost hit the wall on the last curve before the exit. The car was gaining on her. The security arm usually took so long to move once she'd slid her parking card into the slot. Should she just crash through it? She hazarded a glance in the rearview mirror. The car was still a half a lane behind her.

She stopped at the gate.

"How's it going, ma'am? Were your flights smooth?" Ruddy-face Ralph had worked this shift as long as she'd been parking there.

"See that car? He's following me. Could you do something?"

"Sure can. Be safe." With a conspiratorial smile, he saluted her as she eased past the window.

Once out of the parking garage, she floored the pedal and glanced in her rearview mirror. She'd be sure to thank Ralph for the wide gap he had provided. She sped toward a shortcut she'd used before to avoid traffic—a side road filled with houses needing paint and driveways full of trucks. The lawns needed mowing. Another corner brought her down a road skirting a lake overgrown with reeds. She modulated her voice and asked one more time. "Cómo te llamas?"

Humming, the girl swished the bunny's tail under her nose. "Rosa."

"Rosa is a pretty name. What's your last name?"

No response.

This wasn't getting any easier. "Why are those men following you?" she asked in her best Spanish.

Rosa sucked her thumb, tail swishing under her nose.

I give up, she muttered. Five more intersections and a few miles on the toll road brought them to her Dr. Phillips neighborhood. She was about to take a left into her condo parking lot when a glance in the rearview mirror showed that same car a block behind. How had they found her? She accelerated. No way would she lead them to her home.

At the next corner, she veered onto a street adjacent to a golf course. Another jerk of the wheel brought her back to the toll road. She didn't get it. Maybe she wasn't as good a secret agent as she had imagined. After passing a number of cars, she veered onto an exit, hoping she'd lost them. At a red light, it was time to take stock of her situation. She should go to the police. Not yet. Rosa had been through too much. She glanced at the small girl. Her eyes were closed and her head bobbed rhythmically.

She knew where to go—to Celebration—Julie's new home. It would be empty because she was still in Colombia for two more days. She swerved from the right lane eliciting an angry honk. Speeding off, she headed for Julie's bungalow. Keeping an eye on the nearly deserted road, she opened the glove box and snagged the garage opener so she could hide her car. Lucky for her, she still had it from six months ago. Julie wouldn't mind. Then Angela glanced at the sleeping girl. Yes, she would.

No one followed her mud-spattered Audi into the alley. At last, they slid into the garage, and the door shut them in like a safe cocoon. She woke Rosa up and ushered her through the back hall, through Julie's law office, and into the kitchen.

After flipping on the light, she grasped Rosa's hands. "Would you like something to eat or drink?" The nearly-bare refrigerator held a pitcher of sweet tea. The cheese drawer contained a block of mold-covered cheddar and a stick of salami. She loaded her arms with the meat, mustard, and a box of crackers from the pantry. She put them on the dinette table and brought over two glasses and the pitcher of sweet tea. She plopped Julie's moist wipe container on the table and used one.

Rosa climbed into the chair and sat on her knees, her eyes eager and fearful at the same time. Angela handed her two wipes. Rose stared at them and laid them on the table.

"This is how you use them." She picked them up and demonstrated how to wipe each hand. The cloths darkened to a dull gray.

After pouring her a glass of tea, she placed a plate of crackers and meat in front of her. Rosa's eyes grew into saucers. She peered at Angela and back at the food, her tongue licking her lips.

Angela pointed at the food. "Eat."

Two little hands dove into the plate and then into her mouth. The mustard made Rosa's eyes water, and she clutched the tea with both hands and guzzled it down. Slamming the glass on the table, she commanded, "Más."

"Por favor?" Angela waited.

Rosa's face tightened. Then she repeated, "Por favor, Más." Angela poured more tea. When the food was gone, Rosa stood on the chair and giggled and thrust her mustard-covered hands toward Angela.

Holding her at arm's length, she carried her to the bathroom. While warm water filled the tub, she added some bubble bath hoping Julie wouldn't mind. Soon the room smelled of peaches and cream. Rosa touched the bubbles and shrieked, jumping in with her clothes on.

"Wait, Rosa." Then she stopped. Why not wash both at the same time? They certainly needed it. While Rosa slapped at the bubbles, Angela tried to come up with a plan. She reviewed the facts while working shampoo through Rosa's tangles.

Number one: Julie would not be happy. Stowaways were persona non grata in the US. As an officer of the law, Julie couldn't harbor a child in her house and didn't feel comfortable with children at the best of times. But what was Angela supposed to do? Those men meant harm, she was sure of it.

Number two: She had two days. If the police were called, they'd take Rosa and send her back to Colombia. To what? No parents, she had said. Did the little girl live in the streets? Two days wouldn't make a difference. She could feed her and get her some better clothes and shoes. Julie would understand. Yeah, right.

Rosa stood, dress clinging and dripping, hair streaming water. Angela snatched a bath towel from the rack, enveloped her in it, and rubbed Rosa's hair until only dampness remained. Taking a large-toothed comb, she carefully teased out the tangles until her hair lay smooth. Angela sniffed. The smell of peaches was much more pleasant than the odor of unwashed clothes.

She grasped another towel and rewrapped her before carrying her into the adjacent bedroom, which happened to be Julie's. Bundled tightly, Rosa's eyes closed the minute her head hit the pillow.

Angela stared at the sleeping girl, so angelic and clean. She'd be fired for sure if they found out. But Rosa was worth fighting for—even if it meant losing her job. A shudder traveled down her spine. What had she gotten herself into?

Chapter Four

Julie bowed her head toward Mrs. Lee, who returned the gesture.
It seemed the right thing to do, although she winced at the thought
that she might be stereotyping. Did Asian people even do that
anymore? She waved good-bye to Sun. "Get some sleep. I'll see
you tomorrow."

Once Sun and her mother had reached their second-floor
apartment and shut the door, Julie checked her messages before
driving home. Six awaited her reply. A year ago, she would have
deleted them without a second thought. Now since she had her own
business, that luxury was gone.

The first was from Mr. Perez, the asylum client. Static made it
difficult to understand, but it sounded like he had filled out the
initial application and was mailing her the documents. Good. The
case was a slam dunk. If anyone deserved asylum, it was Kevin
Perez. Maybe she'd even get paid for a change.

She'd check the next three messages when she got home. Two
remained: one from Angela and the other was one she would
savor—from the man who hadn't been too far from her thoughts
during the trip. She'd save it for last and relish every word.

"Julie, Angela here. I'm at your place. I'll explain later. Oh, by
the way, my car's parked in your garage. Hope you don't mind.
See you."

Hmm. Why would Angela be at her house? Of course, she
didn't mind; they'd gotten along swimmingly for six months

before Julie moved to Celebration. Maybe something was wrong at Angela's condo.

The time had come to hear his voice. The voice that had made her homesick, eager to come home. She pressed the voicemail replay button before she pulled out of Sun's parking lot.

"Hey, it's Steve. Call me when you get in. I've … missed you."

And she missed him. The message was short, so like him. She loved the comfort of having Steve care for her. Smart, ruggedly handsome, funny in a sarcastic way, nice when he wasn't grouchy—she couldn't have designed a better boyfriend. They were coming up on their one-year anniversary—the longest relationship she'd ever had.

She thought back to their first date—when they admitted they'd hidden their feelings for each other during law school. All those study sessions where she'd hung on his every word. Where she'd out-laughed others at his jokes and didn't complain when he punched her in the arm like a good old boy. He was older—already ensconced in a career as a police detective. And he'd never seemed interested. Until last summer, when she'd called him for police advice, which had led to their first dinner.

Now, they were … comfortable—that was an apt word to describe their relationship, although he was always busy with his work, and she with hers. He'd finally passed the bar exam, so they could start their plans to open a family law practice together. But lately, the subject never came up.

Her mind drifted to the other guy in her life—the one that got away. Matt Conner. She'd blown it with him when she ordered him out of her house. And when she finally understood and called him, his number was disconnected. He'd moved on or away—she didn't know. It didn't seem possible that a whole year had passed since she last saw him. She didn't like losing. And she had lost him. But Steve had filled that void.

She pressed his number. Never good at relationships, she wouldn't blow it with Steve. Three rings, four rings, five…that deep, gruff, teasing voice she loved.

"Bricker." He must be on duty.

"Hey, Steve."

"You're back? When did you get in?"

"I just dropped off Sun, and I'm driving home."

"You know you shouldn't be talking on the phone while you're driving. I could pull you over and give you a ticket."

"I'm a great driver. And I'm using Blue Tooth. So, how've you been?"

"Good, especially now I know you're back. How was it? I still can't believe you went to South America. What happened to baby steps?"

"It was great, and I only had one panic attack. I think it was the heat more than anything else. And guess what? We found Amber."

"Amber? Name doesn't ring a bell."

"She was the girl in the van with Sun who went missing. The one Sun prays for whenever she says grace."

"Oh that Amber, how did you find her?"

"Sun saw her in a market. You're not going to believe this, but we rescued her from her trafficker. Sun and I whisked her away, and it worked. She's on her way home to her parents in Kansas."

Silence ensued. Somehow she knew what was coming. She steeled herself.

His voice was calm, but every word was clipped. "Do you have any idea who you were dealing with? What were you thinking? That's what the police are for."

"Not in Colombia. She was there on a curb, and there were four of us. In retrospect, we probably should have called the police, but we took advantage of the opportunity."

"Was Angela there? It was probably her idea." A car radio on Steve's end blasted incoherent codes. "I have to go. Can we get together tomorrow? After my brother's track meet. Martin's trying to qualify for Special Olympics. As soon as I drop him off, I'll come over."

He had already hung up. "Sure."

Julie opened the garage door and maneuvered her car beside Angela's. She'd been dreaming of a hot soak with her new peaches and cream bubble bath, a cup of tea, and an early night in her bed with her own pillows and soft satin sheets. The only hitch was Angela, who would probably want to talk. She steeled herself for company as she opened the door.

Every light in the house seemed to be on. "Angela, I'm home. Are you here?"

Angela appeared in the kitchen wearing her robe. "Hi." Her

usual exuberance was subdued. Guilt? Sheepishness?

She moved haltingly toward Julie and hugged her, a bit too long and stiff. What was going on?

"Hi? Did something happen I should know about? You're acting weird."

Angela's eyes peered at the ceiling, the floor, anywhere but at her.

"Okay, when you're ready, you can fill me in, but in the meantime, I'm going to go unpack and take a long, hot bubble bath." She brushed past Angela.

She pulled her arm back. "Wait. Don't go in there."

Julie studied her, a line forming between her brows, ignored Angela's hand, and headed to her room. She didn't know what to expect, but she knew she wasn't going to like it. With Angela on her heels, she opened the door and flicked on the light. Her bed was unmade, but that wasn't unusual. Hoisting her suitcase on the bed, she unzipped it. Something caught her eye—a movement on the floor next to the bed. A balled-up blanket. What was under it— a dog? Had Angela bought a puppy and now wanted her to take care of it? It was so like Angela. "I'm not taking care of your dog," she announced, "I can't believe you'd …"

She approached the blanket, bent down, and lifted one corner.

A tiny sleeping girl sucked her thumb, a stuffed animal resting under her chin. A frown crossed her face as if she were irritated by the unwanted guest exposing her to the light. Julie spun toward Angela who leaned against the doorway. "Who is she?"

"Rosa."

"Okay, what's she doing in my bedroom?"

"You'd better sit down." Angela pointed at the bed. "Remember the little street performer from the corner where we got Amber? That's her."

"But … what is she … how did she get in my bedroom?"

"Long story. Let's make a pot of tea and talk."

"Explain, not talk, explain."

Julie let Angela pull her out of the room. She didn't get it. Children didn't belong in her house any more than gerbils, geckos, or dogs. They're cute and small, but they had their place—zoos, nature areas, other people's houses.

Plopping onto the dinette chair, Julie rubbed her temples.

"Okay, what's going on?"

Angela continued to face away as she busied herself making tea. "It all started in the overhead bin on the flight from Colombia. The passengers had left, and I couldn't get it open for my suitcase. When I finally did, she was there, but she escaped when I went to get help."

The kettle whistled, and Angela filled the teapot with water. Julie noticed that she drained it just the way she had taught her. Then she placed two teabags in the pot and refilled it with boiling water. The tea cozy was placed over the pot before she returned to her story.

"I filed a report about having a stowaway on my flight before I left the terminal. I was so bushed after Colombia and working three flights, all I could think about was getting home and going to bed. But when I got to my car, Rosa was there. I have no idea how she found me. Or why. But she was so little and scared." She stopped long enough to place two cups on the table.

Julie flicked her hand, palm up. "There's more. Keep talking."

"As I was taking her back to the terminal, a car stopped, and two men with guns jumped out. Rosa screamed and ran. I ducked and hid with her." She stopped to pour steaming tea into their cups. "I distracted them."

"How?"

"I threw my hairbrush. I saw it in a movie. We made it to the car and hightailed it out of there. But I couldn't lose them, and they followed me to my condo." Her face held a hint of remorse. "I did all kinds of evasive driving but couldn't lose them, so I hid in your garage. Sorry to get you involved in this. I know you're not particularly comfortable with children." She took a sip of her tea.

"Children? How about stowaways? You know I could get disbarred for harboring one, and we both could be arrested."

Standing abruptly, Angela paced in the small kitchen, rubbing her arms. "Don't you think I've thought about that? I haven't slept since Colombia. Those men were out to hurt her, maybe even me. We had to get to a safe place."

"Why didn't you call the police?"

She slumped back into her chair. "I needed to talk to you first. What would the police do with her—put her in jail or foster care? She doesn't have parents, Julie. Did you notice she wasn't sleeping in the bed? Always on the floor, I find her. All she has in the world is a stuffed bunny with one ear missing. I haven't been out of the house since then. I'm afraid the men know we're in here. Check the front window."

After Angela switched off the living room light, they sneaked to the window, but stayed behind the curtain. "See that car parked across the street? It's been there for two days. The windows are tinted, but you can tell someone's in it. See the smoke coming out of the crack at the top?"

"Great." Julie went to the front door to secure it.

"I already locked all the doors. Rosa wasn't even wearing shoes, and her dress was filthy, so I called a friend with a first-grader to bring me some clothes for her. I also asked her to bring some milk and food until I could get to the store. Now that you're here, I'd like to check out that car. See what's up with it."

Rolling her eyes, Julie said, "Be careful, crazy lady. You don't know who you're dealing with. I think I'll call Steve, if that's all right with you."

Angela whipped around. "He's a cop."

"I know he is. He's my boyfriend."

"I want to be there when you call him. Could you watch from the window so if they kidnap me you can dial 911?"

"Absolutely. Don't do anything stupid, and hurry up, I'm getting sleepy."

Julie stationed herself at the window. The car was parked in front of Mrs. Radnor's house. Mrs. Radnor had a bead on everything that happened on the block. She'd probably already called the homeowners' association.

Angela appeared on the sidewalk, paused, and glanced back at the house. Julie waved at her from behind the curtain. Then Angela crossed to the other side just a few feet from the car. Why did she do that? What if someone jumped out and forced her into it? Angela rubbed her arms, a nervous habit of hers. Good. She needed to be cautious. Her gait slowed as she approached the car; then she picked up speed and rushed past it, her head down. When she veered left at the corner, Julie lost sight of her. The car followed her around the corner.

Julie let go of the curtain edge and stared at the phone. Should she call 911? But what would she say—a car followed her cousin around a corner. Come at once? She teased a cuticle with her teeth.

The backdoor squeaked open little by little. The men from the car were coming to get the girl, she was certain. Plastering herself against the wall, she squeezed her eyes shut and repeated a dozen times under her breath, "God, protect us." A weight pressed on her windpipe issuing in another panic attack. Her eyes darted in search of the paper bag she kept handy in every room. Then her knees buckled beneath her.

"Julie, what are you doing?" Angela stood in the doorway, a puzzled expression on her face. "It's me."

Grasping the wall with her fingers, Julie buoyed up her torso and managed a weak smile. "You scared me to death. What happened?"

"Nothing much. I couldn't see anything because their windows were tinted. I almost knocked on the driver's one but lost my nerve, so once I went around the corner, I doubled back through your neighbors' yards. One of those security lights went on in Mrs. Radnor's; other than that, I don't know more now than I did before."

"So you didn't notice the car followed you around the corner? I thought they got you and were coming to get the girl."

She went to the window and peered out. "The car's back. Let's call Steve."

"It's almost midnight. He'll be ornery if I wake him up." She dialed the number she knew so well. Six rings went to voice mail. After the beep, she said, "Hi, this is Julie. We have a…problem here. If you get this tonight, could you call me?" After disconnecting, she yawned. "Sorry. Guess sleep will have to wait. I'll put the house alarm on."

When she returned, Angela threw an afghan toward her, then dropped onto the sofa. Punching a throw pillow, she pressed a comforter over her shoulders. Julie plopped onto the recliner and pulled the blanket around her. Her eyelids were so heavy, nothing could jar them open. Until the phone rang. Julie managed a weak greeting.

"What's going on?"

She eased to a sitting position. "We have a little problem. It's a bit complicated. Are you at work or at home?"

"I'm on my way home. Do you need me to come to Celebration or can this wait until tomorrow?"

"I put the alarm on. It can wait, I think."

"What do you mean? Are you in danger?"

"Could be. Tomorrow will be just fine." It irked her that she couldn't slam the receiver down on a smart phone.

"I'm on my way."

Julie folded the afghan and glanced at her cousin who was rubbing her eyes. "He didn't sound too happy, but I'm glad he's coming with that car still out there."

"I'm worried about what Steve might do. He could take Rosa into custody or send her back to Colombia. She could end up in an orphanage like the one we worked at, or in juvenile, or worse. Maybe he'd even give her to those men. Who knows—maybe they have a legal claim on her."

Julie folded the comforter. "The longer we keep her without notifying the authorities, the more trouble we're going to be in with both of our jobs, as well as the law." A light tap on the back door stopped their banter. "Well, that was fast. I must have made him worry." After hurrying to the security panel to switch off the alarm, she ran to the back door—eager to see him and smell him, but not so much to hear him.

She stopped a foot shy of the door. Her hand went to the knob, but she pulled it back as if it would burn her. No window or peephole allowed her to peer through, but she was sure two people were mumbling on the other side. Who would Steve bring to her house at this hour? The doorknob jiggled. She stared at it, then backed up through the hall to reset the alarm, but not taking her eyes off the doorknob.

Pulling out her phone, her voice was barely audible. "Those guys are at the back door. They're trying to get in. What should we do?" Her breaths became short and shallow. She struggled for oxygen, but nothing came in. "I. Can't. Breathe." She dropped into the chair and concentrated on taking measured breaths, then said, "It's not working."

"I'll get you a paper bag." Angela rushed to the kitchen, then returned. "Here, put this over your nose and mouth and breathe normally. In and out, in and out. I sound like a flight attendant." She rubbed Julie's back. "Steve will be here in a minute. I'm glad you called him." She flicked off the light and sneaked to the window. "Car's still out there. I can't tell if anyone's in it."

A sharp rap against wood made them stare at each other. The next knock was accompanied by Steve's irritated voice. "I'm here."

Angela strode to the door then stopped. "Oh, almost forgot. I'll go switch off the alarm."

Not wanting Steve to see her with a bag over her nose, Julie shoved it between the cushions and headed for the door, running her fingers through her hair. The minute she saw him, she threw her arms around his shoulders. Firm, strong. She inhaled deeply— Jade East fading, mustard, and a bit of sweat. His five o'clock shadow brushed lightly against her cheek.

He gently untangled her arms from around his shoulders, tipped her chin up, and brushed a kiss on her nose.

She ushered him in but not before glancing past him to see what car he'd brought. "Oh, too bad. I hoped you were driving your patrol car."

He removed his hat and ran fingers through his tousled brown curls. His eyes crinkled. "Missed you too. And what difference does it make what kind of vehicle I'm driving?"

She pulled him in and pointed at the car in front of Mrs. Radnor's house. "It's a long story. See that sedan? The guys in it tried to break in the back door. I'm glad you didn't wait until tomorrow."

"Do tell. Is this going to be an official meeting?"

Angela walked to the door and gave Steve a quick hug. "Maybe, we're not sure yet."

Julie pointed at the sofa. "Angela, why don't you fill him in on your part, and I'll go make some coffee. Steve, would you like some?"

He said, "Just a half a cup," but his attention was on Angela's story starting at the market place in Bogotá. He hardly noticed when Julie handed him a steaming mug.

When Angela reached the end of her tale, her eyes glistened with tears. "I don't know if I did the right thing, but I couldn't let them take Rosa. I'm pretty sure she's had a rough life. I don't want anything else to happen to her. Did I tell you she doesn't have any parents? Please don't make me give her up. She trusts me." A single tear trailed down her cheek as she smiled weakly in Steve's direction.

Julie grinned to herself. How could he say no to that face? This was a new side of Angela—the maternal side. The Angela she was used to blazed her way into every situation without considering the cost. Julie didn't doubt her sincerity, but Maternal Angela was a stretch.

His head tilted to the side, and his lips pursed as if he was torn between Angela's charm and his duty. Finally, he broke his gaze and sniffed. "What do you want me to do?"

What? Julie rolled her eyes. If *she* had asked, he would have said no before she finished her request. "Could you find out who those guys are and what they want? And make them leave us alone."

He stood, linked his thumbs in his belt, and tapped on his holster. "I'll be right back."

Angela watched from the front window while Julie washed the coffee mugs. Her eyes went to the door every few seconds, willing Steve to walk through that door, to be safe.

Meanwhile, Angela gave a play-by-play. "He's opening the car door. The driver's getting out. He appears to be about forty, tall, beefy. Can't tell anything more. The other one's door's opening. He's getting out and leaning against the car. Smoking. Shorter than the other one. They're both wearing dark clothes. Steve's taking notes. The driver's arms are gesturing like he's mad. Steve's hand is on the man's shoulder. They're getting back in the car. What?"

Not a minute later, Steve tapped on the door.

Wiping her hands on a tea towel, she beat Angela to the door. "What happened? Who are they?"

Steve strode to the couch and plopped down on it. He referred to his notes. "Names are Pedro Navarro and Luis Rodriguez from Colombia. They claimed they're the girl's legal guardians but had no papers to show me. They were adamant but couldn't prove it."

Angela's voice was loud enough to wake up the child. "They're lying. You should have seen Rosa's face. She was scared to death when she saw them." Her hands went to her hips. "The men could be traffickers, you know, making money off her as she performs in the streets. I saw marks on her back—scars. Think of what they might do when they get her back—*if* they get her back."

Julie went into legal mode. "She's not a stowaway if she was trying to escape from them. If we could prove she was taken against her will, we could keep her here on asylum or on a T-visa, like Sun got when she ran away. It allows a victim to remain here to testify against a captor."

Angela fidgeted beside Steve on the couch. "What did they say to you? The driver appeared to be threatening you."

"He was mad that I wouldn't do anything to help. He actually teared up and threatened to go to the police and tell them *you* had kidnapped their child. They said they had a right to her, and if you didn't give her back within twenty-four hours, they promised to take action—whatever that means."

"But you're a cop. Why didn't you arrest them?"

Steve stood. "For one thing, they weren't doing anything illegal. It's not a crime to park a car on a public street." He gazed out the window. "They're still there. Ladies, I don't know what to tell you. I agree with you about the guys; they're not her legal guardians, but I don't know if the government would agree. And another thing, I would take their threat seriously. We have twenty-four hours. Rosa needs to be moved." He walked to the door. "Julie, why don't you file the papers for legal remedies? Angela, we could sneak the child out and take her to a shelter of some sort—maybe a woman's shelter. I'll do some research and call you tomorrow. Do you have to fly anywhere in the next few days?"

"Back to Colombia in two days for a three-day trip." Her eyes lit up. "I could get out of it. I've always wondered what those places were like."

"Good. I'll research local shelters. We can all leave at the same time, so they won't know who to follow. We'll keep in touch by phone."

Julie said, "What am I supposed to do about work? I have clients coming tomorrow for appointments. The door needs to be unlocked during business hours, but I won't feel safe with those guys out there."

Steve said, "Keep the doors locked." He paused. "This is a federal matter—out of my jurisdiction. Homeland Security will need to get involved and the FBI. I'll help you get her to a safe place, but then I'll give the case to a friend of mine. It might be a human trafficking issue—a child working as a slave and all. The task force head is a friend. I'll talk to him." Julie held the door open for him; he squeezed her hand and kissed the top of her head. "Until tomorrow, ladies."

While Angela checked on Rosa, Julie groused to herself about not being able to use her bedroom to unpack. She couldn't stand leaving a packed suitcase overnight. "Angela, can we move her? I was counting on sleeping in my own bed."

"Sure, can you help me? We'll put her in the guest bedroom with me. She'll want to sleep on the floor, and I'll use the bed."

Angela bent down and lifted the tiny girl. She gestured with her head at the comforter and pillow on the floor. Julie picked them up and followed her, glancing back to see if she had left anything behind. A dingy bunny without an ear lay on the floor. She picked it up and brought it to her nose. It needed a good cleaning—funny, it jingled—like something was loose inside.

Chapter Five

Angela stretched her arms while she waited for the coffee to perk. Her mind had raced well into the night. Eager anticipation combined with worry about the morning's trip to the shelter kept her checking the clock a dozen times.

"Hola." Holding her rabbit by the ear, Rosa, dressed in pink-striped pajamas, stood in the middle of the kitchen peering up at her, head tilted to one side.

"Buenos dias, Rosa," Kneeling down, Angela grinned. "Guess what? We're going on a little trip today. We're going to be staying at another house."

Rosa's head tilted further to the right, jarring Angela's memory of her charge's primary language. She repeated her news the best she could with her limited Spanish. Rosa's eyes lit up, but stayed that way only a moment. Then she backed up with arms folded across her small chest.

"It will be okay. We're taking you to a safe place." She knelt down and enfolded her hands in hers. "Tell me about the men in the car at the airport. Are they good men or bad men?"

Rosa's face scrunched, and she peered down at her bunny. "Muy mal."

Leading her to the kitchen chair, Angela sat her down so they could face each other. "Porque ellos son mal? Why are they bad?"

Her lips pressed together in a single line with just enough room for a thumb to enter her mouth. The bunny's ear swished under her nose.

So the men had hurt Rosa in some way. She changed the subject. "Breakfast? Cereal? Toast?"

A nod was all Angela was going to get, so she busied herself pouring juice and slicing a banana in a bowl of Cocoa Puffs. A knock on the front door caught her attention. It was probably Steve. Julie wasn't up yet, so she checked in the peep hole before switching off the alarm system. "Good morning. I was making breakfast for Rosa. Come and meet her."

As Steve passed her, she glanced outside. The car was back across the street in front of Mrs. Radnor's. Steve's patrol car was parked in front of the house. Hopefully, a police vehicle would send a message to back off.

Steve waited for her in the living room. He said in a low voice, "I don't want to scare her. You introduce us, okay?"

"With pleasure." Then she stopped. This wasn't her house, and he wasn't her boyfriend. "Julie's still sleeping. Yesterday was a long day for her. Want me to wake her up?"

"No, let her sleep." He let her lead the way into the kitchen.

Rosa was stuffing her mouth with cereal. The spoon rested neatly on the napkin. A puddle of juice encircled the glass. Her mouth was covered with a ring of food and drink. Obviously, they'd have to work on table manners. Angela grasped Steve's hand pulling him toward her. When Rosa saw him, her eyes were as large as doughnuts. She slid off her chair and ducked under the table.

"C'mon, Rosa. This is Steve. He's a police officer. He's going to help you stay safe. Please come out." When Rosa refused to budge, Angela crawled under the table and sat next to the stormy-faced girl. "Please?"

She shook her head.

"Can he join us under here?"

Rosa's expression didn't change, but she scooched over.

"Steve, would you join us?"

"Absolutely." Angela created a space between them for Steve to sit. He didn't seem surprised to be crawling under the already-crowded table, but his knees tangled with the chair legs. A glass tipped over and fell to the floor showering his back with orange juice. His head jerked up causing Cocoa Puffs to crash to the floor.

He said something under his breath and backed up.

After readjusting his six-foot-three body, he backed his way in between them. Angela couldn't help it—laughter and saliva sprayed out of her mouth, and tears streamed down her cheeks. How she wished she had her phone to take a picture. Steve's lips were pursed, but his eyes laughed.

He extended his hand toward Rosa. "Buenos dias, mi nombre es Steve."

She swung it back and forth. "You funny man." Her eyes sparkled.

Julie's furry slippers and striped pajama bottoms faced the table, then her face appeared. "What's going on down there?"

"Morning, Jules." Steve peered up and beamed. "Let's just say, if I wanted to meet this young lady, I had to get down on her level. Want to join us?"

"Don't think there's room for more than three. Interesting way to eat breakfast." She tiptoed over the puddle of orange milk. "Y'all have fun. I'm going to take a shower. I've a client coming in an hour."

"You know what?" Angela touched Steve's arm. "Our girl here likes small spaces—they must be familiar and make her feel safe. Remember I told you I found her in the overhead bin? She's double jointed, so she can fit in anywhere."

"Could be. You might want to make her a tent under a table— throw a blanket over it. Especially when you get to the shelter. It might help her adjust."

Angela noticed she still held on to Steve's arm. And she was reluctant to let go. Her cheeks warmed. Stop it—he's Julie's. Yet, she couldn't deny the electricity their touch caused. She pulled away. "What's the plan?"

"I left my car out front on purpose. Thought we could leave from the alley and take your car. I'll drive. We'll go a round-about way to the shelter. Once you two are situated, I'll bring the car back, and hopefully, your friends out front won't catch on."

Kneeling, Angela swept some hairs away from Rosa's face. "You two keep playing. I'll go pack, but for how long? I have to go to Colombia in a few days."

"Don't know. It wasn't easy getting you into the shelter. They're completely full. We'll work something out before you have to fly out."

After she hustled from under the table, she mopped the floor and rinsed the breakfast dishes, mulling over the effect of that single touch. Don't go there, she reminded herself. Slipping into the bedroom, she closed the door and leaned against it. Just concentrate on the job at hand and nothing else. Rosa didn't have a lot of things to pack, but she did—three changes of clothes, at least; the novel she was reading, and her laptop.

The oak trees in the backyard dappled the lawn with moving shady spots. What would the shelter be like? Would she be able to leave at will? Would there be a lot of rules? After adding a few outfits to her already-stuffed airline bag, she found another suitcase for Rosa's new clothes and the toys her friend had brought over.

Steve and Rosa were sitting at the table playing a game with their hands when she returned to the kitchen. Rosa removed her hand from the bottom of the pile and placed it on top. Angela remembered playing that game with her best friend on her grandmother's porch on hot summer days. Meanwhile, Steve plied Rosa with questions about her life, but his Spanish was limited. Rosa responded to his questions with giggles.

He placed his hand on top of Rosa's. "I have a theory on how she got on the plane. I'm thinking the men hid her in a carry-on bag. When the men weren't paying attention, she managed to unzip it and escape. She probably remembered seeing you in the crowd in Colombia and then again on the flight, so she followed you to the car. Ask her."

"I've tried, but she ignores my questions. I'll try again." She sat next to Rosa and placed her hand on the top of the pile. After three rounds, she asked in Spanish. "Rosa, can you fit in a little suitcase?"

"Si."

"Would you show me?"

When Rosa agreed. she brought out a medium-sized carry-on bag that a passenger might bring on a plane. Opening it, she beckoned for her to get in. Rosa scowled, ran to Steve, and hid behind his leg.

"No quiero." Her eyes filled with tears and her lower lip protruded.

He ruffled her hair. "She connects something traumatic with

that bag. Let her be." He glanced at his watch. "Time to get going."

She pulled Rosa into the bedroom to dress her. As she combed through Rosa's tangles, she called out to Steve, "Come here." When he tapped on the bedroom door, she asked, "What do you know about shelters? What should I expect?"

"Not sure. It will be crowded. Mothers with three or four children in tight quarters. Don't expect much privacy. You might see and hear disturbing things. Mothers and kids with burns and black eyes. It won't be easy, but it'll be over in a few days, as soon as we get rid of the guys out front. I'll be in the kitchen."

Once the bags were packed, Angela clung to the kitchen doorway. Rosa held on to her arm, her thumb in her mouth and her other hand clutching the bunny by the ear.

Steve picked up his keys. "I'm going to leave by the front door, carrying whom I hope they'll think is Rosa and drive around for a few minutes in case they follow. While I'm gone, load up the trunk with your bags. It might not be a bad idea to take bedding. I'm not sure if they'll have any. Meet you in the garage in ten minutes." His expression was hard to read.

Angela busied herself braiding Rosa's hair while Rosa led her around the kitchen, singing at the top of her lungs. A knock on the door silenced her. Wide-eyed, Angela stared at Steve. What if it were the men? She pulled Rosa close. The braids could wait.

Julie yelled, "I'll get it." Angela joined her as Julie peered through the peep hole. "I see the top of Sun's head." She opened the door. "Come in. We have to get to work on some briefs. Do you feel up to typing for hours on end? A client's coming at twelve, and I'm expecting a call from the asylum guy—Kevin Perez early this afternoon." She glanced outside. "Good, the car's gone from in front of Mrs. Radnor's." She slammed the door shut, ran to the alarm, and punched in the code. "Steve, their car is parked right behind yours."

Steve joined Angela at the front window, no longer careful to remain concealed. She asked, "Do we carry on with our plan?"

He went to the door. "They're sending a message by parking there. Would you switch off the alarm? They'll follow me. It'll take me longer to lose them, but let's do it."

Sun cast a sideways glance at him. "Is everything okay?

You're scaring me."

Angela squeezed her arm. "We've had a lot of drama here."

Sun tilted her head. "You had a play here. I like plays."

After switching off the alarm and closing the door after Steve, she paused and scratched her head at the non-sequitur. "Oh, drama. I get it. No, it's American for a difficult situation. Come, I'll introduce you to Rosa."

"Rosa?" Sun followed Angela into the kitchen.

"Check under the table." Angela knelt down and peered underneath. "Come on out. We have to go." Sun bent down next to her. "This is Sun. She's a nice girl."

Sun said, "I seen her before. She was the girl doing flips in Colombia. What she doing here?"

"Show Sun your bunny." They stood. "She prefers small spaces, like the overhead bin on my flight. She followed me home. The men outside want her. They say they have a legal right to her, but we don't think so. Steve is taking us to a shelter to keep her safe, like the one you stayed in last year."

Rosa crept out, and Angela picked her up. "Julie will tell you more, but please keep the doors locked and the alarm on."

Sun's smile was gone. She said, "Of course."

Julie entered the kitchen. "You've filled her in. Good. Let's get to work."

Angela picked up the two bags. "Here, can you carry these pillows?" She hoisted them on her open arms, then led the way to the garage. One pillow fell to the garage floor; the other dragged behind her, but at least, Rosa was in the car without a fight.

They waited. Fifteen minutes morphed into twenty which stretched into thirty. Sweat trickled down her neck. Where was Steve? Had something happened to him? She glanced at Rosa, who sat quietly swishing Bunny's ear under her nose. So patient and compliant.

A rap on the garage door startled her. She put her index finger to her lips. "I'll be right back." She pressed the remote, then started her car. The plan was to pull out so he could pull in. Then she and Rosa would crouch in the backseat as Steve drove them to the shelter.

His patrol car took the Audi's place next to Julie's. They climbed over the front seat. Rosa thought it was a game, laughed, and did a flip into the back.

He leaned in. "Keep your heads down, okay? I'm sure I lost them, but it wasn't easy."

They drove around blocks and doubled back on side roads. His eyes darted between the road and the rear view window.

"I drove past the safe house earlier—it's non-descript, curtains closed. I'll go around the block a few times to make sure nobody's following. When I stop, grab your things and go to the back door. Knock three times and ring the buzzer three times. That's the code." He gazed at her intently. "They think she's your child, so tell her to call you mama."

The neighborhood held rows of bungalows from the fifties and sixties. Lawns needed landscaping; houses begged for cans of paint. She wished she could back out—this wasn't the adventure she had anticipated. The same houses passed her line of vision again. He eased around the corner and parked in the driveway.

"Showtime." Jumping out, Angela shouldered her purse while Steve popped the trunk for the bags. She opened the door for Rosa. "Let's play a game. I'll be the mother and you be the daughter—*mi hija, si?*"

Rosa's eyes lit up. "Okay, mama." Her thumb went in her mouth, and she gripped Angela's hand.

Steve shielded them as they hurried to the side door. "I'll leave you here." He squeezed her arm, his gaze lingering. "I'll be in touch." He patted Rosa's head before he returned to his car.

Three knocks and three buzzes brought footsteps. Someone looked in the peephole, then opened the door a crack. "Who is it?"

Oh no, Steve hadn't told her what their names were to be. "Angela and Rosa."

The door cracked open a few inches. She gave Rosa a reassuring smile and nudged her inside. Whoever had been on the other side of the door had vanished, so they climbed the stairs that led to the kitchen. The room was white—the appliances, the tables, chairs, and the walls. It would have been stark, but for the colorful pictures made by children that dotted the refrigerator and the walls. She sniffed—the smell of cleanser was strong.

A voice from another room reached Angela's ears. "Well, hurry up. I don't have all day."

"C'mon." They walked toward the voice. Rounding the corner,

they found themselves in a large room. A half a dozen women held children on their laps as they conversed in small clusters. A group of older children played Monopoly at a card table. A television was on, but nobody watched it. One woman peeked between the blinds, dabbing at her eyes with a tissue.

A large woman with graying hair and a flushed face joined them, a file in hand. "Welcome. I have to go over some rules with you first, so if you'll follow me, please." She wiped the perspiration off her forehead with the back of her sleeve. For a big woman, she took fast strides. They had to hurry to keep up.

In her small office, the woman offered her hand, and a hint of a smile crossed her face. "I'm Mrs. Foley." She pointed at two chairs. "The police didn't tell us your story. We're quite short on space right now. You'll have to share a room with Kelly and her daughter. The room only has two single beds, so the kids will have to sleep on the floor." She sniffed as if they were a bother.

Angela grinned. "Great. Rosa prefers the floor to a bed anyway." When Mrs. Foley didn't grin in return, Angela cringed.

"Breakfast is at 6:30 sharp. You'll be in charge of cooking one meal each day and cleaning up after another." She gestured toward Rosa. "She'll join the fourteen kids here for school in the mornings and participate in therapy in the afternoons."

Angela cleared her throat. "Um, Rosa doesn't speak English. She just arrived from South America."

Mrs. Foley opened her mouth to say something, then closed it. "Better not to know." She made notations in a file. "Lights out at 9:30. Absolutely no phones. You'll need to give me yours. Do you have any questions?"

Angela pulled her phone out of her pocket, regarded it tenderly, and placed it in Mrs. Foley's open hand.

"Another thing. Don't question the other guests. We value anonymity. We've also found that talking about our problems outside of therapy interferes with the healing process. Do you understand?"

Angela said yes but shuddered inside. Was this a prison?

Mrs. Foley brushed past her, and Angela trudged behind with child and suitcase in tow.

She stopped at the fourth door on the right. "This is Kelly and her daughter Michaela." She pointed at the bed on the right where a small girl played with a doll. "That will be your bed; Kelly has the one on the left." Wiping her brow again, Mrs. Foley grinned at Rosa and left.

Angela was tempted to leave—they didn't have room for them anyway. Instead, she stood in the doorway and regarded her new roommate. "I'm sorry. We don't want to cause any trouble for you or your daughter."

The thin woman pushed straggly hair out of her face. Her hand quivered as she did. The word *unstable* came to mind. "It's fine. Come here, Michaela. We'll manage." Her eyes avoided Angela's, but one of them held the shadow of an old yellowing bruise. Her cheek was marred by a jagged scar.

Rosa scooted from behind her pant legs onto the small space on the floor between the beds. The thumb didn't leave her mouth as she patted the floor beside her, beckoning Michaela to join her, who responded without words. Thrusting the rabbit forward induced Michaela to offer her doll, and in no time, the girls were playing together.

Angela relaxed for the first time since getting out of the car. She placed her two bags on the bed and searched for a closet. Apparently, there wasn't one. The clothes would have to fit under the bed. She sat on hers and watched her roommate, who flipped through a dog-eared magazine at a rate making it unlikely she was reading anything.

Buoyed with years of experience dealing with less than friendly passengers, Angela gave it a try. "How long have you been here?"

"Two months." She didn't meet her eyes, and her words were clipped.

Undaunted, Angela continued, "Would you mind filling me in on the daily routine? Mrs. Foley didn't say much."

She put down her magazine. "After breakfast, we go to group session while the kids are taking their classes. You won't have to talk for the first few days, but after that it's expected. After lunch, we have group with our kids, and then free time until dinner." She yawned. "There's not a whole lot to do. Can't go outside. Kids don't get any exercise."

Angela wanted so badly to hear her story, but she remembered Mrs. Foley's admonition about respecting privacy, so she climbed down on the floor with the girls. Pulling Rosa onto her lap, she asked the little girl across from her. "How old are you, Michaela?"

Her eyes didn't leave her doll. "Four."

"You have pretty blond hair, and you know what they say about freckles—they're kisses from angels."

"That's what my daddy always says. He wuvs my fweckles." Her bottom lip protruded. "I miss my daddy."

Her mother bolted to her feet and swept the child into her arms. "That's enough." Venom dripped from every word. "You've only been here five minutes, and you've already gone too far. I'll not have it." She pivoted and stomped out of the room.

Well, that's great. Five minutes and they'll kick us out. Even Rosa's glaring at me with judgment in her eyes. "C'mon. Let's go into the living room. We'll play cards or watch television. Other kids will be there for you to play with." She grasped her hand. "We'll let Kelly and Michaela have their privacy."

Three boys lazed on the sofa watching *Family Guy*. Toddlers sitting side-by-side built towers with Duplo blocks. One mother knitted and talked about the bridge club she belonged to, the cocktail parties she went to back when things were good. Her voice was too loud for her audience of one—a woman huddled over arms hugging her chest. Angela surmised the woman would put her fingers in her ears if she could.

Guiding Rosa to two little girls who played Snakes and Ladders, she asked, "Can she play with you?" One girl scooted over to make room for Rosa. Her arms were covered with burn marks. Angela took a deep, ragged breath and blinked back tears. Less than an hour, and she didn't know if she could make it through three days. She averted her eyes and forced her voice to be calm. "This is Rosa; she doesn't speak English."

Unfazed, one of the girls held out three different-colored tokens. "Which color? Red, blue or orange?"

Rosa, eyes twinkling, shouted, "Blue," then peering up at Angela, she repeated it three times.

This was going to be an excellent experience for Rosa. She would learn the language far better from her peers than from adults. Angela told her she would be back in a few minutes and returned to her room. It was time to patch up things with Kelly and her daughter. The door was closed, so she knocked lightly.

"Come in," a harried voice said.

Pushing the door open a crack, then a bit further, Angela entered, feeling like a trespasser. Kelly was folding clothes into a small suitcase.

"Are you leaving? I'm sorry if we got off on the wrong foot. I won't ask any more questions."

"It's okay. I've been here long enough. Michaela misses her father, and I'm ready to go back now that I'm stronger."

"Please, please don't do that. You can have your room. We'll find another one. Don't go back."

Kelly folded another shirt and placed it neatly on the others. "It'll be fine. He's learned his lesson. He knows I'm serious this time."

"Your eye is still discolored, and it's been two months."

"My fault. I ran into a door."

Sending a quick prayer to heaven, Angela excused herself and went to Mrs. Foley's office, where she was on the phone. Angela stood outside until she hung up before tapping lightly on the door.

"Enter." When Mrs. Foley saw her, she rolled her eyes. "You made quite an impression on Kelly and her daughter. I've never seen anyone so mad."

She slumped into the chair. "I'm sorry. I just told Michaela she had pretty hair and freckles. That's it." Her eyes filled with tears. "Now she's packing to move back with her husband. I can't believe I caused so much damage." She put her head in her hands.

Mrs. Foley sniffed. "Not to worry. She's been searching for an excuse to move home for a long time. I'll go talk to her. Give me five minutes."

Angela had examined the pictures on the bulletin board and had read every sign hanging on the wall in Spanish and English when Mrs. Foley returned to the room.

"I was too late. Somehow, she got through to her husband. When I got to her room and looked through the window, she was getting into his car. I don't know how—she doesn't have a phone." She plopped in her chair and rubbed her temples.

"What will happen to her?"

"It'll be okay for a day or two; then he'll drink too much and knock her out. She can't come back here now. He knows where the place is."

"Will the child be okay?"

"Not sure." Mrs. Foley stood and went to the door facing away. "You have the room to yourselves now."

Angela left, her head hanging like a naughty child after a scolding. Not here three hours and she'd already driven a battered wife back to an abusive husband. She returned to collect Rosa, but she was so involved with her new friends, Angela sat next to a florid-faced woman fanning herself.

"You're the new one, aren't you?"

"Yes, I'm Angela, and that's Rosa in the green shorts." The girls were now playing a version of *duck duck goose*, and Rosa was as loud and as exuberant as the others. She could tell the woman's eyes were on her. No way would she ask any questions of this one.

"What did your guy do to you?" The question hit her like a brick in the head.

"I thought we weren't supposed to talk about such things."

"Yeah, what they don't know won't hurt them." Her voice was husky and low—a smoker, no doubt. "Me—I got the tar knocked out of me cuz I worked overtime. Can you believe that?"

Angela began to answer when she realized the question was rhetorical.

"You know—you can only put up with so much; then you got to put your foot down. I hope he fries."

She didn't know how to respond, so she watched the girls.

Rosa bounded toward her. "Mama, listen. Blue. Red. Orange. Green. Yellow." She clapped her hands. "Hablo ingles."

The lady coughed. "I thought you said that one was yours. Why she speaking Spanish?"

Not wanting to lie, Angela said, "She's from Colombia, and she hasn't been here long."

"Oh, you adopted her."

Angela searched for a way to change the subject. She noticed marks dotting the arms and legs of one of the girls Rosa was playing with—the quiet one. She was about to ask when the woman interrupted her.

"How did you get someone to approve an adoption if you have an abusive husband?"

Angela rolled her eyes to herself. "Lucky, I guess. Tell me

about that little girl with all the marks."

"Oh, that's an interesting case. Seems the dad wasn't the only one hurting the child; her stepsister did most of the damage."

"You don't say. I've never heard of anything like that before."

"Yeah, apparently the sister was jealous of the little one—afraid her dad would favor the new one over her, so whenever they were alone, she hurt her—bordered on torture. The mother never knew—I guess she was too busy with her new husband to know what was happening to her own flesh and blood."

"Where's the mother?"

"Keeps to herself most the time. Stays in her room."

Angela didn't know if her heart could hold any more hurt. "What happened to the sister?"

"In a psych ward, who knows?"

Angela said, "I didn't get your name."

"Claire." She held out her hand to shake. "I guess that's all you need to know."

"Which one is yours?"

"It's just me. Couldn't have any kids after his boot got done with my stomach." She coughed again. "It's all right. I have plenty of nieces and nephews to keep me occupied." She sniffed and glanced around the room. "Wish I could go out back for a smoke, but they won't let me."

Angela hesitated, remembering her resolve not to ask, but she couldn't help herself. "Where's your husband now?"

"Don't know. Don't care. I finally feel like I can stand on my own two feet. He don't own me anymore."

A call to dinner interrupted their conversation. She got to her feet. "It was nice meeting you. Thanks for filling me in." She joined Rosa on the floor and helped put the game pieces back in the box. "Let's go wash your hands."

Dinner took place in a room Angela hadn't seen before. The children ate together at a small table, the women at a large one with Mrs. Foley on the end. After grace was said, mothers helped serve their children, while the rest dug into fettuccini with chicken in a heavy white sauce. A small salad and a bowl of fruit cocktail completed the meal. Most kept their heads down, focused on their food, and said little while Mrs. Foley reviewed the rules. "Whoever has bathroom duty, make sure to give the shower a good wipe down. Same thing goes for the kitchen sink. Use some muscle, ladies."

Heavy knocking on the front door caused conversation to cease. Children stared at each other with wide eyes. People didn't visit here. People meant trouble.

Wiping her mouth with a napkin, Mrs. Foley stood. "I'm not expecting anyone." No one said a word while she was gone. Forks rested on plates; nobody moved—even the children were silent.

Minutes later, Mrs. Foley returned, her eyes solemn. "Angela, could you come to my office please? Everyone, nothing to worry about. Finish your dinners."

Puzzled, she followed, the office door closing behind them.

"Nobody was there; just this manila envelope." She thrust it toward Angela.

Was this a message from Steve? Wouldn't he call the office rather than drive over? She pulled out a single piece of paper. The words were few and scrawled in red ink, resembling blood.

SEND ROSA OUT OR BURN.

"Call the police. Ask for Officer Bricker." How had they found her? Steve had been so careful. Somehow within hours, the men had discovered their hiding place. All she knew was they had to get out of there.

Mrs. Foley passed the phone to her. "He wants to talk to you."

She brought it to her ear. "They found us."

"It appears that way. She told me about the note."

"We can't stay here. Can you come and get us? What do we do? I don't want to put these people at risk. They've already been through—." She couldn't finish because her throat was devoid of air.

"Get your things together. We have to do this right. We want the perps to know Rosa is not in the house any more, but we don't want to draw any attention to it, or everyone will have to move." His voice was muffled as he put his hand over the receiver. "I'm bringing a few officers with me. We have to assume they're watching. Wait for me to come in and get you."

"Are you going to arrest them? That note must make it a criminal offense."

"It is, but we have to tie it to them. I'll be right over."

After he hung up, Angela stared at the phone; then glanced up at Mrs. Foley. "I'm sorry we've caused you so much trouble. We'll be leaving now." She arose and went to the door, then spun around. "Thank you for taking us in."

Rosa didn't want to go. The corners of her mouth pointed south, and the thumb went back in, but she said nothing. Angela pulled her onto her lap as they sat on the steps leading to the back door. "Do you like adventures? Me too. Steve's coming for us, and it will be fun. You wait and see."

Three knocks and three buzzes got her attention. She opened the door to officers dressed in raincoats dripping with water.

Steve kissed her on the cheek, bent down, and beamed at Rosa.

His light kiss gave her a modicum of comfort.

"Here, put this on." The raincoat was too big, but it covered her. He picked up Rosa. "Are you ready? We're going to form a human shield around you two, okay?"

The next few minutes were a flurry of activity. She made it out to the patrol car. Steam fogged the windows, and the car smelled of wet dogs, but for the moment they were safe.

"Where are you taking us?"

"To the station until we figure out our next step."

Rosa's head rested against her arm; her shallow breathing indicated she was asleep.

"How do they always find her? It's as if she's wearing a homing device or something."

His head jerked up. "A microchip. That must be it. You're brilliant. They've implanted a chip in her somewhere. That's why no amount of losing them worked."

"Is that even legal?"

"Not in this country. I've heard slave owners in developing countries have them implanted in their workers. RFDs—that's what they're called."

She explored Rosa's arms and legs. "How can we find out?"

"Not sure. I'll do some research when we get to the station. In the meantime, you stay with me, okay?" He squeezed her arm. The touch was quick, but her arm continued to tingle.

Her heart filled with warmth. Then guilt put a check on her feelings. What was going on? Was she imagining the spark between them? She wouldn't intentionally hurt Julie. Especially after all she'd been through in losing her parents.

At the precinct, Steve carried Rosa, the long day having worn her out. Her tiny head fit perfectly in the crook of his shoulder. The bright lights and bustle didn't wake her. He carried her into his office, searched for a place to put her, and finally laid her on his coat on the floor.

Gesturing toward a chair next to his, he booted up the computer. Together they searched the Internet for information about microchips and RFDs. They discovered that many states had banned them for constitutional reasons, but Florida wasn't one of them.

Steve saw someone he needed to talk to and excused himself. Out of the corner of her eye, she watched him. She'd never noticed before how utterly attractive he was. Her mind chastised her—control yourself. Focusing again on the screen, she read three articles about RFDs until her eyes grew heavy. She was falling asleep when he returned.

"Good news, bad news," lowering his voice when Rosa squirmed. "They're illegal almost everywhere. It's hard to find a scanner—which is what we need to see if Rosa has one." He picked up the receiver. "But the good news is I have a friend who can find anything. I'll give him a call."

Angela tried to follow the cryptic conversation. It seemed they were setting the terms of a bargain. She returned to her reading. Although at one time, people believed implants caused cancer, nothing was ever proven. The biggest hurdle to overcome was the legal one—invasion of privacy.

He hung up, walked to the door, and stopped. "Okay, tomorrow morning, we'll take her to the Maitland branch of the FBI. It's the only one close by with a scanner. A doctor will meet us there and take out the implant if the scanner reveals one. Rosa will have to be told. Would you do it? My Spanish doesn't include words like *scanner*."

She said she would, not sure if she could do any better. The dim lights and the quiet made her eyes heavy. The clock read 6:20 when she opened her eyes. She bolted up and peered around. A blanket enveloped her shoulders, and Rosa still slept on the floor, but Steve was gone. In minutes, Rosa stirred and sat up.

"Buenos dias. You're in Steve's oficina. Today, we are going to another safe place, but this one's a secret." She pulled Rosa onto her lap. "Did the bad men put something small under your skin—this small?" She held her fingers apart by an inch.

Rosa ignored her and rubbed Bunny against her cheek.

"Today we're going to a special place to see if they did. If we take it out, the bad men can't follow you anymore, and you'll be free. Will that be good?"

She went back to sucking her thumb.

Steve entered. "Here's juice and doughnuts from the vending machine. The feds will send a car to pick us up in thirty minutes. Did you tell her?"

Angela said, "Yes. Will it hurt?" She opened the juice and handed it to Rosa and put the doughnut on a napkin.

"I'm not sure. The transponder is no thicker than a piece of paper and smaller than a penny. It's implanted under a single layer of skin. The pictures show it's usually near the wrist." He sat next to Rosa. Gently taking her arm, he tickled her.

She laughed and pulled her arm back, scooted closer to Angela, but kept her eyes on Steve. "Más."

"Ha. She's asking for more."

He walked his fingers up the inside of Rosa's arm. She squealed but didn't pull away. "Araña."

Angela said, "No spiders."

"There." He touched Angela's hand. "Feel that little square near her armpit? I think that's it."

She walked her fingers up Rosa's arm. Rosa giggled. "I wonder why they'd do that to her. It must have hurt."

"They probably gave her something to make her sleep. That's why she doesn't know. She must be valuable. They don't want to lose her."

"She's talented. Remember I told you the first time I saw her was performing acrobatics on the streets of Bogotá. She mesmerized the crowd. Do you want to see what she can do?"

Steve stroked Rosa's hair. "If she's up to it."

"Could you do some stunts for Steve?"

Rosa jumped on Steve's desk, did a back flip onto the floor, and landed in the splits, her toes touching her head.

"Whoa," Steve said, and they applauded. Then he put his arm around Angela's shoulders as if he had a proprietary right to do so. And it felt good. "She's amazing."

Angela inched away before she succumbed to the attraction that was drawing her like an undertow. It had something to do with the three of them—Rosa, Steve and her, and the bond forming. It felt natural—like a ready-made family, but she couldn't do that to her cousin.

Rosa wasn't done. She sprang around the room like Road Runner, bouncing off walls and landed on the top of a bookshelf. On the ground again, she twirled around the room like a graceful ballerina and ended in Angela's lap.

His kiss grazed Angela's cheek, and he patted Rosa's head. "You're quite the acrobat." He moved behind his desk, his eyes sparkling. "I think I got it. In Colombia she brought in money from the crowds in the street, but they smuggled her into this country to make some real money. Since she didn't enter legally, they were going to sell her to a buyer for some nefarious purpose. But she got away."

When the phone rang, Steve snapped it up. "We'll be right down."

***

Angela's first thought as she climbed in the back of the sleek, black town car was—this is where my taxes are going.

Rosa sat on her lap, Steve next to her. He hooked Angela's fingers in his when they passed the Orlando Eye, the new Ferris wheel. Did he realize what he was doing?

"Rosa," he pointed at the sphere. "Do you want to go on that?"

She clapped her hands and asked, "Ahora?"

"Not now, but soon." His finger still held Angela's. She knew she had to let go; it wasn't right. Julie didn't love easily, but when she did, it was forever. Of all the men in the world, it appeared they wanted the same one. She removed her hand and slipped it in her pocket.

At the guard's station, the security bar lifted, and they drove into an underground garage, the door closing behind them. Angela focused on Rosa. The next few hours would be traumatic; she wasn't sure if Rosa trusted her enough to make it through the procedure.

A security guard directed them into a sterile waiting area with lights so bright Angela shielded her eyes. Steve leafed through a magazine, so she pulled out a *Dora the Explorer* book and did her best to translate it into Spanish. Rosa's giggles morphed into a belly laugh. What had she said?

A nurse poked her head around the corner. "Rosa?" They followed her to a small, equally sterile room. "The doctor will be right in."

Stark white walls surrounded them with nary a picture of internal organs to break up the monotony. She said, "I didn't know the feds had their own hospital."

Rosa whimpered and lifted her arms.

Steve swung her up. "It will be all right."

Her eyes darted around the room and landed on the door. "No" Her fingers dug into Steve's back.

The doctor entered. "So this is Rosa. How are you?"

She tucked her head into Steve's chest and refused to look at him.

"I'll give her something."

Angela had to avert her eyes when the doctor prepared a small syringe, then injected it into the back of Rosa's thigh. She jerked and whimpered, and Angela felt like a traitor.

Rosa's eyes were closed when Steve placed her on the examining table. The doctor brought out a hand-held device that emitted a low buzzing noise, reminding Angela of the metal detectors retirees waved back and forth on Florida beaches. Moving it in a zigzag pattern over her body, the buzzing changed to little blips when it got close to Rosa's arm.

"We found the culprit. I'll go and scrub. This will be over in a minute."

Angela couldn't watch. She leafed through the magazine Steve had been reading. How could they do this to a little girl who trusted them?

The doctor was right—it was over in a minute. He advised them to change the bandage once a day and give her something for pain if she needed it.

Angela asked, "What happens now?"

Steve rubbed the five-o'clock shadow forming on his cheeks. "She can't go home with you; at least not until we apprehend the perps. Miriam, one of my friends with the force and a mom herself, has agreed to take Rosa home until this is all over." He tipped

Angela's chin up with his finger. "Okay? We have to do what's best for Rosa." His eyes held compassion even if his words didn't.

Angela stroked Rosa's hair. "Will I get to visit her?"

"We'll see. The men are onto us, so we'll have to be careful. On the plus side, you'll be able to go back to work." He paused and peered at the door. "Miriam will be coming any minute to get her."

A tear formed. She used the back of her hand to wipe it off before Steve saw it.

When the nurse entered, Steve said, "Let's go while she's still asleep." He guided her out of the room with a light touch on her back.

"Wait. Could I leave the bunny with the nurse so Rosa sees it when she wakes up?" She rushed back into the room where Rosa slept, placing it next to her cheek.

Once she returned, Steve guided her out to the town car—his hand burning the skin on her back with electricity, with guilt. No, she *wasn't* imagining things had changed between them. The driver stepped up and opened the door for them.

Steve's finger went under her chin. "I know this is hard for you, but you can't protect her, and she's not a pet that you can keep. She's somebody's little girl."

She gazed out the window past the fast food restaurants and strip malls. She made a resolution to herself—someday soon, whatever it took, Rosa would come to live with her as her own daughter.

Chapter Six

The phone rang jarring Julie from the brief she was writing. Why didn't Sun answer it? Oh right, she had gone to get food from the deli—a twenty-minute walk from the house. It was going to be an eat-while-working lunch. Placing the receiver in the crook of her neck, she snagged it on her earring. "Ouch, Richards Law—Julie speaking."

"That's quite the greeting. Angela here. Where's Sun? I thought she was working today."

"Sorry. I got the phone caught in my earring. I sent her for some lunch. What's happening? They let you use the phone at the shelter?"

"No, we're out. In one day, I sent my roommate back to her abusive husband, and because of me, the place might be torched." Angela's voice broke. "I'm so tired. They took her, and I couldn't do a thing about it."

"What do you mean they took her? Who's they?"

"The FBI. Turns out the reason those men were able to find Rosa was because she had a tracking device implanted under her arm. So the kidnappers showed up at the shelter and threatened to set fire to the place. Steve drove us to the FBI office in Maitland, where a doctor—at least, he dressed like one—removed the microchip." Her voice quivered, "And a lady with a lot of kids is minding Rosa until they catch the guys."

"The FBI has a hospital?"

"Go figure."

Julie said, "It's for the best. You can't take care of her with your schedule."

"Yes I can. Lots of flight attendants have children."

Knowing she wasn't going to win, Julie changed the subject. "At least they have enough to arrest the guys—that's good news."

"That's what Steve said. But they have to find them first. They probably got rid of the car and are using fake names."

Julie whined, "Now Steve will be too busy to go out. Our timing is horrendous. We haven't spent any time together since I got back. He's always busy."

"Well, he's had a big job to do, and it's not over yet."

"Whose side are you on?"

The other line rang. Apparently, Sun hadn't returned yet. "I have to go. Someone's calling." She pressed line two. "Richards Law, Julie speaking."

The line was crackly and hollow. "Miss Richards? This is Kevin Perez. We met in Colombia about my asylum case?"

"I remember. How are you, Mr. Perez?" She sifted through a hill of documents for his file.

"Not so good. I just received word that the US government denied my application for asylum. I don't understand."

"Are you sure?" She couldn't believe it. This was supposed to be an easy case. "The government doesn't work that fast. It's only been a few days. I haven't received any notification from them yet. Did they send you a document?"

"Yes ma'am. I have it here in front of me. It says they have denied asylum because I don't meet the standard of proof."

"I can't believe it. Your case is so strong. Did they give any other reasons for the denial?"

"They checked off two boxes. The first one is for not belonging to an identifiable group, and the second one is for not having a well-founded fear of persecution. And at the bottom—it's hard to read, but it says I gave material support to a terrorist group. What does that mean?"

"A terrorist group? That gang that stopped you. But they forced you at gunpoint to take money out of an ATM machine. What was it—eighty dollars?"

"Eighty-six dollars. At the bottom of the letter, it says I can appeal the decision, but I must do so within ten days from the date on the letter. That leaves eight days."

Julie scribbled notes on the blotter. Now she would be busy. "Would you fax me that letter? I'll get right on this. We'll certainly appeal their decision."

His voice broke, and there was a pause. "Thank you, Miss Richards. I'm worried about my family."

"Has something else happened? Tell me everything so I can add it to the brief."

"At first, there were the phone calls in the middle of the night. Sometimes nobody was there; sometimes laughter, and once when my wife answered, a voice said, 'Remember who you're dealing with.' That was it. But yesterday my daughter Lucinda was walking to a mall with her friend, and a car drove alongside them for a few blocks. They ran the rest of the way and told the security guard, but the car was gone by then."

"It sounds like things *are* getting worse. Is there somewhere you can go to be safe?"

"We're talking about putting our house up for sale. My kids will go to their grandmother's next week, but my wife and I need to stay in the area for work."

"I wish you would all go. What is the name of the government in Colombia?"

"I don't know what you mean."

"What department of the government do you work for? Also, did the group that held you up—FARC—did they know you worked for the government?"

"At first, I would have said no. Our truck was unmarked, and the equipment wasn't labeled in any special way. But they stole our identification cards, which clearly indicated that we worked for the Colombian government, and one of them said, 'we know who you work for'."

"This is good. Didn't you say they left a threat in blood on your car? What was the threat?"

"It said, 'You're dead,' and it was signed 'FARC'."

"Okay, Mr. Perez, I'm going to file for appeal. I think I have enough to go on. We'll be speaking later. Stay safe."

It would be a long night, but she wouldn't go to bed until she finished the best brief she'd ever written. Mr. Kevin Perez deserved a great defense—he'd only get one shot. It had been easier when she worked for the firm. She could have delegated issues to different interns, and they could have helped with the research.

She spent the first three hours doing research on case law regarding "material support." It was ludicrous that the US government did not view money taken at gunpoint as an exception to the "material support" rule. A call to her former employer didn't help much. He advised her to concentrate on the smallness of the amount taken from the ATM machine in order to disprove the word "material." But that wasn't the issue. What was at stake was the forceful nature of the crime. Simply put, FARC had committed a robbery against Mr. Perez. They had taken the money by force; it was not freely given.

Next, she sought to prove through case law that the Perez family was being persecuted because of his ties to the government. While she couldn't prove that FARC knew about the link when they held Perez and his crew at gunpoint at the truck, they knew once they had seen the identification cards. It was a long shot, but she'd try anything.

The last question she had to tackle was whether FARC's motive was to persecute the Perez family because of Perez's association with the government or because they wanted to scare the family into being quiet. Her mind was dead. Thumbing through old law books didn't help. Calling other attorneys didn't work— they had never done a case like this one. She decided to make a cup of tea and close her eyes for a few minutes. Sun had gone home hours before. The house was like a mausoleum. Where did that thought come from?

She took a sip of her tea and leaned against the headrest. Her eyelids were as heavy as trapdoors. A little nap would make everything better. Five minutes was all she needed.

Everything blurred and moved in slow motion. A little girl with a dirty face tugged on the hem of her skirt, but when she reached over to touch her, the child laughed and dodged her grasp. She sprang from the sofa to the piano to the wall and back. Every place her foot landed left a trace of blood. Then the girl jumped up and down on the dining room table, making her head pound.

She was rubbing her temples when her eyes flicked open. The

noise wasn't coming from the direction of the dining room. The pounding came from the front door.

The room was dark. She switched on the light; then thought better of it, and turned it off. What if those men were at the door? It was better to pretend she wasn't home. She approached the door and stopped three feet from it. Had she locked it? She couldn't remember. Was the alarm on? Probably not, since she hadn't left her desk since Sun had gone home. Did she dare peer through the keyhole? What if they shot at the door like in gangster movies and she lost an eye? Nothing good happened in the dark. If it was Steve, he would have called or texted her.

She tiptoed closer, glad for the darkness. The knocking stopped, but she knew someone was on the other side, and the person wasn't friendly.

She hazarded a glimpse in the keyhole, then jerked her head back. The night masked the caller. She was probably imagining things again—letting her fears control her mind.

Taking three cleansing breaths as she'd learned from an agoraphobia help site, she remembered the back door. Was it open? How could she have been so careless? She hurried to the back door and slammed it shut, engaged the deadbolt, and ran to set the alarm. A single thought penetrated her fear. What if a neighbor needed help? Irrational thinking had plagued her for years, crippling her ability to help others; she would not let it happen again.

With a resolve that defied caution, she switched off the alarm, strode to the door, and threw it open before Cowering Julie could immobilize her. Darkness met her. Except for the paper sticking out from under the welcome mat.

Except for the sprawled writing that read *tell us where Rosa is if you care about your house.*

Those men were on her porch, and they were going to destroy her house. She slammed the door shut, engaged the dead bolt, and backed up, never taking her eyes off the door. Falling into a chair, she whipped out her phone and speed dialed Steve. When it went to voicemail, she left an incoherent message and hung up.

She wished she could hang a *Rosa's not here* sign outside her door, but it wouldn't make any difference. Nothing to do but pace until she heard Steve's voice.

Returning to her desk, she put pen in hand to finish the brief. Then it hit her. THE NOTE. Mr. Perez had said the threatening note the gang had put on the car window was signed *FARC.* They revealed their name. If the gang's intention had been to scare Perez and his family so they wouldn't go to the authorities, they wouldn't have left their calling card. She knew how to end the brief with a punch.

***

Her head ached, the words blurred on the page, but the brief was finished. And it was magnificent. She'd take it to the post office and send it registered mail the next morning, which was only a few hours away. Proud of her accomplishment, she allowed herself to strut to her bedroom. The threatening note hadn't kept her from finishing a tough job. Last year, it would have set her back weeks. Tonight represented a gigantic stride forward.

But the note still weighed heavy on her mind. Where was Steve? Didn't he know she needed him?

She was brushing her teeth when the phone rang. Great. Spitting in the direction of the sink but missing it by a foot, she hurried to snag the phone.

"It's me. Got your message. What happened?"

She snatched the paper from her blotter. "It was about 9:00. Someone knocked on the door—hard. I didn't answer it, of course, but a few minutes later, I got curious. That's when I found the note. It said, 'If you value your house, tell us where she is.'"

"Fantastic."

"I hope you're being sarcastic. What's so fantastic about it?"

He laughed. "Sorry, I didn't mean it the way it sounded. What's fantastic is they don't know where Rosa is. That means they didn't follow us to the FBI."

"But they think I know where she is, and you know I don't need this in my life right now."

"From what Angela said, you can take care of yourself pretty well."

She glanced at the blotter where she had drawn a big hole. In it was a girl's head, eyes fearful, mouth agape. "I wish I had a big neon sign in my front yard saying, 'She's not here. I don't know where she is.'" With her pencil, she attached arms to the screaming girl in the hole. "Can't you catch them? They're probably hanging around some place close."

"We're trying." He whistled. "I got it. The chip is what allowed the men to follow Rosa. What if I retrieved it from the FBI office and used it to draw the perps out of hiding?"

"Sounds like a good plan. Can I come?" Then she hit her forehead with the palm of her hand. She didn't have time for this with the brief and all, and how could she possibly help? "Sorry, probably not such a good idea." Of course, it was a stupid suggestion. She'd have a panic attack and have to breathe into a paper bag. Yet she longed to spend time with Steve. They'd been so distant lately. Something was different, but she didn't know what.

"No, I think it's a great idea for you to come along. If they follow your car to Maitland, it'll be more authentic—like you're going to pick Rosa up. But it might be dangerous. I don't want to put you in harm's way."

She inhaled. Baby steps. "I'll be okay. Will you be there with me?"

"Of course, and there will be back up as well. Can you go now?"

She peered at the slippers on her feet, the note on the desk. She wasn't going to get any sleep anyway. If they could catch the guys, she wouldn't have to lock her door anymore during the day. And Steve would be forced to spend time with her. Hm. "Sure, I can be ready in fifteen minutes."

As she searched through her closet for something to wear, black seemed to be appropriate. She wished she had a Kevlar vest. Who knew what the early morning hours would hold? She ended up wearing dark jeans, a black tee-shirt sporting Latin words from law review, and a baseball cap.

A tap on the back door made her stop short. She thought to herself, *Silly girl.* Then she switched off the alarm and went to the door.

Steve leaned over and kissed her cheek. He smelled like—Brut. The stubble on his chin burned against her face, but she didn't care. It had been almost three weeks since he'd done more than ruffle her hair.

Lifting her chin with his index finger, he did a quick inspection. "You look like Emma Peel."

She stared up at him. "Who?"

"From the original Avengers, or Angelina Jolie—Lara Croft, Tomb Raider. Tough women. I like it." He hit her playfully in the arm.

She rubbed it. "I don't feel like a tough woman. You sure I won't get in the way?"

"Just do what I say, and you'll be fine. You can do that, can't you?" He grasped her hands and pulled her out.

"Wait. I need my purse and keys." Her bag sat on a chair in the kitchen. A quick glance into it before she left confirmed she had the bottle of hairspray—in case she needed to squirt someone in the eyes.

Steve climbed in the front passenger seat and slouched as low as his tall frame would allow. "You drive. I'll tell you where to go."

When nervous, she tended to drive under the speed limit. Her eyes darted between the road ahead and the rearview mirror. It was past midnight, so traffic was at a minimum. No headlights followed her. After hearing Steve click his teeth, she sped up to the speed limit. The thirty-mile trip to Maitland passed quickly as Steve filled her in on what had transpired at the shelter and at the FBI office.

"Who's taking care of Rosa now?"

"I'm not free to say. She's with a good family. The mother is from Puerto Rico, so they'll be able to understand each other. She'll be safe, and they'll try to find out more about Rosa's background." He popped his head up. "You're getting close. Just one more left, and you'll see a parking garage on your right. Pull in there."

She drove to the security guard's station and opened her window. Now sitting up, Steve gave the guard his ID badge. After it was verified, the gate opened. The structure was as somber and eerie as a crypt. The air smelled damp like dark basements from her childhood.

As she pulled into a space on the third level, he said, "You wait here. I'll be right back with the chip."

The minute he was gone, she locked the doors and sank down. *Silly girl. What could be safer than the FBI?* To make the time go by faster, she made herself review the brief in her head. There was still time to make changes on it before she carried it to the post office in the morning.

A tap on the window made her jump. "It's me. I got it. Unlock the door and let me drive."

"Absolutely." She stepped out of the car while he checked his phone. He threw an immense bag in the backseat before he got in. Walking around the car, her eyes took in her surroundings—dimly lit, she imagined gangsters hiding behind cars. She shook her head at her irrational fears. It was the FBI parking lot.

Steve's fingers tapped on the seat as he maneuvered the car out of the parking space. "Are you ready for this? The chip's in my pocket. I'm going to attach it to the teddy bear in the back seat. I thought we'd drive to your place and then cruise around Celebration for a while—places you might go. Then my partner and another officer will meet us at a restaurant parking lot on 192. Hopefully, the men take the bait."

"Why Celebration?"

He glanced at her and then back at the road. "This is your car, so it's got to appear like you've picked up Rosa and are taking her back to your house, but you stop to get a coffee. We want them to follow us, but the actual takedown will be in Kissimmee."

She was too tired for it all to make sense. "Then why are *you* driving? What if they see you?"

"It doesn't matter if they see me. These guys are desperate. They want the girl back—they'll follow." He removed his hand from her neck as he merged onto the highway. "Oh, I forgot to tell you—I saw Rosa when I got the chip."

"Seriously? What's she doing up so late?"

"The agent, who shall remain nameless, and I had to debrief, and where she goes, Rosa goes. When she saw me, she leaped into my arms. She's a natural gymnast. If we can keep her in this country, I'd like to get her into a good program. At her age, she can already do so much; think about the gold medals she could win after she's had some proper training."

"Don't get too attached to her. Immigration has no sympathy for stowaways, no matter how much I try to show that she's a victim. I said the same thing to Ange. She's ready to adopt Rosa." A shiver went down her spine. She lowered the air conditioner. "Are you sure Rosa's safe?"

His brow knit together in a single line. "Why did you say that?"

She rubbed her arms. "I don't know. Just a weird feeling, I guess. It's been a strange night."

"She's in a safe place."

Resting her head against the back of the seat, she let her eyes close. The drone of middle-of-the-night music lulled her to sleep. She was giving the best opening statement of her law career when a jab in her back made her eyes fly open. "What happened?"

Steve glanced at her, eyebrows raised. "Nothing except your snoring."

"I don't snore."

"Um, yes you do, but it's a cute snore—like a babbling brook interspersed with an outboard motor. I'm glad you're awake. I think we're being followed."

When she glimpsed over her shoulder, he said, "Not like that."

She pulled the sun visor down and checked in the mirror. One car's headlights followed close behind although there was ample room for it to pass. "How long has it been behind us?"

"Last ten miles or so. I'm going to speed up and change lanes. Let's see what happens." Her Volvo complained but complied as Steve veered into the far left lane. Julie kept her eyes trained in the mirror. Sure enough, the headlights changed lanes as well but maintained the same distance.

Steve said, "This is going to get tricky. I've got to exit in less than a mile. I'm glad the morning traffic hasn't started yet."

"I'm just happy I'm with a cop." She studied his profile out of the corner of her eye. His strong chin inspired a sense of security. "Do cops get speeding tickets?"

"Sure, I got one once. They gave me a choice between the ticket and having it handled administratively. I chose the ticket." He glanced at Julie and back. "Okay, here we go. I'm going to change our meeting place with back up to the Celebration Hospital parking lot because it'll seem more like somewhere you'd go with Rosa. I'll call my partner." He picked up his cell. "Siri, call Chip."

As they veered onto Celebration Avenue, Julie unclenched her hand on the door handle. The white picket fences, the retaining ponds with egrets lined up, the houses with wide porches brought a sense of calm to her tense nerves. How could anything bad happen here? They inched past her house. It appeared normal and asleep as did the others on the block. They circled back through the alley and passed her house once more. There it was. The car with the tinted windows, sitting in front of her next-door neighbor's property. Its headlights came on once the Volvo passed it.

"He took the bait. Now let's take him on a tour of the town. I wish the speed limit was faster. Never been in a car chase at 25 mph." His fingers gripped the wheel.

"Are you nervous?"

He chuckled. "No, I'm impatient. I can't stand driving this slow. It's not natural."

They passed Lakeside Park on their left. A Muscovy mother led her ducklings over the sidewalk to the water. A one-eyed cat sat in the middle of the street and moved only after they came to a stop. When they passed Columbia's Restaurant and the movie theatre on the right, a glance in the sun-visor mirror indicated the car still followed them. The darkness was giving way to the dawn sky, and joggers ran solo on the sidewalk circling the lake. Steve slowed in front of Starbucks.

"Go inside and order something. I'll stay here and see what they'll do."

Despite her nerves, Julie's stomach rumbled. "Do you want something? I'm thinking of a Mocha latte and an egg sandwich."

He drummed on the dashboard. "I'm good."

She leaped out and headed toward the door. The lights were on but the door was locked. She returned to the car. "It opens at six. Can we wait?"

"Not now. I want them to think Rosa's in the back seat, and we're on our way elsewhere."

Once she buckled her seatbelt, they circled in front of the Bohemian Hotel. She gazed at the elegant entryway with the 1930s car parked out front and vowed to put staying at the hotel on her bucket list. As they continued around the block, the tailing car pulled out of an adjacent parking space.

"Time to go to the hospital." They detoured down Water Street and made their way to the road circling the golf course that would take them to their destination.

The hospital parking lot was half full. A few women carrying yoga mats made their way to the gym. A tired-looking man in scrubs climbed into his car. Steve drove up and down the aisles until he saw Chip's car. After parking, he handed her the tiny implant. It slipped through her fingers and fell to the car floor.

"Sorry." She bent down and clenched it in her fist.

"This is where it gets tricky. Get out and make your way between the cars toward the hospital. Walk swiftly and carry this." He snagged an enormous stuffed bear and a blanket from the back seat and handed them to her. "Wrap the bear in the blanket and carry it like you're carrying Rosa. And don't drop the implant."

She stared at him with her mouth open. "I'll put it in my pocket. What if, what if something happens?"

"Don't worry. I won't let anything happen to you." His fingers lingered on her cheek for a moment. "You're doing a brave thing. I'm proud of you."

She had difficulty breaking the moment; how could she say no? She inhaled one more whiff of the aftershave that emanated from his finger and opened the door. "Say a prayer for me."

The ungainly teddy bear coupled with her purse made it hard to see where she was going. She had to trust Steve knew what he was doing. Her gait was unsteady as she maneuvered between parked cars. She bumped into a side mirror; then almost tripped over a cement abutment. She'd traversed three rows and was getting closer. What she wouldn't do for her bed in her locked room in her locked house. But Steve needed her, and she wouldn't let him down.

Only one more row of parked cars before she reached the crosswalk to the hospital's entrance. Spots appeared in front of her eyes. Blinking didn't make them go away. She concentrated on her breathing—one thousand one, one thousand two. The bear's fur stuck out through the blanket folds and tickled her nose. She sneezed.

Her eyes were closed when her body was propelled into the right bumper of a car. Her hands straightened to break the impact. At the same time, the bear went flying, and hands captured it and disappeared. It wasn't her clumsiness that sent her into the car; someone had shoved her. And now they had the bear.

She had failed. Again.

How could she be so careless? She should have had a better grip on it. Her knee hit the pavement first, then her hip. Her elbow smacked into a hubcap as she sprawled to the ground in the narrow space between two vehicles. Nobody saw her. She tried to scream Steve's name. Nothing came out but a raspy whimper.

Voices and scuffling reached her ears. "Hands above your heads. Down on the ground. Slowly."

Julie reached to her side and used a tire to hoist herself up. Slowly. Blood trickled from her knee. Her favorite black jeans were ripped and soaked with blood. She kept herself low and peered through a car window watching the drama unfold. Steve and his partner Chip trained their guns on two men kneeling with their fingers linked behind their heads.

A heavy-set man with a black beard was spitting a diatribe of Spanish words. The other shouted, "You have our little girl. We want her back."

"Tell us your name."

Silence.

"Why do you want the girl? Are you the girl's parent?"

Silence.

Steve's partner stuck his gun in his back belt, cuffed, and did a slow pat down of each man, extracting a revolver and a knife from a shoe from one man and another weapon from the second. He stuffed them in his belt.

From the pocket of each, he retrieved wallets. "This one's name is Luis Rodriguez from Colombia—picture resembles him, although he's put on fifty pounds. The other one's name is Pedro Navarro—age 26, from Honduras."

Steve caught hold of the bigger one by the arm and twisted him around. "These your real names?"

The man spat in his direction, just missing his face.

The smaller man said, "Please, please, we just want our little girl back. We won't make any trouble."

Steve said, "Trouble? You threatened to blow up two houses. Arson's a felony in this country. Chip, read them their rights."

The men stared at each other and smirked. The larger one said, "You got the wrong men. We didn't do that. Maybe you're profiling us. We want a lawyer."

Steve said, "Fine. But for your information, we don't have her. What we do have is the chip you implanted in her arm. No, you're going down."

Chip led the heavy man to the patrol car and helped him in.

As he went for the second one, the guy yelled, "Check your car, Officer." His head motioned toward the Volvo's hood. He jumped up and down. "Rosa. Come to Daddy."

Hands on her hips, Rosa resembled an action figure. She shook her head at the man and stuck out her tongue.

Julie forgot her pain. She rushed from her hiding place to the car. "Rosa, come down from there." She slowed her pace, not wanting to frighten her. "How did you get…Por que?"

Rosa glanced down at her and grinned. "Hola."

Steve joined Julie, "How did she…I'd better call the agent." Then he said, "C'mon, Rosa. Come down from there." He inched toward her as if he were trying to catch a cornered animal. "C'mon, sweetie."

Rosa giggled and jumped to the hood; then pranced from car to car before she disappeared from their line of vision.

The handcuffed men howled from the squad cars. One hollered, "These American cops can't catch a small girl."

Steve barked orders over his shoulders. "Jules, go left. I'll head her off on the right. Chip, stay with the perps."

Crouching low enough to search under the cars, Julie scoured the space between each vehicle, knowing it was futile. If Rosa wanted to hide, mere humans wouldn't find her. She was right—no Rosa. Steve was waiting for her at the crosswalk linking the parking lot with the hospital's entrance.

Wiping the sweat off his forehead, Steve's grim face did little to encourage her. "Can I borrow your car to take one of the guys to the precinct? As soon as he's booked, I'll come back and get you." He wiped his face with his sleeve. "I don't want them in the same car, so we need both vehicles."

She nodded yes, her heart yelled no. How was she going to find the little escape artist in a place as big as a hospital? Plodding toward the car where she'd dropped her purse, fatigue made it hard to keep her eyes open. She hadn't had a good night's sleep in days. Outside of a few minutes on their way to the FBI, she hadn't closed her eyes in more than twenty-four hours.

Coffee was what she needed. Retracing her steps to the crosswalk, she headed for the hospital's entrance, her eyes aware of areas where Rosa might hide—behind a flowering bush or the row of wheelchairs.

Two valets leaned against their post chatting. A middle-aged woman helped a frail man move from a car to a wheelchair.

Julie approached the valets. "Have you seen a little girl—dark hair, orange shorts, about seven?"

Glancing at each other, they shook their heads, and one said, "No, ma'am."

"She, um, disappeared from the car in the parking lot, so she should be around here somewhere. Her name is Rosa. She's doesn't speak English. If you see her, call me." She removed a card from her purse.

"Ma'am?"

"What?" She hated it when people called her ma'am; after all, she was only thirty-two.

"I asked if you were the girl's mother."

"No, I'm her—her lawyer." She didn't have time for a cross-examination from guys barely out of high school. She plucked the card back from them, removed a pen from her purse, and added Steve's number. "If it'll make you feel better, call Officer Bricker. He knows about her case." She whirled around and headed for the door. Honestly, the world would be better if people weren't in it.

First, coffee. Everything would be better after caffeine entered her bloodstream or frontal lobe—wherever it entered. When she caught a glimpse of herself in a glass door, she made a detour to the restroom. Her hair was sticking out at right angles; her pants were soaked with blood. Her eyes were wild and red-rimmed. No wonder the valets had questioned her.

She splashed her face with water and used a wet paper towel to dab at her knee. Her hair didn't appear much better after a finger comb, nor did her eyes, smudged and circled with fatigue. She vowed to carry a brush and some make-up in her purse for situations like this one, but then she'd have to buy a bigger purse. Hers was so small it could almost fit in her pocket. Big purses were girly.

Coffee.

The cafeteria was filling with people in scrubs queuing to get their breakfasts. Julie put the largest cup she could find under the amber liquid stream and inhaled its nutty aroma. She didn't care if it burned her tongue as she sipped the dark brew. Everything would be better in a moment. Snatching a banana and a yogurt, she got in the shortest cashier line and paid. Time to collect her thoughts and come up with a plan. She bit into her banana. If Rosa could hide in the overhead bin of an airplane, imagine the places she could hide in a building as massive as a hospital. She needed more than help. She needed divine help.

Setting her coffee cup down, she closed her eyes to pray, but instead almost drifted off to sleep. Then she remembered why she was here. Rosa. She got to her feet before she fell asleep again. What was that little Catholic poem Angela's mother had taught her when she was a child? Something about St. Anthony. *Tony, Tony, look around; Rosa's lost and must be found.*

The place to start, she surmised, was at the information desk in the front lobby. She supposed there was a security guard at such a large place. But wouldn't they want to know why she was searching for the girl? She needed Steve. Once the cup was half-empty, she headed for the lobby, rehearsing what she'd say. "You're not going to believe this, but I've lost…no, that wouldn't do." Tell the truth; she'd try that.

She was so immersed in her thoughts, she didn't notice the person on her right when she took a sharp turn and smacked into him. Oomph. Her knees gave out, and she sprawled to the ground, taking the man with her. Her legs tangled with his. Coffee splattered on her clothes, hair, and shoes. A puddle formed at her feet. Now she smelled like a Colombian blend with a nutty aroma.

"Whoa, sorry. I didn't see you," the voice next to her said. The person scrambled to his feet and extended a hand, which she grasped. She glanced up to see green scrubs spattered with stains matching hers. Her eyes moved up to see Bradley Cooper. No, but close. Better than Bradley Cooper. Taller, younger. Dimples. She loved dimples.

She wiped her hands on her pants and brushed the hair out of her face. "Sorry, my fault. I should have signaled before I took a right."

"Quite all right." He studied her knee. "It looks like you're injured." He pointed at a nearby seat. "Here, let me check it out." Gently, he rolled up her torn pants. "This isn't a new cut, is it? You won't need stitches, but I can clean it up for you." When he smiled at her, his teeth were white and straight—perfect. Did she see a sparkle reflect off an incisor?

Extending his hand, he said, "I'm Doctor Moyer."

She held it in hers—warm, perfect. "Julie, Julie…." It required too much effort to remember the rest.

His head tilted a perfect amount. "That's easy to remember. The back side of the ER is just around the corner. Come with me and tell me how you injured your knee."

"I fell in your parking lot."

He chuckled—deep, melodious, perfect. "Most people injure themselves before they arrive at the hospital parking lot."

She stopped. "Yes, well, I should be going."

"Why don't you let me clean that up for you? It's what I do."

She blustered. "No, I'll be fine." The room started spinning.

He caught hold of her arm. "Whoa, sit for a minute. I'll be right back. Don't move. I mean it."

Her main concern was her frazzled appearance. She wished she had a mirror, but if she did, it would make her feel worse. Her fingers combed through the snarls the best they could. Her second concern was time. She didn't have any minutes to spare. She should be searching for Rosa.

But he took her breath away. Literally.

She peered out the window behind her that looked out on an alcove or a patio—the kind hospitals offer their visitors for privacy and quiet. Benches surrounded a fountain spewing water from a vertical fish's mouth. Too many places for Rosa to hide. Julie couldn't find her on her own. She needed to seek help. Closing her eyes, she whispered a prayer.

Something cold on her skin made her eyes pop open. Dr. Moyer was on his knees in front of her patting the wound with alcohol wipes.

"Sorry, didn't mean to scare you. I brought the ER to you. Were you praying?"

She felt her cheeks warm. "Um, yes."

He was quietly attentive to her bloody knee. Had she offended him? After applying a bandage, his hand remained on her knee as he gazed at her. "The wound isn't that bad. You won't need stitches. Just keep it clean and change the bandage every day."

"I will, but I wasn't praying about my knee." Seriously? He didn't care what she prayed about.

His head cocked to the side as if he didn't follow her segue. Standing, he held out his hands to help her up. "I don't mean to pry. Are you visiting family or going to the gym?"

"Neither. It's a long story. And a complicated one. I don't to want to take any more of your time." She peered out the window. "I should be going. Thanks for your help. Should I pay you or the hospital?"

He bowed. "On the house. It's been a pleasure. Maybe I'll see you again some time."

Her insides warmed—if only. "Maybe so." She had no desire to leave, but his quizzical expression prompted her to head toward the lobby, being careful not to run into anyone. She could sense his eyes on her back, and it thrilled her. What did he mean by *I'll see you again some time*? Probably nothing. People said that all the time.

The information desk had only one volunteer, and a long line waited. Patience wasn't her strong suit, but her mind was on the good Doctor Moyer—playing back every word he said. She was at the head of the line before she knew it.

The lady's reading glasses rested low on her nose, her hair bordered on purple, but her voice was kind. "What may I help you with?"

"I'm searching for a lost girl. She disappeared in the parking lot here, and we haven't been able to find her. Where do I go? Do you have a lost and found?" She glanced at the nametag and added, "Eunice."

For some reason, Eunice sat back in her chair and fanned herself. "No, can't say I've heard about a lost child. Are you her mother?"

That question again. "No, I'm her lawyer. Her name is Rosa; she doesn't speak English, and she ran away from me and the police."

"Is she a teenager?"

"No, she's about six or seven—I'm not sure. Is there someone I can talk to? A security guard?"

She dialed a number. "Vinny, could you stop by my desk for a minute?" After hanging up the receiver, she pointed toward a cluster of chairs. "Please, have a seat. The security guard will be here in a minute."

Julie sat on the edge of the chair. Somehow, she felt guilty, like she didn't have a right to ask about a child who wasn't hers, and negligent as if it was her fault Rosa had disappeared. Five minutes increased to ten. Checking her watch for the third time didn't help. She should be doing something to find Rosa, but where to start? After switching on her phone to call Angela, she realized her cousin was probably at the airport ready to board a flight. Not wanting to bother Steve, she pressed the cancel button.

A tap on her shoulder made her pivot toward a middle-aged man with a badge on his crisp uniform and a seriously large mustache. If his hair wasn't salt and pepper, he could have been a clone of Super Mario.

"You've lost your daughter?"

She wanted to kick the table in front of her; instead, she said in a measured tone, "No, I'm her attorney. Her name is Rosa. She's a kidnapped victim from Colombia. The FBI had her in custody, but she escaped in your parking lot. Now I'm searching for her. Have you seen her? She's small, about six or seven. Doesn't speak English."

He didn't answer her question. "We should call the police."

Her head ached, and she fought to keep the edge out of her voice. "The police already know about her. Officer Steve Bricker and his partners arrested the kidnappers this morning here in your parking lot. That's when she disappeared. Steve—Officer Bricker will be back any minute to pick me up. He'll be able to vouch for me."

Mario pulled out his phone. "I'm going to call the police."

"Please, can we go find her? She's probably frightened, and we're wasting precious minutes."

Facing her, he said, "Maybe so, but I'll let the police handle it."

Julie slumped on the chair. What was the use of having a security guard if he wouldn't do his job? And where was Steve? She closed her eyes. It wasn't her problem anyway. What she needed was a short nap. Then she could think straight—straight enough to go home and take Mr. Perez's petition to the post office. But with what? Steve had her car. Sun would be at her house wondering why she wasn't there. Fortunately, the spare key was hidden in the fake bottom of a terra cotta planter. She called Sun.

As she waited for her to answer, a commotion drew her

attention behind her. The people in line at the information desk were indignant—that sense of righteous injustice that pops up when someone cuts into the line. Her eyes went to the source—the extremely good Dr. Moyer. He struggled to carry a screaming, careening child with wild hair and orange shorts.

Bolting up, she rushed to him. "Rosa, stop."

Dr. Moyer corralled the child by the waist with one hand and fended off her kicking legs with the other. "Is this your daughter?"

Julie backed up, as had the others in line to avoid the whirling dervish with feet. "No, I'm *not* her mother. As I've told everyone else, she's my *client*. Her name is Rosa. She doesn't speak English." Julie knelt in front of her and opened her arms.

"What do you mean, she's your client? Are a social worker?"

Julie embraced Rosa. "No I'm an immigration attorney. She was kidnapped and brought into this country. The police apprehended the kidnappers in the parking lot this morning, but she got away. She's scared."

His eyes opened wide. "This—scared? A temper tantrum is more like it. How do we keep her from bolting?"

"I've got her. She knows me. Where did you find her?"

"In an x-ray room, playing with the buttons."

Rosa twisted toward the doctor and tensed.

"Maybe we should restrain her—hand cuffs, one of those straitjackets?"

"'Fraid not. Let's take her to the office I use."

"Wait, I've got to tell the security guard we've found her." She leaned down and held Rosa's face with her hands. "Honey, I want you to go with Dr. Moyer." Her eyes directed Rosa to the doctor. "And be good. Promise?"

The guard was still on the phone. She tapped on his shoulder.

He glanced up, "I'm still on hold."

"Too late. We've found her."

He waved her on, so she hurried to catch up with Dr. Moyer and Rosa, already at the elevator.

Rosa dragged her steps and keened like a wounded animal. People stared at them and shook their heads as if they were bad parents. She felt like one.

It was a relief when they stepped into the elevator and its doors closed. She didn't know what to say, but she was patently aware of his proximity. It saddened her when the elevator stopped at the third floor and he moved away. Rosa's cry morphed into a tired moan. He stopped at an unmarked door. "Let me get the keys from my pocket. Have you got her?"

"Um, sure." The office was the size of a broom closet, reminiscent of Julie's first one—something they had in common.

Another door opened to an interior hall. Using his leg, he shoved it shut. "Lock it from the inside please."

The second she blocked it with her body, Rosa jerked away from her.

He barricaded the other door. "Okay, fill me in."

Starting with the trip to Colombia, she told him the whole story. The words poured out—for some reason, she trusted him. Perhaps it was his scrubs, or the way he'd dabbed at her torn-up knee, or the smile that should be in a portrait in the Louvre. Meanwhile, Rosa bounced from wall to wall, careening off them like a caged marsupial.

His head tilted slightly to the right, as if he was having trouble making sense of the situation.

"You can call Steve Bricker or the FBI to verify the story."

"What I don't understand is how she got from the Maitland FBI office to our parking lot without anyone noticing."

She lifted her palms. "She sneaked through customs and onto a full airplane. She's a master gymnast and an escape artist. That's probably why she was brought to this county—to make money for her kidnappers." She paused, "You know, it most likely happened when Steve and I changed seats. Come to think of it, I fell asleep on the way back, and I remember being jarred awake by a jab in my back. I thought I was dreaming. She was probably crouched behind my seat."

Rosa was tiring. She lay on the floor, sucked her thumb, and twisted her hair with her free hand, but her eyes darted from door to door. Where was her bunny? Maybe that was the problem. She'd probably dropped it, and it was gone for good.

Dr. Moyer moved a chair close to Rosa and touched her foot with the toe of his shoe. She didn't resist. "Wonder what will happen to her now."

"We found her—that's what's important. The government will classify her as a stowaway and take her into custody for removal to

Colombia. Rosa said she doesn't have parents, so they'll probably dump her in an orphanage. I just came from one of those places—not nice at all."

Rosa and the doctor silently played footsy.

"My job is to find a way to keep her here. The US doesn't like stowaways, but I can apply for a stay to buy some time. Then I'll apply for a visa based on the fact that she was kidnapped. Or perhaps asylum." Why was she talking so much? He didn't care about visas.

A knock made them glance at each other. Julie whispered, "You're better able to hold her than I am." As he folded Rosa into his arms, she went to the door. "Who's there?"

"Officer Bricker."

Inching the door open, a pang of guilt rippled through her. She sloughed it off. "Come in."

Steve flashed his badge at the doctor. "I hear you're the one who rescued her."

Julie said, "Steve, this is Dr. Moyer. He found Rosa in an X-ray room. Thanks to him, she didn't get away again."

Steve saluted him. "I'm grateful. She's a handful." He leaned toward Julie. "You're probably ready for sleep. How are we going to get her out to your car?"

Dr. Moyer held his hand out, and Rosa gripped it. "I've got her. Let's go." She was surprisingly compliant. Like a proper little lady, she walked by the doctor's side with no resistance out to the car.

Steve had parked at the valet curb. Doctor Moyer opened the back door and helped her into the seat.

Steve asked Julie, "Why don't you sit in the back with Rosa?"

She climbed in, fastened Rosa's seatbelt, and held her hand.

Before shutting the door, Dr. Moyer bent toward her, his deep blue eyes flooding her heart. "It's been an interesting day. I'd like to call you…" He glanced at Steve, who was on the phone, "… to check on your knee."

She nodded a bit too eagerly, she thought. But Doctor Moyer was intriguing, and she wanted to know more, a lot more. After he closed the door, she sat back, inhaled deeply, and caressed Rosa's hair with a distracted finger. Her eyes went to Steve's head. Good Julie spouted words about loyalty and faithfulness. She pushed the mute button.

It was then her leg brushed against something soft. She leaned forward and fingered it. "Hey Rosa…your rabbit. It's been in the back seat all this time." As she lifted it up, a sharp-cornered object inside it jabbed her in the wrist. "Ow."

"What's that?"

"Nothing, the rabbit just fought back."

Before pulling away from the curb, Steve glanced in his rearview mirror. "That's why she didn't fight us when we put her in the car. How do you suppose she got in without either of us noticing?"

She played with Rosa's hair. "I have no idea. It's a gift."

As he merged onto the main road, he said, "From now on, nobody will capitalize on that gift except Rosa."

"Here, here." Her eyes caught a glimpse of the card Dr. Moyer had given her. What was his first name? Brett. Brett Moyer. Julie Moyer. Stop it. She hoped he wouldn't forget to call her.

About her knee.

Chapter Seven

Sun had never been alone in the office before. Nobody had
answered the door when she knocked, but she found the key in the
fake bottom of a flowerpot as Miss Julie had taught her. There was
usually a list of tasks on her desk, which a teenager with less-than-
perfect English could do, but today nothing. Drumming her fingers
on the desk blotter failed to make time pass more quickly, but she
had nothing else to do.

The house felt dreary and lifeless. Moving to the front porch,
she plopped into a deck chair and waited. It didn't seem right to be
in Julie's house when she wasn't home. Her eyes took in the other
houses on the street—quiet, safe. She watched seven ducks waddle
single-file across the street. She loved her life in this country—her
friends in youth group and a home-school program that allowed
her to accelerate in math and science—her first and second loves.
Not to mention this job, which gave her the chance to give back to
Julie, who had reconnected her with her mother and brought her
family here from South Korea. The paycheck was a bonus.

Enough sitting around. She needed to make herself useful.

After she rinsed the coffee cups left on the living room table
and Miss Julie's desk, she noticed the thick manila envelope
addressed and ready to be mailed. She also noted the doodling on
Miss Julie's blotter of a girl that had fallen into a pit. Her boss's
drawings always spoke volumes about her feelings. What
happened after she left the office yesterday?

After putting the cups in the dishwasher, she waited for her laptop to boot up so she could read Miss Julie's e-mails—the ones she could handle by herself. Why didn't Miss Julie call? Sixteen e-mail messages. Eleven were junk, but the others seemed important. The shrill ring of the phone interrupted her. Hopefully, Miss Julie was checking in.

"Good morning, Julie Richards Law, Sun Lee speaking."

"Good morning. I'd like to have a word with Ms. Richards, please."

Taking hold of the pink message pad, she carefully pronounced the words she had memorized, "I am sorry. Miss Richards not here—is not here. May I take a message please?"

"I'm Pastor Siemens. My daughter Amber met her in South America a week ago."

Not able to contain herself, Sun interrupted. "Oh, you Amber's father. I know Amber. How is she? I hope she is doing good—so sorry, you didn't call me; you called Miss Julie."

"Sun ... yes, Amber mentioned you. You were the one who helped rescue her. I—my wife and I are grateful to you and Ms. Richards. That's why I called—to thank you."

"I am most grateful you called. I was worried about her. Is she well?"

"Physically, she's fine. We had our family doctor check her over. She's a bit malnourished, and some of her teeth need work, but she'll survive. Sadly, she's having trouble adjusting. That's another reason I called. If her mother and I had a fuller picture of what she'd gone through, we would be better able to help her. Amber doesn't want to talk. Would you and Ms. Richards be willing to answer our questions? It would mean the world to my wife."

"I am sure Miss Julie will talk to you, and I will too. Would you tell Amber I miss her and pray for her all the time please?"

There was a pause. "She doesn't know we called you. We found Ms. Richards' card in her things. I don't want to tell her right now; the way she is. When would be a good time to call back?"

"Tomorrow morning? Miss Julie is not here now."

"Well then, until tomorrow."

The back door opened, voices of Officer Steve and Miss Julie saying their good-byes. "Wait, she's back. Can you hold please?"

Julie entered the waiting room, plunked onto the couch, and closed her eyes. "I'm too tired to even talk." She opened one eye. "Sun, could you reschedule my appointment for another day? I need sleep."

"Certainly, Miss Julie, but," pointing at the phone she held in her hand.

Julie whispered, "Who is it?"

"It's Amber's dad."

Opening the other eye, she yawned and pushed herself to her feet. Taking the phone, she grumbled, "Good morning. This is Julie, may I help you?"

Sun rocked back and forth on her heels, wanting to hear what the pastor was saying.

Julie put her hand over the phone, "Sun, stop rocking. Take this, and I'll get on the line in my room."

Sun couldn't help herself. "Pastor Siemens, is something wrong with Amber?" She heard the light breath of Julie listening in.

"As I said, physically, she's fine, but she's a different girl. Frankly, we don't know what to do. Our whole family is in turmoil. I think if we understood what she's been through, we'd be better able to help her. But if things don't change, she'll run away again."

Julie said, "I just met Amber, but Sun can tell you more. Sun?"

Oh, this wasn't going to be easy. Sun knew how Amber felt. She wouldn't want her parents to know everything. She'd be too ashamed. Sending a prayer for wisdom up to heaven, she began, her words halting and unsure. "I met her in the van. She was the only nice one. There were nine girls and one master—Dae. He in jail now." She corrected herself. "He *is* in jail now."

"What do you mean *master*?"

"Dae had his girls do jobs for him." She lowered her voice when she said the word *jobs*. "The first thing Amber said to me was, 'I want to go home.'" The muffled sob on the other end made her pause.

"Then what happened?"

"One night, I did not know where we were—Dae made us dance in a big place. People made bids. Amber was behind me when I went on the stage. After, she didn't get back in the van. Dae made us leave without her." Her voice caught in her throat.

Julie spoke up. "We rescued Sun and the other girls here in Orlando, and they arrested the man Sun spoke of, along with two others. As long as I've known Sun, she has never stopped praying for Amber."

"How did you find my daughter?"

"Sun found her. She saw her in a market in Bogotá while we were on a trip with our church, and Sun wouldn't let us rest until we rescued her."

The pastor's voice was thick. "I don't know how to thank you, Sun. And you too, Ms. Richards."

Sun spoke up. "Thank you for calling. We want to help her now, don't we, Miss Julie?"

"Um, sure. Whatever we can do."

Pastor Siemens said, "Okay, let me fill you in. As you probably know, Amber's a twin. The two sisters have not been close in the last few years. Aubrey is the outgoing one. She's always had a lot of friends. She plays on the school teams and is a cheerleader. Amber has always been the shy one. She hung back from joining clubs, preferred to read."

Julie asked, "I'm taking notes. Is it okay with you?"

"As you wish," he coughed, "I'm afraid her mother and I were partly to blame for their problems. We were always pushing Amber to be more like her sister, not realizing how it was hurting her. In the process, we pushed her away. She found new friends, ones we didn't approve of. Her grades suffered, which led to huge arguments. She ran away after one of them." He lamented, "Oh, if we could go back and do it over."

Sun piped in, "She's home now, and that is good."

"It hasn't been so good. You see, when she ran away, her mother and I spent all our time and resources searching for her. We formed groups, we went on television, and we started a non-profit organization. Our minds were always on finding Amber, so we had little time for Aubrey and her younger brother, Oliver."

Julie said, "I'm sure they understood."

He coughed again. "Oliver is fine, but Aubrey's had difficulty with the fact that we were so distracted all the time. So when Amber came home, we were overjoyed—the whole town was overjoyed. The only two who weren't were the twins. Aubrey has been sullen and non-talkative since Amber came home, and Amber—well, she feels out of place."

"That's terrible," Julie said.

"It's only been a week, but Amber stays in her room—doesn't come out, doesn't eat, and she didn't come home last night. My wife's worried sick. What's more—Aubrey told us Amber's been, well, she's been cutting herself."

"What?" Sun and Julie said at the same time.

"She hides razor blades—anything with an edge, and cuts her arms and legs—places she can hide under clothes."

"I'm so sorry," Julie said.

Sun interrupted, "Excuse me, sir. Miss Julie, I would like to talk to you in private, please."

"Excuse us, Pastor."

They met in the kitchen. Sun peered up at her boss, eyes hopeful. "Could Amber stay with us?"

She backed into the refrigerator. "Oh, I don't think so. We have so much going on, and she needs more help than we can give her."

Sun's shoulders drooped, and despair threatened to take over like a heavy weight. She needed to help her friend. "I have an idea, Miss Julie. Amber could stay at the safe house—the one I stayed at. They have classes and people to help. We can take her to McDonalds and church like you did with me."

"We shouldn't leave Pastor Siemens on the phone. Let me see what he thinks."

Sun returned to her desk and picked up the extension.

Julie cleared her throat. "Sorry to keep you. We were wondering if Amber would benefit from coming here. When Sun and the other girls were rescued, they lived in a safe house. Counselors helped them deal with what had happened to them, and they even received an education."

"I hate to lose her so soon after finding her again." After a long pause, he said, "but I see the value of what you're suggesting."

Julie said, "I can't promise she'll get in, but with your permission, I'll talk to my friend and see if it's a possibility."

"Please do. I don't know how my wife will react to losing her daughter again, but if it will help Amber, we won't stand in her way."

Once Julie had hung up, Sun bounded into the room. "I can't wait to see her."

She rested her hand on Sun's shoulder to calm her down and cautioned, "We don't even know if she'll be able to come. Don't get your hopes up."

"I'm going to pray real hard. She needs us."

***

Always amazed at Sun's childlike faith, Julie didn't want to discourage her. She called Steve instead.

His gruff voice answered on the third ring. "Bricker."

How could one word make her feel so good? "It's me. I have a request."

"I got too much work to do."

"Not about me. Apparently, Amber's having trouble adjusting to living with her family. Her dad called and is worried she'll run away again."

"That's not good. She'd be fair game for more trafficking."

"So Sun thought it might be good if Amber could stay at the same safe house she did; you know, with girls dealing with the same issues."

"I can check, but it won't be easy. There's hardly room for the victims from the Orlando area."

"True, but Amber would have been with Sun when she was rescued here if she hadn't been forced away."

"Counselor, you don't have to convince me." Papers rustled. "I'll do some checking and get back with you."

"I guess I should tell you. Amber's cutting herself. Would that be a reason they wouldn't accept her?"

"I'll find out. By the way, Rosa's back with the agent. She's calmed down and hasn't tried to escape. But she won't talk—just sucks her thumb and twists her hair."

"What about the kidnappers?"

"They'll be indicted tomorrow for kidnapping a minor, making terroristic threats, and attempted arson. The DA is throwing a lot of charges at the wall hoping some will stick. We've notified ICE, you know, immigration enforcement, and when the accused leave criminal court, they'll be detained for removal."

"If we could get Rosa to talk, I could work on a visa for her to remain in the United States—the same one we got for Sun."

"Could work. Human trafficking also involves forced labor. If she was brought here to perform, that's child labor. If she didn't receive compensation, you got slavery."

An awkward pause followed. Then he said, "Have you heard from the doctor?"

"What doctor?"

"The one at the hospital who found Rosa."

"No, why would he call me?"

He sounded cranky. "I don't know. I'll talk to you later." The phone was dead before she could say good-bye. Well, that was weird. He wasn't jealous, was he? Things were improving.

Sun popped her head around the corner. "Would you like some coffee or tea?"

"Tea sounds good. I'm going to take a nap soon. It's been a long day and night."

Julie pulled up the T-visa online. It wouldn't be as easy to fill out as it was with Sun's application without Rosa's background information. She didn't know her birthplace or birthday. Pressing save, she exited out of the program. A yawn resurrected her need for sleep. Sun set a cup on her desk. Inhaling the cozy aroma of chamomile, she said, "Thanks, and good night."

A knock on the door made her spill a few drops of tea on the hall floor. "Sun, do I have any appointments?"

"No, miss. I cancelled your three o'clock. I'll get it."

Great, she could hardly keep her eyes open. She sipped the tea and placed it on the hall bookshelf. She wanted to escape into her room, take out some fresh pajamas, and bury herself in the cool, crisp sheets up to her neck. Of course, she'd have to read a chapter of one of the many novels on her bed stand. It was a superstition with her—no matter how tired she was, she had a ritual of three before closing her eyes: One, read a chapter of a book; two, rub her mother's handkerchief on her cheek and kiss it, and three, pray. Sun could handle whomever was at door.

No such luck.

"Miss Julie? You need to come here, please."

So much for her plans. She rounded the corner to the living room. The smell of the street assailed her nose before she saw the baggy jeans, disheveled jacket, and matted blond hair. She took measured steps forward.

"Miss Julie, Amber's here."

Chapter Eight

Angela dropped her pumps on the bedroom rug and massaged her ankle. It had taken all the self-control she could muster to be cordial to her business-class passengers. The flight from New York to Washington wasn't her favorite turnaround because of the martini drinkers who ordered one after another. But trading for this flight allowed her to stay one extra day with Rosa.

Where was Rosa? And how was she getting along after the safe-house catastrophe? Her mind went to the shelter. She cringed when Kelly came to mind, and how she had triggered her return to an abusive husband. She tried not to think about the little girl with the scars running up and down her legs and arms. The weight of that memory was hard to bear; how much heavier a burden for the girl to carry. Yet on the surface she'd seemed happy. Children were more resilient and forgiving than adults.

She marveled at the paradox of her two worlds which rarely merged—little girls with scars and kids like Rosa who lived in the street versus rich, inebriated passengers who networked over martinis on flights. Did those two worlds ever intersect? Probably not. Her own work revolved around airports and resort hotels. To meet Rosa, she had to leave normal and go to the streets. To her surprise, she much preferred the smell of unwashed clothes to that of vermouth and olives.

Pulling herself off her satin duvet, she carried her uniform to the closet. She hated ironing—a necessary evil for flight attendants, so she did what she could to keep her uniform wrinkle-free. Her phone rang. The muffled song meant it was either in a coat pocket or her purse. She hurried to the chair where her purse sat and dug in it. Ah. Steve. Energy flooded her voice. "Hi there."

"How was your trip?"

"Over. Excessive amounts of alcohol for the commuters. What's up? How's Rosa?"

"A whole lot has happened since I last saw you. Do you have a minute?"

She gazed at her inviting pillows, so plump and soft. "Yes," she answered with a tone that said "no."

He filled her in on Rosa's escape at the hospital and the kidnappers' arrest.

"I can't believe it—*our* Julie Richards helped with their capture?"

"All true. She was great. Couldn't have done it without her. But now I need you."

"Who, me? Sure, for what? Did Rosa escape again?"

"No, nothing like that. But it does involve her. She won't talk to anyone. She just wants the plane lady."

"You sure she didn't say the *p-l-a-i-n lady*?"

"No, she said it in Spanish. Anyway, the agent and I figured Rosa might open up to you. Would you be willing to meet with her and see if you can get anything out of her? Like a last name, anything—brothers, sisters, school, neighborhood. We'll have a better chance of putting those two guys away if we can connect her to something we can use."

"When would you like to do this?"

"I can tell from your frequent yawns you need some sleep. How about when you wake up, you give me a call, and I'll arrange a meeting."

"Sorry," she yawned, "can't help it. Sure, I'll call you in a couple hours."

###

Another adventure were the last words tumbling through her mind when she fell into a deep sleep. Now she waited on the porch for Steve. Wearing a new top with a colorful squared neck she'd bartered for at the market in Bogotá, she paired it with light green capris and her favorite sandals. She'd taken extra care putting on her makeup.

Why was she so excited? Must be the potential adventure—she was going to the FBI and seeing her Rosa. Hmm. Why did she say *her Rosa*? Julie would be more than upset with her for forming a relationship with a child who might have a family in South America.

She'd keep her dream of adopting Rosa to herself for the time being and pray about it. This strange longing had to come from a place other than from within. Kids had never been part of her plans.

Steve ambled toward her. He had a luscious smile. Delete. He extended his hand and helped her up. Then he folded her into a bear hug. He smelled—what was the word? *Beguiling.* That was odd. She'd never used that word before in her life. But it had never fit someone so perfectly.

From the moment he opened the door of his truck for her to the moment they arrived at their destination, they talked about nothing but Rosa. She would be sent back if Angela couldn't get the right answers. At the last minute, she'd asked him to stop at a convenience store, where she bought a bag of penny candy—such a misnomer; nothing cost a penny any more. But a little bribery might help Rosa open up.

Steve led her through a number of stark white hallways, past nondescript offices and closed doors. Arriving at one, he knocked twice.

"A secret code?"

He smirked. "You watch too many spy shows."

When the door opened, Steve introduced a petite woman with dark hair and inquisitive eyes. "This is Miriam. She's been watching Rosa." Angela shook her hand—a firm handshake belied Miriam's small stature.

Steve called out, "Rosa, check out who's here."

She was sitting on the far side of a table eating a cookie when their eyes met. She stopped mid bite.

"Hola, Rosa," Angela said.

Her eyes lit up. Jumping upon the table, Rosa ran toward her, papers flying in all directions. She threw herself into Angela's arms, sticky fingers gripping the back of her neck.

Thrown off balance, she loosened one of Rosa's hands and with it strands of hair that stuck to her fingers and carried her to the sofa. "I missed you," she said in Spanish. Rosa answered with words Angela didn't understand.

Funny, she thought as she wiped crumbs off Rosa's mouth; she'd never felt a tinge of maternal instinct before. Children were for moms and dads. She was a career woman, always eager for the next trip or vacation. But for the first time, every child on the flights she worked reminded her of Rosa. Thoughts like *I bet Rosa would like that game*, or *how good Rosa would look in that outfit* played in her mind.

Now here she was—close enough to tickle. Instead, Angela remembered her mission. She started with a game in Spanish. "What's the bunny's name?"

Rosa shook her head.

"Is it Ferdinand?"

Rosa giggled and shook her head.

After several rounds of unusual names, Rosa revealed its name was Nayeli.

"Nayeli what?"

Silence and a thumb.

"Is it Nayeli Lopez? Ramirez? Hernandez? Fernandez? She listed every name south of the border she could think of.

Rosa's eyes widened at the twentieth one. "Buenos dias, Nayeli Colón."

A twinge of guilt passed through her for treating a child like a seal with a fish as she took out a Mike n' Ike and handed it to Rosa. She stuffed it in her mouth. Another round of questions revealed Rosa's last name was Colón as well—at least, her eyes lit up the same way. Miriam rushed out at Steve's request to check the database. Angela gave her another piece of candy.

Next, she used the bunny to find out where she was from. It cost three Mike and Ikes to extract a location—Medellín. Steve left the room.

Rosa rubbed her eyes and leaned her head against Angela's chest. Enough for a while. She rocked her gently. Her thoughts were conflicted. The more information they learned, the more likely it was she had roots elsewhere. She was going to lose her. Closing her eyes, she asked God to help her distance herself, so her heart wouldn't break when Rosa was taken home.

The door opened, and Steve bustled in carrying a projector. While he set it up, he said they had located some information about the town and sent a request to its police. Up popped pictures of a beautiful city. Medellín, according to Steve, was listed as one of the top most innovative cities in the world, rivaling Tel Aviv and New York, as of 2012. However, it had been one of the most dangerous cities in the eighties. But it had rid itself of major crime groups like FARC, and now most of the city was safe, although crime still occurred in the poorer areas.

As Steve continued to project pictures of shopping areas, schools, and parks, Rosa bolted up and pointed at the screen.

"Mi parque—Bolívar."

Steve's eyes danced with excitement. "That's right. Have you been there?"

She said something that sounded like gibberish.

"Ask her if she went to the park with her mother."

This time she ignored them and swished the bunny's tail under her nose. They were getting closer to some unpleasant truth. Miriam tiptoed into the room, said something near Steve's ear, and handed him a slip of paper. His face grew solemn, and lines appeared around his mouth.

"Miriam got through to the people in her town. Two years ago, a four-year-old was abducted from that park. Her name: Rosa Maria Colón, birthday March 18, 2009, two siblings, father Jesus Colón—an industrial engineer. Mother Isabella—a nurse. Family lives in a safe, affluent gated community. They're notifying the family as we speak."

Hugging Rosa, Angela kissed her on her head. God had fit the pieces together perfectly. If they hadn't been about to rescue Amber, she wouldn't have been in the crowd that witnessed Rosa perform, and Rosa wouldn't have followed her. Now she would be reunited with her family. With therapy and time, Rosa could have a normal life.

"Would you like to go home?" But Rosa was busy digging into Angela's pockets for more candy. She found the bag and stuffed a fistful into her mouth before Angela hid it away.

Steve said, "We have her house on satellite. Let me hone in on it." Pointing at the screen, he said, "Rosa, See?"

She pointed and clapped her hands. "Mi casa." Then her lower lip quivered, and tears erupted. Burying her head into Angela's neck, she wailed, her words muffled by her crying.

"What's she saying?"

Angela pulled the hair out of her eyes. "She wants her mother and father."

The phone rang. Steve's face was grim when he replied, "Uh huh. Okay." He hung up. "The police are having trouble locating her parents. They moved a year ago, and they have no intel on their whereabouts."

"Did they check at the father's work or the siblings' school?"

"Everywhere. They said it's as if the family dropped off the planet, but they're still checking."

Angela bit her cuticle. "What do we do now?"

Steve leaned back in his chair and massaged his temples. "Status quo for the girl. But we have information to use against the kidnappers. The police will start plans to extradite them to face charges after we're through."

"Good riddance. Can I take her for a walk? She's getting antsy after all that sugar."

He stood. "Sure, but be careful. She's a runner."

The empty halls and lack of windows made Angela wonder what it would be like to work in such an environment. Rosa bounded from one wall to another, clearly needing some physical activity. They played tag, hide and seek, and Rosa entertained her with gymnastic stunts.

Steve joined them and leaned against the wall, arms across his chest. His lips pressed together in a single line.

Angela asked, "What's wrong?"

"Got a call from the police in Colombia. They don't know for sure, but they think her family was killed. Apparently, after the ransom was paid, Rosa's older brother witnessed one of the guys we have in custody. His parents called the police, but someone on the inside must have tipped off the kidnappers. Never saw the family again."

"Could they be in hiding?"

Steve avoided her eyes. "Probably not, they're most likely dead."

Angela pulled Rosa toward her and held her tight. No mom or

dad to kiss her good night. She rested her lips on her cheek.

Someday, Rosa.

Chapter Nine

Seizing Amber's hand, Sun pulled her into the reception room/ living room and onto the sofa. "You are ashen—not the word—pale. What's wrong?"

Amber stared at her lap, her stringy blond hair shielding her face. A shaky hand pulled the hair away to no avail. Her jacket and baggy jeans smelled of the street. Her fingers scratched her neck, causing pink blotches to form. "I had to split. I've ruined all their lives, at least that's what Aubrey says. I never should have gone back." Her voice held a shudder.

Sun wanted to say something encouraging, but her limited English made it hard to find the right words. "That is not true. They love you very much."

"How would you know? I wish—I wish I'd never left Miguel. He would've taken care of me."

Sun knew better than to argue. Instead she ventured a quiet question. "Tell me what happened."

"I don't know what I expected, but I thought everything would be better. Mom and Daddy were cool at first. They've been in bad shape since I ran away." Her eyes brightened. "Oliver—he's my little brother—he's gotten big in the last two years. I feel bad I wasn't there for him. But…" She rubbed her temples.

"It sounds like your family loves you."

"Not Aubrey." Her fists clenched. "That first night, she walked into my room and talked smack—told me I ruined her life. Said the family fell apart because of me. The last thing she said was she wished I was dead." Amber stared at her hands, her face grim and devoid of color. Sun rubbed her back.

Sun said, "I am sure she didn't mean it."

Amber's chin jutted out. "Oh, she meant it. Whenever I come in a room, she runs out and slams the door. She refuses to eat when I'm at the table." She sank into herself like a candle melting in the sun.

Sun couldn't imagine how it felt to be scorned by one's sister.

Amber rocked, gripping her arms around her chest. "She's right. I should've stayed away. They'd be better off without me. I started cutting, you know. One of the girls in the van did it, remember? It felt good at first. I cleaned the razor blade real good. The plan was to make a design—art plus pain is a beautiful combination, don't you think?" A cold, matter-of-fact expression darkened her face.

"How could you cut yourself?"

"Don't know. Something I could hide. I cleaned up so nobody would know."

Sun touched her jacket sleeve. "Can I see?"

Scooting to the other side of the sofa, Amber averted her eyes. "No, don't." Her body language let Sun know the conversation was over.

Sun was at a loss. Should she stay or leave her alone? Amber needed someone with more experience than she had. She got up to leave when Amber began talking again.

"One night, Aubrey said I was hogging the bathroom, barged in, and caught me etching the most awesome tattoo on my thigh. She couldn't wait to tell everyone. Now my mom cries every time she sees me. My parents keep asking me if I'm cutting. They say they love me, but how could they? Anyway, I couldn't take it anymore—especially being in the same house with Aubrey."

Sun interrupted. "I have an idea. When we were rescued from Dae, Miss Julie and Officer Steve found a safe house for us. It wasn't bad at all. Maybe you could stay there."

Amber whipped around. "No way. I couldn't stand spending another day locked up. It was bad enough at my parents'. And why would I want to stay with *those* girls again? They were—mean to you and me." Her eyes said it all. Horrified and betrayed, as if a friend would never suggest such a thing. Then her eyes changed—trance-like, distant. "It wasn't so bad in Colombia. Miguel loves me. He always said so. He said I was his best girl."

Sun fought an urge to shake her. Instead, she slid closer and touched her arm lightly. Nothing to say, but her mind whirled with conflicting thoughts. *This is too big for me. I don't know how to help her.*

The phone rang. "Excuse me. I have to answer it." She inhaled deeply and reviewed her memorized greeting, which came out haltingly.

"Hey Sun, Steve here. I've checked with the trafficking people. There's no room for your friend, but I'll keep on their case."

"What is this 'keep on their case'?"

"Uh, I'll continue to ask them if there are openings at the shelter."

Amber's eyes were closed, her head rested against the back of the couch. "I understand. Thank you."

Seizing a comforter from the bedroom, she tucked it around her friend's shoulders, then went to Julie's office. "She has no place to go. Officer Steve called and said the shelters are full. Could she stay here? If not, I'll ask my mother if she can stay with us."

Julie swiveled around. "You have no room in your two-bedroom apartment for anyone other than your sisters and your mother." She paused. "Okay, she can stay here until we find a place for her." She went back to her computer.

Prancing back to the living room, she sat next to Amber and waited for her to open her eyes. When it didn't happen, she bounced enough to wake her.

"What's up?"

"Miss Julie said you can stay here. I am so happy. We can go to McDonald's and to the mall and to church."

Amber glanced toward the window. "I didn't bring many clothes. Wanna go to a mall?"

"Of course, I'll ask Miss Julie." She leaped to her feet, but her boss was on the phone, so she fidgeted by the door.

Hanging up the receiver, Julie said, "What is it?"

"Amber needs clothes and wants to go to the mall. Would you please take us when you're finished with your work?"

"I can drop you off at the Florida Mall, but I don't have time to stay with you. Does Amber have money?"

Leaning her head around the office corner, Sun said, "Do you have money?"

She held up a small handbag, but her eyes remained closed.

"Miss Julie is going to drive us. You ready?"

Amber sat up. "I've got to clean myself up and put on some makeup. Be right back."

Sun poked her head in Julie's office. "Excuse me. I have an idea—maybe good, maybe bad."

She removed her reading glasses, her head cocked to the side. "What's your idea?"

She tried to arrange her words before she released them. "Amber said her twin sister Aubrey is angry with her. Didn't we learn in church it's important to forgive each other right away—no waiting?"

Julie's eyebrows furrowed. "Yes, but ….?"

Sun gulped. "I had this idea. What if we invited Aubrey here to meet with Amber? They could talk about their problems and say they're sorry—and maybe become friends again."

"Sounds like a good plan, but what if things get worse—here in this house? I don't know how to deal with teenagers. They're … young."

"We could ask her father for his opinion."

"I can call her father and see what he thinks while you guys are at the mall."

Amber's voice at Sun's back startled her. "Why do you need to call my father?"

Julie answered, "Your dad called earlier today. He was worried about you."

Sun added, "We asked him if you could come here, so it was great when you showed yourself."

Julie picked up her handbag and keys. "Showed up. Let's go, girls."

***

The parking lot was full, but it didn't matter since Miss Julie was dropping them off. This was the first time she had ever gone shopping with a friend—without an adult present.

Julie stopped at the side entrance of a department store. "I'll pick you up here in two hours. Is that enough time?" She glanced at her watch. "Four o'clock. Call me if you need me."

Sun restrained herself from jumping up and down. "See you later."

Amber's steps quickened as they entered the store. "Hello, world," she said. Her eyes perked up, and it seemed to Sun she walked with confidence and a new sense of purpose. Her eyes darted from the umbrellas on the left to women's scarves on the right. She plucked one from a rack and held it up to her neck. "What do you think? Too old fashioned? Do you have a Hot Topic here?"

"Not sure." They headed for the mall entrance and found the directory. "There's one on the second floor." Amber dragged her up the stairs.

Dark. Sun took in Hot Topic's atmosphere, and a slight tinge of ill-ease made her wrap her arms around her chest. Her first thought was this was a store her mother would object to— a place where her friend Dae would buy his leather vests and bandanas. Everything was black—not such a good color for Florida summer weather. But Amber didn't seem to mind—she scurried from display to display.

"Check these out. I want them, and those black boots. Maybe a tee-shirt or two."

"Remember it's hot here, especially now."

"I don't care. Oooh! Look at this sweet hat. Gotta get it." As Amber swung around, two guys jumped out of the way before she stumbled into them.

"Whoa, girl. Watch out."

Amber backed up, laughing. "My bad."

A tall reed of a boy with long dirty-blond hair and peach fuzz sprouting around his lips grinned and nudged her arm. His shorter partner, twice as wide, wore a red and white knitted cap and sported a tattoo of a tear under his eye.

The slender one said, "You buying the store out?"

"Sure, why not?"

"You live around here? Haven't seen you before."

Their clothes smelled of old smoke. Sun held her breath.

Amber didn't seem to mind. Running her hands through her hair, she nudged him back. "Just arrived. I'm staying with my friend here." She touched Sun's arm.

Sun didn't say anything, motionless as a mannequin. Her mother wouldn't want her talking to guys she didn't know, but Amber seemed to welcome their attention.

"What do you think of these caps? Which one do you like the best?" She modelled each one.

"Girl, buy them both. No, give me the blue one. I'll get it for you."

Giggling, Amber placed it on his head and dropped the pile of clothes on his open arms to carry to the cashier. Sun followed behind but felt like an unwelcome spectator. A hand touched her back causing an uncomfortable chill to run down her spine. Hurrying her pace, she moved to Amber's side. "Can we go?"

Amber whirled toward her. "What's your hurry? Don't you love this place? This is where I buy all my clothes back in Wichita." She pulled the tall boy to her side. "This is Trent— something, and his friend is Moog—did I pronounce it right?" The guy with the tear nodded, his eyes half opened, half closed. One twitched.

Sun managed a quiet hello. She focused on the colorful lava lamps on the counter.

After Amber had completed her transaction, she headed toward the exit dragging her large shopping bag behind. Trent offered to carry it for her, and they sauntered side by side, clearly intrigued with each other. Sun glanced at her watch. Only twenty-seven minutes had passed, and she couldn't wait for Miss Julie to pick them up. This was not how she had envisioned their time at the mall.

"Sun, hurry up. We're going to the food court."

Moog kept pace with her as she quickened her step. No, her mother would not be happy if she knew Sun walked with a stranger, but she had been taught to be polite. She asked, "Do you go to school near here?"

"Not any more, I was taking a course through Virtual School but got behind so I quit. Don't have time because I work construction with my uncle." He shrugged, "The money's good."

"What do you want to be when you grow up?"

His eyebrows knit together, as if he hadn't considered the idea before. "Dunno. I like to work with my hands. Maybe a carpenter or a welder or something. I don't want to do construction for the rest of my life, but it's cool for the time being. What about you?"

"Something with math or science—those are my favorite subjects. I do virtual school too, but I still have two more years of high school."

"You look like you're from China, are you?"

"No, I'm from South Korea—Seoul."

"Oh, sorry, they're all the same to me." He guffawed. "You speak English good."

The food court was packed. Families with shopping bags draped over stroller handles tried to rein in their children. Teenagers lounged next to each other as they checked their messages. Amber led them to a table for four. The boy named Trent dropped Amber's shopping bag on the floor beside it and said he was going to get some drinks. Amber said she'd go with him. She caught up, linking her arm through his.

Conversation dried up with Moog. He didn't seem to notice. His attention was on his phone, his back to her. She felt like a stranger in this world, but Amber was a member.

Amber returned carrying fries bathed in catsup, followed by Trent who balanced a tray of Cokes. They sat close to each other. She fed him a french fry, and they giggled about something only the two of them understood.

Laughing, she hit his arm playfully, "Stop it." She sipped her drink, stood, and announced, "We're gonna walk around. I'll meet you back in an hour—where we arrived, okay?"

"Don't you think we should ...?"

Amber wasn't listening. Her arm was linked in Trent's. They laughed about something. She cast a glance over her shoulder at Sun. "See you later."

Moog was still focused on his phone. Sun excused herself— mumbled that she was going to the bookstore. In reality, she didn't feel comfortable spending the next hour with a person she hardly knew. How could Amber leave her like that?

She checked the directory and headed for her destination. Books felt safe, and she needed to feel safe. Upon arriving at the store, she inhaled deeply—she loved the smell of books, but now all she smelled was coffee.

Mentioning Korea to Moog made her homesick. Heading for

the travel section, she found three books about South Korea and leafed through them, searching for familiar places. Pictures of parks, high-rises, and bridges brought tears to her eyes—memories of her dad pushing her on a swing so high she had shrieked. Memories of her early life cascaded over each other, causing more tears to spill down her cheeks. She peered around to make sure nobody noticed her. They didn't. She used her shirt to wipe her face.

She missed him. Life had certainly changed since the day her mother had sat her down and said her daddy had died, that they would be moving to a smaller place, and she would be changing schools. That was the day her life of innocence and ease evaporated. They had moved into a small apartment above Mr. Park's grocery store. She grinned at the memory of him. He always pretended to be stern, but she saw the glint of amusement in his eye. He always let her take handfuls of rice and overripe vegetables up to her mom. Life had been simple then. And she hadn't appreciated it.

She glanced at her watch and realized an hour had lapsed, and she had to hurry in order to meet Miss Julie. She hadn't thought to get Amber's phone number. She didn't even know if Amber had a phone. They hadn't talked once the guys showed up. Worry erupted and filled her with uneasiness. If she could just get Amber back to Julie's house, she'd feel better.

Amber wasn't there. Sun scanned the place where Amber had tried on scarves. Julie's car was at the curb. She waited five more minutes, past the time they were supposed to meet. She said a silent prayer for Amber to show up quickly. Maybe she was already in the car. That must be it.

Julie's eyes jerked open when Sun opened the car door.

"Have you seen Amber?"

She yawned, "No, I've only been here for a few minutes. Did you lose her?"

"No, she told me she'd meet me, but she's not here."

Julie straightened and put the car in gear. "Go wait inside for her. I'll park the car and come in to help find her. Don't worry. She probably forgot about the time."

As Sun entered the store, she knew Amber wasn't going to be there, although she didn't know why. Maybe if Moog was still in the food court, he would know how to get in touch with his friend. Miss Julie's face was grim when she joined her. Maybe she had the same feeling.

"Why isn't Amber with you?"

Too ashamed to meet her boss's eyes, she focused on the terrazzo floor. "We met these guys."

"What? What happened?"

"We went to a store Amber likes to shop at—Hot Topic. Two guys started talking to her—Trent and Moog. We went to the food court with them; then she said she was going to walk with Trent and would meet me here in an hour. That's the last time I saw her."

Julie inhaled and closed her eyes. "Okay, let's retrace your steps. Maybe she went back to the store."

"Moog might still be in the food court. That's where I left him before I went to the bookstore."

Julie grasped Sun's hand and hurried in the direction of the food court, winding through crowds of teens and tourists wandering the aisles. When they arrived, their tray full of drinks and soggy fries was still on the table, but Moog had vanished.

Julie spun around. "How about we circle the mall, and if we don't find her, we'll go to the mall security and ask for their help. I don't want to panic yet."

"Shouldn't one of us wait at the entrance? What if she shows herself—shows up?"

"Good question. I don't have an answer. Wish we had her phone number. Maybe her dad does. I don't want to upset him though." They returned to the entrance. No Amber anywhere. "Let's walk around the mall, but first let's pray." She pulled Sun into a narrow aisle between two racks of men's shirts. "Help us find her, Lord. Keep her safe. Lead us to her."

If it were anyone else, their trip around the mall from one anchor store to another would have been fun for Sun, but considering Amber's past, they exchanged few words. Sun agreed to survey all the stores on the right side of the aisle. As her eyes darted from a group of teens in a shoe store to the lone customer in a perfume shop, her mind filled with calculations involving the statistical probability of finding a moving person when the searchers were mobile as well. She didn't like the odds.

When they had returned to their starting point, Miss Julie's grim expression said it all.

"It's time to go to the security office. I'm going to call Steve." Julie pulled out her phone as they waited in line at a mall information desk. She grimaced and held the phone away from her ear. "Okay, we'll meet you here." Her eyebrows raised. "Not a happy camper. He'll be here soon."

Sun was perplexed. "If he is in a state park, how can he be here soon?"

Julie said, "Huh? Oh, no, he's working. He just said there's a dark cloud that follows me wherever I go."

A pink-haired girl with a nametag that read "Hi, I'm Lauren" said, "How can I help you?"

Julie said, "How do we find someone we lost? Can you page her or something?"

Pushing her glasses up, Lauren said, "No, we can only use the PA system for emergencies. You can have your friend paged in the department stores though. I could call on your behalf. What's her name?"

"Amber Siemens. Could you direct us toward the security office, please?"

Lauren sniffed and rolled her eyes. "This is the second time today I've had to ask for a security officer."

Sun touched Miss Julie's sleeve. "We have to stay here. Officer Steve will be here from the forest soon."

"What?" She leaned toward Lauren. "Could you ask a security guard to meet us here? We have to remain in the area for the police."

The teen pursed her lips and picked up the receiver. A line formed behind them. Miss Julie motioned her toward a circular bench surrounding a fountain where they sat. Pennies abounded in its water. Where did the money go at the end of the day? Did they give it to a poor family? She hoped so.

Twenty minutes passed before Officer Steve and a stocky man in uniform with a mall security badge arrived at the same time from different directions. After they shook hands and talked about police things, Officer Steve bent down to Sun's level. "Tell us what happened to Amber."

Ashamed of herself, she kept her eyes on the floor as she repeated everything she had told Julie.

When she glanced up, both men were staring at her. Hanging her head, she said, "I'm sorry. It's my fault."

Steve touched her shoulder. "You didn't do anything wrong, Sweetie. It's just that this mall is a breeding ground for traffickers. Happens all the time. A group of guys seeks out the shyest girl and tells her she's pretty to buoy up her confidence. It's called grooming. Then they get her to leave the mall for a party, or they tell her she should be a model and entice her to leave with them to get professional pictures taken."

Sun wanted to say they got the wrong girl. Amber was the fun, outgoing one while she was the shy one. But Moog and Trent were clearly more interested in Amber. She kept her thoughts to herself.

Steve shifted his attention to the other officer. "We have to find this girl. Could you give us access to your security cameras? Maybe we can locate her in time."

"Sure." He put his hand on her shoulder. "Describe the two males please."

Her lips quivered. What did he mean by *locate her in time*? "The boy named Trent had long blond hair. He was tall and wore black."

"Everyone's tall to you. Was he as tall as I am?"

She stared at the floor. "I think so."

"Did he have any tattoos, scars, or piercings?"

Closing her eyes to picture him, nothing about Trent came to mind. "I don't remember. But Moog had a tattoo of a tear right here." She pointed under her eye. "And he wore a red wool cap. He had curly dark hair."

The officer's expression twisted. "I remember that cap. That one's here almost every day. Don't know about the other one." He beckoned with his finger. "My office is this way."

Wheelchairs and scooters lined the wall outside an office barely big enough to hold two people much less four. Sun hovered by the door until Julie moved her close to where the two men huddled over a computer. The images on the screen were grainy.

Officer Steve said, "At least, we have an approximate time frame to follow them from Hot Topic to the food court."

"There." Sun watched a thin male with long hair take Amber's shopping bag. Her gait was playful. She punched Trent's arm. Then she saw herself, long black hair to her waist, solemn and tentative—tiny compared to Moog, who sauntered next to her. His body language said he didn't want to be stuck with her. A chill travelled down her back, and she shivered to think a mere two hours ago, they walked side by side.

She watched herself join the others at the table in the food court. Amber's attention was on Trent. Moog's back was to her as he focused on his phone. She sat in the middle, clearly uncomfortable. Then Amber and Trent left, the shopping bag draped over his shoulder.

The story unfolded as the security officer downloaded the files from different cameras. Amber ran to a display of bottles and sprayed herself at a bath store. Trent planted his hand on her back as she sniffed candles at another shop. Trent talked on his phone as Amber headed for the restroom. When she returned, he said something in her ear and she laughed and hit his arm. Turning at the nearest exit, they left the mall.

An exterior camera showed the pair waiting. Amber laughed at something he said. A late-model Cadillac pulled up at the curb, Trent guided her to the car and opened the back door, throwing the Hot Topic bag in the backseat. The last view of Amber showed her gazing back toward the entrance to the mall—bothered by something. Then he made her laugh, and she climbed in.

Julie said, "Seems like she had second thoughts."

The security officer added, "Like a lamb to the slaughter." When he glanced at Sun's trembling lip, he added, "Sorry, we'll find her."

As the car pulled away, Officer Steve asked, "Can you pause it right there? Zoom in on the license plate." He wrote the number on a pad of paper. Then he pulled out his phone. "You're not going to believe this," he said, "We need to issue an Amber Alert on said car. The hostage's name is Amber--," he leaned toward Julie. "What's her last name? Also, give me a brief description of what she was wearing and her appearance."

Julie glanced at Sun. "Her last name is Siemens. She was wearing long jeans and a blue jacket. Her hair is long and blond. She's fifteen, is that right?"

"Yes," Sun said, "Her arms and legs have tattoos she cut on them. She bought black jeans, a tee-shirt, and a cap at the store."

Officer Steve asked, "Did she pay with cash?"

"No, she used a credit card, and the boy named Trent bought her another cap. I don't know how he paid for it."

After he repeated the information to his contact, he said, "Let's go to the store—Hot Topic, was it? And get a read on Amber's purchases. They might use her card, and we'll be able to follow their trail."

As they headed to the store, Officer Steve's phone rang. After a short conversation, he said, "Bad news, good news. The car was stolen from another mall's parking lot earlier today. But the good news is the Amber Alert is up and running."

Sun peered up at him. "What is this Amber Alert—something that will help Amber?"

"It's a bulletin to all drivers to be on the lookout for a car that may be transporting a child." He patted Sun's shoulder. "We'll find her. Not to worry."

Sun's eyes filled. She knew better. Amber was gone forever.

Chapter Ten

"Go in circles like this." Angela placed her hand over Rosa's little fist and showed her how to stir the Jell-O liquid. "Carefully. Yes, you've got it." Cherry-colored liquid streamed over the sides of the bowl and onto the counter. Seizing her phone, she snapped a picture of Rosa standing atop a chair at the counter, an oversized apron covering her clothes, already stained with mustard and chocolate. "Smile." Rosa waved the wooden spoon, red liquid flying in all directions.

"Oh, you're a funny one." She checked the kitchen clock. Where was Steve? Now that the men were in custody, he'd allowed Rosa to stay with her for the time being.

But as he left, he grasped her hand. "Don't get too attached. I can see it in your eyes. You want to keep her. It doesn't work like that." He'd pulled her toward him. "Don't give her your heart."

He kissed her on the cheek—warmth engulfing her. It was becoming so difficult to read his intentions. He advised her not to give Rosa her heart, but he had gone over the line with her. She couldn't help herself—she was falling in love with both of them, and she didn't know how to turn off her feelings.

Rosa needed a bath; the house needed a bath. She didn't care. She'd take Rosa any way she could get her—chocolate-stained and sticky or neat and clean. What Steve didn't know was she *was* going to adopt Rosa, come hale or high water as her mother used to say. And he also didn't know she had a contact that could help her with the adoption.

Squirting some lavender-scented bubble bath under the faucet, she slipped off Rosa's dirty clothes and directed her into the tub. Rosa's guttural laugh was loud and raucous as she splashed her arms spilling water over the sides. Wiping drops off her cheek, Angela sat on the bathroom tile and called her friend Jo-Ann McEwan, a flight attendant who had adopted a child from Honduras the year before. They talked about their flights, the schedule for the upcoming month, and then she got to the point. "I need your help. I want to adopt a little girl from Colombia. I know it usually takes a while and there are rules to follow, but what if I want to get this done fast? Are there shortcuts?"

"I went through an organization called Lutheran Refugee Service. They helped me find Manuel. My husband and I had to go through several interviews and a background check, but we had Manny in about four months. Normally it takes at least two years, but we were lucky. But it cost over ten thousand dollars."

Rosa was putting her face under the water and blowing bubbles. Angela trailed her hand in the water. "Here's the thing. Rosa's with me right now. You're not going to believe this, but she was a stowaway on my flight from Bogotá."

"Oh dear, you can't keep her. You got to call the police and file a report and a bunch of other things."

"It's more complicated than that. All those things are done. She was kidnapped onto my flight, so in reality, she's not a stowaway; she's a kidnapped child. Anyway, she escaped and ended up near my car. We had to flee from her kidnappers, but they're in jail now. Steve Bricker—he's with the police department has been helping me. He found out her family was probably killed by the kidnappers because they've been missing for two years.

Silence. Then, "Wow, you have the most exciting life. I think you should contact a certain organization. Give me a minute. I'll call you back." She hung up.

Angela used the break to envelop Rosa in a fluffy bath towel. Carrying her into her guest bedroom, she dropped her on the bed eliciting another bout of guttural laughter. She found some pajamas in the overnight bag Steve had retrieved from Miriam and put them on her. It must be time for a nap, she thought. Kissing her on the forehead, she enfolded little hands in hers and recited a prayer

Julie's mother had taught her when she was a child. Probably during one of the many weekends she'd stayed with her aunt and uncle while her mother was on one of her trips. While she prayed, Rosa closed her eyes and mumbled something unintelligible but precious. Her eyes remained shut, so she tiptoed to the door and closed it halfway.

Her phone was ringing as she returned to the bathroom to clean up the mess. It was Jo-Ann.

"I have a place for you to contact. It's called Foster Care for Unaccompanied Refugee and Immigrant Children USCCB. Once you've talked to them, make an appointment to meet with the Lutheran organization. Hope this helps."

"What will they ask me? I have no clue how to take care of a child."

"Well, don't tell them that. Just be yourself. They'll want to be assured that you're ready to make an eighteen-year commitment to the child. And that you're reliable and have good character. You'll make a great mom."

"Thanks. You've been a big help." Once disconnected, she wasted no time making the calls. The refugee center asked for her information and said they'd mail her forms to fill out. Then she dialed the Lutheran organization. She hoped they wouldn't ask too many questions. After three rings, a New England-accented voice answered.

"I'd like to talk to someone about adopting a child from Colombia."

"Wonderful. If you'll give me your address, I'll mail you an information packet to begin the process."

She hesitated, "Actually, I was wondering if I could come in and talk to someone. I'm in Orlando. Do you have an office in Florida?"

"Sorry, our headquarters is in Baltimore. We often do skype interviews with clients. The gentleman who would best be able to answer your questions will have some free time around four Eastern Time. Would you like me to pencil you in?"

"Sure, that would be great." Everything was moving fast, the way she liked it, but it felt out-of-control as well. After leaving her name and phone number, she sat on the floor in the bathroom staring at the puddles forming between the cracks in the tile. What was she getting herself into? Could she be a good mother to Rosa—all by herself?

A light tap on the door made her start. It must be Steve. How would he react? Would he scold her? She opened an inch. His eyes drew her in. The next thing she knew, her head was tucked under his chin. Like a puzzle piece, she fit perfectly.

He laced his fingers around her waist. "Whoa, what did Rosa do to you?"

"Nothing of course. I have lots to tell you." Backing up, she ran a hand through her hair. Then she hooked her finger in his and led him to her sofa. They didn't need to talk; the contact of their knees was enough. She loved how his eyes crinkled, as if he was mulling over something humorous or planning some mischief. She bet he'd been a handful as a child.

"What's going on?"

"Hmm?" She'd never noticed he had freckles before.

He grinned. "You said you had lots to tell me."

"Oh, earth to me. Yes, I've been checking into adopting Rosa."

"What did I tell you?"

"Something about guarding my heart. But I can't—she already has it, and so…."

"And so?"

"Nothing. Anyway, a representative from an organization called the Lutheran Refugee Service is going to skype me this afternoon, and I was wondering if you could—if you could be there with me."

"What do you know about them?"

"What do you mean?"

"There are a lot of fly-by-night companies out to make a buck."

"Well, it has *Lutheran* in the title. That's worth something, isn't it?"

"You can name a company anything."

"My friend Jo-Ann adopted a child from South America, and she recommended the organization and another one. I haven't signed up for anything yet. Today's meeting is solely to get information." She glanced at her watch. "They should be calling any minute."

He held her hand in his. His was warm and reassuring, and she didn't want to pull hers away, but Julie's face came to mind. She stood and paced—everything was too complicated. People would get hurt. People who mattered to her. And how could she hurt Julie? Steve was her first and only boyfriend. Then there was Rosa. Didn't she need to do everything within her power to find her parents?

She sat next to him again. "What if Rosa's parents are still alive?"

"Families don't vanish for any good reason. Colombia doesn't have a Witness Protection program."

He brought her hand to his lips. A shiver went down her spine.

She stood abruptly and strode to the window. She couldn't let him see her face. "You said they had money. Maybe they used it to move out of the country."

"We thought about that. Their house was intact; the wife's purse and cell phone were on the kitchen counter. Even the kids' backpacks were ready for school, as if life was going on when they vanished. But the thing is—one of their cars was found in a remote area— destroyed by fire. No bodies were found in it or in the immediate area. The police closed the case months ago. It just took them a while to locate it after we called."

She checked her watch. "Time to open skype. I'll be right back. The lighting is good in here. Will you sit with me?"

"I don't think this is a good idea." He hesitated. "Okay."

Once the laptop was on the coffee table ready for the interview, she leaned toward him. "What do you think they'll ask me?"

"Don't have a clue. I assume they'll want to know why you want to adopt Rosa. And they'll want to know if you'll be a good mother."

"Do we have to tell them the whole story? It's so complicated."

"They can't organize an adoption of a child without having all the facts."

A beeping indicated the other party had entered the program. An intelligent older man with tufts of white hair surrounding a bald head appeared. He wore spectacles and had kind eyes. "I'm Chet Ross, director of Lutheran Refugee Service. You called for information about adopting a child from Colombia, is that right?"

She cleared her throat; her voice uncharacteristically shaky. She hoped he wouldn't notice. "Yes, my name is Angela Howell, and this is Steven Bricker. I have a little girl named Rosa Colón staying with me temporarily, and I'd like to adopt her. It's a long story. Before I go into it, could you go over the requirements first?"

"Pleased to meet you, Angela, Steven. We'll need to know about this child named Rosa. But to answer your question, we have to make sure the child will be raised in a loving home. Faith is important to us, so we'd want to be assured Rosa would be raised in a godly home by parents who could provide a safe environment."

Angela's expression changed. "Oh."

"Is there a problem, Miss Howell?"

"The godly home wouldn't be a problem, and I can assure you Rosa would be brought up in a safe, loving environment, but I'm not married."

Mr. Ross removed his glasses and wiped the lens with a tissue. "That may be a problem. We'd prefer that the child be brought up in a two-parent family. Usually these children have endured multiple hardships. We've found they do best in a home with a father and a mother."

Steve squeezed Angela's arm. "She meant to say she's not married *yet*."

She gazed at him. What did he mean?

"Would you excuse us for a minute, Mr. Ross? It will only take a minute."

"Sure, no problem."

He led her to the other room and spun her around to face him. "Let's do it. Let's get married. You feel it. I feel it. I'm in love with you, Angela Howell."

Her mouth moved, but nothing came out at first. "But what about….?"

"She'll understand. Rosa needs us." He pulled her close and kissed her on the lips—tenderly, sweetly. Then he tipped her chin with his finger. "What do you say?"

She inhaled deeply. His eyes drew her in. His expression was tentative. "Okay, I accept."

He brushed her cheek with a kiss. "Let's do this." They returned to the couch, his arm around her. "Sir, we're getting married. Rosa will have a mother and a father."

He appeared surprised. "Very well. Tell me about this little girl." He wrote notes as Steve and Angela told him the story, each interrupting with extra details. When they were finished, he pulled out a handkerchief and mopped his forehead. "This is a bit of a cart before the horse, but I don't see why it can't work. We'll send you forms to fill out, and there'll be a formal interview here in Baltimore. When is the wedding date?"

They gazed at each other, speechless. Steve glanced at Angela and said, "Soon. Very soon."

Chapter Eleven

Julie pushed all extraneous thoughts from her mind. The worry
about where Amber was. Sun pouting in the next room. She
thought they should be out searching for Amber. But what Sun
didn't understand was there was nothing they could do. It was in
the police's hands. Steve had said the human trafficking task force
was involved, and it was merely a matter of time before they found
her.

Why had Amber shown up at her door anyway? She didn't
have time for all this drama. Not when she'd just received notice
that her client Kevin Perez's hearing for asylum was the next day.
Not only did she have to write a compelling opening statement, but
she also had to prep her client for the hearing.

A sense of malaise overtook her as she thought about
immigration court. She hadn't been there in over a year. Most of
her work was done at her desk by E-mail or phone. What would
she wear? How could she possibly be ready by tomorrow to stand
before the judge?

Dropping her pen, she closed her eyes and prayed for wisdom.
Her client needed her best defense. He'd only get one chance.

Fortunately, she had already done the research on case law. Her
first point: the definition of robbery was taking the personal
property of another through force or intimidation. The money
taken from Mr. Perez's ATM account was done with a gun to his
head. He did not freely give material support to a terrorist

organization. In criminal court, the members of FARC would be convicted of armed robbery, but immigration court was not bound by the rules of other courts. To convince an immigration judge that robbery was different than giving material support would be a challenge.

Her second point—FARC did not harass the Perez family because it was trying to intimidate Mr. Perez into not going to the police. The fact that it had written the word FARC on his car proved the group was not concealing its identity. A good point, but she needed a third.

She leafed through her notes. What was missing? She reviewed the requirements for asylum. The asylee had to belong to an identifiable group, and because of that association, he had a well-founded fear of persecution. Her client's association with the government fulfilled one part of the definition. The gang had stolen his government identification. They knew he worked for the government. For some reason, they continued to harass the family. Why? Either because they wanted more money or because he worked for the government. They hadn't demanded more money. She closed her eyes and rubbed them. Time was running out. She had to call Mr. Perez.

She spent the next thirty minutes preparing him for the hearing. She told him to answer the judge's questions with confidence but not to elaborate. Before she said good-bye, she asked if FARC had done anything else rising to the level of harassment.

"They left a message on our front door. It said, 'Your wife is very beautiful.' It was signed FARC. I snapped a picture of it. Do you want me to send it to you?"

"Absolutely. It will help. Plus, it will prove they're not hiding their identity."

"My wife's last day of work is tomorrow. Then she's taking the kids and moving to her parents' house for the next few months."

"That's a good idea. I wish you'd go with her for your own safety. I'll see you, or rather hear you in court tomorrow."

After she disconnected, she reflected on how to capitalize on the picture. The case was solid—even more solid with the new evidence. She didn't see how the immigration judge could not rule in her client's favor.

Her phone buzzed indicated a new message. Angela. She

wanted to know if she and Steve could stop by. They had something to discuss with her. Hmm. That sounded ominous. It must be something to do with Rosa.

She hurried to put together her file for court before they arrived. Usually, this was her favorite part of preparing for a case. The file would be in a perfect order with colorful tabs she could refer to without delay if she needed them. Next, she took a quick shower. It was where she practiced and refined her opening statement. Judge Boyd was fair but busy. He didn't appreciate grandstanding. She'd keep her opening remarks to three or four minutes. Then the judge would ask Mr. Perez questions. If everything went according to plan, Perez would be moving to the US in a matter of days.

She was climbing out of the shower when Sun knocked on the bathroom door, saying Miss Angela and Officer Steve had arrived. Great. She quickly put her clothes on over her damp body and ran a comb through her wet snarls. After pinching her cheeks to add a bit of color, she applied some lip gloss and put on her earrings. She smirked at her reflection in the mirror. It would have to do.

"Hi guys. Sorry, I was in the show…." What was this? Steve's hand was on Angela's back. Angela appeared to be sick to her stomach. "What's going on? Are you ill?"

Angela glanced up at Steve. "I—we have something to tell you. You might want to sit." With an audible gulp, Angela gripped Julie's arm and pulled her to the couch. Something was off. The tension in the air was palpable.

"It kinda just happened. We didn't plan it."

"Plan what?"

"Don't get mad. But we've decided—to get married."

What? Her cousin with her boyfriend? Her mind couldn't wrap around what she had just heard. There must be some mistake— some big joke on her. Angela was her best friend. What was she missing? "Very funny. Are we on one of those hidden camera shows like Punk'd?"

Angela peered up at Steve, her eyes filled with tears. "Not a joke. I'm so sorry. You're like a sister to me. I would never ever hurt you, but it happened. We're going to get married and adopt Rosa."

Julie bit her lip to keep it from quivering, but she couldn't keep the hurt out of her voice. "Do you think it's wise to use marriage to adopt a child?"

Steve's arm rested on Angela's arm. "It's more than that." He hesitated. "I love her."

Bile rose in Julie's throat. "And you?"

Angela stared at the floor and whispered a single word. "Yes."

Julie bolted from the sofa. They had to leave before she lost it. "Congratulations. I'm … happy for both of you." Keeping her eyes on the door, she hugged Angela and touched Steve's arm. Never had she felt so awkward. "When's it going to happen—the wedding?"

Steve answered, "Not sure yet, but soon. We have to be married to adopt Rosa."

Oh, their main reason was to adopt Rosa. It was a marriage of convenience. How noble. "I have to get ready to go to court tomorrow. We'll talk soon." She ushered them to the door and managed to keep her expression pleasant. "Really, congratulations."

The minute they were out the door, she leaned against it and crumbled to the floor. She could lose it now or she could go to her room and lose it there. "Sun?" Her voice cracked. "You can go home early if you like. I'm going to lie down. I'll lock up."

Betrayal. Memories of Steve's attention to whatever came out of Angela's mouth. His short, gruff responses when she called him. Like she was bothering him. And Angela—beautiful, exciting Angela, who could flutter her lashes and guys melted like Crisco.

When Sun finally left, she trudged to the security box and poked in the code. The dishes could sit in the sink for a week—she didn't care. Falling onto the couch, she pulled her earrings off, but one got loose and fell behind the sofa cushion. Feeling for it, her forefinger circled the clasp, but her hand brushed something else. Paper. She stood and pulled off the cushion. It was obvious she needed to vacuum more than just the carpet.

What was this? Stuck deep between the crevasses of the sofa almost hidden from sight was an envelope. She pulled it out carefully so as not to tear it. The handwriting wasn't familiar. The letter had been forwarded to her new address in Celebration. It didn't appear to be a bill—that was good news. The postmark was dated January 6th from North Carolina—seven months earlier. Who did she know there? She opened it.

Dear Julie,

It's been six months since our last conversation—since you ordered me out of your house. You were angry, but I thought when you cooled down you would have wanted to talk. We had something, at least I felt we did. Since it was evident you didn't feel the same way, I had to leave. Everything reminded me of you. So I moved to Ashville, North Carolina. I do my best writing here, and I can hike whenever I want. There was no reason to stay in Florida.

I think about you often. If you get the urge, give me a call. Maybe we can make it work.

Love,

Matt

No way. Matthew Conner. The man she had thrown out of her house because she couldn't deal with the truth. It was easier to tell him to leave. Now here was proof that he wanted a relationship. He must have thought she still harbored bad feelings. But she didn't. His handsome, intense eyes, his intelligence, his loyalty. Her head hurt. Timing had never been her friend. She *had* called him, but his phone was disconnected. Six months ago, she would have responded to this letter in a heartbeat. Now all she wanted to do was go to bed and forget today ever happened.

***

Opening one eye half way allowed her to see it was an hour too early for the alarm to go off but too late to go back to sleep. When her other eye opened, she stared at the ceiling, and then it hit her. Heavy despair—how could she ever face her cousin or Steve again? It would be too awkward, too painful. At first, she'd avoid any contact. She'd delete every message; she'd be out or wouldn't answer the door. She'd work on forgetting them tomorrow. Now it was time to put them out of her mind and concentrate on her client's case.

As she pulled her navy blue suit off its hanger and wiped the dust off its shoulders, she recited her opening statement. Repeating it a dozen times would cement it into her long-term memory so when nerves overtook her, she could rely on her memory to carry her through. Next, she practiced answering the questions the judge might ask her. But she wasn't worried—how could she not win this case?

***

As soon as she'd pulled into the closest parking space to the courthouse, she checked her watch. Time to pray—a short one was all she had time for. She was ready.

An elderly couple helped each other out of a car in a handicapped parking space. The man leaned over his wife and unbuckled her seatbelt and gently pulled her to her feet, handing her a cane. So cute together—like Angela and Steve. They were a better fit than she and Steve. Life wasn't fair. Why did God take away everyone she loved? No, her life wasn't fair, but whoever said it was? Her dad used to say life wasn't fair, and then you die. Sigh.

She opened the car door, the heat punching her in the throat. Florida summer heat. Funny. She remembered saying to God she wanted to become a lawyer to make life more fair. Well, she'd do her best for Mr. Perez. Clutching her briefcase, she wiped the sweat off her face with her free hand, careful not to destroy her makeup. Walking up the courthouse stairs, she reminded herself of the elements of the case. Well-founded fear of persecution, association with a group. Money taken by force and violence. Those would be her points.

It was a short twenty minutes before Judge Boyd called her to the podium. After summarizing the case for his recorder, he counseled her to be brief in her opening remarks.

Stepping to the podium, she said, "Good morning, Your Honor. Julie Richards, attorney for Mr. Kevin Perez in absentia, who seeks asylum for himself and his family. I believe when you hear what he has to say via the telephone, you will be convinced he has a well-founded fear of persecution in Colombia because of his association with the government of his country.

Shuffling papers, Judge Boyd brushed his hand through the air. "Proceed with your opening statement, counselor, but keep it short. When you are finished, we'll call Mr. Perez."

No jury was present to direct her comments to; no room to pace as she liked to do when she talked. Instead, she leaned toward the microphone, knocking it against her chin. The sound was deafening and awkward. Glancing behind her, a dozen people stared in her direction. She breathed in deeply, apologized, and said what she had memorized, stopping at cogent points for emphasis. Once the judge yawned; another time, he peered at his watch.

"Thank you, Counsel. I'll call Mr. Perez and put him on speaker phone."

Mr. Perez answered on the second ring. That was a relief. What if he hadn't been home?

"Mr. Perez, my name is Judge Boyd. We are here to determine your petition for asylum. Our conversation will be recorded. Is that all right with you?"

"That is fine, Your Honor."

"Tell us, Mr. Perez, why should the United States offer you asylum?"

"Well sir, ever since the group named FARC attacked me, my family has been living in fear. They've followed my little girl to school, left messages on our house threatening our lives. They've even…"

"Have they actually followed through on a threat? Have they harmed any member of your family?"

The pause was too long before Mr. Perez said, "No, Your Honor, but they said they were going to rape my wife. They left a dead dog in our driveway with a message written in the dog's blood for us to read. You have no idea how this is affecting my daughter. She can't sleep. And she saw one of the men watching in her bedroom window."

The judge groaned as if he'd heard it all before. "Again, I'll ask you—has any member of this group called FARC actually touched a member of your family?"

"No, Your Honor."

Picking up the file, he said, "You haven't met the standard of persecution, Mr. Perez. The best I can do is continue your case for another month. Counselor, do you have anything else to add?"

Her heart fell. She had nothing. "No, Your Honor." Her face heated up. If she argued with the judge, he could dismiss it with a single word. A continuance was better than nothing.

If the Perez family could make it that long.

She wished she could console her client. He must be desolate. Another unfair thing happening to her. Maybe if she had Angela's eyelashes, she could have fared better with the judge. No, that was unfair of her.

The judge set a new date, and she was dismissed. If she were a better attorney, she could have won this one. If she had more experience or worked for a firm with clout, Mr. Perez would be safe. Her best wasn't good enough. Maybe she should just give it up pretending she was competent. A new attorney could have won the case. Mr. Perez deserved better.

Her shoulders sagged as her confidence plummeted to new-found depths; she trudged out of the courthouse. If she couldn't get Kevin Perez asylum, she didn't deserve to call herself an attorney. Maybe it was time to take the shingle down.

All she wanted was to lock herself in her house away from all people. Like a year ago, when the very thought of leaving her house caused her throat to constrict. Agoraphobia—her cousin called it, and then insisted she make an appointment with a grief counselor. She always agreed and then changed the subject. Honestly, she wasn't crazy. She drove herself to work and back every day. It was just everything else. Pushing the delete button was easier than dealing with her friends' platitudes. "They're in a better place," "time heals all wounds," and "you need to get on with your life." Nobody understood how hard it was to lose both parents at the same time.

Lost in the past, she almost missed the first step of the courthouse stairs. High heels were hard enough to walk in on level ground. She held onto the bannister and began her descent. Her whole life was going downhill. Maybe it was time to isolate herself for a while. Not like last year. Just until she had time to process what was happening to her. Lucky for her, it was Sun's day off. She wouldn't have to plaster a fake smile on and say nice things. The only thing she had to do was call Mr. Perez. It wasn't a conversation she was fondly anticipating.

One good thing—the judge hadn't dismissed the case. It was almost as if he was waiting for something bad to happen to the family so he could rule in Mr. Perez's favor. A wait-and-see was better than an outright denial. But what if a member of his family was killed?

It was on the third step from the bottom that her heel stuck in a rut on the stair. Like a slow motion movie, her arms and legs flailed to regain control, but gravity won. Down she plummeted.

Had she been alert, she would have seen the crack. But she'd been distracted, and she wasn't especially adept at walking in heels on a good day. Her ankle bone, protruding at an unusual angle, was beginning to swell and discolor. A file folder full of papers was carried off in the wind. She lay there sprawled across three steps. Glancing around to see who had witnessed her clumsiness, she spied a woman standing on the top step looking down on her literally. Instead of offering to help, she continued to talk to her companion. A mosquito buzzed close to her ear. She swiped at it, to no avail. Even mosquitoes had better luck than she.

The palm of her hand, which had tried to break her fall, was scraped and bleeding. The heel to her shoe lay on the second step. She put all her weight on her elbows to hoist herself up, but the ankle said no. Now what was she supposed to do? She couldn't make it to the parking lot by herself. She'd have to just sit there until someone came along to help. Angry tears threatened to erupt. How was she supposed to gather her papers when she couldn't move? *God, please help me. Tell me what to do.*

A lady wearing polka dot capris pushed a stroller and stopped when she approached Julie. "What happened?"

Resisting the urge to roll her eyes, she said, "My heel got caught in a crack. I think I twisted my ankle."

"Here, let me help you." She pulled her child from the stroller. "Sweetie, go get the papers and bring them here. I'll hold your lollipop." She nabbed the sucker as the child ran from step to step. "I'll go get the ones on the lawn."

Julie inched her ankle toward her torso. Who could she call for help? The only one who came to mind was Angela. No, no way she could call that … that vixen, that traitor. Staring at her phone, she wished she could call her parents. Sun couldn't drive. There was nobody, only her cousin.

The phone went to voice mail. Of course, it did. At least, she didn't have to *talk* to her. "Hi, it's Julie. I need a favor. I fell on the stairs at immigration court. Could you come and get me?"

The woman and her son returned carrying a pile of wrinkled, muddied papers. "Here you go. Hope we got them all."

"Thank you for your help." She tried to stand. "Before you leave, could you help me to that chair over there? I think I'll be more comfortable waiting for my ride on the bench, but I don't know if I can make it on my own."

"Of course." She pointed toward the purse sitting on the edge of a small puddle. "Kyle, could you bring the lady her purse? That's a good boy."

Leaning against the lady's shoulder, she slipped off her shoe and hopped to the bench. Every step sent shock waves of pain through her foot. It took all her effort not to scare the child. When they reached the bench, she eased herself down and inhaled. "You've been so kind. Can I pay you for your trouble? I don't have much cash, but I can write a check."

"Don't be silly. It was our pleasure, wasn't it, Kyle? Is there anything else we can do for you?"

"No, it's just been one of those days. You've been a big help. Bless you."

"Yes ma'am. He has blessed me. C'mon Kylie."

Well, that was nice, she thought. With teeth clenched, she raised her foot to rest it on the bench. The ankle was twice its normal size and had morphed into stormy colors. She wished she had some ice. Pulling her phone from her purse, she checked to see if Angela had called back. No. It was just as well. She wasn't ready to talk to her yet. Calling her back, she left a message telling her not to bother. She'd call a cab instead.

Once she found a taxi company and left directions to find her on the bench, she disconnected and chafed at her luck. The last twenty-four hours hadn't been her finest, but she'd survive. It wouldn't be easy. She was a failure at love and a failure at work; now, she couldn't even walk on her own. Was it too much to ask for a little success?

***

Julie paid the cabdriver, then waited impatiently for him to come around and help her out. It hadn't been easy for him to hoist her up and load her into the cab at the courthouse. For his extra work, she'd added an extra five-dollar bill to the tip. Her eyes automatically drifted to her neighbor's curb, forgetting that the guys were in custody now. No need to worry any more. She surveyed the neighborhood, her eyes finally landing on her porch. Two people sat on her swing chair. Was that Amber? She planted her foot on the curb and yelled her name when pain surged up her leg. "Ow." She hated having to rely on people.

Leaning on the cabdriver's shoulder, she limped—one painful step at a time. The man on the swing hurried down to help her climb the stairs. She didn't recognize him, but the girl with him was a cleaner version of the girl who had rung her doorbell yesterday. Maybe he had rescued her. She repeated, "Amber?"

The girl shook her head and held back.

Once the men had lifted her to the top step of the porch and gently put her down, she thanked them and smoothed the wrinkles off her skirt. With her torn nylons and bare feet, she wished these people would go away and come back when she was decent. Instead, she thrust out her hand toward the girl; then removed it when she noticed how dirty it was. "You must be Aubrey, Amber's sister."

The man joined the girl. "Yes, this is Aubrey, and I'm her father, Jeremy Siemens." He put forth his hand to take hers, not appearing to notice the dirt and scrapes that covered her palm. The girl nodded in her direction but didn't say anything.

"Pleased to meet you two. I'm sorry. It's been a rough day. Come in." She entered the code and opened the door. "I hope you haven't been waiting long. Sun didn't tell me you were coming."

He guided her elbow to the sofa and helped ease her down. "After Sun called us about Amber's disappearance, we got here as soon as we could. What's being done to find her?"

She'd kick herself if it didn't hurt so bad. In all that had been happening, she'd forgotten to call Amber's parents. With the case on her mind, Amber's disappearance had slipped between her synapses. Putting on her most reassuring face, she said, "The police will find her, don't you worry. They have the security videos, which will help identify the boy Amber was with."

"You'll remember we've been through this before. Same thing happened. I don't think we can stand another two years of this. Her mother's worried sick. But we're here to help. Whatever we can do."

Her throbbing ankle resembled a baseball. "Would you mind getting me some ice for my ankle? The kitchen's in there."

"Absolutely." He moved to Aubrey. "Tell her what you had in mind while I go get an icepack." He moved a few steps before he glanced over his shoulder. "Can I get you anything else—some coffee or water?"

"Maybe some aspirin and a glass of water. Check the cupboard next to the refrigerator."

Once Pastor Siemens left, she focused her attention on the girl, who sat on the sofa next to her. "You resemble Amber so much. Could you get me my purse? I think I need to call a doctor." It occurred to her Aubrey hadn't spoken a single word.

Fishing through her purse, she found the card Dr. Moyer had given her, stared at it for a moment, and almost put it back in her purse. Dr. Brett Moyer. She didn't want to appear needy, like she couldn't take care of herself. That's what Steve had told her more than once. He'd said he dealt with enough problems at work and didn't want to handle any more in his private life. Now here she was needing help again from this doctor.

Another glimpse of her ankle made her dial the number. The call went to voice mail. She loved his voice, even if it was just a recording.

"This is Julie Richards. We met at the hospital. Remember, I was the one with Rosa, the little girl who had run away. I'm calling about me this time. I—um—tripped at the courthouse and I think I twisted my ankle. It's swollen and hurts a lot. I can't put weight on it. Anyway, I'm not sure what to do next. Would you call me back?" She left her number before disconnecting.

Moving toward Aubrey who stared out the window, she said, "Sorry about that. What did your dad want you to tell me?"

Aubrey's voice was tentative, hardly above a whisper. "Me and Amber haven't been close, not since we were little kids." She gazed at the door as if she wanted to run through it. "It's my fault Amber ran away again. I haven't been nice to her since she came back home."

Julie went to touch her arm then thought better of it. She didn't know a lot about teenagers—only Sun—and she didn't know if they liked being touched. Aubrey didn't jerk away. "It must not have been easy to have all that media attention on your family."

A tremulous giggle erupted from her mouth. "No, it wasn't. My parents forgot about me and my little brother for the last couple years. Don't get me wrong. I wanted Amber to come home, but everything changed after she left. I guess I wanted Amber to know how we felt." She gazed at her hands. "I told her I wished she was dead."

"We all say things we don't mean."

She jerked her head up, her eyes intense. "No, I meant it at the time. It was about then she started cutting herself. It's always something with her. Another thing to worry about."

"So, I take it you're not as eager to find her as your father is."

"Oh I want to find her. She's a train wreck, but I love her, and I feel responsible for her running away. That's why I'm here—to try to find her."

It didn't make sense. The girl still seemed to hold a grudge; yet here she sat. "Did your dad make you come?"

"I came on my own. It was Dad's sermon last Sunday that made me want to come. He talked about the prodigal son and how happy he was to have Amber home. Then he gazed at me, and his eyes were so sad. It hit me then—the problem in the parable wasn't the prodigal son; it was his brother. I was the brother—jealous, resentful. That's why my dad's eyes were so sad."

"Wow, I never thought of the parable that way."

She grinned for the first time, and her eyes brightened. "Yeah, me neither until last Sunday. I'm still mad at my sister, but now I realize I haven't been Miss Perfect either. So here I am—ready to help."

Pastor Siemens returned with a towel wrapped around some ice cubes. Handing it to her, he said, "Aubrey had this crazy idea, and I don't like it, but she wants to help. Tell her, Aubrey." He handed Julie a glass of water and a bottle of pain relievers.

"I was thinking I could pretend to be my sister. We used to do it when we were little, and we even fooled our parents some of the time. I could dress like her and hang out at the mall. Maybe the guys who abducted Amber would be fooled into thinking she got away. The police can be watching and catch them in the act."

Reaching for her phone, she pressed Steve's number, then thought better of it. She didn't know if she was ready to talk to him yet. It would be awkward, uncomfortable. Then she glanced at Aubrey's eyes. Unsure of herself, full of mixed feelings, but willing to risk her life for her twin sister.

He answered on the first ring. "Bricker."

She was hoping for voicemail. "It's me, Julie. Amber's father and sister are here. Anything new on your search for Amber?"

His voice cracked. "We've shown pictures of the guy around, but nobody has identified him. If they know, they're not talking. The picture's pretty grainy, so it's hard to tell."

"Well, Amber's sister Aubrey has an idea you might want to hear."

Papers shuffled, and he covered the phone to say something. "I'm swamped. Could you give me the short version?"

"Sure," she glanced at Pastor Siemens' downtrodden face. Why weren't the police putting everything else aside to find his daughter? "Aubrey looks exactly like Amber. You can't tell them apart if their clothes are the same. Aubrey thought she could pretend to be Amber at the mall and smoke the guys out." Silence ensued. "Did you hear me?"

"Yes, I heard you. Could work. We could get Sun to go with her. They could go to the same stores and the food court and see what happens. But it could be dangerous. We could place a wire on the girls and put some plain-clothes detectives in the area. It might work."

"When?"

"How about later today? You get Sun and take the girls to the mall. I could be there by five or six."

"I don't think I can make it to the mall. I've twisted my ankle and can't walk. Could you get Angela to do it?"

"How did you twist your ankle? I thought you were going to court today."

"That's where it happened. I twisted it as I was going down the steps outside. Anyway, I'm waiting on a call from the doctor." She knew he was shaking his head at her clumsiness.

"I've got too much going on here at work to call. How about you call Angela. I don't care who brings the girls to the mall. We'll be in touch." He hung up before she could say good-bye.

Her heart felt empty, as if the end of the story was written on their relationship, and she wasn't ready to read the last page. But she couldn't deal with that now. She'd have to wait to grieve.

She repositioned herself on the couch and put the throw underneath her ankle, which was dripping melted water onto the couch. "Steve Bricker is the officer handling the case. He likes your idea, Aubrey. He said you should meet at the mall today at five or six. He'll have officers watching you. I can't go with you because of this ankle, so he suggested Sun accompany you because she was with Amber and knows where they went. I'm going to call my cousin Angela to drive you. She'll be there for you."

She wasn't eager to talk to Angela, but what choice did she have? She answered on the second ring. "Angela, want an adventure?"

"I'm flying out at five in the morning, but I'm free tonight. What's up?"

Once Julie stopped talking, Angela's shrieking and clapping let her know she was eager to help. She even volunteered to call Sun and pick up the girls. Obviously, Angela didn't feel uncomfortable talking to her. She'd have to find a way to make their relationship work. After all, Angela was her one and only relative.

Her eyes went to Aubrey. There was a difference between the twins. Aubrey was too fresh-faced with that peaches-and-cream complexion, and that healthy, shiny hair wouldn't fool anyone. "Did you bring any jeans with you? Or tee-shirts? Amber was a mess when she showed up. Kind of like she'd been sleeping in a bus station." Then she winced—her father didn't need to hear that.

Aubrey's radiant face contrasted with Amber's dower expression. "No, I didn't bring any jeans. I should have thought of that."

Inching her ankle to the side, she said. "I have some jeans, a blue hoodie, and a tee-shirt in my dresser in the bedroom. Why don't you see if you can find something? We have to make you resemble Amber as she was on the day she went missing. Also, you might want to wet your hair and mess it up a bit."

When Aubrey left the room, Julie allowed herself a chance to close her eyes for a minute. If she could erase the last twenty-four hours, that would be good. A nap would at least give her a reprieve.

A masculine voice brought her back to reality. "Any jobs for me?"

What? "Pardon me? How long have I been sleeping?" She squinted to give her eyes a chance to adjust to the light. Pastor Siemens sat across the living room in her mom's striped Queen Anne chair, hands and feet tapping like a caged bear. She'd forgotten about him.

"Fifteen minutes or so. I want to do something. I can't just sit here twiddling my thumbs. My daughter's life is at stake."

Groaning as she readjusted herself to a sitting positon, she said, "I can understand how you feel, but the boys won't get near the girls if you're there. You could sit in the car with Angela."

Her words seemed to appease him, and his knees settled down. "What if they don't take the bait?"

"Hadn't thought of that. We'll keep doing it until the guys show up. Angela can't go tomorrow, but my ankle should be better so I could take them. Maybe you could drive."

Amber's clone walked into the room. With hair hiding her profile, Aubrey was the image of her twin. She even lumbered like her sister.

At that moment, the front door opened and Sun and Angela walked in. "We got here as fast as we …."

Sun's eyes popped. "Amber?" Approaching the sofa tentatively, she interrupted herself. "I don't believe it. You look so much like her. I mean, you fooled me." The minute Sun plopped down next to Julie, her weight made the cushion shift, eliciting a yelp.

Her hands covered her mouth. "Oh, Miss, I'm sorry. You've hurt your foot. And I made it worse."

"It's all right. I should've warned you. Could you get me more ice?" She took in a ragged breath as she moved her foot a few inches. Then she remembered her manners. "Sun, Angela, this is Pastor Siemens, Amber's father, and you've already figured out who Aubrey is."

When Sun left the room to get ice, Angela honed in on Julie's ankle. "Whoa. What happened?"

"I fell at the courthouse, tripped on the steps. I called you, but it went to voicemail."

"I got your messages, but I didn't realize it was that bad. Are you going to be all right?"

Julie said, "Yes, I'll live. I called a doctor I met at the hospital. The one that found Rosa hiding in the X-Ray imaging room. Hopefully, he'll make a house call. They do that nowadays, don't they?"

Angela laughed, "Um, not since the sixties, but Steve said the doctor was quite taken with you, and he also said you didn't seem to mind."

She blushed. "Puhlease." She hoped Angela, who knew her so well, wouldn't make a big deal about him. "He's the only doctor I have a card for." Redirecting the conversation away from herself, she asked, "Where's Rosa?"

"One of the girls on my line—Corky Martin—has a daughter her age. She's the one who gave me the clothes for Rosa to wear. She told me if I ever needed a babysitter she'd be available. And she was. Available."

The thought of Angela, Steve, and Rosa playing house made her stomach crawl. She changed the subject again. "So, what's the plan? How's Sun feeling about repeating the same ordeal at the mall?"

Glancing toward the kitchen door, Angela said, "She's a bit scared. But you know Sun—she tries to hide it. She feels responsible for Amber's disappearance. Like it wouldn't have happened if she hadn't let Amber talk her into things."

Pastor Siemens leaned forward, his voice low, "It wasn't Sun's fault. Amber does whatever her heart desires. If Sun hadn't gone with her, she would have found a way to go by herself. Sun mustn't blame herself."

Angela said, "I agree. I'll talk to her on the way to the mall." Rubbing her hands together, she said, "Okay, here's the plan. Steve, his partner, and two security guards from the mall will be posing as customers. They won't take their eyes off of Aubrey and Sun, so don't worry. The girls will shop for a while and sit in the food court, and if nothing happens, they'll come back another day."

Julie asked, "What will you do? Pastor Siemens wants to go with you."

Grinning at him, Angela said, "Of course, we'll play the parents. We drop them off and pick them up at a predetermined time. Do you have any errands to do, Pastor? It may be a while."

"Call me Jeremy. No, I'm just along for the ride, literally. I imagine we should be ready for multiple days at the mall."

"According to the security dude, one of the guys shows up at the mall every day."

For the first time, Aubrey spoke up. "So what should I do?"

As Sun handed a fresh ice pack to Julie, she shifted her attention to Aubrey. "First we went to a store called Hot Topic. It was a dark store, but Amber—she loved it. She tried on hats and scarves and bought some jeans. I've never seen her so happy." She bit her lip; then she faced Amber's father. "I am so sorry I lost your daughter." A tear trickled down her delicate face, and her hand went to her mouth to cover her trembling lips.

Pastor Siemens put his hand on her shoulder. "It's not your fault. Please don't even think that. Amber needs help, and once she gets it, she'll be good as new. We'll find her."

Once she blotted her eyes and collected herself, she said, "The two guys were at the store. Trent and Moog, but I don't think Moog was his real name. Moog is big sideways." She motioned with her hands to show Moog's girth. "Trent is very tall, and he liked Amber. He carried her bag and walked with her to the food court. Don't know anything about Trent. But Moog said he went to virtual school, but he quit. He's a constructor."

Angela cast a sideways glance at her. "A conductor?"

"No, a constructor. He builds houses."

"Ah."

Aubrey interrupted. "What do we do if they see us?"

"That's where those theatre lessons will come in handy. You need to act like your sister. A free spirit. Act like you know Trent."

Angela broke in. "Maybe she should act like she doesn't know him. Like she's had amnesia or something. If he imprisoned her somewhere, he'll wonder how she got away." She pivoted toward the girls. "Steve gave me these wires for you to wear. Sun, could you get me some tape—the kind you put over bandages? He showed me how to attach them." She said to Jeremy, "Steve didn't want to blow the girls' cover by doing this at the mall."

Julie said, "Check the first aid kit under the sink in the kitchen."

Once Sun had returned with a roll of tape, Julie said to Angela, "Could you prop me up and help me get to the bedroom? I'd like to help."

Angela offered her assistance; then she herded the girls into the bedroom. As she taped the wires on their stomachs, she said, "Steve and the others will hear your conversations. You should have a code word if you feel like you're in trouble. What word comes to mind?"

"Prodigal." Aubrey blurted out, then covered her mouth.

Julie laughed, "It's a great word, but hard to fit into a normal conversation with boys."

Sun's face scrunched. "I thought of ten-four like in movies, but I like prodigal better. I just don't know what it means."

"Prodigal it is—I'm not sure what it means either." Angela pulled out her phone and texted a message. "There. Steve knows the code word. Oh, he already responded. He wrote LOL. He also said to be there within the next thirty minutes." She spun toward Julie, "Sorry you can't go with us. Do you want anything before we leave?"

"No, I'll be fine. Just leave me with the remote and my phone." The girls helped her out to the couch. The pain was lessening, but fatigue was rolling in like waves. "Be careful, and I'll pray for you."

The pastor added, "I'd feel a lot better if we all prayed before we go." They huddled around Julie and held hands. He prayed for protection, opportunity, and guidance. When the last amen was said, they hugged each other. Nobody talked as they walked out the door.

The house was finally silent, just the way she liked it. Now she could get some work done. The Perez file sat on the table, muddied and bent. Trying hard not to move her ankle, she stretched to reach for it, grasping the file by the corner. She carefully inched it toward herself, but gravity won, and the file fell to the floor— papers spreading in all directions. Well, now what? At least, the pages were numbered, so she could make a copy. If she could just get off the couch and make it to her desk. But it was so far away. She groaned. What was the use?

Closing her eyes, she repositioned her head on the armrest so she could get the kink out of her neck. Of course, the doorbell rang. Now what? She had told Sun to cancel her appointments. She raised up on one elbow, brushed her skirt to get rid of the wrinkles, and yelled, "Come in."

He poked his head around the corner—Adonis would have been jealous of that face. "Is it okay if I come in? Sorry I didn't call. Thought I'd sneak in a visit."

He took a step into the living room, clearly unsure of what to do next, clearly exquisite. A younger, better version of George and Brad and Bradley Cooper. All such thoughts ran circles in her mind as she stared at his face. Her tongue was thick and her manners paralyzed by his presence in her house. What was wrong with her? Surely, looks were only superficial; it was the inner man that was important. She came back to herself. "Please come in. You're here. *Obviously.* You make house calls. That's nice." *Was that the best she could come up with?*

He beamed and approached her tentatively—taking her hand in his warm, soft one. "I'm on my dinner break. Here, let me see that ankle." Once she had released his hand, he knelt down and touched her foot gently. "I bet that hurts. Can you stand on it?"

"Not without help. Maybe I can now."

His arm went behind her; he smelled like lime—no, that wasn't it—something tropical like a mai-tai. Seriously? A cocktail? Her nose was pointed at his neck as he lifted her to her feet. She knew she had to move it, but first one more inhale. There.

Her arm slung over his neck and shoulder, she put tentative pressure on the foot but pulled it back as she inhaled sharply. "Ooch. That hurts." Trying one more time, she managed a few steps. "I guess I'm going to live."

"Yes, you are. Let's get you seated again. How about I drive you to the hospital to get some x-rays? They're open late tonight."

"You don't have to go to so much trouble. I can get someone to take me tomorrow."

When he smiled perfect white teeth, she noticed a small gap between them. Somehow, it made him even better. Slightly flawed perfection. God did good. Well.

"I insist. C'mon. Let's go."

He helped her to the door, and she didn't mind, though the pain was present and jarring with every step. To walk down the porch steps, he had her circle her arms around his neck; then he picked her up and carried her. When they reached the bottom, she held on a second longer than was necessary. Who cared what Mrs. Radnor thought?

He helped her into a shiny red Volvo parked at the curb. Her eyes took in the whole interior of the car for clues. Clues to a wife or children. She had to know, but how to ask? Before he started the engine, she asked, "Are you married, Dr. Moyer?"

He said nothing at first. He blinked, and his eyes narrowed. "No, my wife died. Cancer."

How utterly stupid of her. Wasn't the saying in law, "don't ask a question for which you don't already know the answer?" Her breath caught, and she hunched her shoulders. "I'm sorry—for your loss, and my rudeness."

"It's okay. Let's get you to the hospital." She hazarded a glance at his grim face and was at a loss for words.

***

The wheelchair at the hospital entrance made for a quicker, less painful trip. He whisked her to the imaging department, left her in the care of the receptionist, but not before handing her the key to his office. "I have to get back to work. Do you remember where my office is? Would you mind waiting for me there? I'm not sure how long I'll be, but I'll hurry." He swept her cheek with his finger and left.

Warmth radiated from the spot where he had made contact. She touched it lightly wanting the feeling to last. Then it hit her. Was there something on her cheek? That must be it. She hadn't glanced at herself in a mirror since earlier in the morning before court, when she had reapplied lipstick in her car. She said to herself, "Sure, take your time. I can entertain myself." She could, but it would have been a better use of her time if she had brought a file or two.

As it came to pass, the x-ray tech was gentle with her ankle and quick, and before she knew it, an orderly was rolling her to Brett Moyer's office. Once inside, she sat for a minute, content to do nothing but rest in the thought she had been allowed into his inner sanctum. Surely, it must mean something. Of course not, she chided herself. What choice did he have but to ask her to wait in his office while he worked? It wasn't like he had given her any indication their relationship was more than professional.

But he touched her cheek. No doctor had ever touched her cheek—except her dentist.

Wheeling around the best she could, this was the smallest office ever—even more cramped than the mudroom where her old desk was located. Her eyes went to a bookshelf on the wall behind his desk. A single row of books lined the shelf—all medical textbooks, but there were photographs in gilded frames—clues to Brett's private life. She simply had to see them, but how? The wheelchair would never fit behind the desk, and what if he walked in and found her snooping?

Pushing herself to a standing position, six hops brought her to the desk. It was harder than she thought, and she had to stop to catch her breath. A few tentative and painful steps brought her face to face with two colored photographs taken at a beach. One was of a short-haired, blond woman wearing sunglasses, a large sun hat, and a white terrycloth cover up. She held onto the hat with one hand and covered her face with the other, as if the photographer had caught her off-guard. She was pretty in an unpretentious way and had a natural smile.

The other picture showed the same woman holding a chubby toddler with brown pigtails dressed for the beach. The young woman's finger pointed at the camera. Brett Moyer's wife. Brett Moyer's daughter. She touched the pictures. A happy moment frozen in time followed by tragedy and loss. They probably didn't know that her life would be cut short. She wondered how old the pictures were; where the little girl lived. How had she coped with her mother's death?

Jealous thoughts tugged at the corners of her mind. She did her best not to dwell on them. Yet it was true that Dr. Moyer had loved and lost, and maybe that's all he had room for. Like when her parents died, it was years before she would let anyone in. Four years before she'd even consider getting together with friends or going on a date. Her timing was terrible. Better to let him go before it was too late.

The phone jarred her thoughts and she almost fell. Nabbing the receiver, she said, "Yes?"

A pause ensued before a deep, musical voice said, "Is this Julie?"

Oh no, he'd know she was snooping near his desk. "Yes, is this Dr. Moyer?"

"Call me Brett. How did the x-ray go?"

"Fine, but they wouldn't tell me anything."

"I have the x-rays here in front of me, and I'd say it's a twisted ankle. That's good news. It'll heal fast as long as you stay off it. I'll write you a prescription for pain and wrap it when I'm finished here. They let me borrow some crutches for you. I won't be too long."

Flipping through a medical journal, she didn't find the articles interesting. Her eyes strayed to the desk, the walls, and the bookshelf again. He was a neat man—neater than she was, but she knew where everything was. No other clues about his life, his past, his present. Only the pictures.

She was sitting in his chair behind the desk staring at the pictures when he walked in. She whirled around to face him. Her neck felt warm and blotchy at being caught snooping.

He came behind her, placed his hands on her shoulders, and twirled her toward the picture. "That's my daughter Jennifer—Jenny for short, and her mother, Lisa. My wife. He picked up the picture and handed it to her. "We were at Sanibel Island that day. We'd gotten up early to pick shells. I'll never forget that sunrise."

"Your wife and daughter appear happy."

"We were. It was a special day." He gazed at it before putting the picture back on the shelf.

Feeling awkward, like she was breaking in on a private moment between Brett and his past, she said, "I went to Sanibel many times with my parents when I was young."

"So did my family. Maybe we were there at the same time."

She giggled. "Doubt it. How old is your daughter?"

"Jenny's six. She's with my mother. It's too hard with me finishing my residency here and working all the time. But I go and see her whenever I can."

"Where do they live?" She kicked herself. If he wanted her to know, he would have told her.

"She lives in Winter Park, a mere hour away. She'll be starting first grade this fall at our church's school. She can't wait." He twirled her around and bent down, taking her hands in his. "You remind me of Jenny."

Her eyes met his. "How so?"

He brushed a strand of her hair behind her ears and got his hand caught in a snarl. "Your hair is similar—thick and curly. But it's more than appearance. You act like her too. I can't put my finger on it, but the similarity is remarkable."

Then it hit her. "You go to church?"

"Yes ma'am, my mom wouldn't have let me loose unless I did." He grinned. "How about you?"

"Absolutely." Her face warmed. Stop. You've already been hurt once this week. Don't give your heart away so easily. She leaned against the desk to hoist herself up. "Could you bring the wheelchair over here please? It's getting late."

His eyebrows raised. "Sure. I'll get you home right away." He spun it around and said, "Your chariot, Madame." He wheeled her to the elevator and pressed the button. "Do you mind if we stop at the desk. I have to sign some charts. It'll take a minute—no more."

"I'm not in a big hurry, except my house has become a meeting place for a sting operation at the mall today."

"Do tell."

When she had finished talking about Amber's disappearance and Aubrey and Sun's trip to the mall, he whistled. "You have the most exciting life of anyone I know."

"No I don't. Why do you say that?"

"First you hurt yourself running interference for some kidnappers to save a little girl's life; then she runs away and you mount a search in the hospital, and you find her. Now you're a part of a rescue team for another kidnapped girl, after you've been to court to help a man who's seeking asylum in this country."

She thought about it. "You're right. No wonder I'm exhausted." She felt a yawn coming on. When they reached the car, he gently helped her in. She couldn't help but make comparisons between Steve and Brett. Whenever Steve heard what she was involved in, he grumbled about how helpless she was—always getting herself in trouble. This guy wasn't put off at all; he was impressed. Stop it, she told herself, you have to guard your heart. He's taken.

Maybe. Maybe not.

When they reached her house, he showed her how to use the crutches. Once they had made it to the top of the stairs, her energy was spent. "Could we sit on the swing for a moment? That was harder than I thought." She picked up the crutches, hopped to the swing, and sat down.

He bent over her. "Could I have your keys? I'll go get you some ice."

She managed a weak smile, fished them out of her purse, and handed them to him.

While he was gone, it occurred to her that she had given him the wrong impression of her life. She liked order, routine. Angela was the exciting one, not her. Not her at all. Oh no, maybe he'd prefer Angela once he met her.

He returned with a dishtowel wrapped around a few ice cubes and placed it on her ankle. "How does that feel? Good? Let me have a glance at that knee while we're at it."

She'd forgotten about the knee. Cringing, she lifted her skirt a little, which exposed a torn hole in her stocking and matted blood where the wound had opened up again.

"Wow, that's a mess. I'll be right back."

"The first aid kit is in the kitchen under the sink," she yelled to him. Well, that was embarrassing. Now Brett would think she was needy. She didn't want that. When he returned, he sat next to her and gently dabbed at her knee with hydrogen peroxide.

"You have little pieces of gravel stuck in it that have to come out. It's going to hurt as I debride it. Hold onto my arm."

She didn't need a second request. Circling her fingers around his biceps, she couldn't help noticing his well-defined muscles moved like a machine as he tended to her knee. Wincing, she bit her tongue and held her breath. When he was finished, she sat back in the swinging chair, reluctantly releasing her grip on his arm.

He leaned toward her and grinned. "You're all set." He paused and peered at his hands, then returned his gaze to her. "I like you, Julie Richards. I'm not good at this. But would you consider going out with me?"

Holding herself back for once, she said, "I think you have the wrong impression of my life. I'm not exciting at all. My cousin Angela got the exciting genes; not I. A year ago, I wouldn't leave my house except to go to work. I'd have panic attacks whenever I opened the door. I'm over it now, but I do best when there's order and routine in my life." She glanced at her hands and said in a low voice. "I thought you should know that about me."

"You could have fooled me." He grasped her hand, causing a warm shiver to travel through her. "Believe me, there's enough excitement in the emergency department for me to handle. I was merely making an observation."

The swing rocked back and forth, lulling in its rhythm, squeaking when it moved forward, again when it moved back. A bird tweeted in the tree above, a squirrel darted up an oak tree on the front lawn and jumped from branch to branch. The smell of freshly-mown grass filled the summer air. But nothing in nature compared to the beauty of the moment. All the worry, anguish, and self-loathing vanished with the touch of his hand.

Yet she had to say it. "No, I don't think I should go out with you."

Silence. "Okay." He retracted his hand and faced her after an eternal moment. "Is there someone else?"

She wished she could take the words back, but it was too late. "Sort of."

"Sort of?" His eyes narrowed. "It's the cop, isn't it?"

She used her hands to reposition her leg because it was falling asleep. "It was. He just informed me he's marrying my cousin and best friend so they can adopt Rosa. I've been trying to make sense of it all." She leaned toward him; the hurt in his eyes made her want to embrace him, but she held herself back. Her hand betrayed her and went to his cheek to brush it. "Friends?"

His hand covered hers. "Friends." Standing up, "Well, I should be heading home." He bent down to help her up. Her arms went around his neck, and she couldn't help languishing in the scent of his closeness.

He said, "I have Sunday off. Jenny wants to go biking and have a picnic. How would you like to join us? As friends." He stressed the last word, his mouth contorting as if he was chewing on a pickle. "If you don't have a bike, you can use my mom's."

The empty feeling washed away, and hope replaced it. He hadn't cut her off. "Don't think I'm ready to ride a bike, but I can do picnics."

His eyes widened, "With you so close, I forgot; I thought we were just having a moment. No, bikes are out of the question for the time being, but a picnic would be good for you—doctor's orders." He grinned and kissed her cheek. "Let me help you in." He hoisted her up so high her toes barely touched the porch floor.

"Could you drop me at my desk? I need to get some work done."

Before she allowed him to help her into her seat, her arms encircled his neck, and she brushed his cheek with her lips. "Thanks for understanding." How brazen of her, but she couldn't help it.

"I'll pick you up about one on Sunday. Does that work for you?"

She stifled a yawn and said, "yes," too quickly. What would work was some sleep. She waved as he walked out of her office. A sense of peace filled her, and the thought that when God closes a window, he opens a door. Was Brett a door or a diversion? Closing her eyes, "Please God, let him be a door." She couldn't imagine going through the hurt she was feeling ever again.

The phone rang, jarring her awake. She picked up the receiver. "Richards law, Julie speaking."

"Jules, Angela here."

"What's going on?"

"We've been waiting out here in the parking lot for three hours. Once every fifteen minutes or so, Sun calls with an update. So far, she and Aubrey have circled the mall two or three times, but nothing's happened. Steve said we'll give it another hour or so, and then call it a night."

"Sorry you have to give up your day for this. I know you have to fly out early."

"I'm glad to do it."

There was a pause. Julie didn't know or feel like filling in the uncomfortable gap.

Finally, Angela cleared her throat. "I have a favor to ask, and I want you to think about it before you give me an answer, okay?"

"All right. What is it?" A car door creaked open, and Angela asked Jeremy to take her place in the driver's seat while she went for a short walk.

"Julie, I know you think I'm the biggest Judas in the world. Please know I never wanted this to happen between me and Steve."

"Do we have to talk about this now? I'm tired, and my ankle hurts. Can you save it?" Her shoulders tensed, and her words were clipped. How could Angela presume to ask for a favor? She wished she could put her in her place with a single word.

"Well, here's the thing. Our appointment with the adoption agency in Baltimore is next week, and we have to be—married before we go."

Every word sliced into her like a butcher knife. If she wasn't so sleepy, she'd hang up. "Great. So what does this have to do with me? I'm tired and I want to go to bed."

"You're my closest relative and my best friend. I tried texting Mom. Last I heard she was on a cruise with another one of her

'this is the one—I just know it' men. But she hasn't written back."
She coughed, and her breath was becoming labored as if she was
walking fast. "I know this is asking a lot, but here goes—would
you consider being my maid of honor? I need you. Please?"

Maid of honor for you and Steve? Never in a thousand years.
Why don't you just impale me? Instead she said, "I guess so. What
do I need to do?" Angela was the only family she had left.

"Vegas? No, it'll be a quick, no-frills ceremony at the church.
Saturday night, if that's okay. One of the assistant pastors will
perform the service."

"Are you sure you know what you're doing? You used to
dream of a wedding on a beach in Hawaii. Aren't you settling?"

"Things change. Rosa needs us. You remember what it was
like in that orphanage? If we don't adopt her, she'll be sent back to
one of those places—where the ladies sit all day watching the
soaps, and it's almost impossible to adopt them because they make
so much government money off the children."

Julie couldn't help herself—she had to know. "Do you love
him?"

Another pause although her breathing was audible. "Yes, very
much."

"How long?"

"I don't know. I didn't plan this. I only know that I do. You
won't back out on me, will you?"

She moaned. It would be hard, but she'd been through difficult
circumstances before, and surprise, she made it through. She sent a
quick prayer to heaven. Then she took a deep. ragged breath. "No,
I'll do it."

"You're great. I can't thank you enough. I hate to put you in
such a position." A car door opened and slammed shut. "I'm back
in the car. I'll keep you posted. Get some sleep."

Once Angela hung up, Julie stared at the phone. Nothing like
getting her nose rubbed in a marriage that should have been hers.
But it was one hour out of her life, like a root canal. She'd have to
make herself focus on the positive. It might even help bring
closure. She'd never been good at closure.

Maid of honor for her boyfriend and cousin's marriage. Life
couldn't get any worse.

Chapter Twelve

Sun removed her shoe and rubbed her foot. Keeping up with
Aubrey was a combination of a sprint and a marathon. Aubrey felt
as at home in the mall as her twin had. Every shop window was a
source of fascination. But for Sun, they all blurred together. She
felt older than her sixteen years. From what well did Aubrey get
her energy? And should they be shopping when their main
objective was to root out the bad guys?

Aubrey danced to the bench where Sun sat. "I'll be right back.
I want to try some of the moisturizer samples. Then when you're
ready, we'll make one last circuit around the mall. Can't wait." She
hurried to a bath store display, and then made a beeline to the
surrounding stores.

Sun rested her chin on her propped-up palms. She vaguely
remembered how she'd liked to shop with her friends in South
Korea. Before everything changed. Her life was divided into two
parts: before her father died, and after. Since his death, life lost its
frivolity and became a quest for survival.

She was grateful, she was. Life was better in this country. The
apartment the church let them stay in was clean and safe. Mother
was happier, and the worry lines were fading from her forehead.
Her sisters were almost fluent in English now and were making
friends with their schoolmates. Her part-time job at Miss Julie's
helped with expenses.

Still, something was missing—she watched Aubrey spraying

different colognes on her wrists. What she wouldn't do to be a carefree teenager like Aubrey. She wanted to go back to that place where her biggest decision involved what color to wear to school or what present to buy for a friend's birthday.

Dae's face, like a dark cloud, broke into her musings about life in Korea. He'd been her cherished friend once—until he forced her to do unspeakable things. She hadn't thought of him in months— weeks. Her eyes closed to block out the vision of his face. How did they treat Korean boys in prison? She shook her head to loosen the thoughts—more important things to think about than Dae Kim. But his face wouldn't leave. Sympathy for the boy she'd known battled with memories of hurt and betrayal.

Was he sorry? Should she visit him in prison? Out of respect for the childhood friend he'd been.

Aubrey returned and pulled Sun's arm toward her. "You seem to be in another world. C'mon. Let's go back to Hot Topic. You have no idea how much I made fun of that place back in Wichita— probably because Amber loved it. Now I kind of see why she liked it." She rubbed her stomach. "This wire itches. Does yours?"

"Not so much." They began walking, or Sun did. Aubrey zigzagged from store to store. When she'd slowed her pace enough for conversation, Sun asked, "What does 'prodigal' mean? I don't know that word."

"I had to look it up in the dictionary. It means 'wasteful; someone who spends too much money.' It comes from a parable about a brother who asked his father for his inheritance, moved away, and wasted it all."

Sun's eyes brightened. "I'm familiar with this story. So you chose that code word because Amber was prodigal?"

"I used to think so, but the story was told to the church leaders of the day, not to runaways. It was all about the good brother who stayed home with the father, and how he hated his younger brother for coming home. Just like I did Amber. That's why I chose the word."

They arrived at the store. Sun shuddered as they entered. The walls were covered with music posters interspersed with shelves of jeans in different colors. Loud, screeching music blared out of the speakers. A cloying, sweet smell filled the shop. Amber had called it incense. It was hard to hear. As Amber had done, Aubrey found a mirror and tried on hats of all sorts.

Sun checked the piles but didn't see anything small enough to fit her. Dozens of tee-shirts sat in neat stacks against the wall. Her finger trailed the design on one. She wished they could leave. A tap on her shoulder got her attention.

"Hey, you're the Chinese girl from the other day. How's it going?" Moog. Same cap covering his long curly hair, same plaid shirt and tee-shirt.

She bowed but caught herself. "Hello, Moog. How are you?"

"Great. Who you here with?"

"Same one. Amber." She averted her eyes when she realized she hadn't told the truth.

"Where is she?" His head jerked up and he pursed his lips at the mention of her name, then he took in the whole store. "I don't see her."

She pointed. "Over by the hats. See her?"

His eyes were wide. "I'll be right back." He headed toward a shelf full of strobe lights and candles. When he pulled out his phone, Sun hurried to find Aubrey, but she wasn't near the hats. Where was she? The store wasn't that big. Then she saw her bent down, scanning the sizes of fringed leather vests.

Before Sun had a chance to alert her, Aubrey giggled with glee. "Check these out. I have to buy one if I can find my size. What do you think?" She bounced to her feet and held a vest in front of her shirt.

"It's nice. The boy named Moog is here. He asked where you were. I think it's time to use the code word."

"Can you wait until I try this shirt and vest on? I'll be in the fitting room if you need me." She bounded away.

Helplessness washed over Sun. She should do something, but Aubrey's personality was too strong to argue with, as was Amber's.

Moog was still on the phone. His eyes went to her, to the fitting room, and back. She had let down Amber last time by not listening to the little voice inside her. She wouldn't make the same mistake with her twin. It was time. Covering her mouth, she enunciated, "Prodigal."

"What did you say?" Moog was right behind her. "Who you talking to?"

Before she had time to answer, he pulled her toward a display of belts. "Have you seen these buckles? I collect them, you know. What do you think of this one?"

Her eyes went to the fitting room, then back. "It's nice. Are you going to buy it?"

"Nah, I have enough already." His eyes darted around the store.

"Are you expecting someone? Is Trent coming?"

"Dunno. Haven't seen him in a while."

Backing up, she said, "Excuse me. I have to check on Amber."

"I'll go with you." His hand touched her back.

"No, I can do it." He must not have heard her. She inched away from him. "Please, I'll be right back."

She rushed ahead of a group of girls who inadvertently created a gap between her and Moog. "Leave me alone," she said under her breath.

Voices emanated from the second fitting room. The first one was empty. Sun pulled the door shut, and locked it, the click loud in her ear.

"Let me go." Aubrey's voice. Something bumped against the wall.

Then a male voice. Was that Trent? "How did you get loose? Schroeder isn't going to be happy. Let's go."

"I don't know what you're talking about." Sounds of a struggle. "I'm not going anywhere with you. Prodigal."

"What did you say?" Fabric ripped. "Check this out. She's wearing a wire. Help me get her out of here."

Moog's voice. "Where's the Chinese girl? She headed this way."

"Don't know. Don't care. Let's get this one back before he notices she's missing."

Footsteps and Aubrey's resisting whimpers passed Sun's hiding place. All she could do was sit on the bench, hugging her shaking legs. What should she do? Where was Officer Steve and the others? God, help. Nobody else would.

***

Not usually lost for words, Angela racked her brain for things to talk about with Jeremy Siemens. Hours in the car waiting for the girls to come out was taking a toll on her. In the summer heat, the car warmed quickly. They fluctuated between running the air conditioning, opening the windows, and fanning themselves. She consoled herself with the thought that the girls should be finishing their last lap around the mall within the next fifteen minutes. She and Jeremy had discussed life with twins, hurricanes versus tornadoes, capital punishment, and circled around predestination.

Stifling a yawn, she hoped this adventure was coming to an end. When her alarm went off at three thirty in the morning, she wanted to have enjoyed at least six hours of sleep.

"Check that out." Jeremy pointed ahead of them.

"What are you pointing at?" She tried to see around the group of teens making their way to the parking lot in front of their car.

"That car just drove up in front of the entrance."

"Can you see the driver?" The glass doors pushed open and two guys—one tall, bone thin, with long blond hair tied back in a ponytail; the other larger, darker, and hairier—held Aubrey's arms behind her and pushed her toward the open door of the sedan. She struggled against their grips but was overpowered. "Honk the horn."

"No," he said, "we have to follow them."

Putting the car in gear, she said. "Get the license number and call Steve." She threw her phone at him. "Hurry."

Out of the corner of her eye, she noticed Jeremy's shaky hand scrolling for Steve's number. Under his breath, he vacillated from, "Oh God, please protect her," to "What have I done?" She couldn't imagine the torment he must be feeling losing two daughters—one because of a plan he'd agreed to.

As the car ahead pulled away from the curb, she was careful not to follow too closely. "Tell Steve it's an Oldsmobile, a Toronado, I think—light blue." Veering onto Sand Lake, she had to hurry to keep up. A VW Beetle moved into the lane filling the gap between them. The sun hit her in the eyes, forcing her to pull down the visor.

Jeremy's monosyllabic responses didn't offer much information, but he stayed on the line. Finally, he pulled the phone away from his ears. "The police are with Sun. She's upset. They got to Aubrey when she was trying on clothes. They found the wire and ripped it off her. That's why Steve and the security guards couldn't follow her."

She craned her neck to see over the car ahead of them. "Why didn't they take Sun?"

"She locked herself in the next fitting room but could hear them through the wall. Steve said they missed them by minutes. He said to stay on them but don't do anything stupid."

"What does he mean by that?"

"Not sure. Just keep them in sight, but don't approach them." He pointed. "They're turning onto Orange Blossom Trail."

"Great." She wasn't familiar with the area, but she knew OBT was a busy street. Now they were behind the car, but a U-Haul threatened to change lanes in front of them. Accelerating, she hoped the driver of the Oldsmobile wouldn't look in his rear-view mirror. At least, the sun was out of her eyes. Another corner brought them onto a two-lane in an industrial area. "Tell Steve we turned onto Boice."

Once he relayed the information, Jeremy said, "That's wonderful. I appreciate it more than you'll ever know." He shifted his attention to her. "They're right behind us. And they've called for backup. Just stay on their tail."

"They're speeding up. Should I go faster or hang back?" Her natural inclination was to stay with them, but she didn't want to do anything to jeopardize the chase. She let up on the accelerator.

Four blocks separated their two cars. The sedan made a quick turn into a residential neighborhood. By the time Angela reached the corner, the car had vanished. Bungalows in various pastel colors lined the street. The neighborhood had seen better days. Lawns were in desperate need of sprinklers; Carports were filled with trucks and late model cars, and satellite dishes rested on patched roofs. She nosed the car to the next corner and swallowed for the first time since the chase began. Had she lost them? Then her eye caught movement on a driveway two blocks ahead on the right. She stayed where she was. "Give me the phone."

"Here's Angela."

"They stopped at a house about two or three blocks from where we're parked." She gave him the street name.

Static made it difficult to hear. "Wait until the coast is clear, then drive by and give me the address. Don't let them see you."

She gulped, then she pressed the speaker phone button and veered around the corner. "Green house, arched driveway. The number is 1571."

"Good work. Don't slow down or stop. We're right behind you."

With eyes trained on her rear view mirror, she drove another three blocks and did a U-turn. "Let's park here and watch."

Two squad cars appeared around the corner, came to a quick stop in front of the house, and blocked the driveway. No lights, no sirens. Another police car joined them in front of the house. She counted eight police officers rushing up the driveway.

Jeremy seized Angela's hand. "Could we say a prayer?" He didn't wait for a response as he sought heaven's protection for his girls.

Once he finished, she said, "Let's move a little closer." She inched forward one block and parked in front of a house that appeared to be vacant. Opening the window, she breathed in the smell of freshly mowed grass. From all over the neighborhood, people came out of their houses and stood on their lawns or joined others on the sidewalks. Fingers pointed at the police cars. Quiet murmurs filled the air. Children circled their bikes around the area where the squad cars were parked. All eyes were on the house with the circular driveway.

Angela inched the car forward another block. Driving as close as she could, she parked where she had a good view of the front door. None of the neighbors seemed to notice; all eyes were focused on the house.

Moments later, an ambulance swung around the corner, alarm blaring. Pre-teens on bikes swerved onto driveways or leaned against the curbs to get out of its way. The ambulance came to a screeching halt next to the patrol cars, and two paramedics jumped out. One carried a stretcher. The door to the house burst open. Four police officers rushed out, accompanying two sullen-faced guys. The ones from the mall. The tall one's head was down, his face stormy. The other one sporting a woolen cap resisted, his body language communicated his assertion of innocence.

"That must be the one called Moog."

Once they were pushed into the back of the police cruiser, and it maneuvered its way around the ambulance, Angela returned her focus to the front door. There should have been three. The driver of the sedan still hadn't exited the house. Had he escaped out the back?

The door burst open again, and paramedics juggled a stretcher down the step and across the front lawn. Steve followed the stretcher.

Jeremy was out of the car in an instant, screaming "Amber, Aubrey?"

Forgetting Steve's admonition to stay put, Angela jumped out of the car and rushed toward him. "Is it Amber? What happened to her?"

"It's Amber."

Jeremy kept pace with the paramedics, his hand on his daughter's arm. Her eyes were closed. Even from a distance, Amber's face was ashen, and her lips had a bluish tint.

Steve hooked Angela's elbow and stopped her. "Whoa. Let them do their jobs."

He approached Jeremy and extended his hand. "You must be Pastor Siemens. I'm Steve Bricker, OCPD. She's in pretty bad shape, but she's alive. They're taking her to the hospital if you want to follow the ambulance."

"But what about Aubrey?" At that moment, the door flew open, and Aubrey, Sun, and two more officers appeared.

"Dad." Jumping off the porch, Aubrey rushed toward her father.

Tears streamed down his face unchecked. "Aubrey, I thought I lost you. What did they do to you?"

"Nothing. I'm fine. But Amber isn't." She covered her face with her hands. "What they did to Amber—."

Taking Angela by the elbow, Steve walked her back to the car and opened the door.

"What did they do to her?"

He shook his head. "They had her handcuffed and her feet shackled to a bed. She's been fed a lot of drugs. Don't know if she even knows what's going on. I can only guess what she's been through." His face was grim. "Let's not get into it."

"I noticed only two guys were arrested. What happened to the driver?"

He helped her on with her seatbelt. "Who knows? Probably went out the back when we drove up. Let his friends take the fall." He glanced back. "Okay, here comes the Siemens. I know you have to go to work, but could you drop them off at the hospital? I'm sure they'll want to be with Amber in the next couple hours."

"Sure. What will happen to the guys you arrested?"

"Hopefully they'll be put away for a good while since she's a minor. We have a great human trafficking organization here."

She glowered. "I was hoping for life." He brushed a kiss against her cheek and closed the door. The others approached the car and got in, their faces solemn. She didn't understand their sadness. "Steve said she's going to be fine with a little time and care."

Jeremy said, "You're right. Both of my girls are back safe. Thank you for giving up your time to help us."

"Glad to help," she shifted her attention to Aubrey. "What happened to you?"

"It was scary. I was trying on clothes when those two guys took me from the mall and forced me into a car. A whole lot of people at the mall saw them do it and didn't do anything to help. Then they asked me a bunch of questions. They still thought I was Amber at that point. They kept asking me where I got the wire. Since I didn't know the answers, I kept my mouth shut."

Sun said, "You are a brave girl."

"I was scared to death. Once we got to the house, they locked me in a closet. It was so dark—I couldn't see anything. They put something heavy against the door so I couldn't get out. I stood there until I heard loud footsteps. Then I started banging on the door until a cop opened it."

"So you never saw Amber?"

"No, not until the paramedics showed up and brought her out on a stretcher"

Angela peered at Sun in the mirror. "Sun, you did a great job."

Her face was grim. "No. It was all my fault."

Aubrey chimed in. "No it wasn't. You don't know my sister. If she wanted to go with that guy, nothing you could have said would have stopped her."

Her father said, "Aubrey's right. We don't hold you responsible. It happened, but now it's over, and Amber will recover in time and get a chance to turn over a new leaf."

They followed the ambulance to the emergency entrance. Everyone piled out of the car except Sun. Angela asked, "Are you going to stay with the Siemens or do you want me to take you home?"

Aubrey poked her head in the car and grasped Sun's hand. "C'mon. Amber will want to see you when she wakes up."

A small smile struggled to form on Sun's lips, and eventually she scooted out of the car. Before she joined the Siemens at the hospital entrance, she spun around and returned to Angela's half-open window. Her face was grim. "It was *my* fault that Amber was hurt, wasn't it?"

"Sun, you did what you could. Some people just learn the hard way."

Chapter Thirteen

Julie stifled a yawn, then realized she had the house to herself, which meant she could yawn as loudly as she wanted. She plodded into the bedroom, pulled down the eiderdown comforter exposing crisp Egyptian sheets. Without a moment of hesitation, she jumped in, nestling into her favorite pillow. Never had sleep been so welcome, so easy.

It occurred to her she'd forgotten to say good night to her mother, but it would have to happen with her eyes closed. Feeling under the pillow, she located the handkerchief, brought it to her lips, and kissed it. Her mother's Shalimar was fading. Should she spray it when she got up in the morning? Tomorrow, she'd put it on her list. The lulling rhythm of the ceiling fan made it easy to drift off.

Until the phone rang. Her eyes flickered open, and the room gradually came into focus. The clock read eleven thirty. Morning or evening? No light peeked through the slats of the blinds. Who'd call so late at night? She felt for the phone. "Yes?" Her voice sounded like a bulldog. Or a bullfrog.

"Julie? Sorry to call this late, but we're in a bit of a pickle here at the hospital."

"Hmm? Oh, Pastor Siemens. What's the matter? Is Amber okay?"

"She's still out of it, but resting comfortably."

She pushed herself to a sitting position. "I'm glad to hear it. So what can I help you with?"

He cleared his throat. "We left our car at your place, so we don't have any way to get from the hospital to our hotel. Sun's here and needs a ride home, so if it's not too big of an imposition, could you come get us?"

She fell back onto the pillow; sweet slumber would have to wait. "By all means. Give me ten minutes."

***

A somber group climbed into her car. Sun climbed into the front seat while the other two sat in the back. Julie spoke into the swelling silence. "What did the doctors say about Amber's condition?"

Pastor Siemens said, "She's unconscious, but the doctors believe she'll be back to her old self in no time, at least physically. But she'll need some time to heal emotionally."

"Dad, don't be such a pessimist. The doctors said she can come home in a day or two."

His voice was weary. "Don't get your hopes up. She'll have to go through withdrawal, which will be hard for her and us. But at least we have our little girl back."

Julie glanced in her rearview mirror. "What do you mean 'withdrawal'?"

"The guys that abducted her filled her to the brim with narcotics. The doctors were surprised she's still alive, but it's only been a few days, so maybe it won't be so bad."

Sun was quiet. Julie patted her hand. "How are you doing? This must have been hard for you."

"I'm fine now that we have her back." She said, "You should have seen Aubrey, Miss. She held Amber's hand and talked to her about how they were going to be best friends—*bffs*—she called them. And guess what? Amber smiled when she said that."

"That's wonderful." She pulled into a parking space in front of Sun's apartment. "Are you coming into work tomorrow?"

Sun giggled. "No, tomorrow is Saturday. I have to babysit my sisters while my mom goes to English class. Sorry."

Julie covered her yawn. "My days have all blended together. Have a good weekend."

Sun opened the door, then glanced in the back seat. "I'm sorry."

165

Once Julie dropped the Siemens at their car, the anticipation of crisp sheets—cold just the way she liked them—drew her to the bedroom, a trail of clothes falling to the ground behind her. She peeled off the clothes she wore over her pajamas and jumped back into bed. The clock read midnight, the last thing she saw. Her early morning errands would have to wait until the afternoon, or she'd have to reduce her to-do list. Normally, she had to make herself sleep until eight, but tomorrow, she'd break the rules and stay in bed until she felt like getting up.

Until the phone rang.

At first she thought it was the alarm—a distant but annoying one. One eye opened as she glanced at the clock. Four twenty. Who calls at four twenty? Nobody likeable.

She brought the phone to her ear, kept her eyes closed, and croaked, "Yes?"

"Miss Richards? It's Kevin Perez, from Colombia."

Sitting up, she shook her head to get rid of the sleep fugue. "Yes, what is it, Mr. Perez? Couldn't this wait until the morning?"

"I'm sorry, but I don't know what to do. I'm at the hospital with my wife. She's in a coma."

"Oh no. What happened?"

"She was waiting outside her office for me to pick her up this evening; they had a party for her because it was her last day of work." His voice was wistful. "Her last day. They got her, Miss Richards. A custodian found her behind the building by the dumpster. Like a piece of trash."

"Who got her? FARC?"

"I assume so. She hasn't regained consciousness, so I can't tell." He blew his nose. "It's all my fault. I should have made her go to her parents' when the threats began. Now I might lose her. Excuse me." His sobs were muffled.

"I am sorry, Mr. Perez, Kevin." Pangs of guilt ran through her. His wife was hurt because of her. Because she was a bad lawyer. Despair hit her like an anvil. "I'll call Judge Boyd and petition for an emergency hearing. Please keep me posted about your wife's condition. I'll be praying for your whole family." When she disconnected, she lay back and stared at the ceiling. How could she contact the judge on the weekend? She had to find a way. It was the least she could do for her client.

Sleep was out of the question. A pot of strong coffee and four uninterrupted hours to research emergency hearings in immigration court was what was needed. She'd have one shot to plead for the court's mercy on Kevin's behalf.

Case law and court procedures filled her attention until the sun's rays filled the office with light. Switching off the desk lamp, she stretched. What she'd found discouraged her. The practice manual indicated the average asylum case ranged from forty-five days to six months. Two weeks was unheard of, but she had to try anyway. She prayed for the judge's favor.

The Westminster clock in the living room sounded nine chimes. No time like the present to call the judge, but first she had to find his number. She called her former boss whom she knew played golf with him at his club. She'd only talked to Mr. Freed once in the last year—when she faced a legal conundrum. While she knew the law, it required years of networking and golf games to know the loopholes. Mr. Freed was the epitome of a schmoozer. He was more successful winning a case with a phone call to a judge than by going through normal channels. If anyone could get her a judge's phone number, it was Barry Freed.

The ping of a driver's contact with a ball was the first sound she heard when he answered. "Julie Richards, how are you, girl? How's that little boutique practice of yours going?"

"Reasonably well. I don't want to take up too much of your time, but I need a favor."

"I'd be glad to help." Laughter in the background let her know he wasn't alone.

"I need Judge Boyd's home phone number."

"You gotta be kidding. Why?"

"I have an asylum client from Colombia whose wife was just attacked and is in a coma. Our case was continued until September, so I need an emergency hearing."

"Tell your client to get out of the country ASAP."

"I told him to move to safety, but he can't leave now until his wife is better, and there are kids."

"All right, I'll text you the phone number, but he's not going to be happy."

"I know. Thanks. I owe you one."

While she finished printing some cases about emergency

hearings and harm caused to family members, a warble on her phone let her know Mr. Freed had come through. She mumbled another quick prayer for favor and dialed the number.

A brusque voice answered.

Hers came out squeakier than normal. "Judge Boyd? This is Julie Richards, attorney for asylum petitioner Kevin Perez from Colombia. I would…"

"Why are you calling me on a Saturday? Where did you get my number?"

"Please don't be angry. Barry Freed gave me the number because there's been a new development, and I need an emergency hearing. I know this isn't the way things are done, but I don't know what else to do."

"Highly irregular, Ms. Richards. You're overstepping the mercy of the court."

"Yes, Your Honor. Mr. Perez's wife was attacked last night and is in a coma. I don't think we can wait until September for the case to come to trial."

After a pause, he asked, "How did it happen?"

"It was her last day of work before going into hiding. She was waiting outside her office building for Mr. Perez to pick her up. A custodian found her in the back by a dumpster."

"Who attacked her?"

"He assumes it was FARC, the paramilitary group that attacked him the first time."

"Did she say anything?"

"She's unconscious, Your Honor."

"I can't do anything until there's proof that it was FARC who attacked her. I mean anybody could have done it. Get me proof, and I'll move the case up."

"But…"

"Is there anything else, Ms. Richards?"

"No sir." The phone went dead.

Slumping in her seat, she closed her eyes. If Mr. Freed had been her client's lawyer, his wife would be safe. Waves of failure and despair coursed through her. A failure in her career, a failure in her personal life. She should tell Perez to call Mr. Freed and not trust his future to her.

She dialed her client's number. After she gave him the news, there was silence.

Then he said, "What if she doesn't know who attacked her?"

"We won't know until she wakes up."

"You're right. I'll let you know as soon as that happens."

"Before you go, perhaps it would be better if you found another attorney, one that has more experience working with asylum cases." She closed her eyes.

His silence was longer than she could take. She held her breath and waited for the strike. When he finally spoke, his voice was low and modulated. "It was no accident my nephew met you at the orphanage. It was a God thing. I'm sticking with you."

She hadn't expected that response. His words were like a warm hug, but she shivered at the unknown future. "All right then. We'll be in touch."

Even if she didn't know how to schmooze or find a loophole, God was still God.

Standing in front of the mirror, Julie surveyed her reflection. A month ago, the dress had fit with room to spare. Now it showed every roll and bump. It wasn't fair. She hadn't eaten a normal meal for a week, and she had gained weight. It didn't matter anyway, she thought, as she tugged on her pantyhose. Steve's eyes would be on his *bride*. Certainly, not on her. The tears were coming—she had to stop them. That's all she needed—red, swollen eyes drooling with black mascara.

Angela had texted her to be at the church at seven. She would be going from the airport to the church after having worked a turn-around flight. Only Angela could manage work and a wedding on the same day.

Julie glanced at the clock. Two hours until the ceremony began. Three hours until she got her life back.

The stuffed squid on her pillow wrenched her heart. Steve had given it to her following a visit to an aquarium when she had remarked that she didn't care for normal stuffed animals. Cephy the cephalopod was a constant reminder of a time when she'd been deliriously happy. Cephy needed to leave. She seized him to stuff him in the trash but stopped—why should he have to suffer?

Pulling open the bottom drawer of her dresser, she hid him behind wool socks and turtleneck sweaters.

Buck it up, she told herself. This whole situation—the marriage and the adoption is all about the child, isn't it? Rosa needed parents, or she'd end up like all those orphans in Colombia. Angela and Steve were doing a good thing, but her cousin's words pricked at her. Angela loved Steve, and he had said he loved her too.

She went to the bathroom to run a comb through her tangles. Makeup didn't matter. She'd cry it off anyway, but not until she was alone in the car after the wedding. Until then she'd put her best natural face on and wish them well. All this while leaning on a cane.

During the drive to the church, a mental battle ignited in her head. Memories of Steve flashed unannounced and unwelcome on one side. Their first date at her favorite Italian restaurant overlooking the lake. The way he had intertwined her fingers with his, brought them to his lips, and told her he'd always had a thing for her.

No, don't go there, the reasoning side of her brain ordered. You need to arrive with a happy face, head up, nothing but well wishes and good thoughts.

The rational side won for a moment; then thoughts of Steve's quirky habits played like a movie in her head. The way he drummed on his belt buckle when worried about something; the way his eyes sparkled when he teased her about her tendency to take things literally.

He's gone. He doesn't belong to you anymore. Get a grip. Her knuckles paled on the steering wheel. Relax. It will be over before you know it. She turned into the church parking lot. Only four cars lined the closest spaces. Her Volvo joined them.

Putting one foot in front of the other with the aid of the cane she had found in the closet, she willed herself to open the church door and enter the hall surrounding the sanctuary. Ordinarily it was full of people—ushers greeting new arrivals, parents with children searching for Sunday-school classes, teens conversing in small groups. Now the bookstore on the right was dark and empty—like her heart.

Her phone went off, and Angela's face filled the screen. "We're in the chapel."

"On my way." Her voice sounded monotone and forced.

A single light slivered into the hall. The cloying smell of flowers sickened her. Was it just the flowers? Angela's melodic laughter reached Julie's ears. Still time to change her mind and run—limp. Swallowing her apprehension, she entered and plastered a small grin on her face—not so large as to be noticeable, but big enough so Angela and Steve wouldn't pity her.

She wanted everyone to forget she was there.

"She's here." Angela ran to her and hooked arms with her, the scent of her tasteful cologne leaving a trail behind her. She was stunning. Her sleeveless, white-silk dress ended at her knees showing her tan legs. Elegant and classic came to mind.

Steve's eyes never left Angela. He moved close to her, "I've never seen you more beautiful."

Julie backed up to hide behind the stage curtain, but the cane betrayed her with a thunk.

Steve's eyes twinkled. "Where you going? Thanks for doing this for us, Jules."

She opened her mouth to answer, but his eyes had already returned to his bride. The assistant pastor gestured to Steve to approach the altar. His hand went to Angela's back. She remembered when Steve's hand had burnt a hole on *her* back. The cavern of despair inside her deepened. She wondered if she could just sneak out the door. She couldn't go through with it. Then the pastor grasped her arm and moved her to the left of Angela, who faced the altar. Angela took hold of her hand and squeezed. She squeezed back a little.

Four of them made up the wedding party. Martin, Steve's younger brother, was on the other side of him. He waved at her. He wasn't a teenager anymore. She'd been so busy with the move to Celebration and getting her practice going, she hadn't attended his track meets as promised. She'd always known Steve was devoted to his little brother. Sweat poured down Martin's face, and he pulled at the neckline of his shirt. At least, she wasn't the only one who was miserable.

The ceremony lasted seventeen minutes, and she didn't hear a word of it. When Angela and Steve were pronounced husband and wife, they clung to each other. It was the first time she had seen them kiss. *Tender* came to mind. He never kissed her like that. The pastor snapped a picture. She pasted on a smile, but she was sure it was more of a smirk. Someone asked her to sign a document, and then she walked as swiftly as she could to the door. Once out in the hall, the cloying smell of flowers would vanish. Certainly they wouldn't mind if she left. She'd done her duty.

A hand seized her elbow. Steve gazed down at her, his eyes sparkling, which made the knot in her throat double. How dare his eyes sparkle. "We're going to The Big Fin for dinner, and we want you to be there."

"No, I'm sorry. I really can't. I have to wash my hair."

"C'mon. It won't be the same without you."

She glanced at the door. "No, I've got a lot of work to do back home. Congratulations." She broke from his grasp and limped out into the hall, leaning against the door once it closed. With the help of the cane, she hobbled down the tiled hallway. She'd gotten through the ceremony without weeping. Now she needed to get safely home. Her cousin's voice called for her to come back, but it was too much.

Tears of embarrassment and despair blinded her as the heat of the summer hit her outside. She didn't hold them back. Thirty-one years old and her one and only—the man she thought would be with her forever was married to her best friend. Thoughts of future Christmases sitting across the living room from them and their children plagued her. It wasn't fair.

Nothing in her life was fair.

Her breath caught in her lungs like a barrier and no amount of deep breathing helped. A panic attack threatened to pounce. Black spots surfaced and floated before her eyes. She closed them to block the spots, but they showed up in the darkness. Not now. Why? She hadn't had a panic attack in ten days, and she'd been able to hide the last one. Leaning against her car, she focused on three even breaths. In out. In out. In out. The overpowering smell of flowers still clung to her.

She clenched her fist, then pressed her shaky hand against the button to open the car door. Sliding in, she leaned back against the headrest until the pain in her chest ebbed. Thoughts of leaving before the newlyweds came out motivated her to sit up and start the engine.

It wasn't fair. How could God let this happen after all she'd been through? Two parents dead. Two guys gone. Two injuries. An easy case lost. People said when God closed a door, he opened a window. Where were the windows?

###

A headache pounded her awake, and she squinted to check the time. Sundays offered the opportunity to sleep an extra hour before she had to get ready for church. Sitting added a wave of dizziness. Was she coming down with the flu? It certainly wasn't a hangover.

Memories of the night before descended like a bad dream. The one she loved married to her cousin. She wasn't sure if she could ever face them again. Had they been in love all along, and she too busy to read the signs? Thinking back, Steve had seemed more irritated than attracted to her in the last few months. Stop it. Dredging up the past wouldn't change the fact that Steve and Angela loved each other and sealed it with a ring. Was there a ring? She couldn't remember.

After she plodded back from starting the Keurig machine, she put the shower on cold—punishment for the doldrums. Normally she went to church with Angela. Today, she would go alone. Then it hit her. The doctor would be picking her up after church. Lumbering into her closet, she chose a pink and white, checked summer dress. She loved that dress—it screamed picnics, county fairs, and cotton candy. And it covered her lacerated knee.

The sermon was on Jonah and his reluctance to go to Nineveh. When her mind wasn't wandering, she caught a smidgen of the message. Jonah didn't think it was fair the people of Ninevah should have the chance to be forgiven, so he refused to obey God and ran in the opposite direction. And he never got over that feeling of injustice.

Life wasn't fair for her either. How could God expect her to celebrate being stabbed in the back by her cousin and boyfriend? And hadn't she prayed for Kevin Perez to get asylum? Where was God when she needed him? The pastor broke into her thoughts. Jonah didn't have a happy ending. He was miserable and wanted to die. Maybe she wouldn't have a happily-ever-after end to her story either if she didn't stop feeling sorry for herself. She peered around to see if anyone could read her thoughts. No, things would improve, although she couldn't see how.

After the service, she kept her head down so she wouldn't have to talk to anyone and fled as fast as her swollen ankle would allow. Twenty minutes got her home, but she didn't notice. Her mind was on the doctor and his daughter. What was her name? Jennifer or Jenny. Brett had said they were a lot alike. Not possible. Children had dirty faces and smelled like the outdoors. They cried and played in the dirt, and fawning parents were oblivious to their offsprings' faults. Look at how Rosa had toppled everyone's lives. She had clearly ruined everything in *her* life, hadn't she?

Stop with the pity party already, she told herself. Pulling her shoulders back, she made a resolution. She'd put on her best face for Dr. Brett because of all he had done for her. And she'd be civil to the girl.

The top was down on his Thunderbird. Sunglasses hid his beautiful brown eyes, but his unabashed smile said it all. How could someone that handsome be interested in her? Pushing herself off the Adirondack chair to her feet, she grimaced as she put weight on her bad ankle.

Smoothing the wrinkles on her dress, she put on a cheery face. "Good afternoon." *She sounded like a Jane Austen character.* "Hey there." *What? Elly Mae Clampett came to mind.*

Jumping to the top of the porch stairs in a single bound, he lifted his glasses and offered her an arm. "My lady."

She leaned on his arm and stopped. She hadn't quite mastered the art of going down stairs with a cane. Earlier, when she'd gone to church, she had to scoot down on her bum. She wouldn't do that now. Tendering her foot on the top stair, she tried to put pressure on it, which caused an involuntary yelp.

"Whoa, I'll take you down."

Her arms went around his neck, and she had nowhere to put her nose except on his shoulder. The scent of his aftershave was intoxicating. Closing her eyes, she inhaled a steady whiff. She was glued to the crook of his neck when he gently put her down, and she had to force her nose to move.

"You look splendid. Jenny can't wait to meet you." He hurried ahead to open the door for her. The car was a rich shade of dark blue with specks of silver that made it pop. White leather bucket seats showed a pride of ownership and care. "This was my dad's car—a 1968. He kept it in pristine condition. I try to do the same in his memory."

"I've never been in a convertible before." She rifled through her purse for a scrunchy to keep her hair from blowing in her face. Once they were on the highway, she took an exhilarating breath. The car smelled of polished leather. The sun combined with the breeze, and her shoulders relaxed. The noise of the wind prevented conversation, so she hazarded a glance at Brett's profile. She hadn't noticed his dimples before. He always appeared happy, and it wasn't fake either. Clearly, he enjoyed living.

Once they'd passed the *Welcome to Winter Park* sign, they curved onto a heavily shaded cul-de-sac with well-kept houses from the sixties. He veered into a driveway that curved around a well-manicured lawn, leading to a stucco bungalow with a large picture window. The door burst open, and a young girl with dark braids threatening to break loose sprang down the stairs and skipped to the car. The moment Brett opened the door, she jumped into his arms and circled his neck.

"Hey, baby."

Her voice was buried in his neck.

He carried her around the car to open the door for Julie with his free hand.

"Let me down." He placed her on the driveway, but she took hold of his fingers and refused to move from her spot, shielding her eyes with her other hand as she assessed Julie.

As he pulled her cane out from the back seat, the girl asked, "Is it a fracture or a sprain?"

Taken aback by the question, she said, "I twisted it, that's all."

"You should put ice on it. What's the acronym, Dad? Ice, compression, elevation. Isn't it cool? It spells ICE."

"Wow, you know your stuff." She removed the scrunchy and shook out the curls.

"I helped Dad study for his tests, didn't I?" She peered up at him with adoring eyes.

"That she did. Let me go get the bikes. I'll say hello to Grandma and be right back. Why don't you climb in the backseat, squirrel?"

Conflicting thoughts collided in her mind as Julie grinned benignly at the girl before she jumped in the backseat. Why didn't he want her to meet his mother? And then again, why would he?

She hardly knew him.

"Daddy says you're an attorney. How cool is that."

Julie peered over the seat at the six-year-old with braids nearly undone. "Pretty cool," was all that came out. Really? She sounded like someone from Disney Channel.

The child didn't appear to notice. "I want to be a pediatrician when I grow up."

"That's a noble goal. It sounds like you already have a good start. Why pediatrics?"

"I like children. I'm a child, you know."

Did she just wink at me?

"Do you put criminals in jail?"

She smoothed her dress. "Not so much. I help immigrants. Do you know what they are?"

"People from other places that want to move here—people who need help making a fresh start."

"Out of the mouth of babes," she murmured.

"Excuse me?" She moved forward, sticking her head through the gap between the front seats.

"You're exactly right." She changed the subject. "Tell me about the park."

"It's by a lake, and me and Daddy ride our bikes around it all the time and stop for ice cream. I like Moose Tracks. What's your favorite flavor?"

"Pralines or anything with chocolate."

The door opened, and Brett climbed in after setting a picnic basket on Julie's lap. "What have you two been talking about?"

Before she could answer, a hand touched her shoulder, causing her to jump. She swiveled to face a woman with short white hair and a radiant smile, not unlike Brett's. "Sorry to startle you, dear. I just wanted to meet you before you left for the park." She offered her hand. "I'm Doe Moyer. Brett tells me you have a sprained ankle. Don't let them push you too hard at the park."

"I won't." Brett's mother's trim form pushed away from the car and waved. "Pleased to meet you, Mrs. Moyer."

She waved back. "Call me Doe."

As they made their way to the park, Brett said, "Did you talk her ear off, squirrel?"

"Not yet." She giggled. "What are you going to do while we

ride around the lake?"

"Just enjoy the quiet, I guess—not that you're not quiet."
Why'd she say that?

When they stopped at a red light, Brett enfolded her hand in
his, sending a pleasant shudder through her stomach. "Guess what,
Jenny? Julie helped rescue a little girl from kidnappers."

"That's so cool. Was she an immigrant?"

"As a matter of fact, she is. Rosa's from Colombia, and she's
an acrobat."

"Will she live with a family here and be safe?"

Her heart ripped open again. She'd been able to suppress
thoughts about the wedding for two hours, but they came back in a
rush. Her voice croaked as she answered.

Brett glanced at her and changed the subject. "What did you
learn in Sunday school?"

"It was about Moses and the burning bush and how he had a
speech imped—impediment. Does that mean he stuttered or
couldn't say certain letters? Remember when I called spaghetti
'pisgetty'?"

"Yes, and you pronounced yellow 'lellow'." He slowed down
after turning into the park and maneuvered into a space under the
shade of a tree. "We're here."

Birds flocked along the shore of the lake, and a trail of ducks
nestled in the shadow of a picnic table. Jenny bounded out of the
car until her dad called her back to get her bike from the rack on
the trunk. Julie clutched the picnic basket and tried to maneuver its
weight while leaning on her cane.

Brett rushed to take it from her. "Let's set up at the picnic table
under the oak tree."

"Daddy, can we eat right away? I'm ferocious."

Julie was impressed. "I think you mean 'voracious.' I applaud
your large vocabulary."

"Thank you." Jenny dropped her bike, ran back, and held
Julie's arm. "I'll be your crutch." When they arrived at the table,
Jenny opened the basket and brought out the tablecloth. "Help me
with this, Julie."

Her fear of not knowing what to say vanished as she followed
Jenny's lead. Brett poured lemonade as Jenny pulled out three
sandwiches. "Roast beef with that yummy mustard." She brought

one to her nose and sniffed. "Pumpernickel. I love that word. It rolls off the tongue, doesn't it?" Her hands dug deeper and pulled out cookies. "Still warm from the oven."

It occurred to Julie she hadn't eaten in twenty-four hours. Brett grasped her hand and his daughter's and said a nice prayer. Then they dove in.

Between bites, Jenny said, "Grandma makes the coolest sandwiches."

Brett wiped mustard off her mouth with a napkin. "You like that word *cool*, don't you?"

"The girls in my class say it all the time, so I'm making myself say it."

"Since when do you care about your peers?"

"Sometimes they make faces when I talk, so I try to fit in."

Julie was awestruck. It was as if the child was her clone. "I had the same problem when I was your age. They said I talked like an adult. I guess that's what comes from being an only child."

She wiped her mouth and stood on the bench. "I like you, Julie Richards. You don't talk down to me. You're my new favorite adult."

Julie felt her cheeks warm. She was thrilled. Two sticky arms wrapped around her neck from behind.

"Do you like me?"

She touched Jenny's wrist under her chin. "Very much."

Seconds later, Jenny said, "Let's go, dad." Jumping off the bench, she hopped on her bike and rode circles around the table.

Julie shook her head as she gazed at braids flying in the wind. "I'm speechless. She's something else."

He laughed and picked up his bike. "It's like looking in a mirror, isn't it?" To his daughter, he said, "Let's get going, squirrel, but not before putting on your helmet." While he donned his own, he said, "We'll be back in a half hour. Don't clean up. We can do it after." Then he did the unbelievable. Putting down his bike, he came to her, kissed her on the cheek, and whispered in her ear, "You're the one." Then he left.

What did that mean—*You're the one?* Like when people play tag and say, *'you're it?'* He was already pedaling toward the lake when it struck her what it might mean. Touching the spot where he'd kissed her, she said aloud, "Maybe so," but they were already too far away to hear.

She sat still for a few minutes. Could he be the one? Could he be the reason Steve was taken from her? She was confused, but it was okay. This was a very fast window.

Once she had finished washing off the plastic tablecloth and placing everything neatly in the picnic basket, she hobbled to a bench that would give her a better view of the lake. Two little boys batted a beach ball back and forth on the grassy area. The pleasant aroma of fried onions and hamburgers wafted in her direction. She sniffed a big whiff. In less than a day, her heart had gone from the deepest abyss to something akin to euphoria—or at the least, a sense of satisfied calm. Then doubts surfaced. What if he meant something else? Never would she let her heart be vulnerable like that again, no matter how charming Brett was or how adorable his daughter was. *Guard your heart* would be her mantra from now on.

Shielding her eyes with her hand, she thought she saw two moving specks on the other side of lake, the larger one following the smaller one. Jenny appeared to be a well-adjusted girl, not as childish as the other two or three children she had met.

She recalled the time she was asked to work in the nursery at church. It was the closest thing to a horror movie she had ever experienced. She was at a complete loss as to what to do when they wouldn't listen to reason. The cries of the babies brought volunteers to the gated door. It wasn't long before they told her she could leave.

The specks were out of sight now. She glanced at her watch. The warm breeze combined with the rhythmic drone of human and wildlife chatter, making her eyes heavy. She felt her head fall back, and she let it. Her phone vibrated in her pocket. Shaking the fog from her head, she brought the phone to her ear.

No one answered at first; then a husky voice with an accent said, "I met your friend."

"Who is this?"

"Don't you want to know which friend?"

"I'm going to hang up unless you tell me who you are."

"That little girl—she's real cute—the way she can ride a bike real good. Ella habla mucho. Does she ever stop talking?"

Her eyes scanned the whole park but saw nothing out of the

ordinary. "What do you want?"

"Rosa—she never learned to ride a bike like that. She belongs to me, and I think you'll give her to me."

"I don't have her. I'm going to call the police." She hobbled toward the lake to search for signs of Brett. Where were they?

He chuckled. "Okay, hold your pants. How 'bout you give me the bunny. As a souvenir?"

She was about to hang up when she realized he had started talking.

"By the way, I met your friend—the Asian dude—A Dae Kim. He told me about the little Asian girl I seen at your house. Ain't it a coincidence? You know 'em both."

Her throat was closing up. She managed to ask, "What do you want?"

"I already told you. By the way, I sent a picture of your little picnic to the doctor, and I'll send it to you too. No charge."

"Why are you doing this? Leave them alone." She hung up, cutting off raucous laughter.

A shudder traveled up and down her spine. She took in the whole park—someone was watching her, but from where? She checked her messages, and up popped a picture of the three of them eating sandwiches, laughing, totally involved in the moment. The thought that a person was recording them, and they had no idea made her want to vomit. The kidnappers were in prison. That's where Dae was. Then how were they able to take a picture of her? Maybe they had an accomplice. Someone on the outside.

Then his words struck her again. He'd mentioned Sun, and he said he'd met Dae Kim. Julie had only seen him once—when he was taken away in a squad car after Sun had escaped from his van. They'd been childhood friends in Korea, but he had betrayed Sun's trust and made her one of his stable. Her little friend—she had come so far since her escape last summer, but she was still fragile. Her newfound faith had allowed her to forgive herself and move forward. A premonition involving Sun, Rosa, Brett, and Jenny made her shiver, and she rubbed her arms to increase the circulation.

She had to call Steve. But for all she knew, he was on his honeymoon with Angela. She couldn't wait. She switched on her phone and pressed his name.

Music played in the background when he answered. Was he in Hawaii? Miami? She felt like jumping in a hole. "Hi." He sounded irritated.

"I'm sorry to interrupt your—honeymoon, but it's important."

He laughed and covered the phone as he said something to someone—probably Angela. "I'm not on my honeymoon. We're in Baltimore meeting with an attorney about the adoption. What's so important?"

"One of Rosa's kidnappers just called me. He must be out of prison because he snapped a picture of me while I was having a picnic lunch with—friends."

"It must be some kind of joke. I assure you both guys are still in prison, but I'll call and see what's going on. What did he say?"

She shuddered. "He said he wanted Rosa back, and he mentioned he had met Dae Kim, the guy who kidnapped Sun. He sent me the picture he had taken. How did he get my number? What do you think he wants?"

"Take a deep breath and calm down. It may mean nothing. He's just trying to scare you."

"Well, he's succeeding. Where's Rosa right now? What should I tell the people I'm with? Do you think they're in danger? What about Sun?"

"Again, it's just a phone call. I'll call you back when I find out more about the guys' whereabouts. Not to worry."

"Okay." She didn't mean it. It was not okay. A hand touched her shoulder, and she jumped a foot in the air.

Brett stood with sweat running down his forehead. A wet spot covered his tee-shirt, but his smile revealed his dimples. "Sorry, I didn't mean to scare you. We're back."

"Great," Remembering Steve was still on the line, she said. "I have to go. Call me." She whirled around to face Brett. Jenny stopped beside the two of them. "Did you have a nice bike ride?"

Jenny laughed, "It was perfect. We saw a baby deer, but when it saw us, it ran back into the woods. And we saw a family of otters dive into the water. It was so cool."

"Wow, I wish I could have been with you." She glanced up at Brett, whose grin had disappeared. "What's wrong?"

He averted his eyes. "Squirrel, could you go get the picnic basket from the table?" Once she had skipped away, he leaned toward her. "Were you talking to that cop?"

She grimaced, uncertain of what to say. Finally, she said, "Check your messages."

"I don't think so. I try to keep my phone off on Sundays."

"Please, just this once."

He pulled it out of his pocket and clicked it on. "Look at that. It's a picture of us. Did you take it? Wait a minute, you're in the picture. How…what?"

"I got the same message sent to me." She paused. "And a phone call. It came from the guy who kidnapped Rosa. He said he wanted her back."

"Isn't he in prison awaiting trial?"

"That's why I called Steve. He's on his honeymoon, but I had to call him."

"Honeymoon?"

"Not exactly. I assumed he was on his honeymoon because he and Angela got married last night."

He whistled. "I'm sorry. I had no idea."

Her neck felt like it was being attacked by a dozen gnats. Scratching made it worse, until she remembered her propensity to break out in hives when she was stressed. She pulled her hand away and sat on it. "There's more."

When Jenny returned, Brett frowned. "Squirrel, see how many times you can circle around this table on your bike. I bet you can't do twenty."

"I'll double that number." Her chin up, she began to circle, screaming the total after each rotation.

Sitting next to Julie, he covered her hand with his. "Continue."

His hand was warm—the good kind—not sweaty. She basked in the moment knowing her next words might create a division between them. It was time. "The man on the phone mentioned your daughter riding around on her bike, so I assume he was the one that snapped the picture." A tear fell, and she brushed it off with the back of her hand. "I'm so sorry to involve you in this. I never in a million years wanted to put you in … in danger."

His finger traced a line on her cheek. "Hey now. It's not your fault. Jenny's fine. I'm crazy about you whether you like it or not. A host of angels will protect us." He gazed at his daughter who had just finished her eighteenth rotation. "How do you suppose he got my number?"

"Not sure. The kidnappers were already arrested when you found Rosa. There must be more than two of them, and one could have been searching for Rosa and saw you in the hospital." She sniffed and wished she had a tissue.

He pulled one out of his pocket. "When you have kids, you always have one of these handy."

She blew as daintily as she could. "It's been a roller coaster since we got back from Colombia. I want things to go back to boring."

He kissed her on her forehead as Jenny returned. "Twenty-five. I can't do any more." She jumped off her bike. "What's wrong with Julie?"

"She's fine. Let's get going." Getting to his feet, he draped Julie's arm over his neck and helped her walk the hundred feet to the car. "I'll come back for my bike if you take yours to the car."

They drove to Brett's mother's house in silence except for the incessant chatter coming from the backseat. When they pulled into the driveway, Jenny's face poked through the front seats. "Will you come next weekend? We're going to the new Dali exhibit. He's a cool cubist. Can she come, Daddy?"

He glanced at Julie and then back at his daughter. "She may already have plans, but we'll see."

He had already written her off. She didn't blame him. It always happened to her.

Once they were on the road, she stared out the window, but somehow the silence was comfortable. Sunday traffic was light, and they made good progress until they came to a dead stop near the theme parks. Stretching his arms, Brett yawned, and then touched her cheek. "Penny for your thoughts."

"The man on the phone's words keep playing in my head. I can't make sense of them."

"Tell me what he said, and maybe we can figure it out together."

"I was so shocked, I don't remember them all, but here goes." Once finished, she pulled down the visor to see if they were being followed. A dark sedan similar to the one parked in front of her neighbor's was on their tail.

"What is it?"

"That car behind us. That's the same one that was parked in front of our house—the one that the kidnappers were in."

He inched into the next lane. "I'll try to lose them. Let's stop at the coffee shop by the hospital." Within a few minutes, they pulled ahead of the slower moving lane.

Once they had arrived and were seated by a window where they could survey the parking lot, Brett returned with two steaming cups of cappuccino. The air conditioning made her hands cold. She sipped the cappuccino, sending the warm liquid coursing through her body and took comfort in its heat.

Brett enfolded her hands in his. "They're freezing." He brought them to his lips and kissed them. "I know we agreed to be friends, but I want more. I want a lot more." His eyes were wistful as if he were steeling himself for rejection but hoping for something else.

"I'm pretty raw right now. Angela asked me to be her maid of honor, and I couldn't say no, although it was so hard being there last night when the pastor pronounced them husband and wife." She removed her hands and rested her chin on one palm. "Maybe it was a good thing—like a funeral—it gave me closure." She sighed. "It's going to be hard. Angela's a big part of my life, so I won't be able to avoid either one of them."

"We're both raw. I thought I died when Lisa died. I've buried myself in work, which has been a salve, and weekends with Jenny have been therapy as well. But now my heart has started beating again." He leaned forward and brushed his lips across her forehead. "I like you, Julie Richards. Maybe more."

His words caused a tremor in her stomach, and the hurt was shoved to the background for a moment, replaced by a warm contentment. Words escaped her, but her manners didn't. "Thank you. How about friends with possibilities?"

He helped her to her feet. A glint of hope or amusement—she didn't know which made his eyes sparkle. "Friends with possibilities. I can live with that."

As they left the coffee shop, she held onto his arm, sinewy and strong. How could she have gone from such depths to these heights in a matter of hours? Maybe there was a hope and a future for her. Was he the one? Maybe he would guard her heart.

When they reached the T-bird, he helped her into her seat; then went to his side of the car. "What's this?" He held up a piece of rolled-up paper. "This was stuck in my door handle."

Unraveling it revealed a colored picture of Jenny riding around the picnic table, braids flying in the wind, eyes closed, mouth open. On the bottom were five words: GET ME ROSA OR ELSE.

He threw it in the front seat and leaned against the car, his back to her. "What am I supposed to do with this?"

Jenny's happy face—not a care in the world. "It's time to call 911." Her phone rang, and Steve's picture popped up. "Hold it a minute. It's Steve. Why don't you talk to him?"

He grabbed it and put it on speaker phone. "This is Dr. Moyer. We met at the hospital. Julie probably told you someone sent both of us a picture of my daughter, which was taken while we were having lunch in the park."

"Yes, she told me. I called to tell Julie that both men are in custody. They must have someone on the outside."

"That same person, I presume, put another picture of my daughter in my car here—we're at a coffee shop not far from Celebration. On the bottom, it reads, 'Get me Rosa or else.' I don't mind telling you, I'm beyond disturbed. Jenny, my little girl, lost her mother, and she's still fragile. Tell me what to do; I'll do it." His voice cracked, and he handed the phone to Julie.

"Steve, that dark sedan followed us. I saw it."

"That's impossible. We impounded it from the hospital parking lot."

She noticed her other hand was caressing Brett's back. She withdrew it. "Why is Rosa so valuable to them? She's just a little girl. Oh, I forgot to tell you, the guy mentioned that he wanted the bunny."

"Interesting. I'll get Chip to check it out. They've lawyered up, but from what I gather, the guys see her as a goldmine—they brought her to America to make money off her—television contracts, Las Vegas, circuses. Sit tight. Tell Dr. Moyer to go home. I'll be back on Tuesday night."

Once Steve had disconnected, she focused on his worried face. "He said the police are working on it. He wants you to fax the picture to his partner, go home, and don't worry about it."

His eyes were red. "Not worry about it? That's my daughter's picture."

She had no response. "I should get home." Her hands were

cold again.

Without a word, he pulled the convertible top up and secured the latches. They arrived at her house within minutes. She opened the door herself. Something had changed—an invisible wall separated them. She hoisted herself up with her cane. "Thank you for a lovely afternoon." She sniffed. "I'm sorry."

"I'm sorry too." His smile didn't reach his eyes. "This isn't going to work. I have to protect her. I'm all she has. You understand."

All she could manage was a single nod. Her body trudged away. She made it up the porch steps somehow. This time, he didn't offer to help. He pulled away without so much as a backward glance.

Chapter Fourteen

When she woke up the next morning, it took Julie a moment to figure out why her heart felt like it had been hit with a sledgehammer. Then it all came back. A perfect picnic ruined—phone calls punctuated with innuendo and veiled threats, pictures of Jenny from a malevolent source. Brett distancing himself from her. She couldn't blame him. If it wasn't for her and the trouble that always followed her, his daughter's life wouldn't be in danger.

The only thing to do was to bury herself in work. She headed to the kitchen, made coffee and toast, and carried them to her office. There were cases to catch up on, and she needed to get to work on Rosa's visa. Luckily, her kidnappers were in jail. Julie chewed on her pencil. Rosa would make the best witness against them when their case came to trial, although the court would never make her testify in the same room with her captors.

In the meantime, she'd apply for a T-visa allowing Rosa to remain in the country for four years. She had helped Sun get the same visa after she'd escaped from Dae Kim. She thought of yesterday's phone call from the guy who had mentioned Dae's name. Did he mean to do Sun harm? She would be here any minute. Then they'd talk.

***

She rubbed her eyes after an hour of reading small print. The

187

ring of the phone jarred her muddled brain. A tingle travelled through her. Maybe Brett was having second thoughts and needed her desperately. She could only hope. "Julie Richards Law, Julie speaking." She managed a quick sip of lukewarm coffee.

A tunnel-like background noise let her know it wasn't Brett. "Miss Julie? This is Kevin Perez, from Colombia. I'm sorry to bother you, but I thought you should know my wife has awakened from her coma."

"That's great news. Has she said anything yet?"

"Not much, but the good news is she recognizes me. The doctor says it's possible she'll make a full recovery."

"Is there some way you could record what she says for the judge?"

He coughed. "I was wondering if you could come to Colombia and talk to her yourself."

Her hands tightened on the chair arms. The suggestion made her blood curdle. It was too much to ask. There was no way she could make a trip like that alone. She could barely leave her house. "I simply couldn't. I'm sorry. But you could record what she says and send it to me."

His voice was weary. "It's all right. I had to try. I'll think of something." An uncomfortable pause followed. "Well then, I'll call you if she says anything."

If her conscience had a body, he'd rant and shake his finger at her. "Wait. I'll come if you think it will help." She sensed his relief. "I'll try to be there by tomorrow."

"Oh, thank you. I'll cover all your costs."

After hanging up, she snipped, "Well, that's just great. I don't have time for this. When will my life slow down?" What he and the rest of the world didn't know was she was still afraid of everything. Julie Richards was a fraud. People thought she had conquered her fear when she moved to Celebration and opened her own practice. She fooled them all. The truth was—working out of her home meant she never had to leave at all.

God put one over on her. Now she had to travel by herself to a foreign country. Her throat seized up just thinking about it. She'd have to pack a lot of paper bags.

Sun poked her head into the room, "Did you say something?"

Her cheeks flamed. "Oh, sorry, I didn't hear you come in. I was just grousing to myself." She arranged the burgeoning hill of papers into neat piles. "I need to talk to you. Have a seat." She motioned to the leather chair she had brought from her mother's house. The wood parts needed a layer of paint, but the bones were good.

Sliding into the seat, Sun put her hands neatly on her lap and waited. "I have to talk to you too."

"I'm all ears."

Her eyebrows formed a V at the bridge of her nose; then she giggled. "That is funny, Miss."

"What is funny?"

"What you said. Your ears are normal size."

Julie joined her, snorting coffee onto the pile of letters in front of her. "Sorry. I'm overreacting. It's been a whirlwind of a week. What I said means I'm listening."

Sun said, "I like this saying. I'm going to practice it often today." A groove formed between her eyebrows. She leaned toward Julie as if someone might be eavesdropping. "I got an email from Dae Kim on my computer here. I don't know what to do."

"That's a coincidence. His name popped up yesterday. One of the men who kidnapped Rosa texted that he had met Dae in prison."

Sun's eyes opened wide. "He is texting you?"

"Yesterday, I was having a picnic with a date and his young daughter. One of the kidnappers apparently had someone taking pictures of us— to scare us." She rubbed her temples. "I don't want to think about it right now. Dae shouldn't be communicating with you. What did he say in his email?"

"Here. I made a copy." She pulled a paper out of her pocket and read it. "He wrote it in Korean. I'll read it to you. 'Dear Sun, I think about you all the time. I am sorry I betrayed our friendship. I don't expect you to forgive me. Someday maybe. My case is coming up for trial. I know you will be there. I hope you will remember our friendship kindly. Signed, Dae.' What do you think I should do?"

"Hmm. How is he able to send emails from prison?"

"I'm not sure. Do you think he means it when he says he's sorry for what he did to me?"

"I don't know. People can change, but you will be testifying against him for what he did to you. He *could* be trying to influence you. Don't respond to his email. Promise me."

"Didn't you tell me to forgive people? I think I should."

"Yes, but that doesn't mean you should let him off the hook for trafficking you. Think about what he did."

The groove deepened on her face. "I try not to, Miss."

Putting on her reading glasses, she reached for the letter. "If you would write a translation of the letter, I will send this to the prosecutor. Dae shouldn't be corresponding with you."

Sun lowered her eyes.

"Okay? I'm going to Colombia tomorrow to meet with Kevin Perez's wife. Could you handle things around here? I don't have any appointments scheduled for the next few days. Just answer phones and emails. Also, would you do some research about children testifying at court? Anything you can find out on Lexis Nexis and Westlaw about the procedures for questioning them. I'm mainly concerned with Rosa being able to testify against her kidnappers, so I'm searching for information about kids from six to eight years old."

"Yes, ma'am." Her eyes brightened. "I wish I could go with you. To visit the babies at the orphanage."

"I don't think I'll have time to go there. It's going to be a quick trip."

"What if something happens that I can't handle here?"

"I trust you. I'm sure you'll do fine." She thumbed at the crutches leaning against the closet. "I'm going to use a cane. Travelling with video equipment and crutches is too much to handle."

***

She felt like an old lady. She'd forgotten to take off her reading glasses. Walking through the plane with a bulky video bag, a computer case, and a cane, she'd had to apologize to numerous people for jarring their seats or knocking them in the head as she passed. Fortunately, she'd never see them again.

The heat hit her hard as she left the airport to join the line of sweating people waiting for a cab. She'd only brought the suit she was wearing, now wilted and dripping wet. Four couples stood ahead of her. Pulling out her phone as she leaned on her cane, she called her client. He picked up on the first ring. "I've arrived."

"That's wonderful, Miss Richards. I'm at the hospital right now. Can you come?"

"I need to unload my bags first. Thank you for taking care of the hotel reservations. I twisted my ankle, so I'm walking with a cane. I'll be there as soon as I can."

Once ensconced in the back of an ancient taxi with two other passengers, she fanned herself with her boarding pass. Her phone buzzed in her pocket. Shifting her bags from one arm to another, she jostled it out. "Is there something else, Mr. Perez?"

"No dear cousin, this is Angela."

A stab of something ugly went through her. "Sorry, I thought you were someone else. How's your honeymoon going?"

"It's no honeymoon. We're still in Baltimore at the adoption agency, and I need your help."

Again? "I don't know how much I can help you. I'm not an adoption attorney."

"No, but you *are* an immigration attorney. I need you, Jules."

"What's up?"

"We have to go to Colombia to obtain Rosa's birth certificate and proof that her parents are deceased. Could you go with us as our attorney? Puleez? I'll never ask for another favor again."

"You're not bringing Rosa down here, are you? Because they can keep her here."

"That's what the adoption lawyer said. She'll be staying with the FBI lady and her family. Rosa likes it there."

A drop of sweat dribbled onto her eyelash. She wiped it off and squeezed her eyes shut when she noticed it landed on the woman next to her. "In fact, I'm in Colombia right now for Mr. Perez, but I suppose I could help you."

Angela's squeal made Julie hold the phone away from her ear. When she finished, "We'll talk when I get there. I love you so much."

Julie put her phone back in her pocket. "Yeah, right."

***

After patting her face and neck with a wet washcloth, she tried

191

to pull a comb through her hair, but it broke in two. She regarded herself in the bathroom mirror—her smudged eyeliner gave her a raccoonish appearance. Her hair had doubled in volume, tendrils sticking to her face. Using the pieces of her comb, she teased out most of the snarls. What she didn't resemble was an attorney. She peered at the broken comb, hair hanging between its teeth. *I surrender.* She pulled her hair into a scrunchy at the back of her head. Then she lined her toiletries on a hotel hand towel.

She padded out to the bedroom. Mr. Perez had been generous. The hotel room was gorgeous, towering over the street from the twenty-sixth floor. Her window looked down on a traffic round-about surrounding a fountain. The cars seemed like ants from her height. What she wouldn't do for a nap with a soap opera running in the background. She used the remote to flick through the channels. The only English-speaking station was the BBC. Good enough to put her to sleep. She gazed at the bed longingly. A short nap would revitalize her energy and make her a better lawyer.

She checked herself. Better not; she was on Mr. Perez's tab. After donning her suit jacket, she snatched her video bag, briefcase, purse, and cane. Following a final sweep of the hotel room, she tugged the door shut.

The trip to the hospital was short in distance but long in duration due to stop-and-go traffic. This was a different, more cosmopolitan version of Bogotá than the one she'd experienced only a short time ago. She called Mr. Perez to tell him she was on her way.

"She's sleeping right now. Been in and out all day."

"Is it a good time for me to come? I brought my camera."

He paused. "As good as any. She hasn't said anything yet, but she recognizes me. She even held my hand today."

Her shoulders sagged. "It would be more effective if she talked rather than me asking leading questions."

"Come anyway—room 34D on the third floor—on your right when you get off the elevator."

She stared out the window at the multitude of people streaming out of shops on either side of the road. Taxis wove in and out of lanes causing brakes to squeal. *Well, this was going to be a waste of time.* The taxi double-parked by the entrance. She gave him some of the leftover Colombian money she had saved from the previous trip and congratulated herself for remembering to pack it.

A strong antiseptic smell assailed her nose when the glass doors parted. Hospitals inspired an increase of her pulse rate. She remembered her visit to Celebration Hospital—the time she had first laid eyes on Brett Moyer—and realized she was talking out loud. Maybe when this was all over and the bad guys were put away for good, Brett would forget she had put his daughter in danger by her mere presence. Guys like him were rare—she would not let him get away without a struggle. He was worth fighting for. She surprised herself with that last thought.

The moment she arrived at room 34D, her pulse quickened heralding a panic attack. She didn't have time for one right now, and she'd forgotten a bag to blow into. She wasn't good with strangers; it was hard enough conversing with people she knew. Wiping the sweat off her neck, it was time for self-talk. *Buck it up and earn your living.*

She pushed the door open. Flowers adorned every table—the air was tepid. The smell of antiseptic combined with lilacs was cloying. The collar of her blouse stuck to her neck. Kevin rose from the chair where he sat at the foot of the bed.

"Thank you for coming, Miss Julie."

"Call me Julie."

"Then you call me Kevin."

A waif of a woman was propped up in the bed, but her swollen eyes were closed. Bruises covered her cheeks, and her lips were swollen. Her hands were folded in a prayer position, rosary beads entwined in them.

"This is my wife Isabel. Sometimes she wakes up for thirty minutes or so. She smiles and holds my hand, but she hasn't said anything yet."

"Do you think she can write? Have you given her a pen and paper?"

He scratched his head. "No, but it's worth a try."

Opening her video bag, she unfolded the tripod and set the camera upon it. Then she remembered the microphone. On the off chance Isabel would talk, she approached her and tried to attach a tiny microphone to the neckline of her nightgown, but her hair became tangled with the wire. She pulled lightly, not wanting to add to her injuries. Not here five minutes, and she was already causing pain.

Hoping Kevin hadn't noticed, Julie gently teased the blond hair away from her face. That's all she needed was to cause her to go back into a coma. What if she screamed? As she tucked loose, curly strands behind Isabel's ear, a dark mark on her neck got her attention. "Did you notice this bruise behind your wife's ear?"

He stood over her, then kneeled to have a closer look as she held back her hair. "Do you think she was hit there?"

She squinted to get a better view. "It almost resembles a tattoo. I wish the lighting was better in here." She switched on her phone's flashlight app, directing the beam at Isabel's neck. "It's fairly new—a cut of some sort. Did the doctors or nurses mention it to you?"

"No, but her hair probably covered it." He pressed the call button. "I'll get the nurse to clean it. Isabel's got enough to deal with, without getting an infection."

While they waited, Julie extracted a pen and a small tablet of paper from her purse. "Let's think about what we can ask her. I don't want to use any leading questions. The judge won't stand for it."

A nurse stepped in and joined Kevin at the patient's bedside. The level of Spanish was beyond Julie's knowledge, but the nurse's expression showed she was surprised at the mark. She left and came back with some alcohol swabs, then gently patted the spot. When she finished, her eyes widened, her voice got shaky, and she spoke under her breath.

Kevin moved toward Julie. "She says her neck was intentionally cut with a knife or a sharp object."

"What do you mean?"

The nurse was about to bandage the wound when Kevin asked her to wait. He summoned Julie closer.

Kevin said, "I might be imagining it, but it seems like her attacker cut a tattoo into her neck. What do you think it looks like?"

Squinting didn't help; she got as close as physically possible. She wished she had her reading glasses. The mark only had a two-inch diameter, but a picture was discernable. "It appears to be two guns or rifles forming an X."

"That's what I thought."

"It could be our imaginations. Ask the nurse."

Once he made his request, the nurse donned her glasses and drew close. Something made her jump back, her face tight with fear. She made the sign of the cross. "La bandera de FARC."

"She said it's the symbol on a FARC flag."

"We have our proof. Ask the nurse if she'll repeat what she just said for the camera."

Upon hearing the request, the wide-eyed nurse backed out of the room, shaking her head.

Julie leaned against the wall. "Well, that's just great." The room was quiet except for the beep of Isabel's monitor. "I've got it." Using her cane to propel her to the bed, she pulled her computer out of her video bag. While she waited for it to warm up, she drummed her fingers. "Patience isn't my best trait."

Kevin peered over her shoulder. "What are you searching for?"

"I don't want to jinx the research. I'll tell you once I find it." Drumming fingers didn't make her old laptop warm up any faster, so she rocked. "If what I find is correct, we'll have the proof we need without the nurse's help." She stared at Isabel's still form and chewed on her lip. "What have the doctors said?"

"About what she went through?" His jawline hardened, and his eyes were slivers of steel. "She was molested. There were deep cuts on her abdomen and thighs. They left her for dead." He stood and paced.

She hesitated before her next question. "This won't be easy, but I have to prove that the extent of your wife's injuries were nearly fatal, and that FARC did it. That means I have to record her injuries as well as the tattoo behind her ear."

He gazed at his wife. "Yes, of course."

She typed in her request. In a minute, she squealed; then glancing Isabel's way, she quieted herself. "See what I found?"

When she moved the screen so he could see, his jawline softened. "We have our proof."

At that moment, a man in scrubs covered with a long white coat entered the room carrying a file. Kevin spoke to him in Spanish. The doctor walked over to Isabel and gently teased the bandage away from behind her ear. His words were too fast to understand.

Julie touched Kevin's arm. He introduced her to the doctor.

Shaking her hand, the doctor apologized that his English was not so good.

She said low enough for Kevin to hear, "Ask him if he would speak about your wife's injuries on camera." She held her breath as he made the request. The doctor glanced at his watch and said yes.

"He says he has five minutes."

As she detached the microphone from Isabel, she thanked God for her good fortune. She pushed *record* and faced the camera.

After stating her location, the date, and the time, she said, "My name is Julie Richards, attorney for Kevin Perez and his family. I present Isabel Perez, who is the victim of a nearly fatal attack and has been in a coma. This is her husband, Kevin Perez, who is seeking asylum for his family in the United States. This is Dr. Luis Gutierrez, who will be speaking about Isabel's injuries."

She calmed herself and passed the microphone to the doctor. Although he spoke in Spanish, she could tell he was talking about his credentials. Then he read from his file. She hoped he was persuasive. Kevin's calm demeanor gave her some encouragement. She would have to hire a professional translator, but she could do that in Florida.

When the doctor stopped talking, she reached for the microphone when he approached the sleeping patient. He lowered the sheet a few inches and exposed her stomach. Garish red slash marks—some deep, some sutured made Julie avert her head. Then he pointed at different places on her neck and her face, making comments she didn't understand. The coup de grace came when he gently tilted Isabel's head, moving the hair out of the way, and exposed the tattoo they had missed before. When he finished talking, she thanked him, and he left.

Once she had put the microphone on her lapel, it took her a moment to collect her thoughts. The words *closing argument* came to mind. With a glance at Isabel Perez, she faced the camera. It was the best impromptu closing of her life. She recapped what she hoped the doctor said; she moved her computer around to show the flag of FARC with its crossed rifles. She finished with a plea for asylum for the Perez family, reiterating that Kevin Perez had a well-founded fear of death based on what happened to his wife, all because he worked for the Colombian government.

She had just switched off the camera when Kevin exclaimed,

"Isabel's awake."

Whirling around, her eyes met a touching scene. Kevin's arm circled Isabel's head. Isabel held on to his other arm. They gazed at each other as if nobody else was in the room.

His eyes remained fixed. "Come over here, Miss Julie. I want you to meet my wife." Then to Isabel, "You don't have to say anything. Julie's the lawyer I was telling you about. She's helping us with our asylum case."

Isabel's eyes moved to focus on Julie.

What to say to a woman who's come out of a coma after being left for dead. She waved like a clown. "I'm glad to see you are awake."

A smile pulled one side of her mouth to the right. "Hello, Julie." Her first words.

"Please don't talk. It must be painful."

She coughed gently and motioned for Kevin to give her some water. Once the straw had left her mouth, she said, "I'm fine." She swallowed with trouble, then smiled another crooked one. "You look just like your mother."

"You knew my mother?"

"I met both your parents."

How could this be? "You must be mistaken. My parents have been ... gone for five years. To my knowledge, they've never been to Colombia."

Kevin grasped her hand. "Maybe we should let you rest."

Batting his hand away, she said, "I'm fine. They said they were proud of you for—how you say—moving on."

Isabel's word had such a profound effect on her, Julie didn't notice right away that she was speaking passable English. Tears formed and ran in rivulets down her cheeks. She used the back of her hand to wipe them off. "Where did you talk to them?"

"Your dad said he liked your new house and is proud of you for starting your own law firm. What were his words? He said, 'that girl has gumption.' I don't know this word."

Her mind went over every conversation she had had with Kevin. Had she told him about her parents and taking that first step to get over her fears by selling their house and moving to Celebration? No, they had never talked about her. Maybe he had done an Internet search and read her profile, but that didn't explain how Isabel knew that her dad used to say *that girl has gumption* all the time.

Kevin smoothed the sheet over his wife's chest. "Sweetie, why don't you close your eyes and get some rest. We can talk later."

Gazing up at her husband, it took all her effort to raise her hand and touch his cheek. "I love you." Then she lowered her hand and beckoned Julie. "Come and sit next to me." She patted the bed beside her.

She took his place near his wife. Her weak hand touched Julie's. "You don't believe me, do you? I know I was attacked. I didn't see his face. I know about the coma. That is where I met your parents."

Julie's tears pinged onto her hands. "What else did they say?"

"Your mother said she likes the doctor. He's a good man. And she said to trust your heart."

A spasm of emotion went through her. It must be her mother. Who else would know about guarding her heart? But it was too late. The doctor was already out of her life.

"One more thing. She said to forgive your cousin. You two need each other. That's all."

She clung to Isabel's hand, not wanting the conversation to end. "How are they doing—my parents?"

Her eyes were half closed. She grimaced slightly. "I think I will sleep now. Your parents are wonderful people. They are happy, and they want you to be happy too."

When her eyes closed, Julie stood, wiped her face with her sleeve, and moved toward Kevin. "I'm sorry I monopolized her time."

"It's quite all right. What do you think she meant? Was she hallucinating?"

A chill travelled up and down her spine. "She knew things about my parents. I can't explain it."

He helped her pack her equipment into the video bag. "Maybe when she was in the coma, she went to heaven. I've heard about people doing that."

Julie frowned. "She doesn't even know me. How could she have met my parents before meeting me?"

"I can't explain it. But it happened." He handed her the video bag and walked her to the door. "Do you think we have enough material to convince the judge?"

"The doctor was a big help, but he spoke in Spanish. I hope the judge will allow me to find a translator."

"I could translate it."

"You have a conflict of interest. It has to be a translator whose credentials are recognized by the court. It won't be hard to find one, but I have no idea what the doctor said."

"He spoke about the rape, about her condition, the coma, of course, and he mentioned the connection with FARC on her neck."

"Bingo. That's what we needed." She paused by the door. "By the way, your wife's English is excellent. Did she grow up in the States like you did?"

He shook his head. "She doesn't speak a word of English."

Chapter Fifteen

Angela tapped her fingers on the armrests and stared at the specks below from her window seat. "I feel guilty sitting here. I should be up serving the passengers."

"Relax. We'll be busy once the plane lands." Steve pressed against her arm as he gazed out the window.

Linking her finger with his, she watched him gaze out. "Do you think we did the right thing?"

A groove formed between his eyebrows. "About what?"

"About getting married."

He removed his hand. "How does anyone know? I think so."

She didn't like his answer. "Would we have done it if Rosa hadn't come along?"

He shook his head. "Don't go there, Ange. What's done is done. Let it go."

Leaning back against the headrest, she closed her eyes. Now he was irritated. Why had she pushed him? Because she couldn't stop herself. "I love you, Steve."

Kissing her cheek, he said, "And I you."

It would have to do.

The minute they stepped off the plane, she was on the phone with Julie. For the first time since she'd given her the news of their upcoming marriage, Julie didn't sound like she was buried alive in an abyss.

Her voice was animated without a hint of sarcasm or deep hurt.

"I have so much to tell you. When can we get together?"

She held the phone away from ears. "Do I have the right number?"

Julie laughed. "What do you mean? Can we meet for an early dinner? I want to finish researching procedures for getting a birth and death certificate for a non-family member. I'm staying at the Palacio. Where are you staying?"

"I'm impressed. How'd you score that hotel? Celebrities stay there."

"My client put me up here. I'm on the twenty-sixth floor. My room is as big as my house and has an awesome view."

"I'm staying at the same hotel I always do with the crew. Steve's going directly to the police station, and once I check in and unload our bags, I'll come to you. I always wanted to see how the other half lives."

***

The luxurious carpeting was not lost on her sandaled feet as Angela checked each room number for Julie's. One could tell a high-end hotel by the plushness of its flooring. A knock at room 2636 brought a squeal and a hug from her cousin. What was going on? *She* was usually the one with unbridled joy compared to her reserved bookworm of a cousin. Something good must have happened to Julie; she couldn't wait to find out.

"I'm so glad you're here. You're not going to believe this place." Julie pulled her into the room.

Her first impression was one of size—larger than her condo in Orlando. Wood, brass, granite, and marble. Double doors into every room. A separate living room with a full bar. A bathroom with a Jacuzzi and double-sized shower. And the view. "Wow is all I can say. I'm in the wrong line of work."

Laughing, Julie hobbled to a chair and rubbed her ankle. "Would you like room service or do you want to go out?"

"Let's go out. I never get to do this when I'm working. We could ask the concierge for his recommendations."

"Great idea, but let's go somewhere close. My ankle's killing me." Julie carried her sweater, although she wouldn't need it in the outside heat. They agreed upon Masa, a popular café-type

201

restaurant in Zona G, close to the hotel.

Once they were seated with their menus, Angela leaned her elbows on the table and stared at Julie, who emanated a *joie de vivre* that she hadn't seen since before Julie's parents died. "Time to spill. What's made you so happy? I want some of that."

She glanced up from her menu. "Let's order first. I'm going with the shrimp pasta."

"I'll take the same." Once the waiter had refilled their water glasses and placed a basket of fresh bread on the table, Angela leaned forward. "Okay, dish."

"Yesterday, I met with my client and his wife at the hospital where she's been in a coma for a few days. It's a long story. In short, she was attacked by FARC, a terrorist organization here in Colombia. My job was to prove to the judge back home that Mrs. Perez's attack was caused by FARC, and not by some random person. She came out of the coma but hadn't spoken yet, although she recognized her husband."

Julie ripped off a piece of brown bread and closed her eyes as she chewed. "Is this ever tasty. Anyway, I was setting up the microphone on Isabel—that's Kevin's wife—and was pushing her hair out of the way, when I saw a wound behind her ear. Kevin called a nurse to take a look, and as she cleaned off the dried blood, the image of two crossed guns appeared. It's the symbol on FARC's flag, so we were able to prove a link between the attack and the terrorist group. When I get back, I'll have some work to do, but I'm sure the judge will grant asylum to this family."

Angela clapped her hands. "That's great. You have such an exciting job."

"That's not all. Mrs. Perez starting talking when I was there. And she told me things about my parents she couldn't have known by herself. She said my parents were happy I'd sold the house and started my own firm. And they liked the doctor."

"What do you think that means? She's a psychic?"

"No, I think she had one of those near-death experiences where she went to heaven. How else could she know anything about my parents?"

"That's a bit hard to believe. And what doctor?"

"I guess we haven't talked in a while, but I met a doctor at the hospital when I was trying to find Rosa. His name is Brett Moyer.

Oh, you should see his face. It's like a work of art—and he's nice and smart. And he's a man of faith." She sighed. "But I blew it."

Their salads arrived. Julie dove into hers, but Angela set her fork down. "What do you mean you blew it?"

"We took Brett's daughter Jenny to a park for a picnic lunch after church. Someone associated with those two guys that wanted Rosa took pictures of us and sent them to our phones."

"They're in jail. How could they do that? Did they have someone on the outside trying to scare you?"

Julie stabbed at her salad and brought a piece of spinach to her mouth. "I suppose so. Anyway, I haven't heard from Brett since that day. He's worried about his daughter. Her mother died of cancer, and Jenny's been through so much. The last thing I want to do is to put her in danger."

"Sweetie, you can get him back."

Peering at the people walking by, Julie said, "I'm not so sure. He was magnificent—like an exceedingly handsome salve after...."

"You can say it. I deserve all your ill will and bad thoughts."

"It still hurts, but I'll be fine. Obviously, God has a different story for me than one with Steve in it."

Angela patted her hand, then glanced at her watch. "So what's the plan?"

Julie opened her purse and pulled out money to pay the check. "Let me get this. I want to use up my Colombian currency."

"By all means, but you're flying back first class with me, as long as you don't mind going standby."

Julie beamed at her cousin, "This nightmare keeps getting better and better. Agreed."

"Why do you say nightmare?"

Julie cleaned her sunglasses with a napkin before speaking. "You know me. I like my routines, my to-do lists, and this trip was a bit of a stretch for me. But if I hadn't come to Colombia, I wouldn't have seen Isabel's neck with the FARC symbol on it, she wouldn't have told me about my parents, and I wouldn't be sitting here with you."

Running around to Julie's side of the table, Angela engulfed her in a long hug. "I couldn't stand it if you weren't in my life."

"Enough already," Julie blustered, "I checked the procedure for getting a birth certificate in Colombia, and you're in luck. You just have to go to the notaria in the county where Rosa was born. If you were in the States, since you're not a parent, you'd be out of luck."

Pulling out her phone and flipping through her notes, Angela said, "I know where she was born—a town called Medellín. It's about one hundred fifty miles from Bogotá."

"I'm sure we can rent a car from our hotel."

Angela hurried to the curb, put two fingers in her mouth as an uncle had taught her, and whistled. A cab pulled up. Using her best Spanish, she asked the driver for the cost of a round-trip to Medellín. The driver didn't appear surprised by the request and gave her a price. She yelled back at her cousin, "Two hundred dollars American."

"Sounds like a good deal, and we won't get lost."

They climbed in the back. The air conditioning didn't reach, so they opened the windows to let the warm breeze in. As the taxi gained speed once they were out of Bogotá, it was hard to carry on a conversation. The breeze brought with it a powdery dust that made Angela's eyes water, but she didn't care. Getting the birth certificate would put her one step closer to Rosa.

When they arrived, the driver asked for full payment. Julie fished in her purse for the money. "Well, there goes dinner and breakfast."

Angela said, "Sorry. I don't feel right about giving him the full amount, but we don't have a choice, do we?" She told the driver to wait for them around the corner.

They got into a line behind a dozen people waiting to enter the notaria. "The sign says the place closes in an hour. I hope we make it in." She pulled out her phone and called Steve, but it went to voicemail. "I'm with Julie. We've gone to Medellín to get Rosa's birth certificate. We travelled by cab. Call me."

The wait wouldn't have been so bad except for the brutal summer sun. The woman ahead of them stood under an umbrella, which threatened to poke them in the eyes. Fortunately, the line moved at a brisk pace, and soon they had advanced to one of three windows. The man at the desk fanned himself with a brochure and asked without glancing up, "Si, Senora?"

Clearing her throat, parched by the hot sandy air, she said with every bit of confidence she could muster, "I would like a copy of the birth certificate for Rosa Maria Colón, born in this city March 18, 2009.”

“What is this for?”

She had to be honest. “I’m adopting her.” Closing her mouth before she said too much, she waited. The next few seconds seemed like minutes.

“Fill this out, sign it at the bottom, and you’ll need to pay the amount listed on the back based on what size document you want.”

She thanked him, not wanting to show how elated she was.

The whole process lasted fifteen minutes. They restrained their excitement until they walked through the door. The minute they were outside, they gripped each other’s hands and danced around in a circle, not caring who saw them. Luckily, the cab was still waiting at the corner when they rounded it.

Climbing in the backseat, Angela said, “Home, James.” It felt good to laugh.

The taxi smelled of sweat and cigarettes, and the breeze was warmer than before. The sounds of slow-moving traffic would have been irritating at any other time, but Angela had the birth certificate safely hidden in her purse. Steve would be waiting for her, and they’d celebrate into the wee hours. Of course, Julie would join them.

As they neared the edge of town, the traffic dwindled, and the taxi groaned as the driver accelerated. Julie’s head leaned against Angela’s shoulder, her rhythmic snore harmonized with the music blasting from the radio.

The driver took a different way back, Angela noticed. She liked this way better—not so commercial; this was the real Colombia. Once in a while, they’d pass a truck with workers piled high on bales of hay in the back. Small cafes and bars in pastel colors dotted the landscape. A family sat under the shade of a tree selling fruits and vegetables. Angela loved this side of Colombia. The best food was in those little, out-of-the-way bistros. Music blared from a fuchsia-colored hot spot although it was still late afternoon. If she could memorize its location, she’d convince Steve and Julie to come back after dinner.

Once they passed the small towns and only scrub could be seen in any direction, the driver slowed down. Good. She could use a restroom break; she had drunk her weight in water today. The driver pulled onto the side of the road by an abandoned fruit and vegetable stand. He got out—probably to relieve himself. She decided to pass on nature's restroom.

He leaned against a stack of tomato crates, cradling a phone to his ear while he smoked a cigarette. When he glanced in her direction, he shifted his back to her. Well, that was rude. Not on her dinero. She opened the door and climbed out. Although the open window had given her an inkling of the sizzling day, a fresh wave of heat accosted her as she stood.

Having lost her shoulder to lean upon, Julie yawned loudly. "What's going on? Why have we stopped?"

"Not sure, sweetie. The driver is talking on his phone. I'll go ask." She sidestepped a gecko and said, "Is there something wrong with the cab?"

Whipping around without taking the phone from his ear, he ordered, "Get back in the car."

She didn't appreciate his tone. After all, it was a natural question when a cab stops out in the boondocks.

Until she noticed the gun.

Gesturing with his weapon, he pointed at the car. "Move. Your friend will be here in a minute."

As she hastened toward the car, doing her best to not lose a heel in a pothole, she whipped around. "What do you mean *your friend*? You mean my husband? Did he contact you?" Three steps brought him so close warm nicotine breathed on her face. The gun poked into her stomach.

"Get in the car and don't try anything stupid, you hear me?"

Her heel got caught in a hole and slowed her progress toward the car. Again, the hollow cylinder dug into her skin. This time, pain from its contact wracked her spine. Throwing herself into the backseat before the gun made contact again, she mouthed to Julie, "Don't say a word."

"What do you mean?"

A bullet flew past Angela's ear, so close she felt its heat.

But it was the sound of the bullet that caused her to scream—at least she thought she screamed. The deafening sound had left her without the ability to hear. Everything moved in slow motion, like a silent film noir. A sulfur odor filled the air. Julie's lips moved, but no sound emanated. Angela shook her head to quiet her. Julie's eyes were frantic. Her mouth opened wide like a fish struggling for air. Her face was ashen, and her hands clawed at her throat as she tried to fill her lungs.

Snatching her hand, Angela dug her fingernails into Julie's palm until she had her attention. Mouthing *quiet*, Julie pressed her lips together. Then she hung her head, struggling to control her breathing. Angela fashioned a bag out of some papers and brought it to Julie's lips. Her eyes filled with tears that splashed onto her shirt. When the rise and fall of her chest became regular, they held hands and burrowed against each other. Julie's heartbeat was palpable.

Then Angela remembered her phone. The cabdriver, blocking the door with his foot, smoked a cigarette with one hand and aimed the gun at their heads with the other. His cold, dark eyes didn't leave their faces. Who was the *friend* the guy said was coming? She didn't have any friends down here and certainly none that would be associated with gunmen.

She had to get through to Steve, but with Taxi Dude guarding them, she didn't know how that was going to happen. If she could just turn on her phone, maybe Steve would realize they were in trouble. Hadn't she heard that a phone could act as a GPS? The phone hid between their laps.

Billowing dust was the first sign that a car was approaching. It blasted through the open window—an uninvited guest, causing both of them to sputter and cough. A maroon sedan that had seen better days pulled up beside them. The *friend* had arrived; his identity masked by tinted windows. Angela was quite sure she wouldn't know him. And he was no friend.

Julie squeezed her hand so hard, she gritted her teeth. Out of the corner of her eyes, Angela gazed at the sedan—and understood for the first time. The one that followed them after they rescued Amber. The one driven by Amber's trafficker—Miguel. What did he want from them? Fear threatened to take over. Her instinct was to run before he got out of the car—before there were two guys instead of one. But her legs betrayed her. She was starting to hear again, but the sounds were muffled. The cabdriver had moved away from the car.

Julie's voice was low. "Should we try to escape?"

"Where could we go? We're out in the middle of nowhere."

"We could at least lock the doors."

"What good would that do? The guy has a key."

The cab driver was back. He yelled at them to be quiet, his gun banging against the side of the car.

The driver of the sedan got out, a phone plastered to his ear. He was young—even younger up close. He wore sunglasses and a white tee-shirt. Approaching the cab, he leaned his arms on the open window, tattoos peeking out from under his short sleeves. He was handsome in an impudent, *Rebel-without-a-Cause* way. His lip curled when he spoke to Julie in Spanish, but she shook her head and pointed at her ear.

He returned to his car. Was he leaving? The slam of his car door was barely audible to Angela.

Julie said under her breath, "Amber's master. Miguel."

He couldn't be more than a teenager, so young to be involved in such a heinous crime. Leaning into the window, he thrust a paper in front of Julie's nose. The paper dropped to her lap.

"It says, 'Where is Amber?'"

Miguel removed his sunglasses. Angela studied his face. A tattoo of a skull was under one eye. His face was hard, yet his eyes hinted at a vulnerability, which allayed some of Angela's fear.

She said in Spanish, "She's with her family."

Miguel gazed at nothing, then he asked, "Is she happy?"

Julie's wide eyes reflected her own disbelief. Who would have thought this kidnapper would care how Amber felt.

Julie said, "Tell him about the hospital."

"Amber's in the hospital in a coma."

The muscles in his jaw worked back and forth. "What happened to her?" His English was surprisingly good.

"She was kidnapped again. The police found her almost dead."

His eyes narrowed, then opened wide. He clenched and unclenched his fists, then slammed one into the door. Was that a tear rolling down his cheek? He brushed it off and averted his head.

Angela couldn't keep the sarcasm out of her voice. "Why do you care? She was just a source of money for you."

She should have seen it coming—the crack across the side of her head that set off a ringing in her ear. He squeezed her arm so tightly, she held her breath. "I wouldn't say that if I were you." He released her. Glancing away, he said under his breath, "I love her."

Remembering Amber's face, she couldn't stop herself. "What you did to her wasn't love—more like abuse."

His lip curled into an ugly sneer as he swung the door open. She winced, knowing she had gone too far. "You don't know what we had. Get out."

The cabdriver stood behind him with the gun trained on their heads. Miguel motioned for them to move toward the abandoned fruit stand with their hands on their heads. A bruise formed on her arm where he had gripped her. Yet she was more concerned about Julie, who must be in the throes of a panic attack although she appeared calm.

Though just a kid, Miguel was in complete control. He retrieved the gun from the driver, who was old enough to be his father. He held it on Angela and Julie while his partner tied them up back to back. Angela searched for a place to run, but the cabdriver blocked the entrance. The place was so small there wasn't room to move around. The smell of rotten vegetables permeated the fetid air. The ground was littered with unidentifiable things of all textures—it was better not to know.

Wriggling her wrists to loosen the twine that bound her was no use. She groped on the ground for anything to use as a weapon. Pebbles and sharp objects bit into her skin. She touched something cold and smooth, the size of a softball and as hard as a rock. After pushing it toward Julie's hand, she continued to feel around. Something else—a soft drink bottle cap, a cigarette butt, a shard of glass. Her hands held it loosely. It could cut the twine.

The two guys stood nearby smoking and talking low enough not to be heard. Angela knew she had said too much, but she couldn't stand it anymore. "What do you want from us?"

Miguel pivoted around and knelt down mere inches from her ear. "Your friend here stole my girl from me. She had no right. I want her back." Fear caused Angela's breath to come in fits and starts. Fear was useless now—she didn't have the luxury of being afraid. She'd concentrate on that tear. A man that cried wouldn't hurt them.

"How did you find us?"

"Bogotá's not that big. I have my contacts."

A shiver went through her, although it was over one hundred

degrees outside. Her throat was parched from the billowing dust. She needed water; her tongue got thick just thinking about it. Hysterical thoughts sped through her mind. How long could they go without water? Animals would find them. Armadillos. Rats. Snakes. Her pulse raced. Then she remembered the phone lodged in her waistband. She hadn't had time to put it in a pocket.

His voice brought her back to the present. "I want her number. You and your friend aren't going back until I get it."

"How do I know you won't kill us?"

"You don't."

Angela's hands were numb from the twine that dug into her wrists. Her feet were full of pins and needles. She translated Miguel's words to Julie; then she asked, "What should we do?"

"Give him the name of the hospital. We can call and warn them once we're back."

Was there room to bargain? What would happen to them when Miguel had what he wanted? She tried a different strategy. "It's hard enough for Amber. If you love her, let her be with her family. Let her heal."

The gun pressed against her temple. "Give me the number."

Tears slipped down her face and her nose ran, but she had no hands to wipe it off. "I don't have it." She gave him the hospital name and the street it was on. "You can get the number from information."

The gun hit her hard. Her neck jerked to the side. Her eyes closed to slits. Noise around her blended into a drone. Her cousin fidgeted and then her head jerked back. The phone vibrated in her pocket. A light sound, but she couldn't reach it. Her head felt like it was split down the middle. Car engines came to life. Smoke combined with dust, filling the air. Then the sounds faded. Her head felt so heavy, she couldn't lift it. Then nothing.

She and Julie were children again, dancing around a beehive. They had their jars ready to catch as many as they could. A few holes in the lids and few piece of grass for nourishment—what more could the bees want? But something was wrong. They were larger than usual, and more aggressive. They swarmed in thick rings around their heads. The noise was deafening.

Opening her eyes, Angela lifted her head with effort—it hurt so much she stopped moving. "Julie? Are you all right?"

"What? Oh, my head. It's bleeding."

"I think he hit you with his gun. Are you bleeding hard?"

"It's streaming in my eyes. I have to keep blinking."

 "We need to get help." She searched around for something to stem the blood. The dark shadows of the fruit stand prevented her from seeing anything clearly, but she could feel movement on her leg. "I think there's a spider on my leg. It's crawling up."

"Oh no, whisk it off."

"I can't. I don't have arms." Whatever it was had reached the pinnacle of her knee. Was it a tarantula or a black widow? She'd heard they liked dark places. With staccato gusts of air, she blew on it, waiting for it to retaliate; waiting for the sting. It stopped moving.

Julie's breathing became ragged and pronounced.

Angela had heard it many times before. She knew a panic attack was coming. "We don't have time for that right now. Breathe in and out. You can do it."

"I'm trying. Do you think they're gone?"

"I heard car engines before I passed out. I don't hear anything now. Let's try to get up. One, two, three." Pushing against each other, they eased themselves up to a squat.

Angelia whined. "It's on my thigh now. What should I do?"

"Is it big? Can you see it? I hope it's not poisonous."

"It's reddish and it kind of looks like a crab—you know—with pinchers, and its tail is curled up."

Julie's voice was surprisingly calm. "That would be a scorpion. Don't make any quick movements. How about we inch toward the wall and use it to make it fall off."

It was climbing—its little beady eyes fastened on hers. Angela's eyes squeezed shut. "Can we get out of here?"

Not wanting to agitate it, she led Julie with small steps to the entrance and into the heat of the sunshine. At least, the men had hidden them in the shade, but now the heat assailed her. Her mouth was so dry, it hurt to swallow, and her lips were swelling. She was thinking of a way to get the scorpion off her leg when her phone vibrated from the waistband of her pants. She was sure it was Steve, but she couldn't answer it.

Then she remembered the shard of glass in her hand. Repositioning her grip on it, she rubbed it over the twine, being careful not to touch the skin on her wrists.

Julie said, "What are you doing?"

"I'm trying to cut the string with a piece of glass I picked up."

"Ingenious. Be careful."

"Once I cut this, I'll call Steve to come and get us, and I can get rid of the monster on my leg."

"Don't forget we have to warn Pastor Siemens about Miguel calling Amber."

"No. I dropped the piece of glass. On a count of three, let's squat down so I can pick it up. One. Two. Three."

As they lowered themselves, Julie screamed and fell, pulling them down. "Ow. My ankle."

Angela said, "What happened?"

"I twisted it again when we went down. It hurts bad."

"Stay calm. Okay, once I find the shard of glass, I'll hurry and cut us loose." Her fingers searched the ground until she almost cut herself with it. This time she didn't care if she tore her wrists. When the twine gave way, she jerked free. Whipping around toward Julie, she cut the twine that bound her. Her hand went to the scorpion to brush it off, but it had vanished—hopefully not in her skirt.

They rubbed their wrists to stop the pins and needles. It was then that Angela noticed a stream of blood falling from her wrists onto her clothes. Julie's head was a mess, but the blood was coagulating. There was nothing to staunch the blood. Nothing—not even a newspaper.

Then it hit her.

"We've lost everything. Our purses, the papers for Rosa—they're in the taxi." For the first time, Angela felt the stirrings of despair. Kneeling down, she hugged herself and rocked as tears erupted. This dark, new sensation was uncharted territory for an optimist.

Julie draped an arm around Angela. "We still have the phone. Call Steve. He'll know what to do."

She had forgotten about the phone. Their one last hope. Otherwise, they'd have to walk—who knew what direction or how far. She couldn't remember hearing any cars go by. She sent a quick prayer to heaven and pressed Steve's name. While she waited for him to answer, something teased at her brain. "Does it seem weird to you that Miguel didn't take our phones?"

"I thought about that. Maybe in the confusion, they got careless."

Angela cast a sideways glance at her. "I don't think they were careless. Did you notice how Miguel seemed genuinely concerned about Amber? He actually cried when he heard she was in a coma."

She was about to hang up when he said, "Steve here."

"Thank God. It's me."

"Where are you? I've been calling all afternoon."

"Not sure where we are. We've gotten ourselves in a bit of trouble. Remember Miguel—the guy in Colombia who had kidnapped Amber? He kidnapped us—sort of. We're out in the country somewhere. I'm not sure where. Can you come and get us—quick?"

His voice was muffled as he talked to someone. Then he said, "We'll find you. Keep your phone on. I'm surprised the guy allowed you to keep your phones."

"I hid mine in my belt. The battery is at ten percent. We had gone to Medellín to get Rosa's birth certificate, so we're somewhere between Bogota and Medellin, but on a rural road by an abandoned fruit stand. Julie's in a lot of pain. She reinjured her ankle, and my wrist is bleeding."

"How bad?"

"Not sure. Quite a bit, I think."

"Rip off a piece of your skirt and wrap it around your wrist."

"Good idea. Hurry." Once he had disconnected, she ran over to Julie. "Here, let me help you to that tree stump over there." Julie leaned on her and hopped on her good leg, crying out with every step.

"Check out my ankle—it's doubled in size."

"If we only had some ice." Angela lugged a crate close to Julie. "Here, elevate your ankle. Do you have your phone?" When Julie pulled it out of her pocket, she told her to switch it on in case her own battery ran out. "If we keep our phones on, Steve will be able to find us." She helped Julie prop her foot on the crate.

She stood too fast, and the world began to spin. Backing up, she leaned against a rusted garbage can until the dizziness stopped. Was it because she got up too quickly, was dehydrated, had lost blood, or all the above?

Once the ground appeared level and still, she hurried to the place where she had dropped the shard of glass. Who would have thought that the little thing was such a lifesaver and could cause so much trouble at the same time? When she found it, she used it to rip off two strips of her skirt. She used one to wrap around Julie's blood-caked head. Then she bound the other one around her wrist. Though the blood soaked through, it slowed down. She ripped off another few inches just to be sure. Glancing at her exposed thighs, she was glad the guys had left. And she hoped Steve would come alone.

She still felt a little woozy. Maybe it was the oppressive heat, or maybe it was the after effects of the unexpected ordeal. She spied a tree stump in the shade of the fruit stand. Hobbling over to it, she sat and closed her eyes for a second. The day had started so well. Everything had gone according to plan. Then this. She should be grateful they weren't dead. She sent a thank you to heaven. Her eyes landed on something familiar beside the dusty grooves of the path.

Two purses and a file. A wrinkled paper peeked out—Rosa's birth certificate. Angela stood too fast again and sat back down. The next time she got up gradually and went to retrieve them. The imprint of tire treads masked some of the words on the certificate, but it was still legible. Unfettered tears ran down her cheek; she didn't care. Tears of joy were always better than the alternative. She hugged the paper to her chest. One step closer to adopting Rosa. As she put the paper back in the file, she noticed handwriting on the back of the document.

"Tell Amber I love her." She shook her head. This written by the guy who had hit them in the head with his gun and left them for dead.

Yet in a strange way, it was kind of romantic.

She picked up the purses and joined Julie, who was rubbing her knee. She checked the back of her head for blood. "It's not too bad."

Meanwhile, Julie searched through her handbag. "Maybe there's something we can use for my ankle and your wrist. Two pieces of gum, my wallet—credit cards intact. Lipstick. Keys. Let's have the gum."

Angela shut hers. "I have nothing. We're just lucky they didn't take our passports or money—although they're not doing us a lot of good out here. Did you know Miguel wrote 'Tell Amber I love her' on the back of the birth certificate?"

Julie's brow furrowed. "Why do you think they did that to us? It doesn't make any sense."

Angela thrust her palms up. "This is Colombia. It's like the wild west here."

"But they left our stuff. It could have been a lot worse."

The sun dipped lower, and with it, tall shadows formed, making it hard to read. An animal howled—a coyote, Angela thought. Where was Steve? She checked her phone's bars—barely a half. Julie slapped a mosquito on her arm and brushed a nettle of insects away from her face. The heat hadn't dissipated with the sun's departure.

"Did you hear that? I don't want to be dinner for a wild animal."

"Steve will be here." Angela checked her watch. Eight thirty. "We can't leave. This is where he'll be searching for us."

"We have the phones." She held hers up. "Mine still has two bars. Anyway, I can't walk. What was I thinking?"

Headlights bounced across bumps in the road, illuminating the area. Angela lunged to her feet. "He's here." She ran to the clearing to flag him down. Then she backed up. It wasn't Steve.

Her stomach clenched as she slunk back into the shadows. She squatted beside Julie and put her finger to her lips. Voices emanated from the vehicle, not Steve-type voices, but wild, raucous curses and laughter. Angela stuffed the file in her shirt and threw both purses over her shoulder. She helped Julie to her feet. They needed to hide, but the only place was the fruit stand. They hobbled toward the little room, the stench increasing with every step. Julie's shoulders tensed—pain or fear or both? Their refuge was even darker now.

At the fruit-stand entrance, Angela changed her mind. They might be followed inside. Instead, she inched around the building and helped lower Julie to the ground. Dusk had morphed into night; the only illumination came from the headlights of the vehicle. The darkness was their friend.

A cacophony of male voices jested in Spanish. Boisterous

laughter and stumbling footsteps approached the building—bottles opened and fell to the ground. Only a thin wall separated them. Angela held her breath and pressed Julie's shaking hand. She was scared; she could only imagine how Julie felt, but her breathing was normal.

Another car arrived. More people and more talk. There had to be at least a dozen of them in the small room. Smoke traveled around the corner into their space. Angela put her arm around her cousin, and they huddled together, trying not to move a muscle or make a sound.

Someone lumbered around the corner, almost tripping on an exposed root. Angela squeezed Julie's hand. It was over for them. Their bodies would be found months later. Unidentifiable. She would not let thoughts like that take over. Instead she prayed.

Belching, he stopped no more than a foot or two from them, relieving himself of a great quantity of fluid. He hummed off-key until finished. After he zipped his pants and left, they allowed themselves to breathe.

"That was close."

The festive tone changed inside. Voices got louder, bottles smashed against walls followed by the sound of bodies being thrown. The fragile stand shook with the weight of the blows.

Julie whispered, "Should we move?"

"I don't know where we can go where we won't be seen."

The smell of acrid smoke hit them. "The place is on fire. We have to move."

"There's no water to put it out." Angela helped Julie to her feet. "Let's hide in the brush. There are no trees, but if we lie down and keep still until they're gone, their headlights won't catch us."

Julie cried. "I don't think I can lie down. There might be snakes and those gila monsters."

"Don't forget scorpions." Angela didn't have time to argue; she gently pushed her down and put her arm tightly around her. "I saw a flashlight beam heading in our direction. Just keep your head down."

Smoke burned her eyes, and the heat from the fire singed the air, flames reflecting off their faces. Angela hazarded a glimpse. Two teenagers stood on top of a truck, laughing and drinking from bottles. Three guys danced around the burning building, yelling unintelligible things and throwing debris from the ground at the fire. Images of *Dante's Inferno* played through her mind. How did the story end? She couldn't remember.

Ants nibbled at Angela's ankles; she didn't care. Her focus was on keeping still. She prayed for protection from the intruders and from the elements. It wouldn't take much for the fire to spread to the brush that hid them. "How are you doing?"

"I've been better."

"Too much of an adventure for me." She patted her hand. "Steve will be here any minute. Don't you ...."

Swirling lights joined the crackling reflection of the flames. The drunken guys jumped from the vehicle's roof to the ground, where they kicked empty bottles under the truck. Others dashed to the spot where she and Julie had hidden earlier.

A police cruiser halted next to the truck. An officer climbed out, his hand on his belt, and ordered the guys who stood next to the truck to line up.

When Steve got out of the car, Angela bolted to her feet and ran at full speed toward him. He didn't see her until she threw her arms around his shoulders and almost knocked him over. He stumbled, caught himself, and held her as she clung to him.

"You're stronger than I thought."

She smirked. "It's about time you noticed."

He lifted her wrist and examined the bloody bandage, still damp. "This doesn't look good."

"I was waiting for you to show up. What took you so long?"

He tilted his head toward an officer. "Sorry. They move at their own speed here. I had to wait for my partner to finish his dinner." His nose crinkled. "You don't smell so good."

She wiped the sweat off her cheek with a dirty hand. "Thanks a lot."

He peered into the darkness. "Where's Julie?"

A weak voice called out, "Over here." She limped toward them, gasping with every step. Steve ran to Julie, draped her arm around his shoulder, and guided her to the police car where he helped her to sit.

He yelled to Angela, "I have to help the officer round up the guys. Then I'll take you back."

The Colombian cop was busy patting down three males, who

leaned against the truck spread eagle. Angela walked over to Steve, who trained a gun on the three men. "There are some more hiding on the other side of the burning hut. They're the ones that started the fire."

Steve's face became hard. "Did they do anything to you two? If they did, I'll kill them."

Angela waved off the comment. "No, we hid in the brush, but I'm glad you showed up when you did."

"Go sit with Julie in the car. I don't want you to get…" He fastened his gaze on her face. "You're a mess. But you look amazing."

He hurried toward the hut, stopping at the corner with his gun poised. An ember fell from the roof barely missing his head. Vanishing from sight, he emerged a minute later with his gun pointed at the backs of three coughing teens in single file, their adolescent joy replaced with somber expressions. One guy scowled when he spotted the girls. Peering back at the others, he muttered something she couldn't hear. Steve ordered them to be quiet.

Another police cruiser arrived. Flashing lights lit the place, although the fire had ebbed to mere smoke that burned their eyes. Angela coughed and couldn't stop rubbing hers. She stole a bottle of water from the front seat, not caring if they charged her with theft. After a long swig, she passed it to Julie, who guzzled more than half the water.

Julie said, "What are they going to do, arrest us?"

Steve walked up holding a scruffy teen, whose hands were cuffed behind him. "You'll have to get out now. They'll need both cruisers."

Julie leaned out and stared at the dark road behind them. "When is the fire truck coming?"

"They won't come for this little building. Nobody's been hurt. They'll let it burn out."

"But what if it spreads to the surrounding brush?"

"Don't know. Do you think you'll be able to climb into that truck with your injured ankle?"

Her eyebrows rose, and she opened her mouth, when Angela said, "I'll help her up. Why do you ask?"

Rubbing the stubble on his chin, he said, "The only way we'll be able to get you back to town is to get rid of the car and take that truck. I'll drive unless you're good with a stick shift."

Angela focused on the dark vehicle. "I can hold my own with a clutch."

A mustached police officer joined them, pointed at one of the cars, and spoke in a low voice to Steve.

"He wants me to ride shotgun in his car. Too many guys in the backseat. How do you feel about following us to the station?"

"Sure, why not? But could you help me hoist Julie into the truck?" They linked arms around Julie's elbows and tried to help her up, but it was too much of a climb. "I could get down on all fours, and she could climb on my back."

Steve laughed, "I can pick her up and put her in the cab."

Julie shook her head. "I don't think so. I'm quite able to get in by myself."

"Stop arguing." With one swift movement, Steve hooked Julie's waist and hoisted her over his shoulder. "Open the door, Angela."

Julie protested, "Let me down." She kicked her legs; then howled from the pain when her foot made contact with Steve's body.

"Will you stop kicking and relax?"

"I can get in myself."

He insisted, "No you can't. Angela, get in the truck and pull her in."

Angela ran around to the driver's side. She leaned across and gently tugged her in. The truck reeked of pot, stale beer, and sweat. In any other situation, she would have gagged. Instead, she blocked the sensation for the time being. Steve slammed the door shut and came around to her side of the truck. The keys dangled in the ignition. She started the engine and peered down at Steve. "There's less than a quarter tank of gas."

"Should be enough. Call me if you have any trouble." He slapped the open window sill. "Gotta go." He strode away.

"My phone's dead." But he had already left.

Julie crossed her arms. "Ooh, he makes me so mad. He always treats me like a child."

Angela grinned and glanced at her cousin. "You couldn't have climbed up with your ankle the way it is."

Julie grabbed a piece of paper from the console and fanned

herself. "You're probably right." Angela forced the stick shift into position. "You do know how to drive this thing, don't you?"

"It's been a while. But I'm sure it's like riding a bike." The engine sputtered as she pushed the gearshift forward.

Julie's voice tightened and raised a couple of notes. "They're leaving."

"I think I've got it." Angela's tongue protruded as the truck jerked forward. "Whew. At least, it didn't stall." She pressed the accelerator, keeping her left foot on the clutch. The engine raced and jerked as she changed to second gear. The truck lurched forward and gained speed.

"Hurry, or we'll lose them."

"I'm trying." Pressing the clutch, she wobbled the stick shift into third, and they were off. She let out an audible breath of relief. "I think we're good to go as long as I don't have to stop on a hill."

They caught up to the police cruiser and both said, "Whew," at the same time.

Julie's hand went to her nose. "What's that smell?"

"I don't want to know." She glanced at her cousin. "How are you doing? I had no idea a simple trip to get a birth certificate would almost get us killed."

Julie's voice broke as she said, "I'm okay. It's a good thing I didn't know what was ahead. You know me—Miss Fraidy Cat."

Angela leaned over and patted her hand. "You're not a 'fraidy cat. Think of all the things we've been through in the last few hours. We were kidnapped, tied up, and left for dead. Then we had to hide from those drunks. You didn't have one panic attack— almost one doesn't count. I officially pronounce you over your fears. The old Julie's back."

"I was scared out there. It felt like snakes were climbing all over my legs, and when that guy almost tripped over me, I thought I was going to faint."

"But you didn't. I was scared too, but we made it through alive," Angela tugged her skirt as far as it would go. "This skirt didn't make it though." The night was black except for the distant rear lights of the police car. Angela yawned and glanced at Julie, who leaned against the door.

When she started giggling, Angela glanced at her. "What are you laughing about? Is that blow to your head finally getting to you?"

Julie belly-laughed and sputtered, "Just look at us."

"What do you mean?"

"We're in exotic South America. Should we take a selfie?"

Angela snorted, "And post it on Facebook."

"Better yet, let's stream a video." She dug out her phone and held it up. "I've still got a half a bar."

Angela tilted her head toward Julie and gave her a ridiculous grin. "How about this?"

Julie clicked one of Angela and then snapped her own picture.

Angela focused on the road. "I feel so much better now, Jules. Don't ever show anyone those pictures."

Julie said, "I have a confession to make."

"What's that?"

"I wasn't looking forward to seeing you or Steve ever again. It was too painful and awkward."

"You have every right to feel that way, but it would have made me devastated to lose you. I don't think I could have stood it."

"But when I saw you with Steve, it didn't hurt like I thought it would. I think you fit him better than I did."

"It *was* all for Rosa at first, but somehow, I have to be honest, I've fallen deeply in love with that man." She paused. "But I'm not sure he feels the same about me."

"He's a hard one to read. I know from experience. It feels good not to be jealous."

The traffic increased as they neared the city limits. Although, it was late, throngs of people swarmed the streets. Pedestrians crossed at will. Angela focused all her attention on staying close to Steve's car and hoped she wouldn't kill or maim any jaywalkers.

When they finally veered into a parking lot, she exhaled loudly. "Made it in one piece." She pulled into a large space, switched off the engine, and grabbed Julie's hand. "I don't think it's an accident that the doctor came into your life when he did."

"I wish. But he's not in my life. He doesn't want to see me." Her voice quivered. "It's like I ruin everything I touch."

"Don't say that."

"It's true. Kevin's wife is in a coma because I didn't do a good enough job of convincing the judge that he deserved asylum."

"You don't know that." Angela swiveled in her seat to face

Julie. "Look at me."

Julie lobbed her head in Angela's direction.

"You always do your best when it comes to the law. You know it and I know it. And look at what happened when your client woke up. She gave you a message from your parents." With a finger, she tipped Julie's chin up. "Am I right or wrong?"

"You're right."

"And don't forget that your parents said they approved of the doctor. What's his name?"

"Brett—Brett Moyer."

"This turned out to be a successful trip. You got your proof. I got a dirty copy of Rosa's birth certificate, and we're back to being pals again."

Julie consulted her watch. "I missed my flight. I was supposed to leave two hours ago."

"Remember, you're going back with me—first class."

Steve climbed onto the runner. "C'mon. Let's get out of here. Good driving, by the way." He landed on the ground and gave Angela his hand.

She asked, "Have you heard anything about Rosa? How's she doing?"

"She's doing good. By the way, when Rosa was sleeping, they examined that bunny. Now we've got a motive."

"Diamonds?"

"No."

"Cash?"

Steve sniffed. "Guess again?"

"Drugs?"

"No, keys—a half a dozen of them."

Angela's eyebrows knit together. "Keys to what?"

"Safety deposit boxes, buried treasure—who knows? They're not talking."

"What's going to happen next?"

"The police have the keys. It's just a matter of time until they find out."

"Were you able to get Rosa's parents' death certificates?"

"We'll talk about it later."

Angela trailed behind as he went to help Julie down. "I want to talk about it now."

He stopped and put his hand on her shoulder, his eyes solemn.

She steeled herself for what she knew would be bad news. "I knew it. You couldn't get the death certificates. Why does everything have to be so difficult?"

His lips were tightly held in a single line. Then he said, "We've located her parents. They're alive."

Chapter Sixteen

For the third time, Sun walked to the front window to see if Julie
had arrived home. Of course, it was an exercise in futility. Julie
would park in the garage behind the house. Returning to Julie's
office, she sharpened pencils and placed a fresh pad of paper in the
center of the desk.

She hated being there all by herself. Clients called with
questions beyond her level of English and knowledge of the law.
Some were even rude when she couldn't give them an immediate
answer. Not only that—her imagination ran wild with every sound.
She drummed her fingers on the desk. Julie had said she'd be home
yesterday. Where was she?

The phone rang. She wanted to say, "She's not here. Call back
after I go home." Instead, she lifted the phone to her ear and
recited the greeting she had memorized.

"Is this Sun Lee?"

A chill went through her. Not many people knew her name.
"Yes, who is this?"

"It's Dae."

At the sound of that name, her hand went to her mouth. What
did he want with her? He was supposed to be in prison. Her eyes
darted around the whole room—was he out there watching? Her
voice was barely audible. "How did you find me?"

"The guy in the next cell mentioned the lawyer's name. Said
she had kidnapped his girl and he intended to get her back one way

or another. And he mentioned a short Asian girl who worked for her. I put the puzzle pieces together and came up with you."

Her hand visibly shook making it difficult to hold the receiver against her ear. All the terror came flooding back—the brutally hot van, the "jobs" he forced her to do, the shackles digging into her ankles. "Are you still in prison?"

"I am." The threatening tone was gone; he sounded like the old Dae she had gone to elementary school with—the one who had walked her home from school in fourth grade; the one who had visited her whenever he returned to Seoul to see his grandmother.

Before he betrayed their friendship and forced her into human trafficking.

She didn't care if her question was dumb. "They let you use the phone?"

"Yes, there's one phone. We line up to use it, so I can't talk long."

She hesitated before asking the next question. "Why are you calling me?"

"Did you get my email? You didn't answer, but I figured the wardens go through our emails and edit them."

She cleared her throat. "I got it." Where was Julie?

"You're busy, I understand." He paused too long. His voice was thick, as if he choked back tears. "I just wanted … to hear your voice."

She closed her eyes. He sounded like the old Dae, but how could he be? "I should be going."

"Not yet. I don't expect you to forgive me." His ragged sigh was audible. "I wish …. "

"What?"

"I wish I could see you face to face."

"I need to go. I forgive you. Good-bye, Dae." She let out a breath. "But please don't call me again." She hung up before he had a chance to respond. She stared at the phone, wondering what she should do, wishing Julie would return. The phone rang again. She let it ring, waiting for it to go to voicemail. Then she remembered she had a job to do and answered. "Please don't call me anymore."

"Sun?" A female voice this time. She cringed at the thought that a client heard her.

"Yes. I am sorry. Who is this?"

"It's Aubrey. I have a favor to ask, or maybe I should ask Julie. Could I talk to her?"

"She's not here. She went to Colombia to interview a client, but she should be back soon." Aubrey's voice was muffled while she talked to someone.

"Dad said to ask you. Would it be okay with Julie if we stayed at her place for a few days? Amber's being released from the hospital today, and our hotel is fully booked for a conference. It would only be for a day or two. Then we'll be returning to Kansas."

"I'm sure it would be okay with Julie. Amber was staying here before she was taken." She hoped it would be fine with Julie. "How is she doing?"

"A bit weak, but she's doing good, but ..."

"What's wrong?"

Aubrey sniffed. "She's not too happy to see me. Whenever I try talking to her, she turns away from me or ignores me."

"I'm sure things will get better with time. When she finds out how much you care for her."

"Hope so. Anyway, we should be there in an hour. Thank you."

Sun hurried into the guest bedroom, searching for things to pick up. With three guests moving in, she'd finally be able to relax. Having other people in the house would be good. Then she would feel safe from Dae. That's silly, she told herself. Dae couldn't hurt her. He was locked up in prison. The mere thought of him filled her with utter dread. What did he want from her? She didn't understand. He sounded sorry, but he had deceived her once; she wouldn't let him do it again.

After plumping the pillows in the guest bedroom and switching on the ceiling fan, she made tea for the Siemens. Her mind went to Amber, and a new wave of guilt assailed her. No matter what everyone said, she should have stood up to Amber at the mall and told her they needed to stay together. But then again, if she had stayed with Amber, both of them would have been taken, and there would have been no one to tell Steve. She hoped Amber would forgive her.

Footsteps pounded up the porch steps. She hurried to check the peephole, then switched off the alarm and threw the door open, glad for voices other than her own. Amber and Aubrey stood in front of their father. The twins were identical except for the gray pallor of Amber's face, the bruises on her cheeks, and her grim expression.

She couldn't help herself; she wrapped her arms around Amber's thin shoulders. "I'm so glad you're okay."

She was about to ask them to come in when Amber shoved her aside and hurried past her. The slam of the bathroom door was her only reply. Sun glanced from Aubrey to Pastor Siemens, but their expressions were non-committal.

Clearing his throat, Pastor Siemens spoke in a low tone, "I think it would be better if we talked out here." He motioned for Sun to join them on the porch.

"What's wrong? Did I say something wrong?"

Aubrey squeezed her arm gently. "No, she's not mad at you. She's mad at me."

Sun wanted to ask why, but it wasn't her place to pry.

Pastor Siemens pointed to the swing where Aubrey sat. He leaned against the column, his face drawn with fresh wrinkles around his eyes. "I guess I should explain. Amber's doctor says she'll be fine. Her injuries are minor; the bruises will fade with time, but she's not a happy camper. She wants to go back to Colombia—to that guy named Miguel. Apparently, she thinks he's the love of her life."

Aubrey agreed. "She blames me for everything. She keeps bringing up the time I told her I wished she was dead and doesn't believe me when I say I'm sorry." Her voice trailed off. She seemed tired. "I don't know how to make her believe I didn't mean it."

Sun glanced from father to daughter. "You have been through so much. Is there someone you can talk to?"

Aubrey bolted off the swing and paced the porch. "I think we should have an intervention with her right here."

"What is this *intervention*?

Her dad piped in, "It's where everybody lays their cards on the table. Aubrey, do you think Amber could handle something like that in the state she's in right now?"

"If we don't do something, she'll run away again, and maybe this time we won't find her."

Sun gazed toward the street, wondering again where Julie was. She wasn't sure if this was the kind of decision she should be making. "I think it would be good if Julie was here for your card game. She's a lawyer, and it is her house."

"What? Oh. An intervention is a conversation about a problem, not a card game." Aubrey said, "When do you expect her back?"

"Not sure. She was supposed to come home yesterday. Anyway, I made some tea. It is too hot out here on the porch. Let's go and sit in the living room." She held the door open for them, then went in the kitchen to put some cookies on a plate and pour the tea. A rustling behind her made her spin around.

Amber stood in the doorway. "Do you have something cold to drink? I'm sweating."

Opening the refrigerator, Sun bought out a pitcher of sweet tea. "Would you like some cold tea?"

"We call it *iced tea* in America."

Iced tea—I have to remember these English words. When she went to get a stool, she almost bumped into Amber, who was tiptoeing toward the back door. "Where are you going?"

She stopped by the door that led to the garage. Her expression was sheepish. "I can't stand it here. I miss Miguel. I want to go back."

"Please, you've been through so much. Could you wait until you're better?"

Amber gripped the knob. "I'll feel better when I'm with Miguel."

Sun approached her with measured steps. She would not let Amber down this time. With all the forcefulness she could muster, she said, "When I ran away, Dae handcuffed my hands to the ceiling of the van. It hurt so much I thought death would be better. I don't want the same thing to happen to you."

"Miguel loves me. He said I was different than the others."

Sun stumbled forward, unsure of her words. "Your sister and father are worried about you."

"My *sister* hates me. She said so. The girls I lived with in Bogotá were more like sisters than Aubrey."

"If you go down there, you may never see your parents or sister or brother again. They want to talk to you. Give them that chance."

She leaned against the door, still gripping the knob. "I know

I've caused them a lot of trouble. They'd be better off without me."

Taking a step closer, she touched her arm. "Don't say that. It's not true." She gently pried Amber's fingers from the doorknob. "Could you at least wait until Julie is back? It should be soon. She went to Colombia to meet with a client."

She allowed Sun to lead her into the living room and sat stiffly on the edge of a chair. She stared at the floor, avoiding eye contact with her sister or her father.

"I'll be right back with the drinks." Sun said a short prayer for reconciliation while she put teacups on a tray. It took her no more than three minutes, but when she returned to the living room, the air was thick with tension and the words were heated. She offered drinks to her guests, but they waved her aside.

"You never paid any attention to me; it was always Aubrey." Amber lashed out at her father.

Aubrey interrupted. "Seriously? Do you have any idea how worried Mom and Dad were about you? It's like Oliver and I didn't exist for the last two years." She began to cry. "That's why I said those mean things to you—because I was jealous of you. I'm sorry, but it's the truth."

"You were jealous of *me*? I've always been jealous of you— you were always the one who made cheerleading and had all the friends. Do you know how hard it was to be asked over and over, 'why can't you be more like your sister?'?"

Pastor Siemens said, "We were wrong to compare you to your sister. We never meant to imply you weren't as good as Aubrey. When you went missing, my heart died every day. It was the worst time of our lives. We missed you so much. Aubrey, I'm sorry we neglected you and Oliver. We haven't been good parents to any of you."

Aubrey's voice was plaintive, but hopeful. "Can't we start over? Won't you give us a second chance?"

Amber gazed at the door as if its magnetic pull was breaking down her resolve to stay. Then she swiveled to face her father. "Only if you'll let me live my life the way I want and stop trying to make me fit into Aubrey's mold." She rose to her feet. "And if you love me the way you say you do, let me go back to Miguel."

The silence was so loud, the clock's ticking sounded like bellows as it marked the time for a response. Aubrey and her father peered at each other. Sun filled the silence. "You know what he will do to you."

"I don't care. It's better than living with people who don't accept me." She ran out of the room, the bathroom door slammed shut, and the click of the lock tolled the end of the intervention.

Chapter Seventeen

Angela craned her neck to see what Julie was doing two rows
back. Her eyes were closed, and her head rested against the leather
of the plush first-class seat. Angela tried to lean her head against
Steve's shoulder, but it didn't feel right. The hollow pit in her gut
wouldn't go away. How different this flight was from the one to
Colombia, when her dream was within reach. So close to adopting
Rosa—just two certificates away. Then four words ruined
everything—*we've located her parents*. She should be happy for
Rosa—she chided herself. Rosa would much rather be with her
family. But it was hard, knowing she'd never see her again. Add to
that, frequent waves of guilt for wanting to keep Rosa for herself.

Ice cubes clinked as she sipped her water. They hadn't
addressed the elephant in the room. What would become of their
marriage now that Rosa was out of the picture? She peered at Steve
out of the corner of her eye. Would he consider their marriage a
fraud now that the reason for it was non-existent?

She was ready to hear the rest of the story. "Where did they
find them?"

He glanced up from his magazine. "Find who?"

"Rosa's parents."

"In a city called Neiva. They were hard to locate because they
changed names. The father is teaching at a university. They've
already been notified about Rosa." He laid his hand over hers—
that tiny gesture filling the pit in her stomach with warmth. "It's

hard, but it's for the best."

"I know, but it hurts—I feel like God put a carrot in front of me and then whisked it away." She dared not move her hand from her lifeline to the future.

He squeezed it. "It doesn't sound like God to me—more like Lucy Van Pelt from Peanuts."

A little voice inside told her to keep quiet, but she'd never been able to obey that little voice. "So what happens to us?"

"What do you mean?"

Her head hurt, still throbbing from the butt of Miguel's gun. "You know. The reason we got married is . . . not a reason anymore."

Peeking at his face, she knew she had gone too far by the vertical groove that deepened between his furrowed brows. "Why do we have to talk about this right now? Let it go."

"I wish I could, but I can't. You didn't marry me for love. You did it for Rosa."

A vein pulsated in his neck, and he removed his hand. "So did you. Do you want a divorce? Is that what you're trying to say?" His voice got louder.

Cringing, she peered around to see if any of the other passengers were paying attention, but the two businessmen sitting across the aisle wore headphones. With a peek back at Sleeping Julie, she knew their conversation remained between the two of them.

"I didn't say that. I'm thinking of you and Julie. It's not too late for you and her." Her trembling voice tapered off at the end, and she stared at her hands. Never had she felt so low.

"If that's what you want." He enunciated every word, and each one dug into her heart.

She wanted to hug him, to tell him that she loved him more each day, but if he didn't feel the same for her, what would be the point? Tears pinged onto her lap and she sniffed. Grabbing the napkin under her beverage, she wiped at them. So Julie *was* still in the picture. He didn't even bother to put up an argument. Even though Julie had said it was over, he was her first love. There was nothing to do but step aside and let them work things out.

Their words erected a thick but invisible wall between them. She couldn't touch him; she couldn't change the tone of their exchange. She sat silently thinking about how life would be without him. They'd only been together a short time, but she treasured every minute. She rushed home from every store, from every errand. Their trip to Baltimore; their first few nights together in her condo. The plans they made, the way he corralled her from behind and wrapped his strong arms around her. All that was gone forever with four little words.

When she couldn't stand it any longer, she grasped his hand and looked him squarely in the eye. "You're Worth Fighting For."

He said nothing. His lips pressed together in a single line, and the vein in his neck still pulsated. Then he pulled his hand away and gazed out the window.

She'd blown it. Was there any way to go back to that place where they were at the start of the flight? No, the elephant had to be trapped and moved or it would always sit between them. She pursed her lips together. Would she ever learn to think, maybe even pray before she opened her mouth? Now she could do little more than watch events unfold as they may.

Her eyes went back to her cousin. Julie must have felt her glance because she opened her eyes and her mouth twitched into a small smile. No, Julie had moved past the hurt, and there was that doctor. Steve had mentioned he looked more like an actor playing a doctor than a real one. Now she wondered if he was jealous. Still unable to hold her tongue when words were burning to come out, she left her seat to join Julie.

Her smile wouldn't fool anyone. "How you doing, Jules?"

"Not bad. You don't look so good."

Once again, she ignored the prompt to keep quiet and unleased the torrent of words. "We had a fight, or at least that's what it felt like."

Julie gazed out the window. "I'm probably not the best person to comfort you."

"We married for Rosa. And now that she's out of the picture, there's no good reason to stay married."

Julie twisted to peer at her. "Do you love him?"

Her lips quivered and tears erupted. All she could manage was a nod.

Julie handed her a napkin. "Well then, there's your answer."

Shaking her head, she said, "I'm not sure he loves me. And

then there's you."

"What do you mean *me*?"

"I don't want Steve to be trapped in a marriage with me if he has feelings for you."

Julie rolled her eyes. "I think our relationship was pretty one-sided. But he was too much of a gentleman to break it to me. I mean if he loved me, he would have stayed with me." She held her palms up. "I'm fine with it. It hurt at first, but I'm over him."

"But what if he were free, would you be interested in him?"

She crossed her arms. "I don't think so."

"Is it because of Brett?"

Julie gazed out the window. "Maybe. But I think I lost my chance with him."

"Why? The danger's over. Rosa's going back to her family."

"Are you going to have a chance to say good-bye to her before she goes?"

Angela said, "I don't know if it would be a good idea. Much as I'd like to hold on to her, it would complicate things. It's hard being an adult." She closed her eyes and relaxed against the headrest.

There was Rosa. Her little hand fit perfectly in Angela's as they walked around a lake shaded by dozens of trees. Rosa wrestled her hand free so she could chase after a squirrel that darted from branch to branch. Angela let her go and pulled out her phone to check her messages. Out of the corner of her eye, she watched Rosa pounce from one place to another following the squirrel with her eyes. Her giggling was a melody, sweet to her ear. She went back to her messages. After deleting all of them, she became aware of the quiet. No more laughter, no more pigtails. She searched everywhere, the panic bubbling up inside of her. Then a man with sunglasses and a swarthy beard came out of nowhere carrying Rosa. When she ran to save her, he said, "She's mine. You can't have her."

"Give her back, give her back." She cried over and over, but an opaque mist enveloped the man and the child until they vanished. She rushed toward the evaporating mist but found herself in the middle of nothing. The wind kicked up and jostled her from side to side. She didn't care. Rosa was gone. Her eyes fluttered open and she sat up. Steve stood in the aisle, his eyes full

of concern.

Julie rubbed her arm. "You were having a bad dream."

She folded her arms across her chest. "I lost Rosa to a man with a beard. It was terrible."

Bending down, Steve spoke low enough for only Julie to hear. "Can I have a moment with my wife?" He stared at the ground, his hands stuffed in his pockets.

"I'll take your seat." Julie stood to swap positions with him but lost her balance and fell in his lap. "Oh, sorry. I'll be moving now."

Steve and Angela sat in silence for interminably long minutes. She refused to be the first one to speak this time. It was her mouth that had gotten her into trouble in the first place. But silence had always been awkward. Her chin rested on her fist as she concentrated on houses that resembled little bugs below.

Finally, he spoke. "Nobody forced me to marry you."

"I know."

"I'm not an idiot."

She didn't glance at him; she was afraid he'd read her eyes. "Never said you were."

"What I mean is . . . I wouldn't have married you if I wasn't in it for the long haul."

What did he mean? She didn't trust her mouth, so she kept it firmly zipped.

"Rosa was *never* a sure thing." He stroked her cheek with the back of his fingers. "But *you* always were."

She allowed her heart to fill with the tiniest bit of hope; she was afraid to jinx it by saying the wrong thing.

"What I'm trying to say is—I can't imagine any kind of future without you in it." He enfolded her hand in his, brought it to his lips, and kissed her fingertips. He chuckled. "Maybe we didn't have the most conventional dating experience, but I'm okay with that."

She felt like her heart was rising out of her chest. He wanted her.

Then he said, "But if you want out, I get it. I won't stand in your way."

No. What should she say? The truth. "I feel the same way you do. At first it was Rosa, but somewhere along the line, it became all about you."

His arm went around her back and he pulled her toward him. She hardly noticed the armrest poking her in the ribs. He rubbed his cheek against hers. "We could always adopt another little girl—if you want. We're on our way to being approved."

She hadn't thought about that. "Maybe." Sadness filled her; she wasn't ready to imagine anyone taking the place of their little contortionist.

"Sure. We'll give it some time, but keep an open mind, okay? God closed a door. Another might open."

She stared at the seat in front of her. It was too soon to think of another child, but it was okay. Gradually, the truth seeped into her consciousness and crystalized—Steven Bricker loved *her*. That's all that mattered.

Chapter Eighteen

Julie pulled into the alley behind her house. Colombia had been the best and the worst of times. She'd made it through being tied up with only a minor panic attack. Her ankle still throbbed, and she'd have to make an appointment with the doctor to have it examined.

The thought of her doctor brought Brett Moyer to mind. On the flight home, she'd come to a decision. She was ready for him. Whatever it cost to get him back in her life, she'd do it. How she didn't know. Tomorrow she'd come up with a plan. Yawning deeply, she pulled into her driveway and pressed the button to open the garage door. Tonight, all she wanted was to relax in a hot bubble bath until the water was lukewarm.

Dragging her suitcase into the kitchen, it occurred to her that she'd lost her cane. She must have left it on the plane. Her ankle throbbed but she could put pressure on it.

Noticing crumbs on the counter, she nabbed a dishcloth and ran it under the faucet; then voices came from the living room. Who was in her house? Must be the pastor—she didn't care. The last thing she wanted to do was talk to people. If she could crawl quietly down the hall to her bedroom, they'd never know. Instead, she made herself take one step and then another toward the living room. She plastered a smile on her face before she entered.

Sun glanced up, "Miss Julie, you're back." Her eyes trailed down to her bruised and swollen ankle. "What happened?"

"It's a long story." She shifted her focus to the pastor and his daughter. "How's Amber?"

Pastor Siemens said, "She's locked herself in your bathroom. She won't come out."

"Is she sick?"

Aubrey answered. "No, she wants to go back to Colombia—to Miguel."

Julie plunked down on the edge of the sofa and pointed at her ankle. "I met him while I was there."

Sun's eyes widened. "You did? What happened? Did he hurt you? "

"Long story short, he kidnapped Angela and me, tied us up, and left us to die out in the country."

Pastor Siemens whistled, "That's awful. Why did he do that to you?"

"He wanted to know how Amber was. Apparently, he loves her." She focused on Aubrey. "He's a thug, but he's a romantic one. He actually teared up when he heard Amber was in the hospital."

"Well, at least he's down there, and she's up here."

Sun leaned her head against Julie's shoulder. "I was worried. I expected you yesterday."

Julie closed her eyes and leaned back. Even a fifteen-minute nap would be nice. "I missed my flight because I was tied up— literally—in an old country fruit stand." She pointed toward the bathroom. "By her boyfriend."

Sun stared at the closed door at the end of the hall. "She's been in there a long time." She faced Julie. "Maybe she'll come out if you ask her."

"All right." The sooner Amber left the bathroom, the sooner she could go to bed. Her footsteps on the wooden floor were the only sound as she approached the door. "Amber? Are you okay? It's Julie."

"Leave me alone."

"C'mon, Sweetie. It's getting late, and I need to take a bath. I'm a mess."

"Go away."

She returned to the living room. "She won't come out. What if I told her I saw Miguel?"

Pastor Siemens stood and rubbed his neck. "That can't be a good idea. It'll just get her stirred up."

Aubrey said, "She's already stirred up."

He stared in the direction of the closed door. "I don't think it's a good idea, but we have to get her out of there."

Julie walked back to the bathroom and put her ear to the door. "I saw Miguel while I was in Colombia."

No response.

"Did you hear what I said?"

Still nothing. She shuffled back to the living room. "She's not answering."

Aubrey peered at her dad, then at Julie. "You don't have any razor blades in there, do you?"

Julie's eyes widened. "You don't think . . ." She rushed back down the hall and wiggled the handle. When it didn't open, she pounded on it with her fists. The noise brought the others to the door. Their pleas produced no response. Julie asked, "What do you think she did? Should I call the police?"

"Get out of the way." The pastor got a running start and slammed into the door. When it didn't budge, he tried again. Rubbing his arm, he pleaded, "Please open the door, honey."

No response.

"Let me." Aubrey pulled a credit card from her purse and shimmied it up and down in the narrow gap until the door lock clicked. She rushed in.

Blood drops spattered the ceiling, trailed down the walls, and pooled on the floor. Julie had seen more than enough blood and violence in the last twenty-four hours. She had reached her limit. Her head started to swim. No, she would not succumb to a panic attack. Not when Amber and her family needed her. With an ounce of resolve, she stepped to the side of the pastor, who crouched by his daughter.

She covered her mouth. Amber leaned against the bathtub, her eyes half closed, her lips slightly moving. Her right hand lay limply over the gaping hole in her left. Blood seeped through her fingers and flowed, staining the grout between the tiles. Aubrey squatted at her side, trying to stem the tide with a blood-soaked tissue.

Her father pressed his hand over Aubrey's to staunch the blood flow.

Amber's head lolled from side to side.

Sun's face paled at the sight of the blood. Julie gently shook her shoulders. "Get some towels. Call 911."

"Yes, Miss."

The fetid odor of blood in the small space assailed Julie's nose, but she couldn't let herself faint. Not now. Holding her breath, she spun toward the linen closet in the hallway, grabbed towels, and threw them in Amber's direction.

Aubrey gently wrapped her sister's arm in a hand towel. "Dad, keep pressure on this." She got up and wet a washcloth, then tenderly patted Amber's face. Aubrey's heaving shoulders announced this was an emotional moment.

Blood seeped through the hand towel. Julie handed fresh ones to Amber's father, who piled them on top and pressed. She didn't get it. Was life so horrendous for this teenager, she couldn't stand the idea of a future? She leaned against the door frame and watched.

Amber's eyes fluttered open and focused on her sister. Her lips still moved, but barely a wisp of sound escaped them.

Then a rare thing happened. Amber raised her free arm to touch Aubrey's cheek. It appeared to take all her effort to do it. Barely above a whisper, she said, "We're all right." Then her eyes closed, her face relaxed, and her head fell to the side.

"No!" Aubrey shook her sister's shoulders. "You can't leave us."

Pastor Siemens pleaded, "No, Amber, stay with us."

In a matter of seconds, noise and lights exploded from the living room. Paramedics forced a gurney through the bathroom door. Retreating out of their way, Julie plastered herself against the wall. Pastor Siemens pleaded with the paramedic to save his daughter. Sun and Aubrey clung to each other.

A paramedic yelled, "We got a heartbeat. A weak one."

Another said, "Let's get her on the gurney … one, two, three."

It seemed like mere seconds and the paramedics were loading Amber into an ambulance. Her father jumped in, and in a blaze of light and sound, the ambulance headed for the hospital.

Julie picked up her purse and gestured to the girls. "Let's go."

The drive to the hospital was silent until they reached the

parking lot. Then Aubrey spoke first, her voice wistful. "Did you hear what she said to me? She said, 'we're all right.' Do you think it means she forgives me?"

Sun said, "It sounds like it. I'm sure she has."

Aubrey's head appeared between the front seats. "What was he like?"

Julie's attention was on finding a free space close to the hospital doors. "Who?"

"Miguel."

Julie parked in an empty one in the furthest row. "Sorry we can't get closer. About Miguel. He was young—he looked like a teenager, but he had to be older. I felt kind of sorry for him. He had that sad puppy-dog expression whenever he said Amber's name. He was a bag of contradictions. A mean thug one minute; a misunderstood romantic the next. But I can't ignore the fact that he was the one who left us to die."

They walked as fast as Julie could tolerate with her swollen ankle. Aubrey slowed down. "How did you meet him?"

She didn't mind talking about Miguel. It took her mind off the pain that hampered every step. "Angela and I had taken a cab to Rosa's birthplace, about an hour's drive from the city, to get her birth certificate. On the way back, I fell asleep. When I woke, the cabdriver had pulled over to an abandoned fruit stand, pulled out a gun, and fired a warning shot that almost hit us. That's when Miguel showed up. He arranged the whole thing."

Once they arrived at the hospital entrance, Sun pointed in the direction of the emergency ward. The pain had increased. Julie held onto the wall, grimacing with every step, but she continued her story. "He seemed genuinely concerned about Amber and got angry with Angela when she criticized him for treating Amber so badly. After tying us up and hitting us both in the head with the butt of his gun, he and the cab driver vanished. But the weird thing was—they left our purses and Rosa's documents. In fact, on the back of the birth certificate, he wrote, 'Tell Amber I love her.'"

"Wow, Miss," Sun said. "You could have been killed. Were you scared?"

"Yeah, but there's something about that guy—he wasn't all bad."

"What you mean?"

"He obviously has an anger problem, and he likes control, but when he talks about Amber, his face lights up."

Sun cleared her throat. "Can I tell you about something that happened to me?"

"Sure."

"Dae called me."

"What did he want?"

"He said he was sorry, and he wanted me to visit him in prison."

Julie peered at her sharply. "I hope you told him no."

"I did, but maybe he's like Miguel—not so bad."

Julie stopped and faced her. "Be careful. You can forgive him, but stay away from him."

Sun stared at the floor. "I feel sorry for him. We were good friends once. But you're right. I'll not contact him."

Julie put her hand on Sun's arm. "It could put your visa in jeopardy and damage the federal case against him. Stay away."

Sun glanced up. "It's easier to forgive him when I know he's sorry, that's all."

They entered the emergency waiting room, full of families with most seats occupied. When people stared, Julie glanced down at their blood-spattered clothes. They looked more like patients than family members. With her limp, she expected to be offered a wheelchair. It didn't happen. Sun and Aubrey found seats in the corner and held one for her.

If Julie hadn't been the designated driver, she would have made some excuse and left. The last thing she wanted to do was run into Dr. Brett Moyer. After all, she hadn't tugged a comb through her tangled hair all day, and her makeup had probably worn off. But if she was honest with herself, it hurt too much. She couldn't take any more rejection—especially from him. It was better to imagine she still had a chance.

Pastor Siemens paced in front of the receptionist desk. His hair was askew, and his shirt covered with blood stains. He rubbed his hands together and his lips moved silently.

Approaching him, she touched his arm. "How's she doing?"

"She's lost a lot of blood. They're going to keep her overnight for observation; then she'll be transferred to Spring Andover—it's a psychiatric hospital." His face had aged ten years in an hour. "I don't know how much more we can take."

"As long as she's alive, there's hope."

Deep crevasses formed around his mouth and on his forehead. "What I don't get is—what could be so horrible in her life that she would choose to bleed to death?"

There was no answer. Silence was better.

The receptionist called him to the desk. "The doctor wants to see you. Wait for the door to open. Once you're in, take a left and go to the nurses' station."

He glanced over his shoulder at Julie. "Come with me?"

"Oh, I don't think . . ."

"Please, it will be easier if you're there."

"What about Aubrey? I can get her."

The double doors opened automatically. He motioned for her to come. "Hurry."

She spun toward Aubrey and Sun and yelled, "C'mon. We're going in." Then she hobbled to catch up with the pastor before the doors shut in her face.

At any other time, she would have been fascinated by the hustle-bustle of the emergency department but not now. Still, she couldn't resist peering into the cubicles they hurried past—patients of different ages, their family members sitting close by. Mothers and wives dabbed at their eyes; fathers and brothers paced. A few patients were alone. White everywhere. The smell of antiseptic and bleach was strong.

Amber's room was the last one on the left. The curtain was slightly ajar. The others rushed in, but Julie and Sun held back. It was a private moment for the family—an inner sanctum she shouldn't be privy to.

But curiosity won out. She peeked in. Amber's eyes were closed, her skin pale as death. Her bandaged wrist lay on top of the sheet. Her face was drawn and etched with tiny lines. The word *corpse* came to Julie's mind, but for the fact that Amber grimaced and thrashed her head as if she was having a bad dream.

It was so pointless. This wasn't how they had foreseen the course the Amber story would take when they rescued her. Maybe it was their fault. Had they made a mistake in forcing her back to a world she clearly didn't want?

A man in scrubs signaled for Amber's dad to follow him.

Papers to sign, he said.

Sun stood on Amber's right, her lips moving slightly as she patted an arm. Aubrey was on Amber's left, her eyes focused, rubbing her sister's arm with a gentle touch. Her words were barely more than a whisper, but they seemed to calm Amber—the lines on her face relaxed.

After a few minutes, Aubrey leaned back and peered at Julie. "I want to stay with her tonight. There's so much I have to say—to make up for lost time. When we were little, we did everything together. Mom used to say we were like two halves of a whole."

Sun's eyes brightened. "I bet it was fun to have a twin. I never had a sister my own age."

"Yeah," she said, gazing into the distance. "It was fun. Mom used to dress us alike. People couldn't tell us apart sometimes although I was taller." A grin crept across her face. "I remember when we played a joke on our gym teacher in fifth grade. I was the athletic one, so I pretended to be Amber and got to miss music, which I didn't like, and played dodge ball for two hours while Amber got to sing. But we got caught when one of my friends yelled my name, and I responded." She smoothed the light blanket covering Amber. "It all changed in middle school; that's when we grew apart. Different friends. Different inter . . ."

"Amber?" A male voice interrupted.

"Miguel." Julie's hand went to her mouth. Everything within her screamed, "Don't get involved. It's not your business anyway." But she was the only adult in the room. She stood in his way. He pushed her aside, his attention directed solely on Amber. He stopped beside the bed. How did he get into the country? No way he could get a visa that fast, or he got in another way. An involuntary shiver travelled down her spine. The system wasn't working.

When Aubrey noticed him, she shielded Amber with her body. But something made her move out of his way. Sun did the same. Maybe it was his eyes. The girls were powerless to stop him, mesmerized by his tenderness.

His finger touched the bandages that covered her wrist, then he wiped his eyes with his sleeve. "Por que, Amber?" Leaning over, he rested his cheek next to hers on the pillow.

Julie had never seen a male so overcome with emotion. His

eyes were red, a day's growth of stubble covered his face, and he looked lost—like a Rottweiler puppy on the loose. Shaking his head, he spoke softly in Spanish—words Julie couldn't understand. He traced her face with his finger. This was not the surly thug who had tightened the ropes on her wrists to the point she couldn't feel them. His tender touch on Amber's wrist reminded her of a brash Romeo, unaccustomed to following the rules, a hotbed of emotions, but capable of great passion and sacrifice.

Julie was so riveted on the love story unfolding before her, she didn't notice Pastor Siemens enter.

"What do you think you're doing? Get away from her."

Miguel stiffened. His eyes flickered across the others in the tiny cubicle, locking on Julie for more than a second. He gestured with his head toward her without saying a word. Then he fastened his gaze on Amber's dad. Shoulders back, he wiped his eyes with the cuff of his jacket, while his other hand remained on Amber's shoulder. "Senor Siemens, I mean no harm. I love your daughter— is all. I come from Colombia to be with her." His lips closed in a tight line.

"You've caused enough trouble." The pastor's fists clenched and unclenched. "You abducted our little girl and made her do unspeakable things." His tremulous voice broke.

Miguel's eyes narrowed. Eyes that Julie remembered. "No sir, I took good care of her. I tell you I love her. I would never hurt her in a million years." His words emphatic, his accent strong but controlled.

Stepping closer, the pastor seethed, "Get. Away. From. Her."

Amber's eyes fluttered open. She squinted as if the light bothered her. Then she saw Miguel, and the lines on her forehead smoothed. Her voice was hardly discernable, although the room was small. "You're here." Her eyes brightened. "I knew you'd come for me." Nobody else was in the room as they spoke to each other in Spanish.

When her father moved forward, Amber said, "Daddy? Let it go."

"But you're just a child. You're *our* child."

"I know and I love you. I'm sorry I've hurt you and Mom and Aubrey and Oliver." She tightened her grip on Miguel's hand. "But *he* has my heart."

Some family matters weren't meant for mere acquaintances. Julie inched toward the door. She didn't belong here.

Her father said, "We'll talk about it later. You need your rest."

Amber leaned toward Miguel. "They're moving me to a mental hospital tomorrow—Spring something." Although the words were in Spanish, Julie recognized the name of the facility.

His reaction was livid. "No. You don't belong there." Before anyone could react, he yanked out the IV lines. "I'm taking you with me."

Amber's father lunged at the bed, grabbed the remote, and pushed the call button. At the same time, Aubrey ran into the hall and screamed.

Simultaneous sensations hit Julie. Amber crying, "No, daddy." Feet running in the hall. Sun shaking her head. Miguel's pained eyes. Antiseptic odors mingling with sweat and leather.

A middle-aged man in blue scrubs rushed in. "What's going on here?" When Miguel lifted Amber out of bed, he roared, "What do you think you're doing?"

Silence and slow motion. A movie gone bad. An accident out of control. Miguel pulled a gun from the back of his belt. Still in slow motion, he pointed it at the man in scrubs whose hands flew up to block his head. Miguel's arm shaking as his finger wrapped around the trigger.

"Stay where you are. Amber comes with me." He helped her up with one arm, his eyes darting between the hospital worker and her father, as dangerous now as a trapped animal.

Shallow breaths—that's all Julie could manage. But she didn't want to draw attention to herself struggling for air. Instead, she concentrated on short silent breaths. Dots played before her eyes. Not enough oxygen. She closed her eyes to make the spots go away, but they remained under her lids. Nobody noticed. They were transfixed on Miguel.

Pastor Siemens broke the silence. "Miguel, can we talk about this? She needs medical help." He inched forward until Miguel jerked the gun toward him.

"Ella no es loca."

"No, Miguel." Amber grasped his free arm. "Don't do this."

For the first time, his glance left the others, his eyebrows furrowed. "But you're not crazy. You know that."

Her eyes drifted closed. "I need help." She held up her forearms crisscrossed with scarred lines. "Do you see my arms?"

Gently touching the scars, his eyes brimmed over with tears, his shoulders racked with sobs. "Por que?"

"No se. I don't know. I need help."

Lowering the gun, Miguel gently embraced Amber—their foreheads touching. Without warning, her father lunged at Miguel, grabbing for the gun. But Miguel's reflexes were faster. He whipped around and pushed him away. They struggled, careening into the wheeled table knocking over the pitcher of water. Aubrey screamed. Sun cowered, covering her face.

Amber cried, "Stop it."

Julie had almost reached the door when the blast of the gun shook the room. Her shoulder exploded. Hot, searing pain. She stared at her hand, tried to lift it. Dead weight. The spots congealed into darkness. Nothing.

Chapter Nineteen

The first thing Julie saw after opening her eyes was a cluster of
tall palm trees outside the window. The next was a ridiculously
tidy room—obviously not her bedroom. It smelled too clean to be
her house. It smelled like a hospital. But nicer—not unlike a hotel
suite—four tall windows, a non-descript sofa, a leather easy chair.
She was impressed. A white blanket covered her feet. She wriggled
her toes and fingers. Feet felt fine; one hand worked; the other
numb. She lifted the numb hand to see if the fingers had
changed—no, still five. An IV line was imbedded in a vein below
her knuckles. Why?

She closed her eyes. What had happened? Miguel and the gun.
Her attempt to leave. A gun's blast and the burning pain. She
rotated her right shoulder. A tightness was all she felt. What time
was it anyway? Her watch was gone as were her clothes. She
shivered. The heron-patterned hospital gown didn't provide much
warmth. Her throat felt like it was stuffed with cotton balls.
Pawing at the table, she reached for the pitcher and tried to pour
some water, but her hand struggled to clench its handle. She spilled
more on the table than she got in the cup. Water seeped onto the
blanket and made its way to the sheet. Great. Now she'd need to
call someone to change her wet gown.

At that moment, Sun walked in and inched toward the bed.
"You're awake, Miss. I was so worried."

She tried to smile, but her lips had a mind of their own. "What happened? How long have I been here?"

"A few hours. Do you remember anything?"

"I remember Pastor Siemens and Miguel fighting over a gun. I think I tried to go get help. I got shot, didn't I?"

Sun gingerly touched her hand. "When you crashed to the floor, I thought he killed you. We were so scared, even Miguel. But the doctor said you would be all right." She glanced around. "Can I get you something? Are you hungry?"

She shook her head. "What happened after I was shot?"

"Miguel and Pastor Siemens stopped fighting. The doctor called for help. You were in the right place to be shot." She grinned. "Pastor Siemens and Miguel kept saying they were sorry they hurt you."

Julie asked, "Then what happened?"

"They put you on a sled and took you away."

"Gurney. Did they arrest Miguel?"

"Not then."

"…so?"

"Miguel and Pastor Siemens forgave each other."

"You're kidding."

"They both love Amber, Miss."

"True, but they were fighting over a gun when I blacked out. What happened next?"

"The hospital police people took Miguel away."

Her arm was starting to ache. She rubbed it with her good hand. "I guess getting shot was worth it then. But my shoulder hurts." She pressed the nurse's call button. "Is Amber still going to the other hospital tomorrow?"

Sun nodded. "She needs help. Even Miguel agreed. They let him kiss her goodbye before they took him, and he said, 'We'll be together someday, but now, you go get better.'"

A nurse poked her head in the door. "You're awake. Good. On a scale of one to ten, how's the pain?" She took her wrist.

"7 or 7.5. I think I need something. Sorry to be a bother, but I spilled water on the bed."

The nurse checked a chart. "It's time. Your doctor will be in soon, but I'll be right back with your medication and some sheets." Her crepe soles swished away.

Julie leaned her head back against the pillow and closed her eyes. "I wonder when they'll let me out."

"Don't know, Miss. I can't stay long. Pastor Siemens is going to take me home if you'll get him borrow your car. I can go to the office tomorrow and take care of things, okay?"

"Thanks. You've been such a help this summer. I'm going to miss you when school starts next month. Tell the pastor it's fine although I don't know where my keys are."

"I'll find them." She opened the closet and rifled through her purse. "Found them. See you tomorrow."

Alone at last. Once they changed her sheets, she'd take a nap. It was hard to get comfortable though, not being able to lie on her side. Was the bullet still in her shoulder or did it go all the way through? She adjusted her upper torso as best she could.

Why did these things always happen to her? She could sense a pity party coming on, and she didn't stop it. The first guest to arrive was the "rejected by two boyfriends" guest. Then she opened the door to the "twisted ankle, head injury, bullet in shoulder" guest. She was just about to let the "betrayed by best friend" guest in when she realized she wasn't enjoying the party much. She was tired about thinking that life wasn't fair.

Actually, life was pretty good. And she was grateful to be alive even if she was uncomfortable. Things were working out for the best. The last few weeks had been a movie-like adventure—the kind Angela and she used to create when they were kids. She got to fly to Colombia not once but twice. And when Kevin Perez's wife came of her coma, she learned about her parents. She wouldn't have met Brett if she hadn't been searching for Rosa in the hospital. Angela and she were close again. Maybe a well-lived life wasn't about being safe. She'd have to stew on that thought for a while before she fully embraced it.

Dorothy might be wrong about Kansas. There are better places than home.

A rustling noise made her open her eyes—wide. At the foot of the bed, dressed in a white coat with a stethoscope draped around his neck, stood Dr. Brett Moyer. The smile on his face appeared genuine. "We've got to stop meeting at the hospital."

She grinned. "Hm. Are you my doctor?"

"I am. I'm Doctor Moyer." He came to her side, glanced toward the door, then taking her hand, he kissed it. "I'm not supposed to do that, but I can't help it."

"Quite a unique bedside manner. Is this your normal practice?"

He straightened, his eyes sparkling. "Just the cute ones."

"How many would that be?"

"Only one."

She felt her cheeks grow warm and squeezed his hand.

"When did the nurse last give you pain medication?"

"She said she was going to bring me some."

He checked the chart, then carefully pulled one corner of the bandage off. "The bleeding has stopped. The bullet just grazed the skin, so it didn't cause much damage. We'll keep you overnight, and if everything's good, you'll go home tomorrow."

She stared at her lap, sure that her face was red. "You must think I'm a hypochondriac."

"No—maybe accident prone. Hypochondriacs don't usually get shot." His eyes were filled with tenderness and warmth. "When I saw you on the floor, my heart gave out. It was like when I lost my wife. I can't lose another person I love."

"You love me?"

His Bradley Cooper eyes beamed. "I was a fool to think I could let you go."

She was afraid to open her mouth in case some unpoetic thing came out like "really?"

"You're the most exciting girl I've ever met."

"Me? Exciting?"

He brushed a lock of hair away from her cheek. "I have a pretty boring life compared to yours. Could you ever be satisfied with a regular guy like me?"

"I love boring. I could out-bore you any day."

He had just taken her hand to his lips when the nurse walked in. When she saw him, she spun around and hurried out.

"Wait, Nurse."

She came back, "Sorry, Doctor. Did you need me?"

"Miss Richards would like her pain medication." He backed out of her way.

After pouring a glass of water, the nurse passed a small cup containing two pills to Julie. "Let me know if you need anything." Then she swiftly left.

"I got a feeling I'm going to be the talk of the nurses' station tonight."

Julie's smile ebbed. "What about your daughter? Aren't you afraid I'll put her in danger?"

"Every night when I call her, she asks about you. Now she wants to be an immigration attorney."

"She's a smart girl—and not only because she asked about me."

"Well, if you can put up with me, you'll have your own personal doctor to take care of you whenever you sprain your ankle or get shot."

She laced her fingers in his. "And a boring one no less—it doesn't get any better than that."

***

She couldn't erase her silly grin even when she dropped her overnight bag on the hall floor. A pile of mail waited for her on the credenza. Sun deserved extra money for taking good care of her office while she was in the hospital. She picked up the mail and then put it down again. Tomorrow would be soon enough.

Mrs. Julie Moyer. She liked the sound of it. God had opened an intriguing door for her to walk through. She was at the threshold ready to take that first step—ready to make the commitment of her life.

Brett was coming over later that night to see how she was. She was glad she'd taken a cab to her hairdresser's and gotten her hair washed and made presentable. Dried blood was never an attractive look. She'd take a bath with her new peaches and cream bubble bath, making sure not to get her shoulder wet. Then she'd spray herself with her favorite Shalimar cologne. Opening her closet door, she chose a silk shirt, which would sit nicely on a pair of black jeans. Add sandals and she was good to go.

As she waited for the water to fill the tub, the smell of peaches enveloped the air around her. She could either put a coat of polish on her nails or read the newspaper. She scanned the headlines— nothing interested her. The sports pages were full of baseball—she kept leafing through the pages until she saw a familiar face in a small picture on the bottom of the society page. His arm was casually draped around the shoulder of a striking woman, one hand on her hip, the other gesturing at the man next to her. *Dr. Brett Moyer and Ms. Billi Osborne share a private moment at the Florida Hospital Ball* read the caption.

She shut off the water—the smell of peaches now cloying to her senses. She wasn't sure what to do, so she sat on the edge of the tub resting her chin on the palm of her hand. Had she imagined something that didn't exist? She replayed their hospital conversation. He had said he couldn't lose another person that he loved. Maybe he meant something different. She examined the picture again. They exuded an aura of delight in each other. Her lips started to quiver. She didn't know if she could take another betrayal. No, she sat up straight. He had said he loved her. There must be a reason for the picture. How was she to bring it up?

She peered at herself in the mirror—the fairy-tale face was gone—the naïve one that believed good always won out in the end against evil. What if the battle was between good and good?

The doorbell rang. She glanced at her watch. She'd been sitting there for thirty minutes. A frozen smile was all she could manage as she left the bathroom.

The moment she opened the door, he folded her into his arms. She fit perfectly against his chest under his chin. He smelled of Burberry and leather. He went to kiss her, but she shifted her cheek to his lips. With his finger, he tipped her chin up, a line formed between his brows.

"What's wrong? Maybe we let you go home too soon."

"No, I'm fine." She managed to maintain the frozen smile. "Come in." She led him to the living room sofa where she sat next to him.

"You're not shivering, are you?"

"Just a chill."

"Well, let me warm you up." Pulling her toward his chest, she stiffened at first, then let herself be enveloped in his embrace. "Okay, what is it?"

Pushing away, she stared at her hands that tormented a tissue. "Nothing much. I saw something that made me think I'd make a mistake."

"Mistake about what?"

"About us."

That line formed between his brows again. "What is it?"

She retrieved the newspaper from the bathroom, knowing their relationship would change in the next few minutes and not for the good. But she had to know the truth.

She inched toward the sofa and handed him the paper.

"What is this?"

"Look on page C1."

Flipping to the page, he stared at the picture; then he glanced up at her, his eyes unreadable. "The picture was taken last weekend. At a hospital benefit for cancer. I was invited to attend in honor of my wife. That's all it was." He handed the paper to her.

Her response was barely discernable. "I'm sorry. I didn't understand."

"It's okay. Maybe you can attend the next one with me. It's an annual event. This year I brought my sister-in-law. That's her in the picture."

She was mortified, then relieved. Her eyes searched his face for some sign of regret or distaste, but his eyes held only amusement. "Let's get a pizza."

"And ice cream?"

"I bet you like pepperoni."

"I bet you like vanilla."

The End

ABOUT THE AUTHOR

Sherri Stewart loves a good suspense novel. When life threw a curve at her family, she started writing and hasn't stopped. Her careers as a teacher, principal, lawyer, and flight attendant have allowed her to draw on personal experiences. Her membership in Word Weavers, Forget Me Not Romance, The Christian Pen, and ACFW have helped hone her skills. She lives near Orlando with her husband Bobby, her son Joshua, and her dog Lily. When not writing or teaching, she likes to walk through the Disney parks for exercise. *A Well-founded Fear of* Death is the second in the Stepping Out series. She has also written four novellas. Please check out her website, www.stewartwriting.com

Sign up for Forget Me Not Romances newsletter and receive a cookbook compiled from Forget Me Not Authors! Check out other great stories at www.forgetmenotromances.com

www.ingramcontent.com/pod-product-compliance
Lightning Source LLC
Chambersburg PA
CBHW071143180726
48291CB00007B/2311